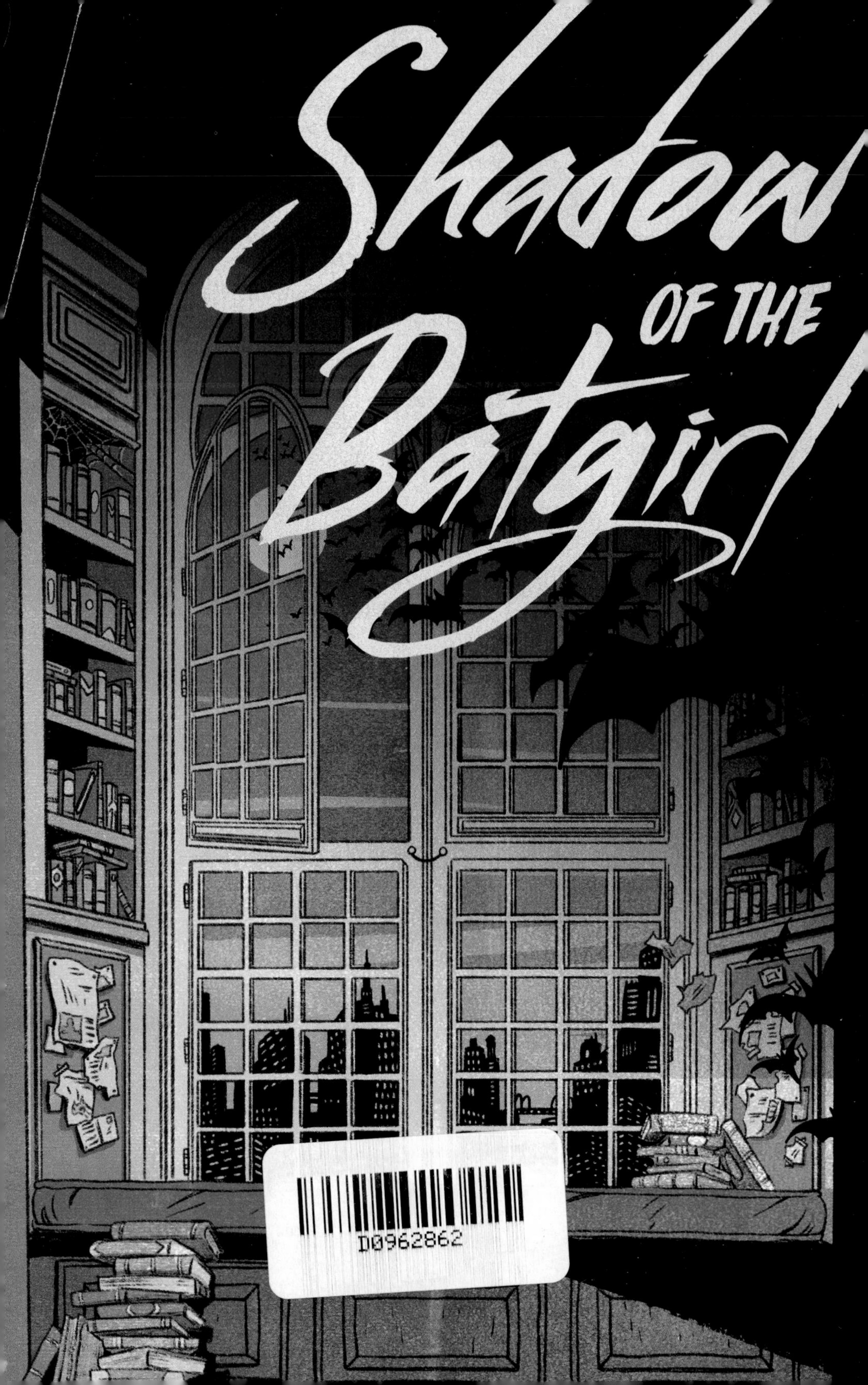
Shadow
OF THE
Batgirl

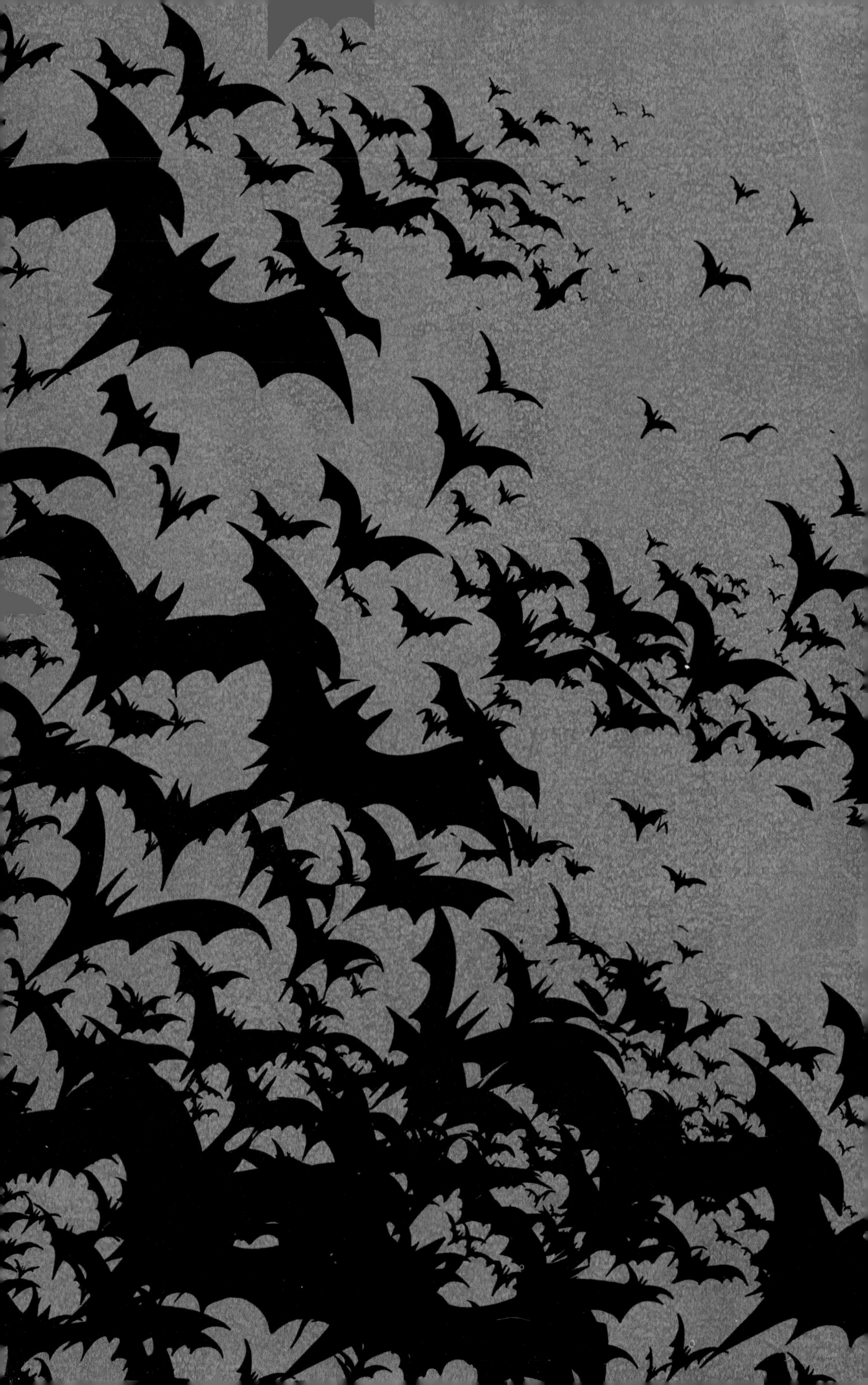

OF THE

Batgirl

SARAH KUHN
author

NICOLE GOUX
illustrator

CRIS PETER
colorist

JANICE CHIANG with
SAIDA TEMOFONTE
letterers

Batgirl based on characters
created by Bob Kane
with Bill Finger.

SARA MILLER Editor
STEVE COOK Design Director – Books
AMIE BROCKWAY-METCALF Publication Design

BOB HARRAS Senior VP – Editor-in-Chief, DC Comics
MICHELE R. WELLS VP & Executive Editor, Young Reader

DAN DiDIO Publisher
JIM LEE Publisher & Chief Creative Officer
BOBBIE CHASE VP – New Publishing Initiatives & Talent Development
DON FALLETTI VP – Manufacturing Operations & Workflow Management
LAWRENCE GANEM VP – Talent Services
ALISON GILL Senior VP – Manufacturing & Operations
HANK KANALZ Senior VP – Publishing Strategy & Support Services
DAN MIRON VP – Publishing Operations
NICK J. NAPOLITANO VP – Manufacturing Administration & Design
NANCY SPEARS VP – Sales

SHADOW OF THE BATGIRL

Published by DC Comics. Copyright © 2020 DC Comics. All Rights
Reserved. All characters, their distinctive likenesses, and related
elements featured in this publication are trademarks of DC Comics.
The stories, characters, and incidents featured in this publication are
entirely fictional. DC Comics does not read or accept unsolicited
submissions of ideas, stories, or artwork. DC – a WarnerMedia Company.

DC Comics, 2900 West Alameda Ave., Burbank, CA 91505
Printed by LSC Communications, Crawfordsville, IN, USA. 12/27/19.
First Printing.
ISBN: 978-1-4012-8978-2

Library of Congress Cataloging-in-Publication Data

Names: Kuhn, Sarah (Author), writer. | Goux, Nicole, artist. | Peter, Cris,
    colourist. | Chiang, Janice, letterer. | Temofonte, Saida, letterer.
Title: Shadow of the Batgirl / a graphic novel Sarah Kuhn, writer ; Nicole
    Goux, artist ; Cris Peter, colorist ; Janice Chiang and Saida Temofonte,
    letterers.
Description: Burbank, CA : DC Comics, [2020] | Audience: Ages 13-17 |
    Summary: Cassandra Cain is the daughter of super-villains and a living
    weapon trained to be the ultimate assassin, but when her father
    threatens the world she has grown to love, she will have to overcome
    that voice inside her head telling her she can never be a hero.
Identifiers: LCCN 2019043896 (print) | LCCN 2019043897 (ebook) | ISBN
    9781401289782 (paperback) | ISBN 9781779502414 (ebook)
Subjects: LCSH: Graphic novels. | CYAC: Graphic novels. |
    Self-confidence--Fiction. | Heroes--Fiction.
Classification: LCC PZ7.7.K857 Sh 2020 (print) | LCC PZ7.7.K857 (ebook) |
    DDC 741.5/973--dc23

PEFC Certified

This product is from
sustainably managed
forests and controlled
sources

PEFC/29-31-337   www.pefc.org

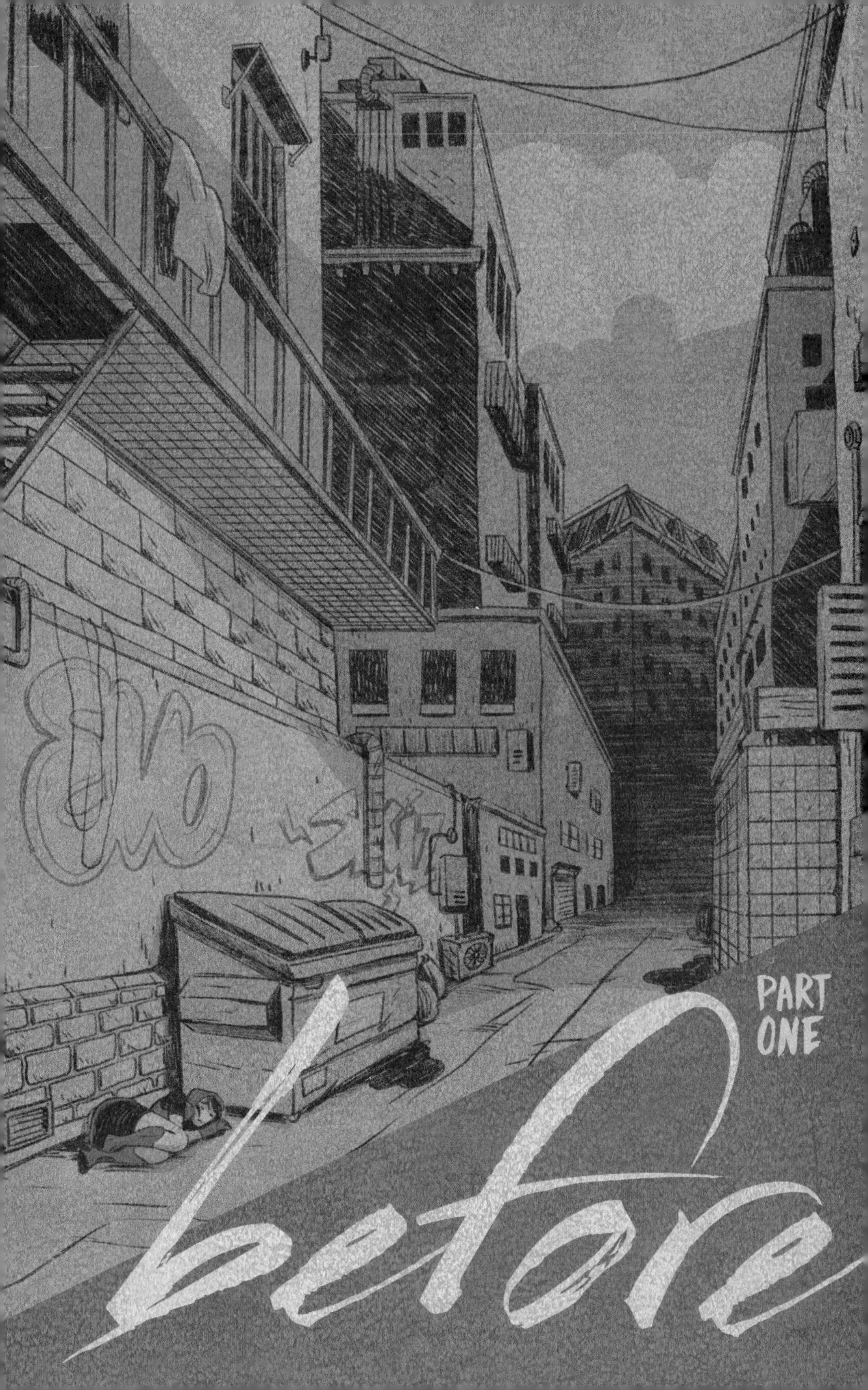
PART ONE
before

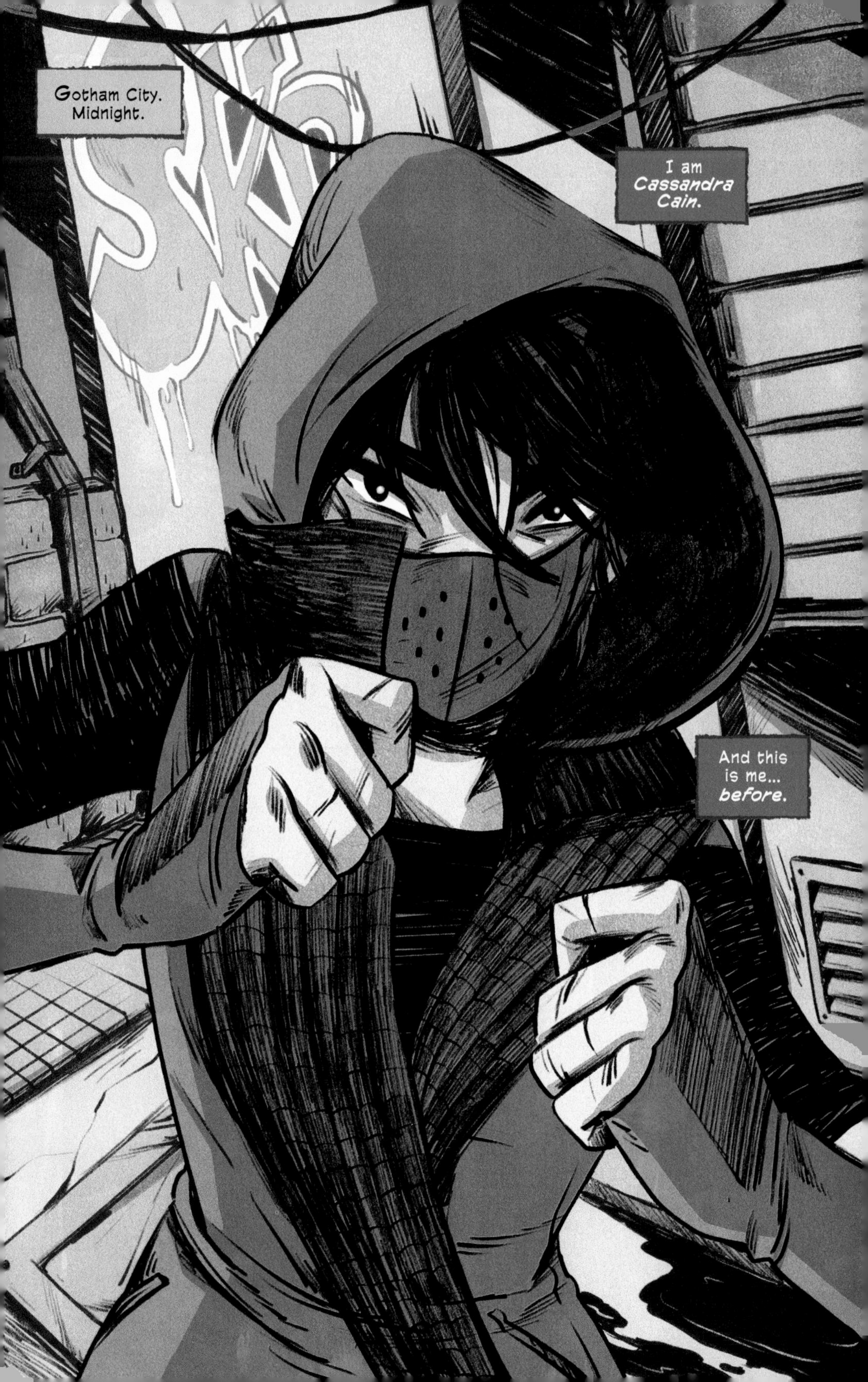
Gotham City. Midnight.
I am *Cassandra Cain.*
And this is me... *before.*

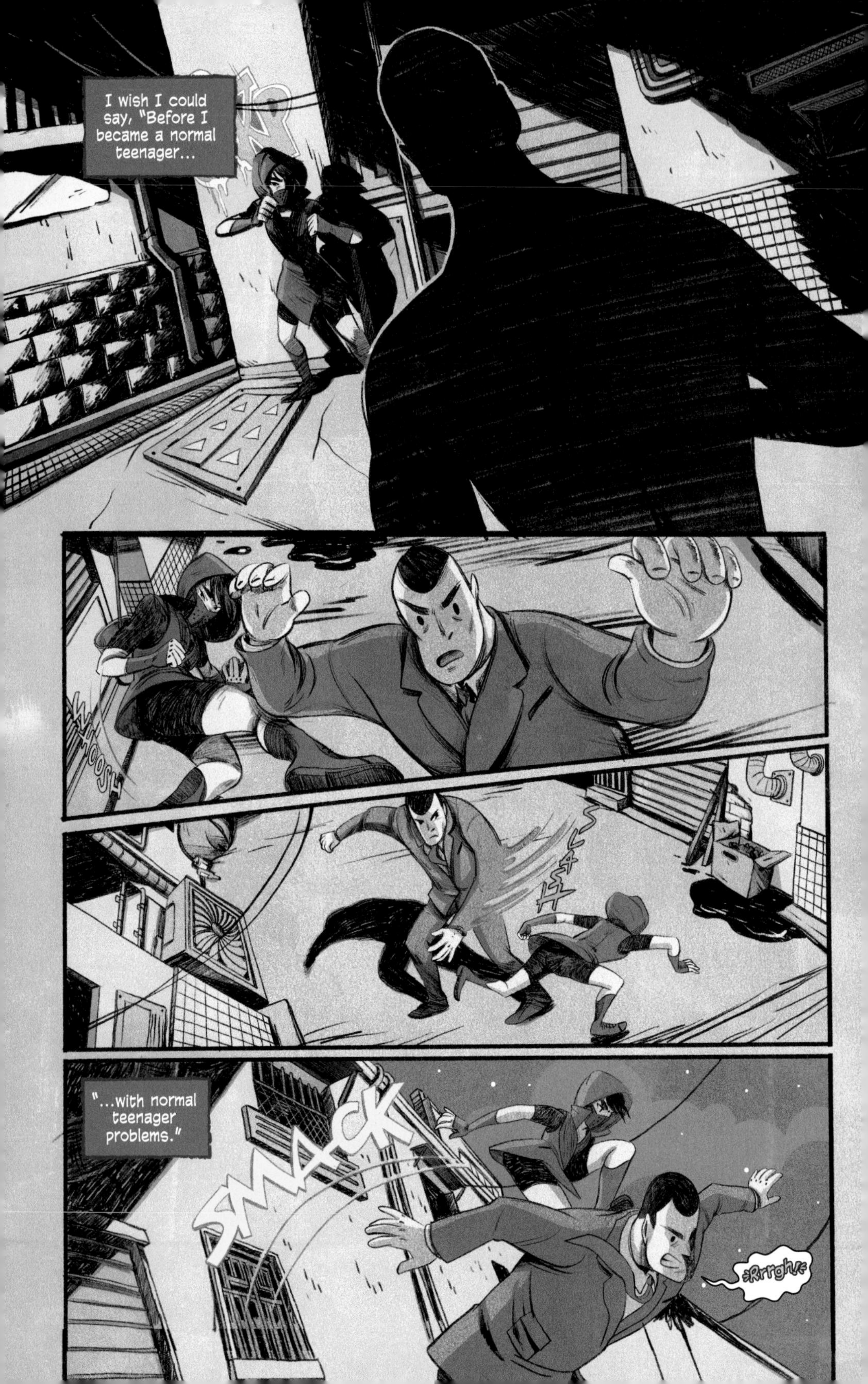

I wish I could say, "Before I became a normal teenager...
WHOOSH
SLASH
"...with normal teenager problems."
SMACK
Rrrgh!

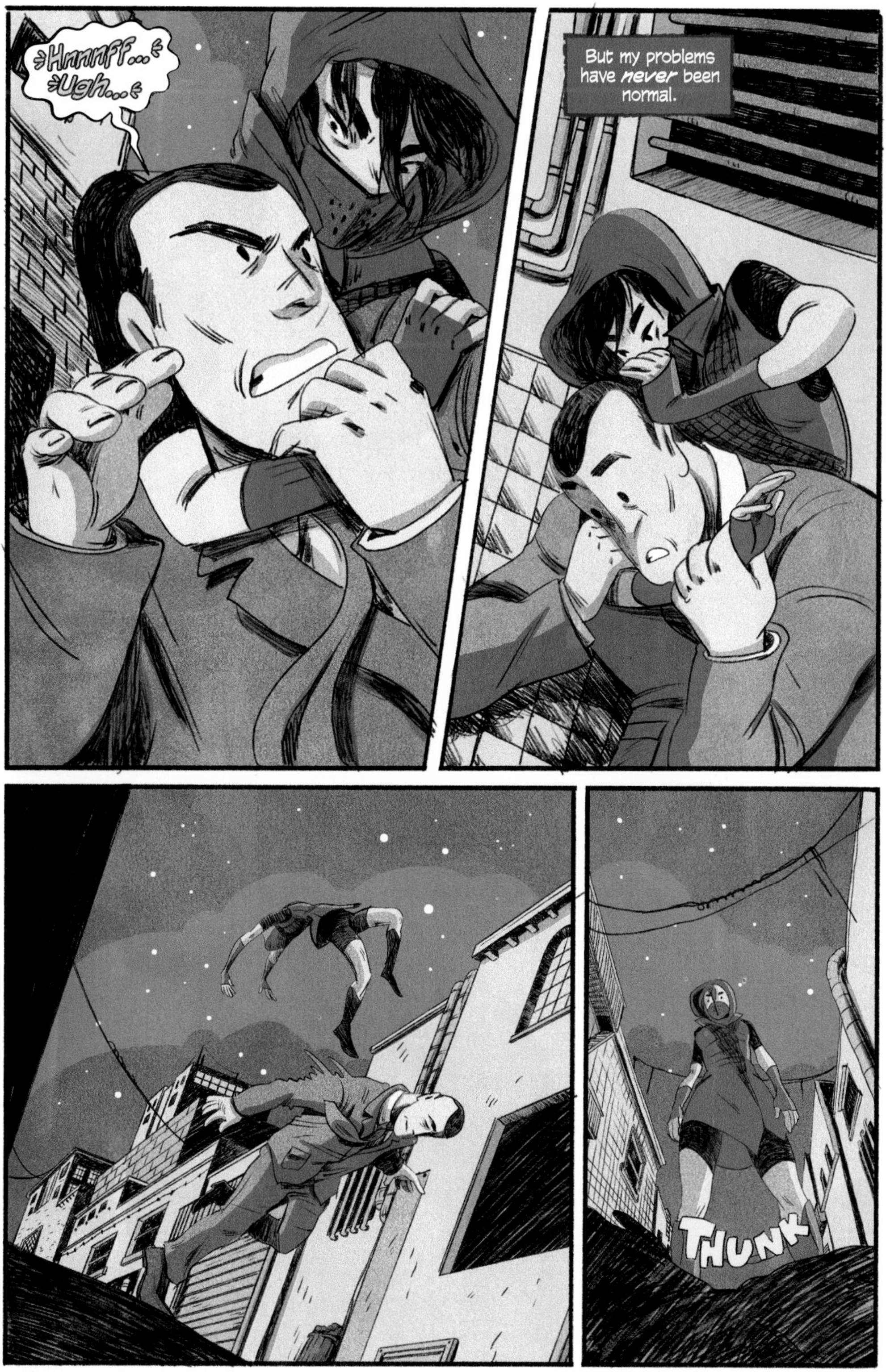
Hnnnff...
Ugh...
But my problems have *never* been normal.
THUNK

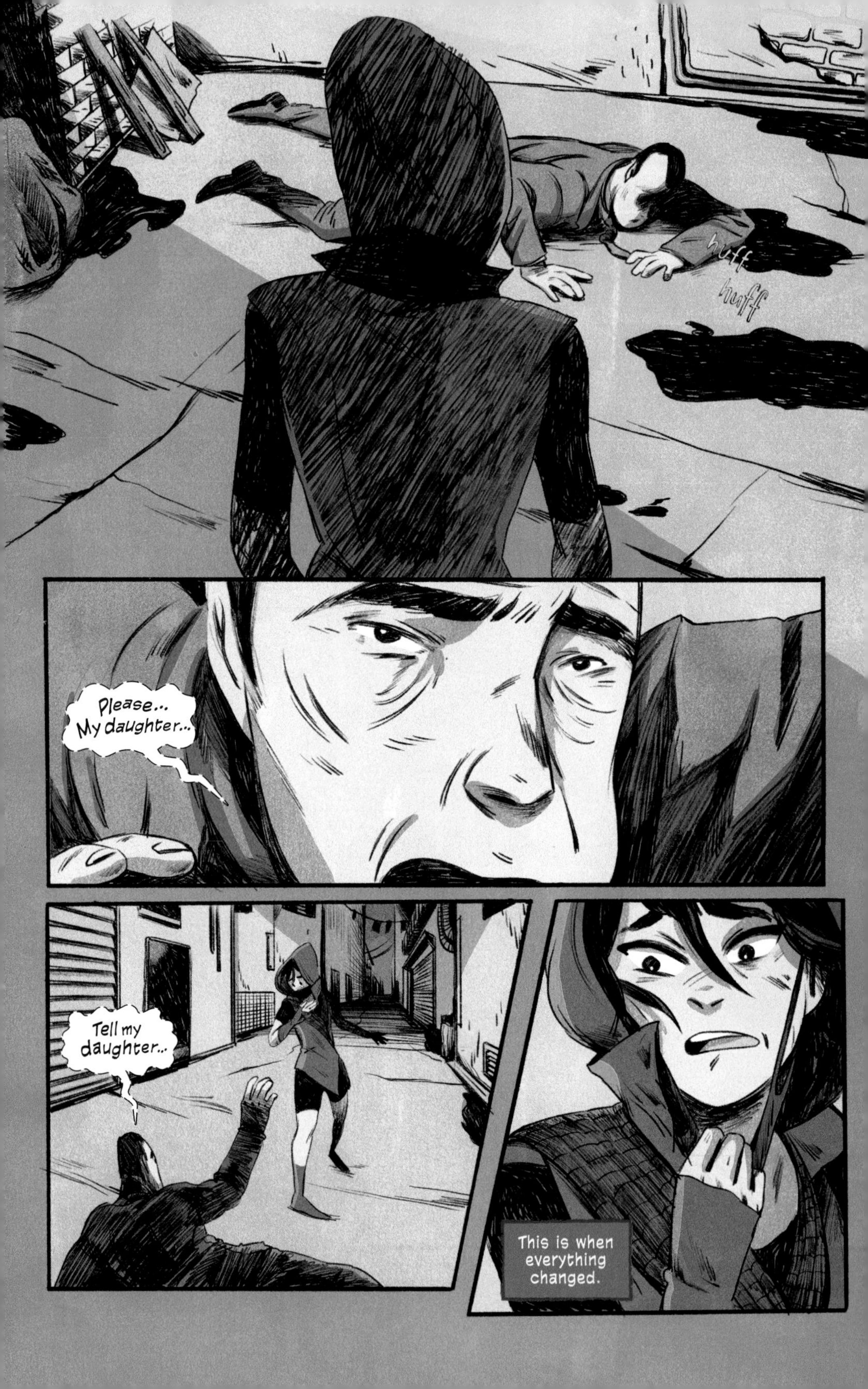
huff
huff
Please... My daughter...
Tell my daughter...
This is when everything changed.

I'd killed in the past. It's what I was *trained* to do.

Please...

This time...for the first time, I couldn't go through with it.

Killing doesn't require words. So I hadn't been raised with many.

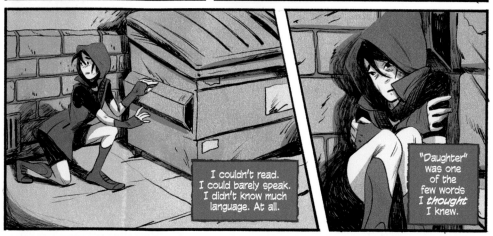

I couldn't read. I could barely speak. I didn't know much language. At all.

"Daughter" was one of the few words I *thought* I knew.

But...the way that man said it. The agony overwhelming his entire body...

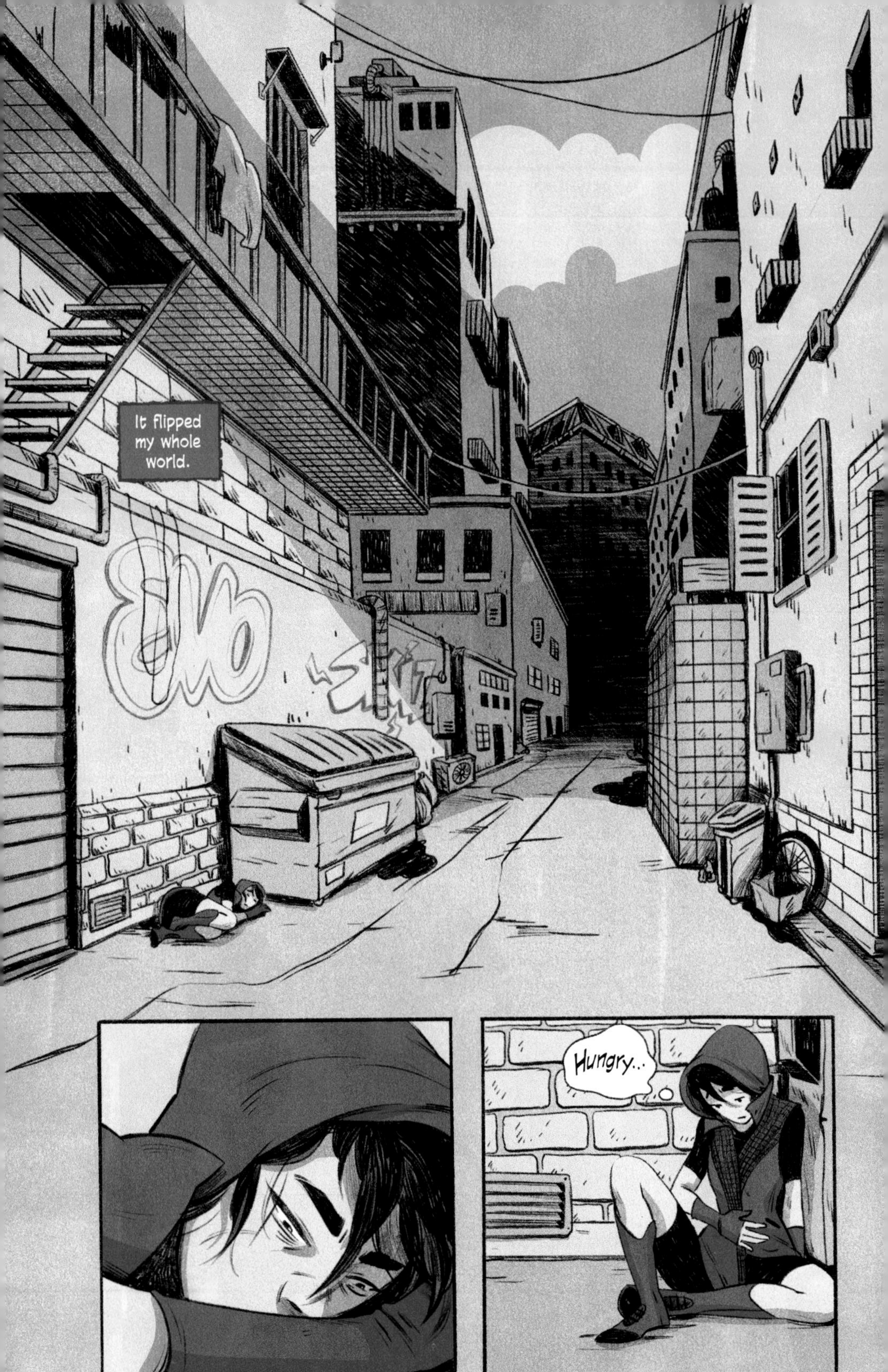
It flipped my whole world.
Hungry...

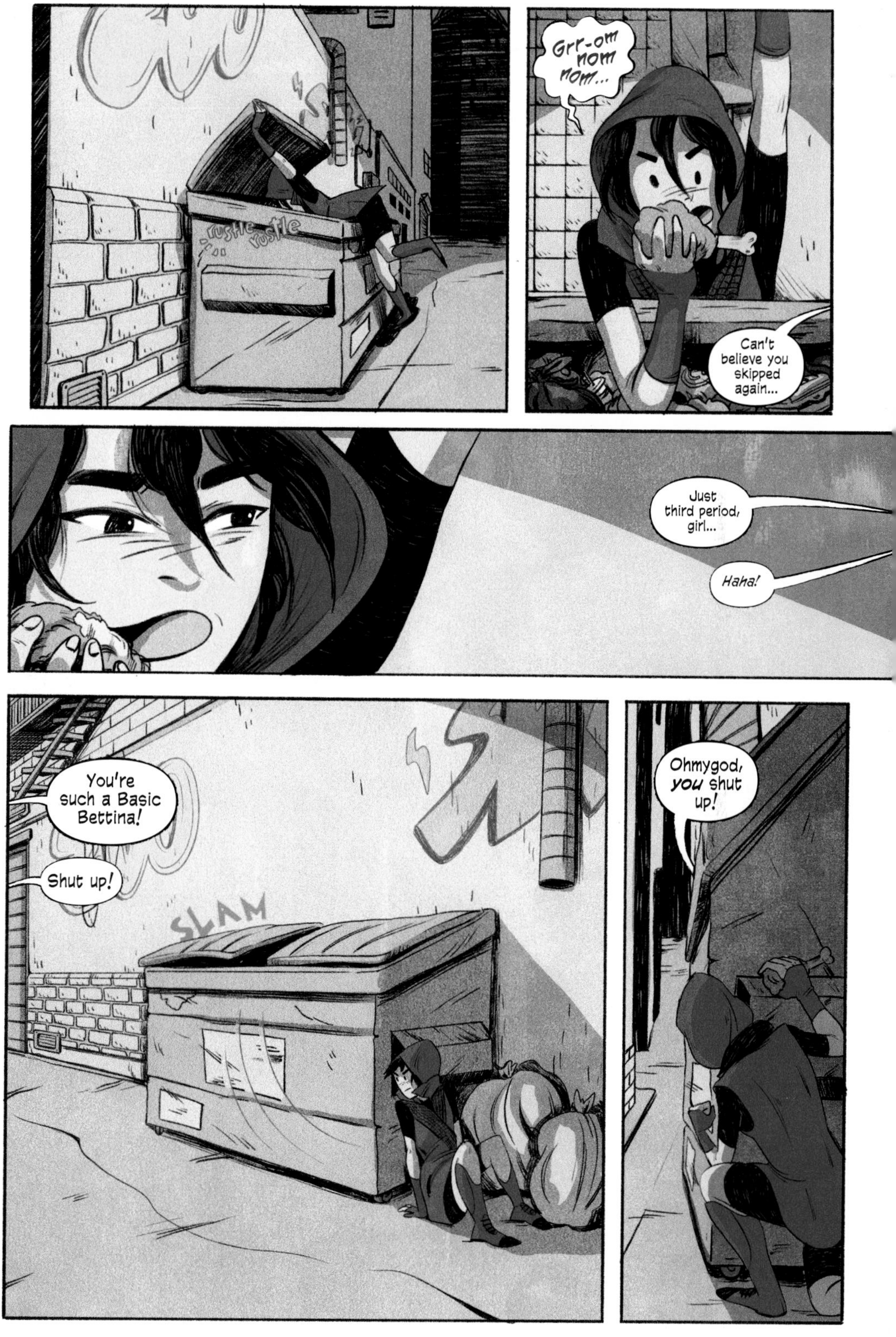
rustle rustle
Grr-om nom nom...
Can't believe you skipped again...
Just third period, girl...
Haha!
You're such a Basic Bettina!
Shut up!
SLAM
Ohmygod, *you* shut up!

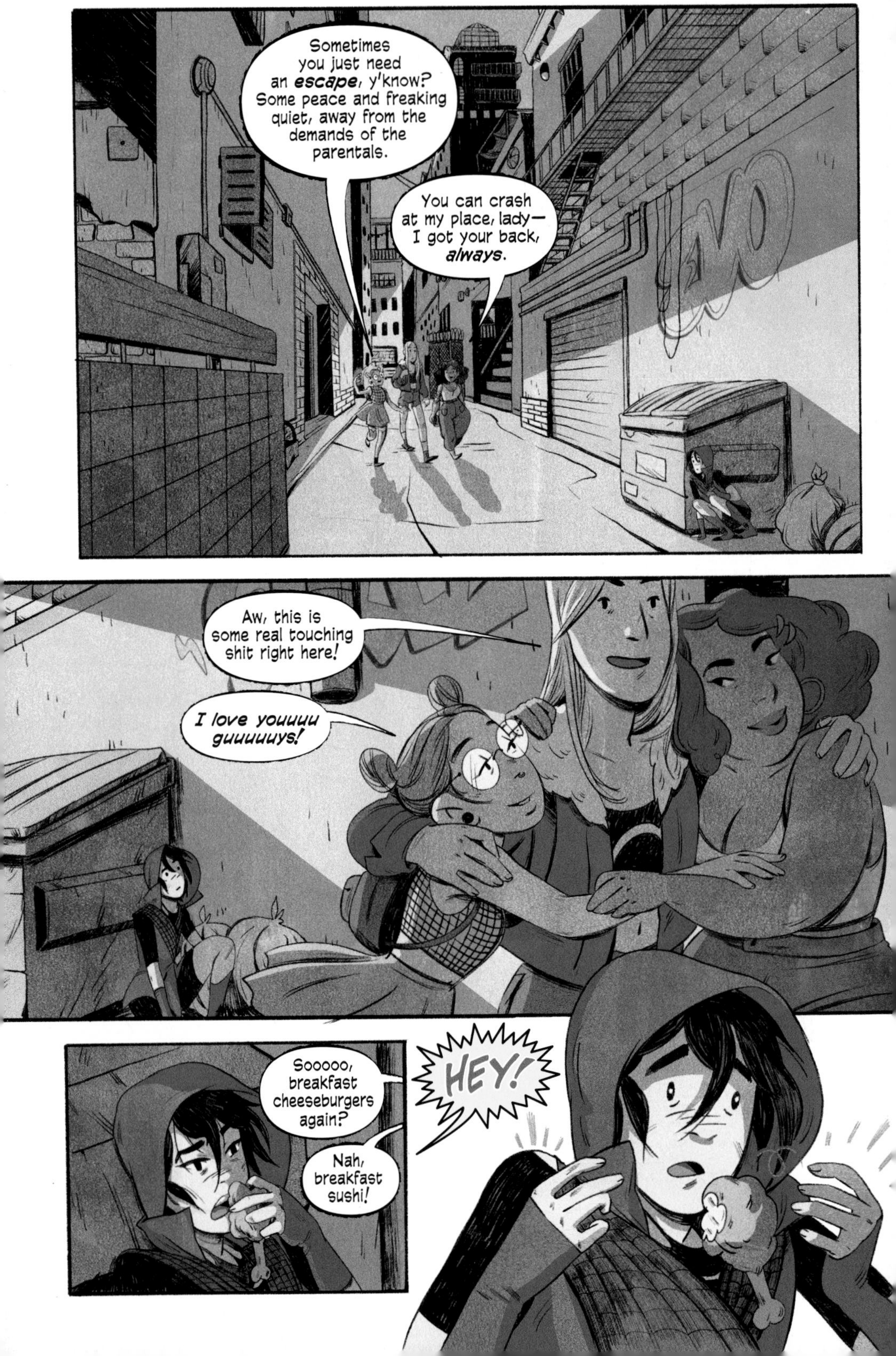

Sometimes you just need an *escape*, y'know? Some peace and freaking quiet, away from the demands of the parentals.
You can crash at my place, lady— I got your back, *always*.
Aw, this is some real touching shit right here!
I love youuuu guuuuuys!
Sooooo, breakfast cheeseburgers again?
Nah, breakfast sushi!
HEY!

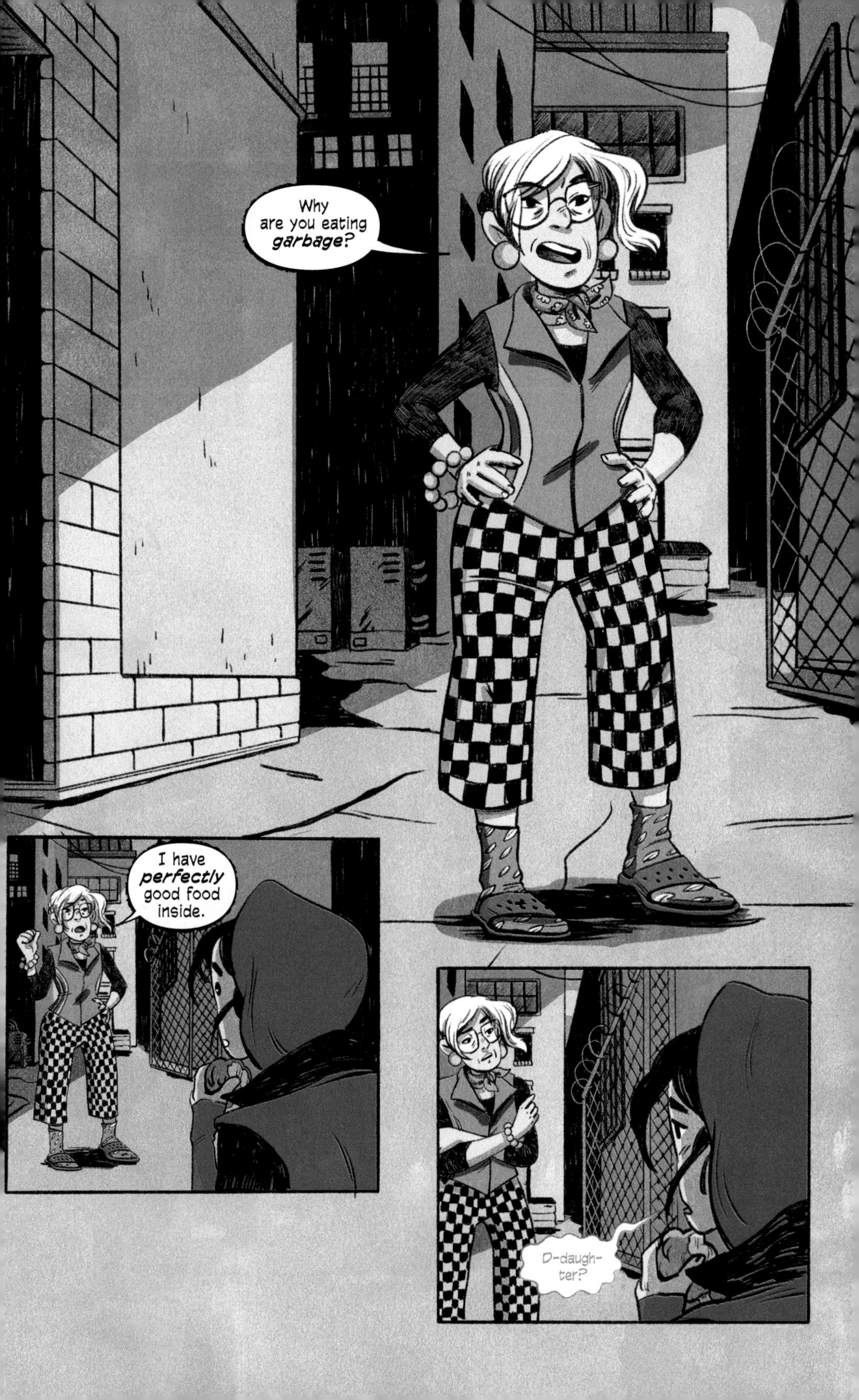
Why are you eating *garbage?*
I have *perfectly* good food inside.
D-daughter?

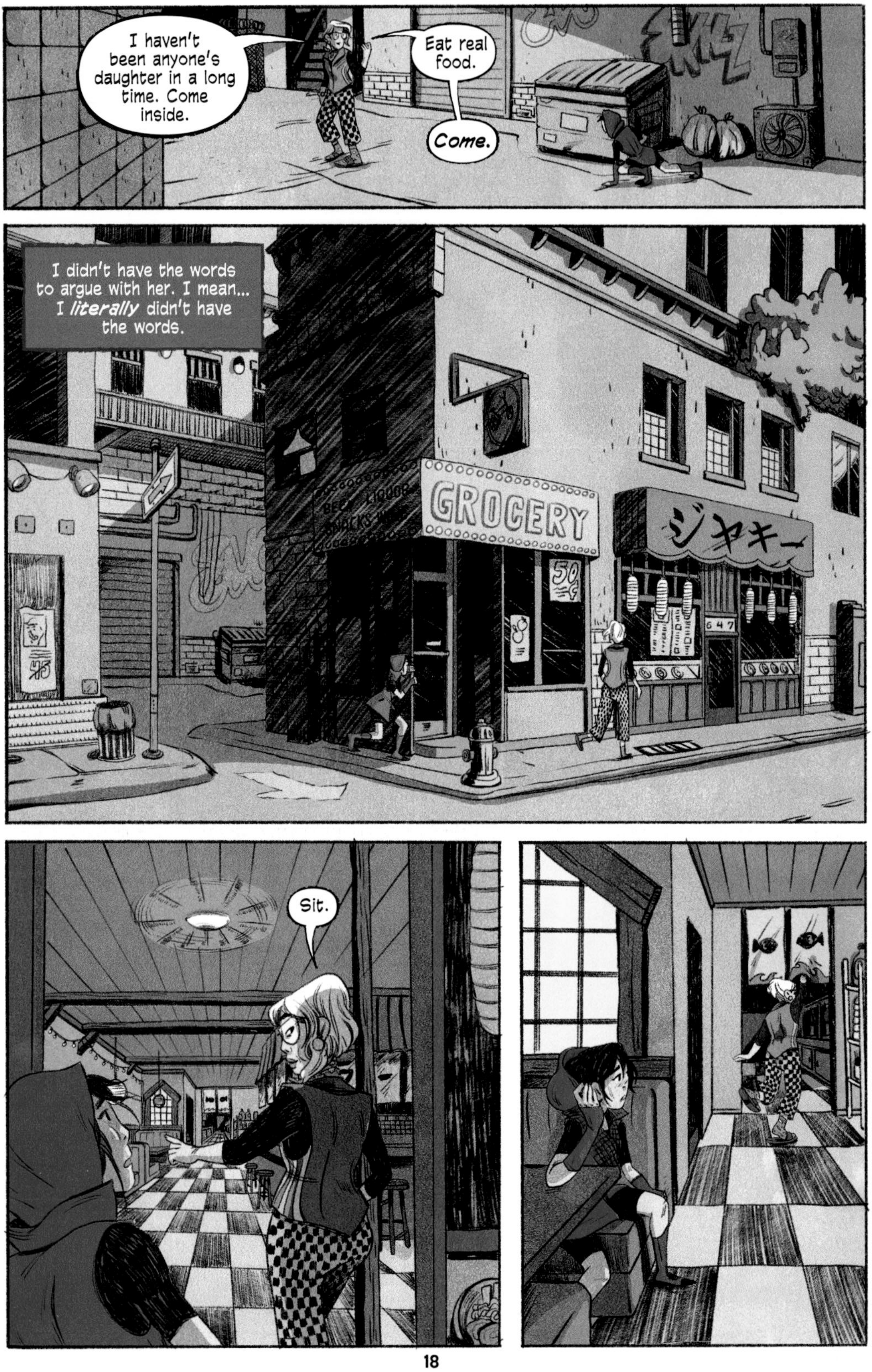

I haven't been anyone's daughter in a long time. Come inside.
Eat real food.
Come.
I didn't have the words to argue with her. I mean... I *literally* didn't have the words.
GROCERY
50¢
ジャキー
647
Sit.

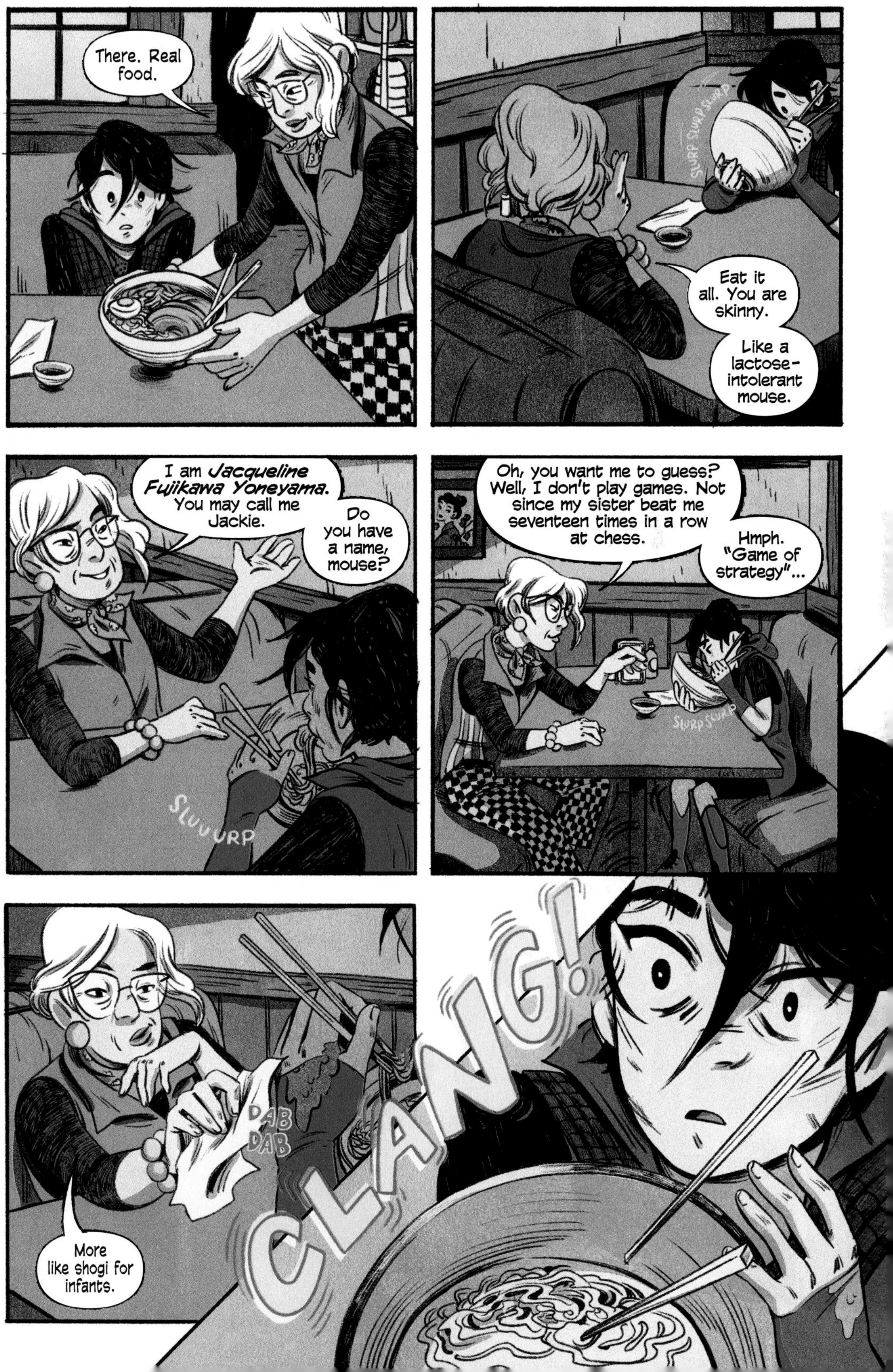
There. Real food.
SLURP SLURP SLURP
Eat it all. You are skinny.
Like a lactose-intolerant mouse.
I am *Jacqueline Fujikawa Yoneyama*. You may call me Jackie.
Do you have a name, mouse?
SLUUURP
Oh, you want me to guess? Well, I don't play games. Not since my sister beat me seventeen times in a row at chess.
Hmph. "Game of strategy"...
SLURP SLURP
DAB DAB
More like shogi for infants.
CLANG!

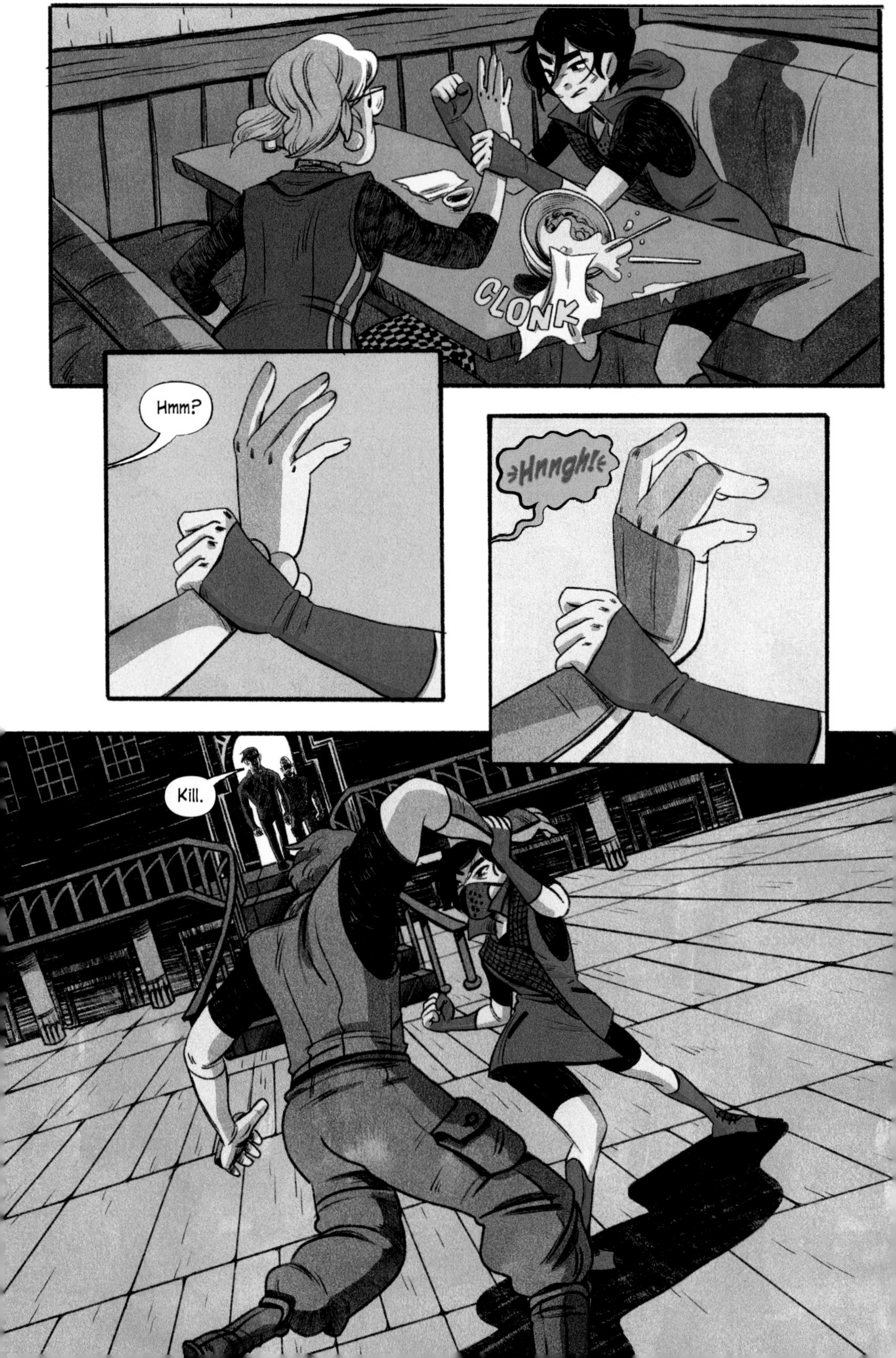
CLONK
Hmm?
Hnngh!
Kill.

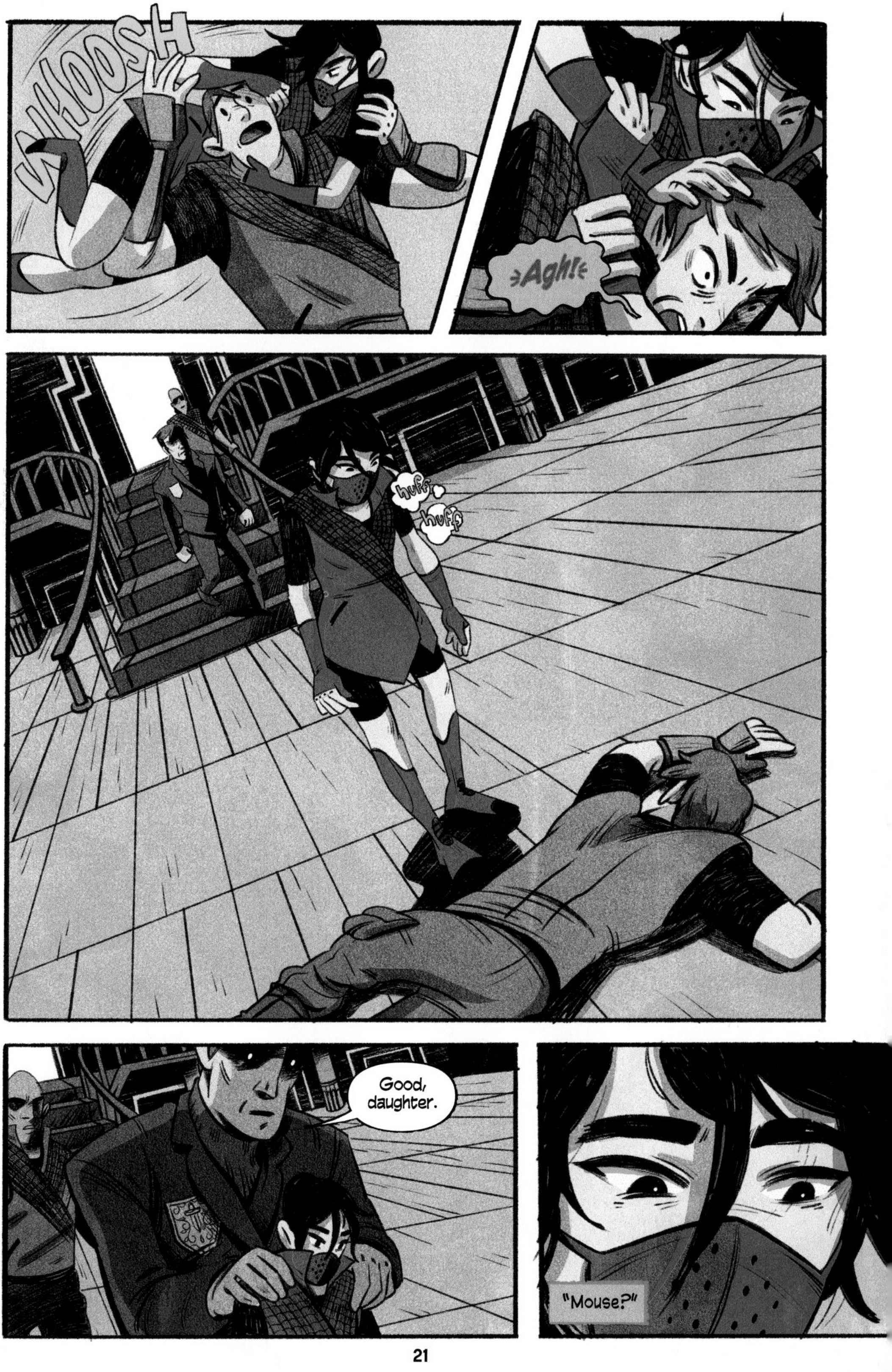
SWOOSH
Agh!
huff
huff
Good, daughter.
"Mouse?"

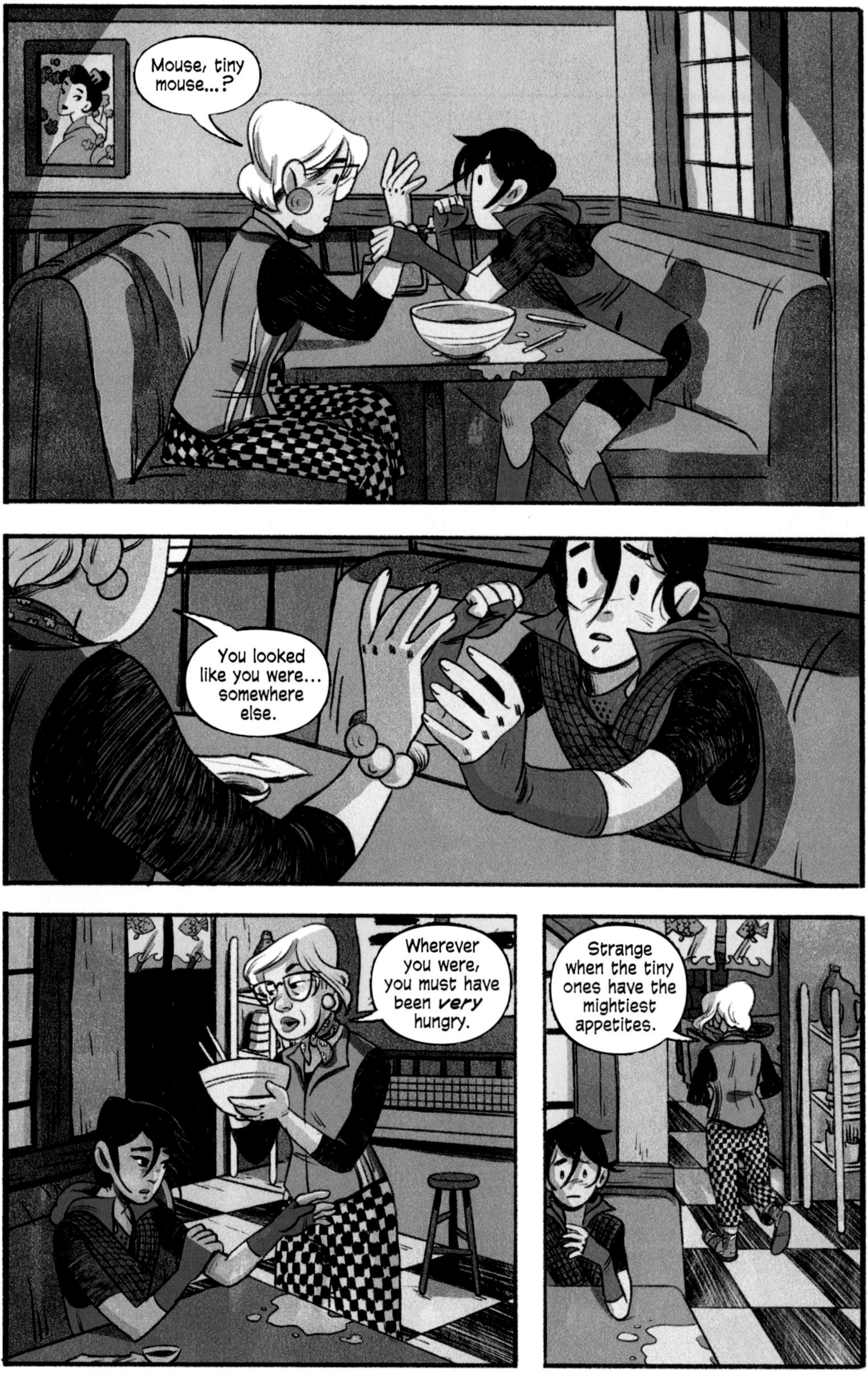
Mouse, tiny mouse...?
You looked like you were... somewhere else.
Wherever you were, you must have been *very* hungry.
Strange when the tiny ones have the mightiest appetites.

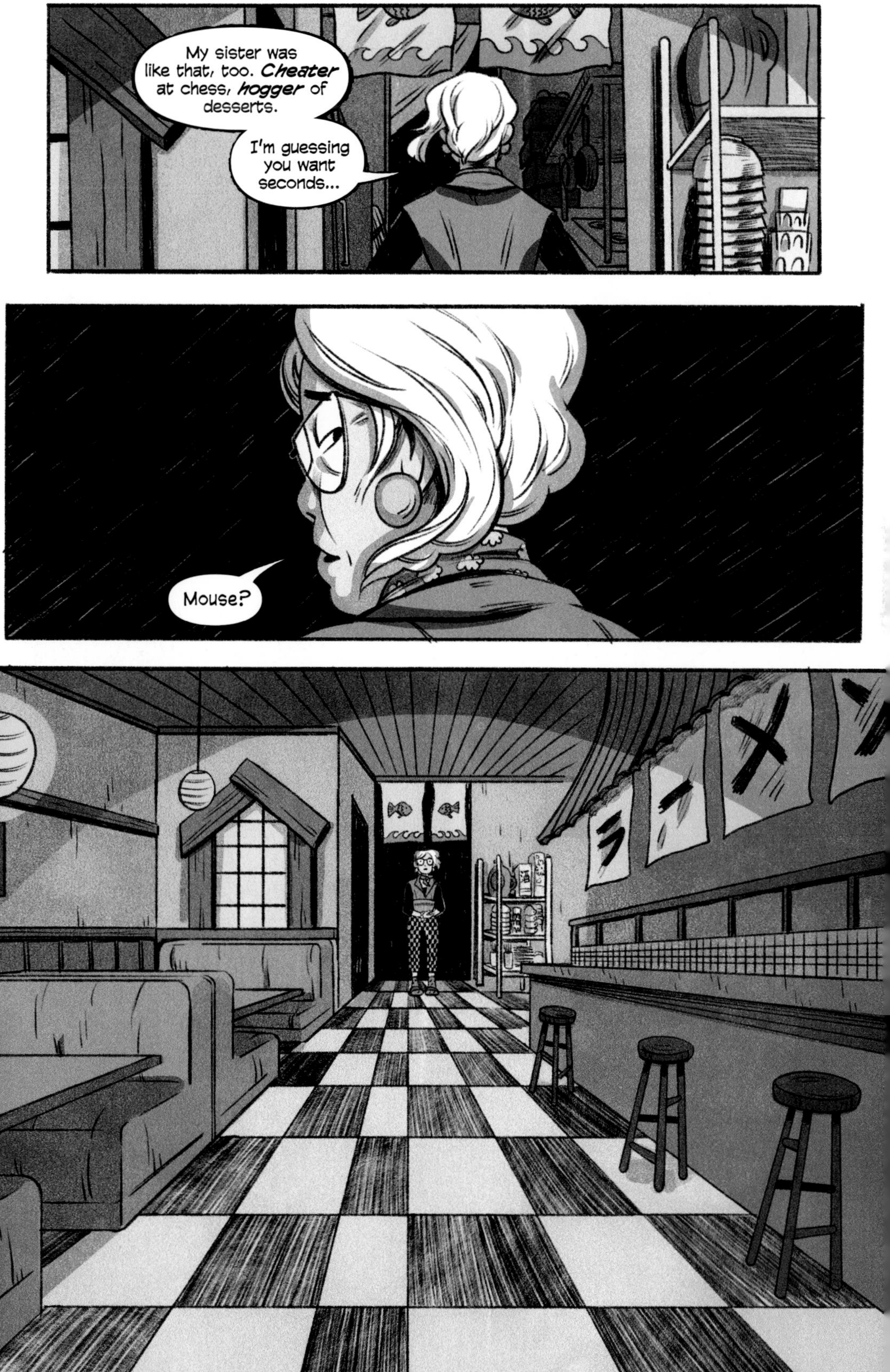
My sister was like that, too. *Cheater* at chess, *hogger* of desserts.
I'm guessing you want seconds...
Mouse?

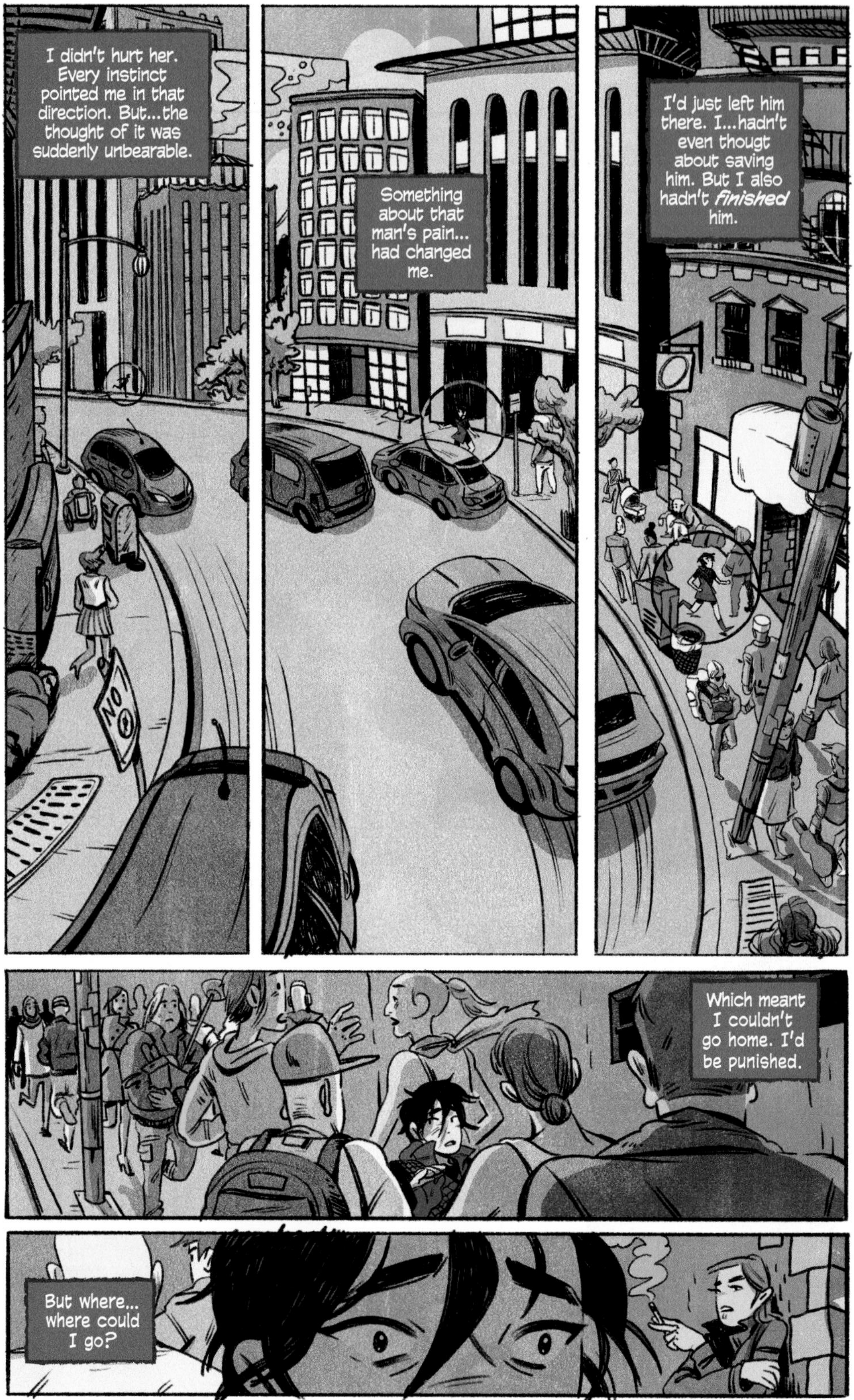
I didn't hurt her. Every instinct pointed me in that direction. But...the thought of it was suddenly unbearable.
NO
Something about that man's pain... had changed me.
I'd just left him there. I...hadn't even thougt about saving him. But I also hadn't *finished* him.
Which meant I couldn't go home. I'd be punished.
But where... where could I go?

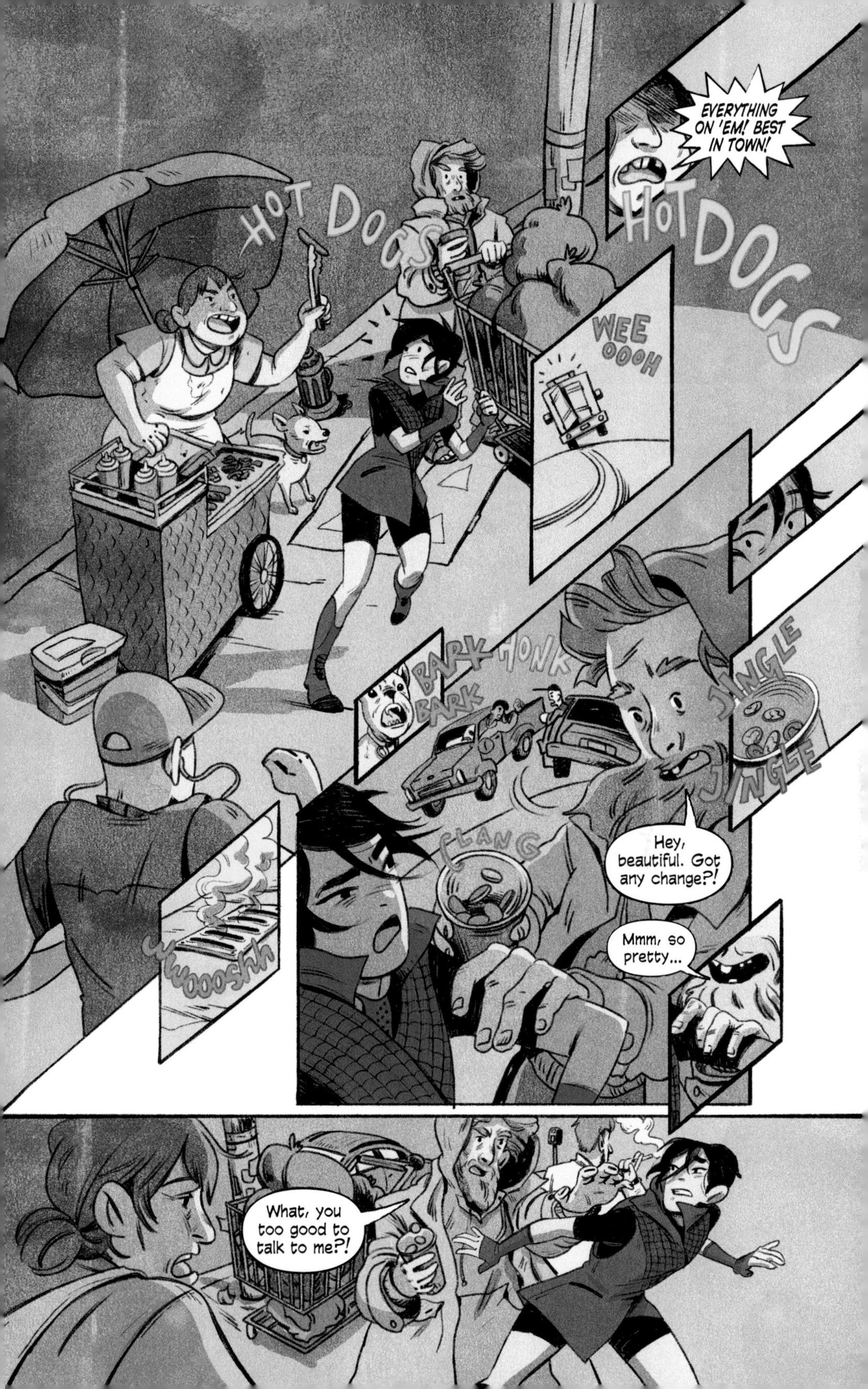
HOT DOGS
EVERYTHING ON 'EM! BEST IN TOWN!
HOT DOGS
WEE OOOH
BARK BARK
HONK
JINGLE JINGLE
CLANG
WHOOOSHH
Hey, beautiful. Got any change?!
Mmm, so pretty...
What, you too good to talk to me?!

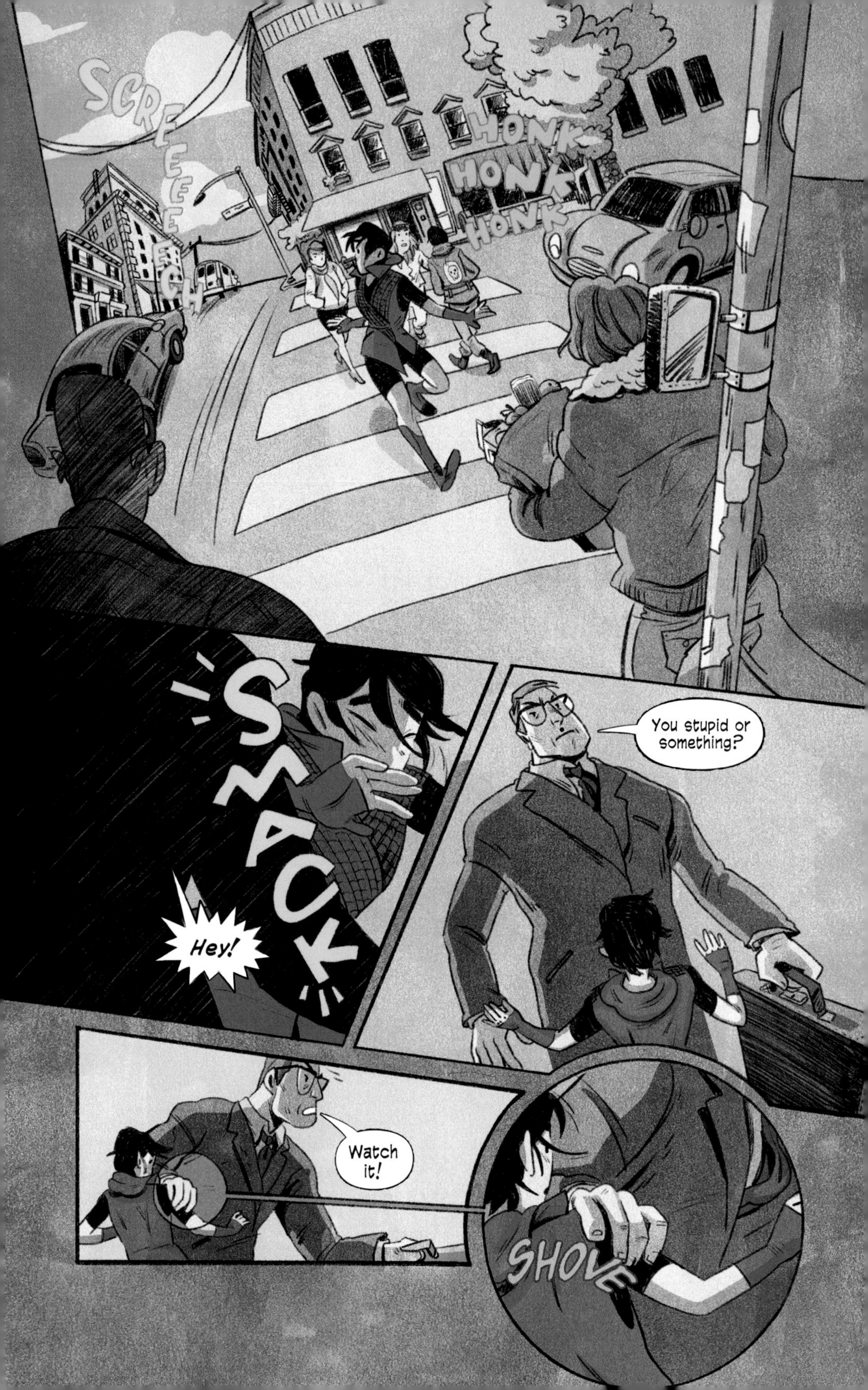
SCREEEEECH
HONK
HONK
HONK
SMACK
Hey!
You stupid or something?
Watch it!
SHOVE

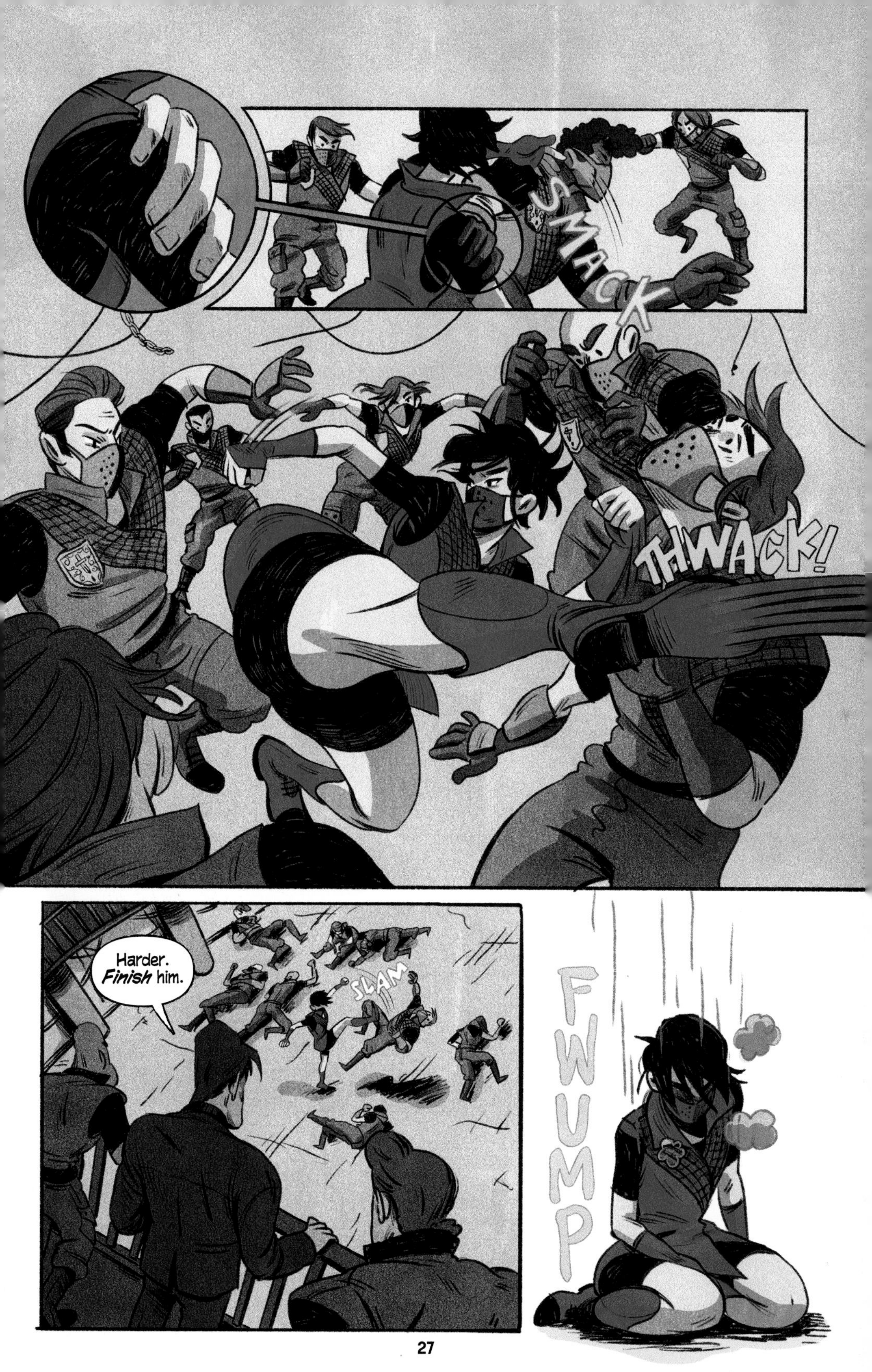
SMACK
THWACK!
Harder. *Finish* him.
SLAM
FWUMP

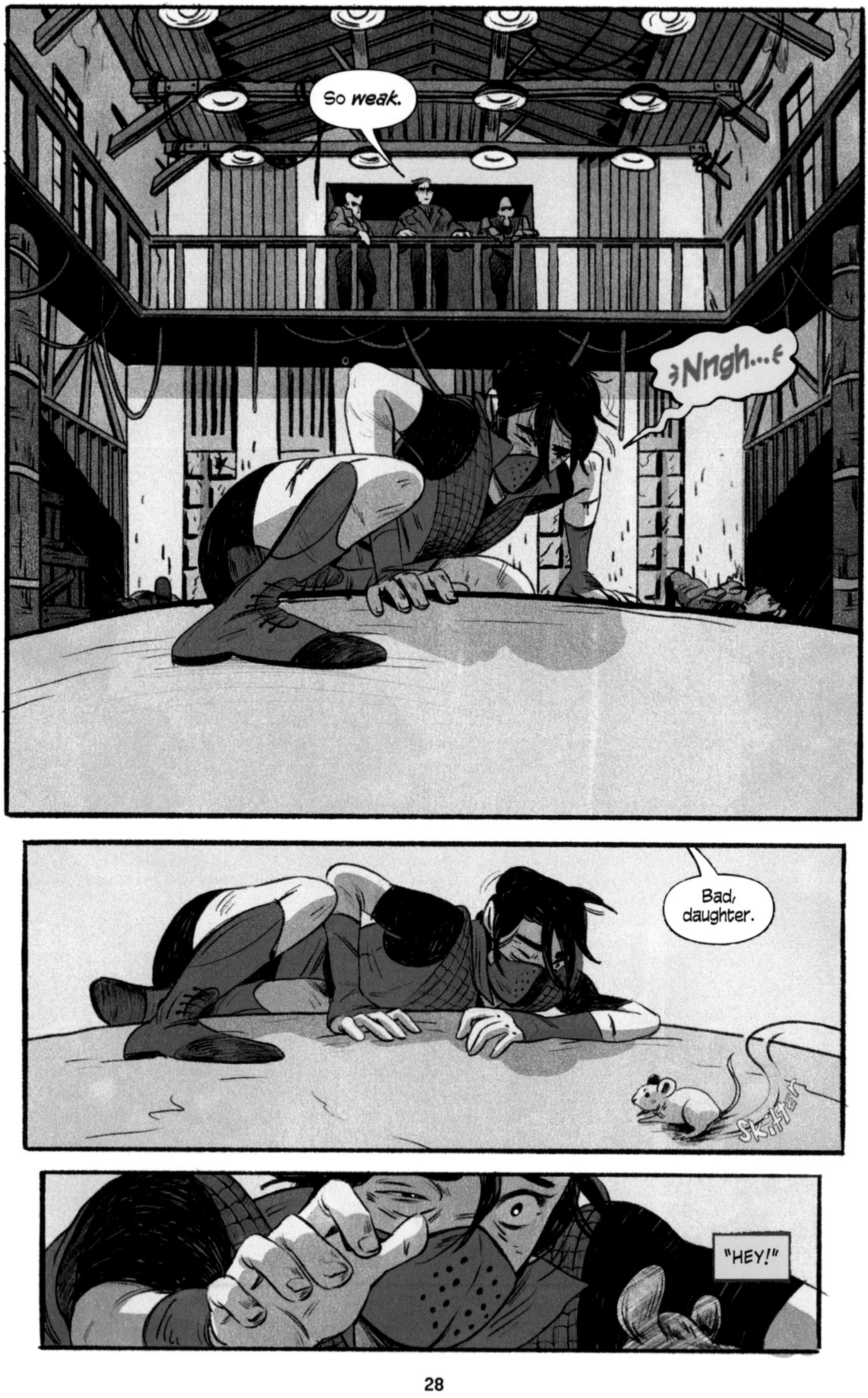
So weak.
Nngh...
Bad, daughter.
Skitter
"HEY!"

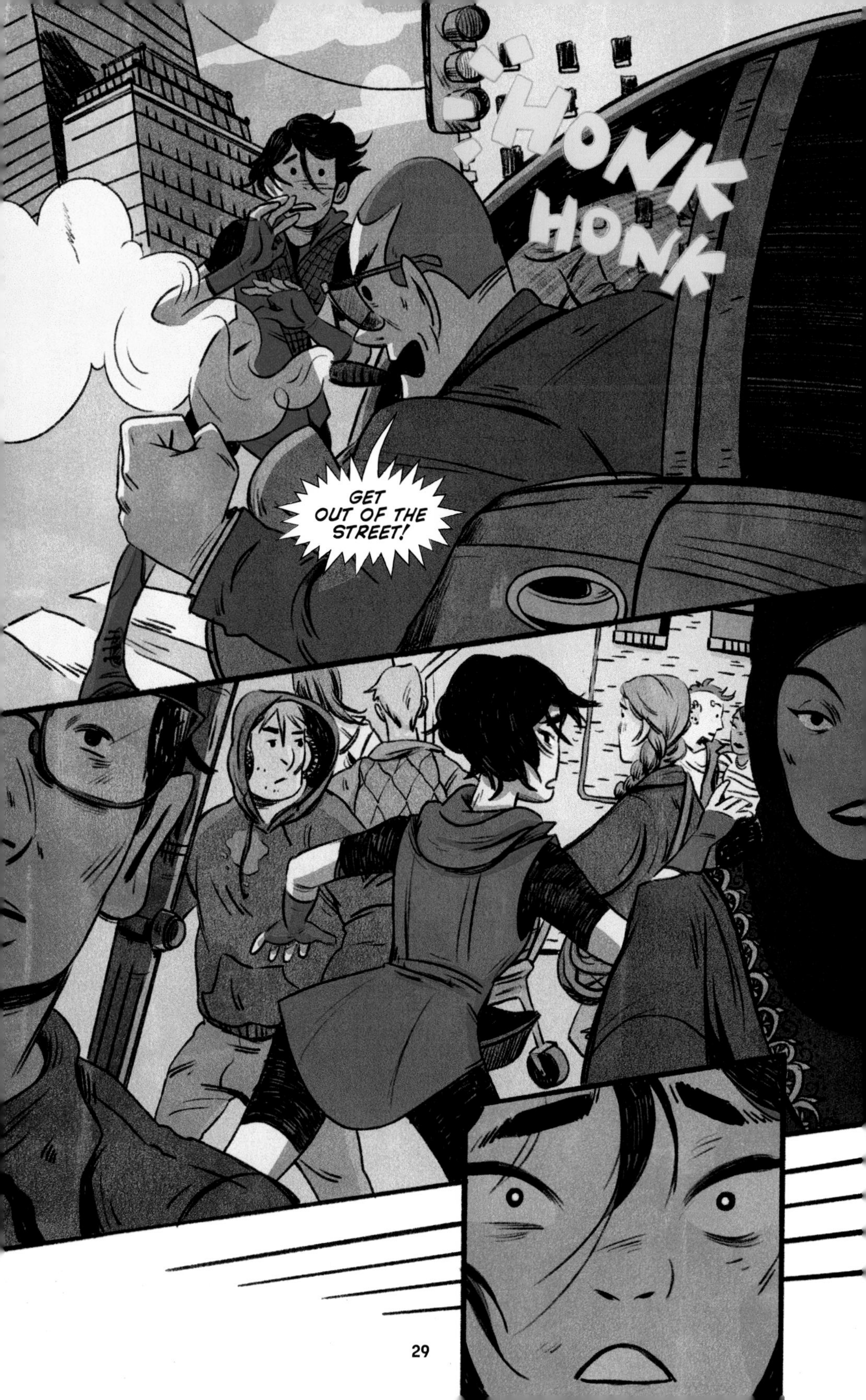
HONK
HONK
GET OUT OF THE STREET!

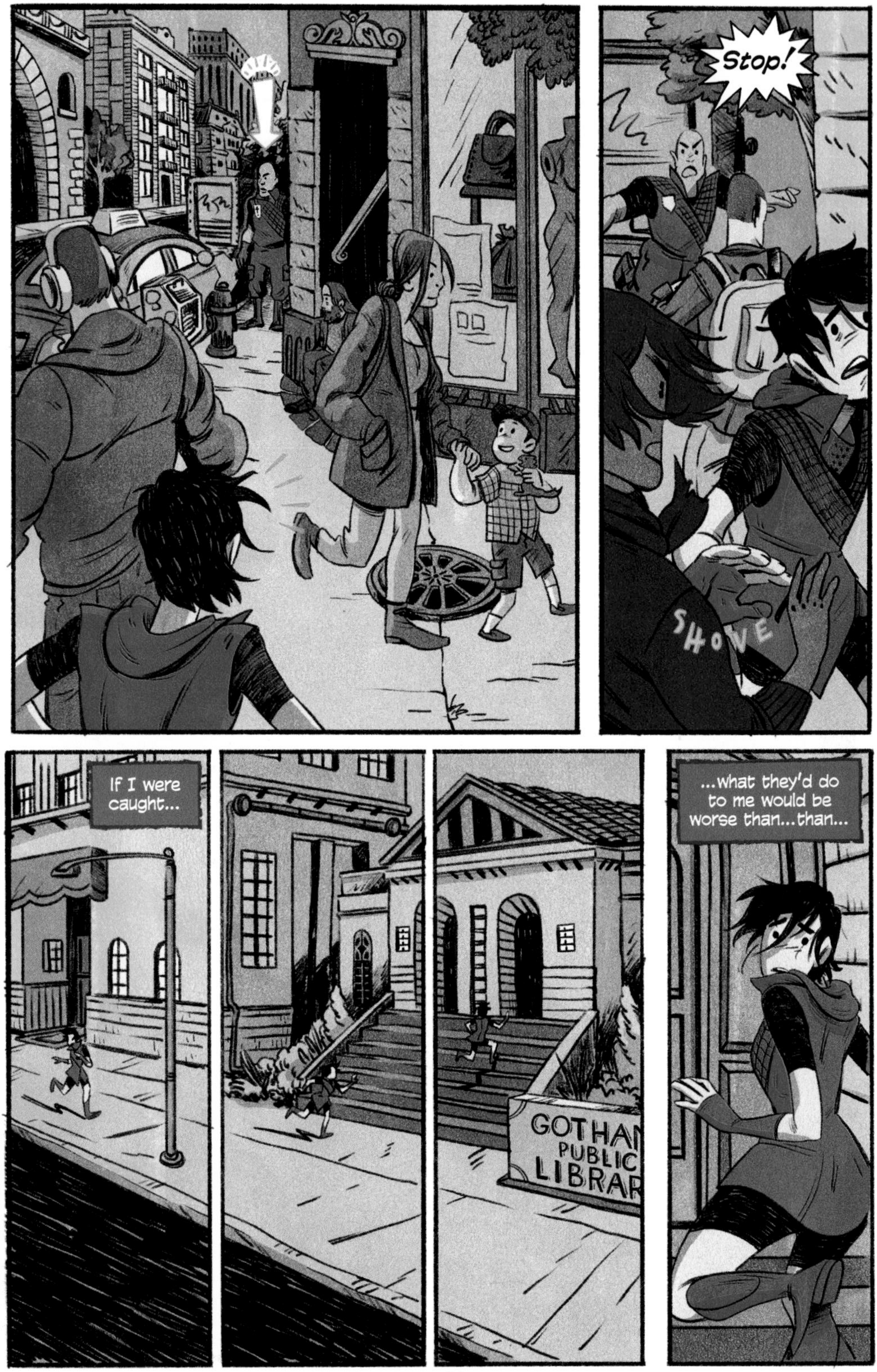
Stop!
SHOVE
If I were caught...
GOTHAM PUBLIC LIBRARY
...what they'd do to me would be worse than...than...

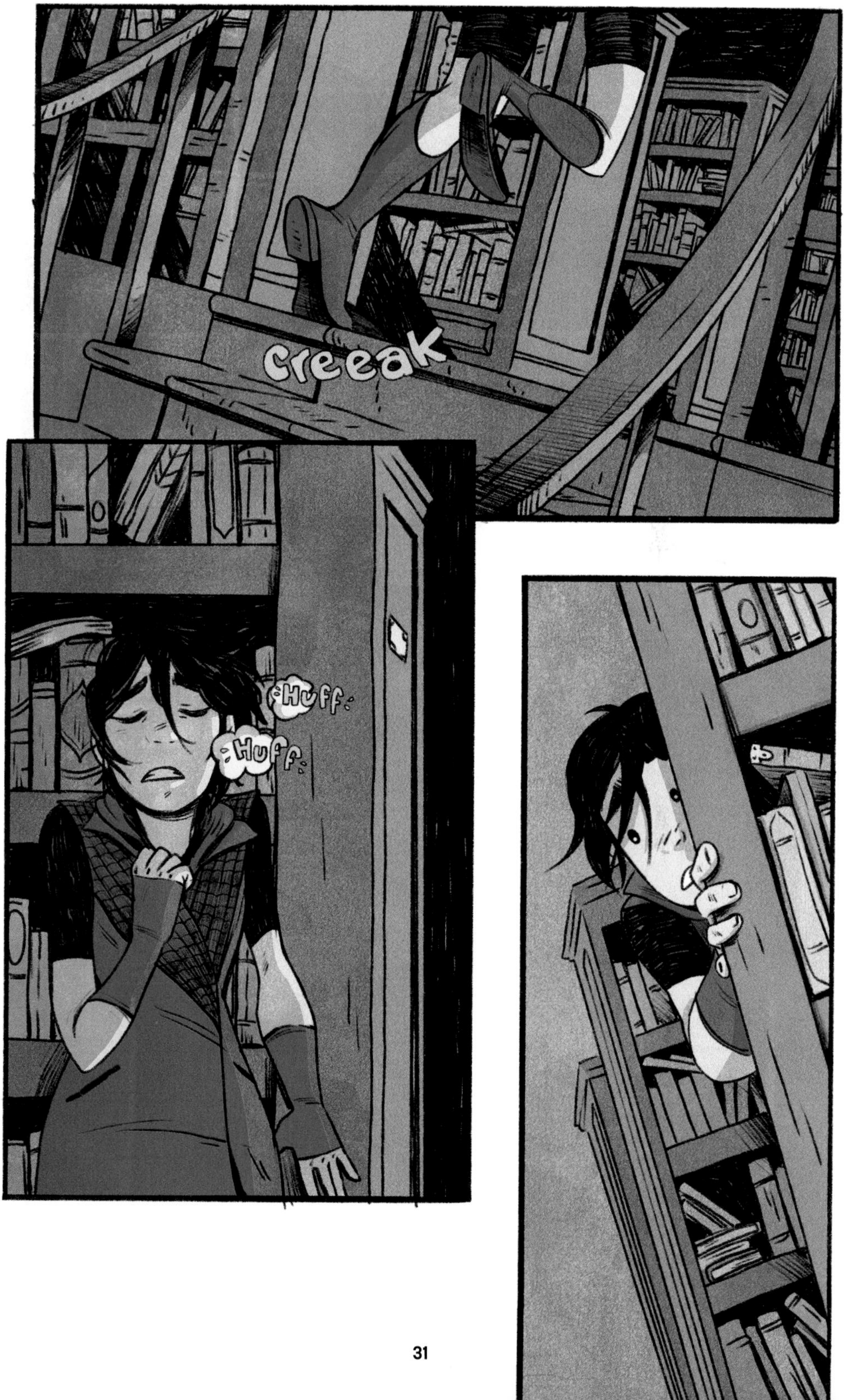
creeak
Huff
Huff

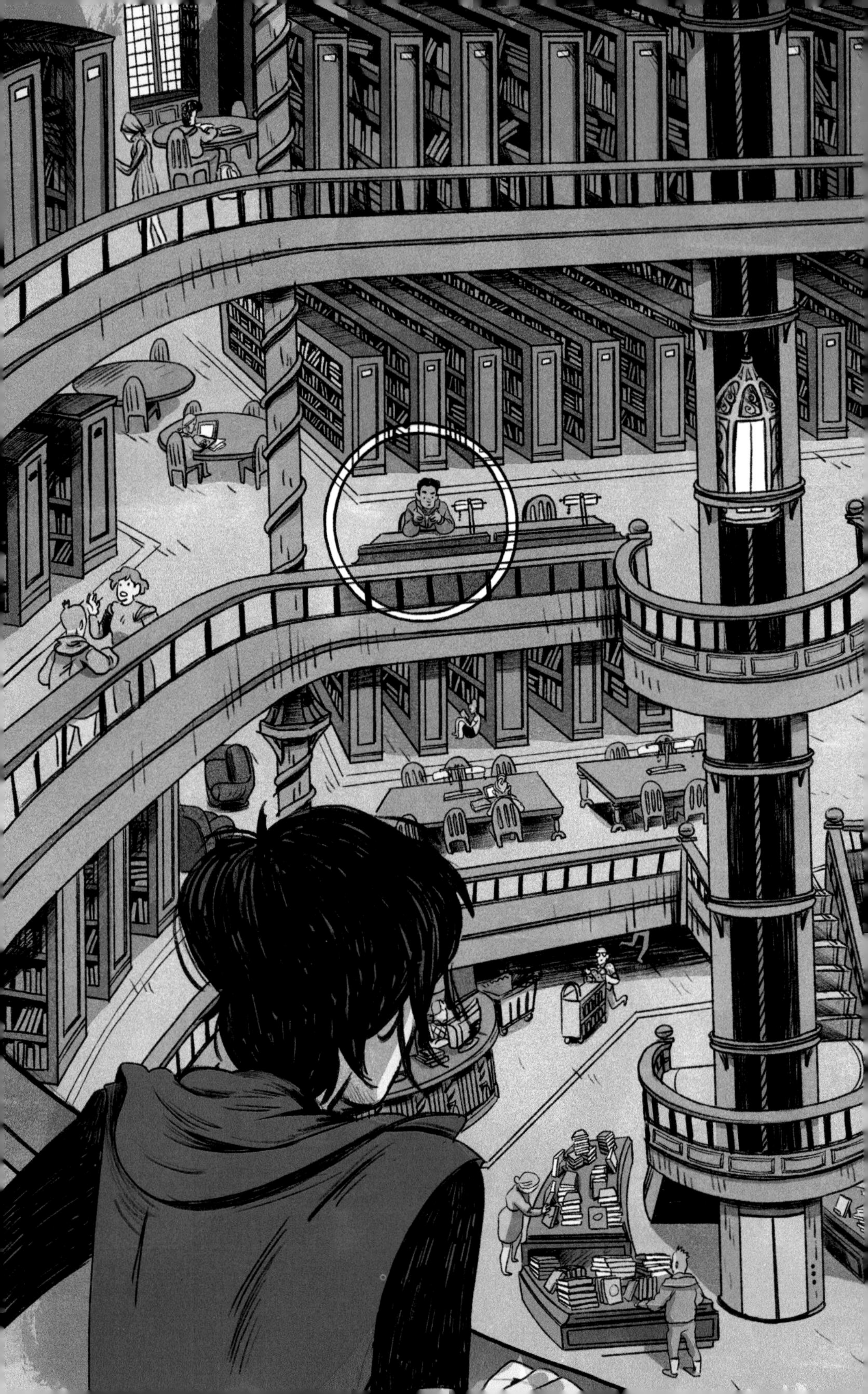

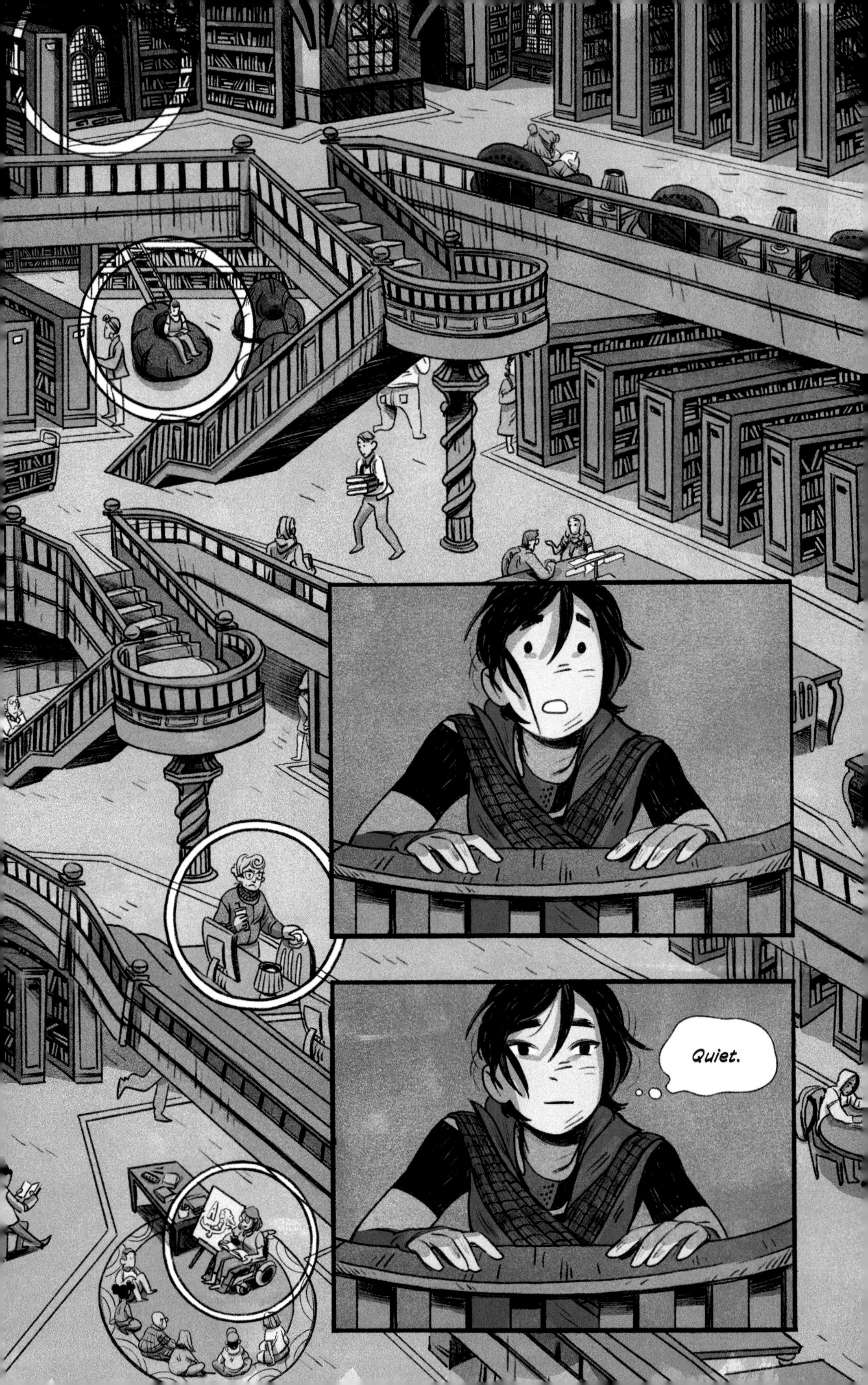
Quiet.

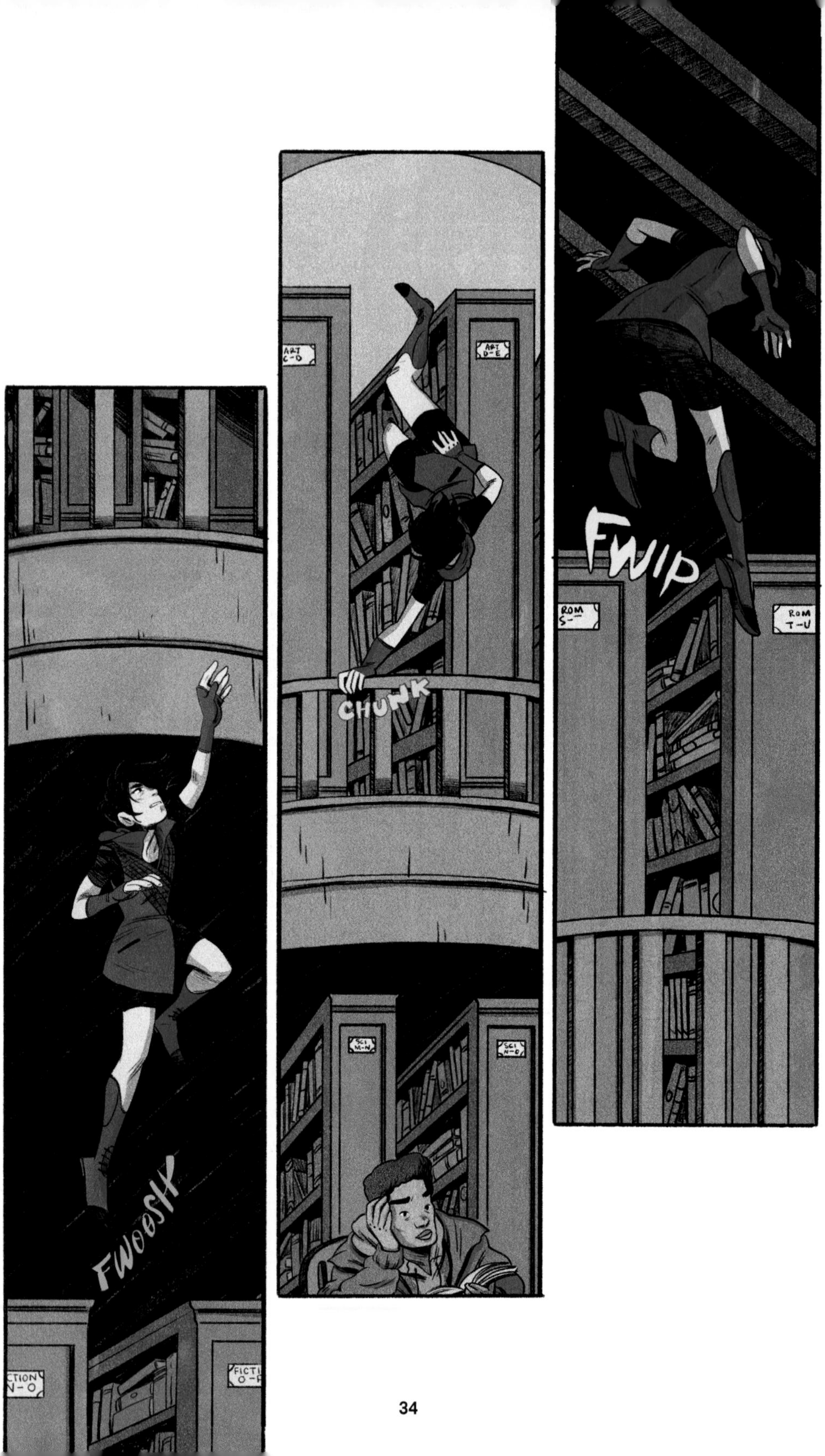
FWOOSH
FICTION N-O
FICTI O-P
ART C-D
ART D-E
CHUNK
SCI M-N
SCI N-O
FWIP
ROM S-
ROM T-U

Creeeeak

Pitter pat

Pitter Pat

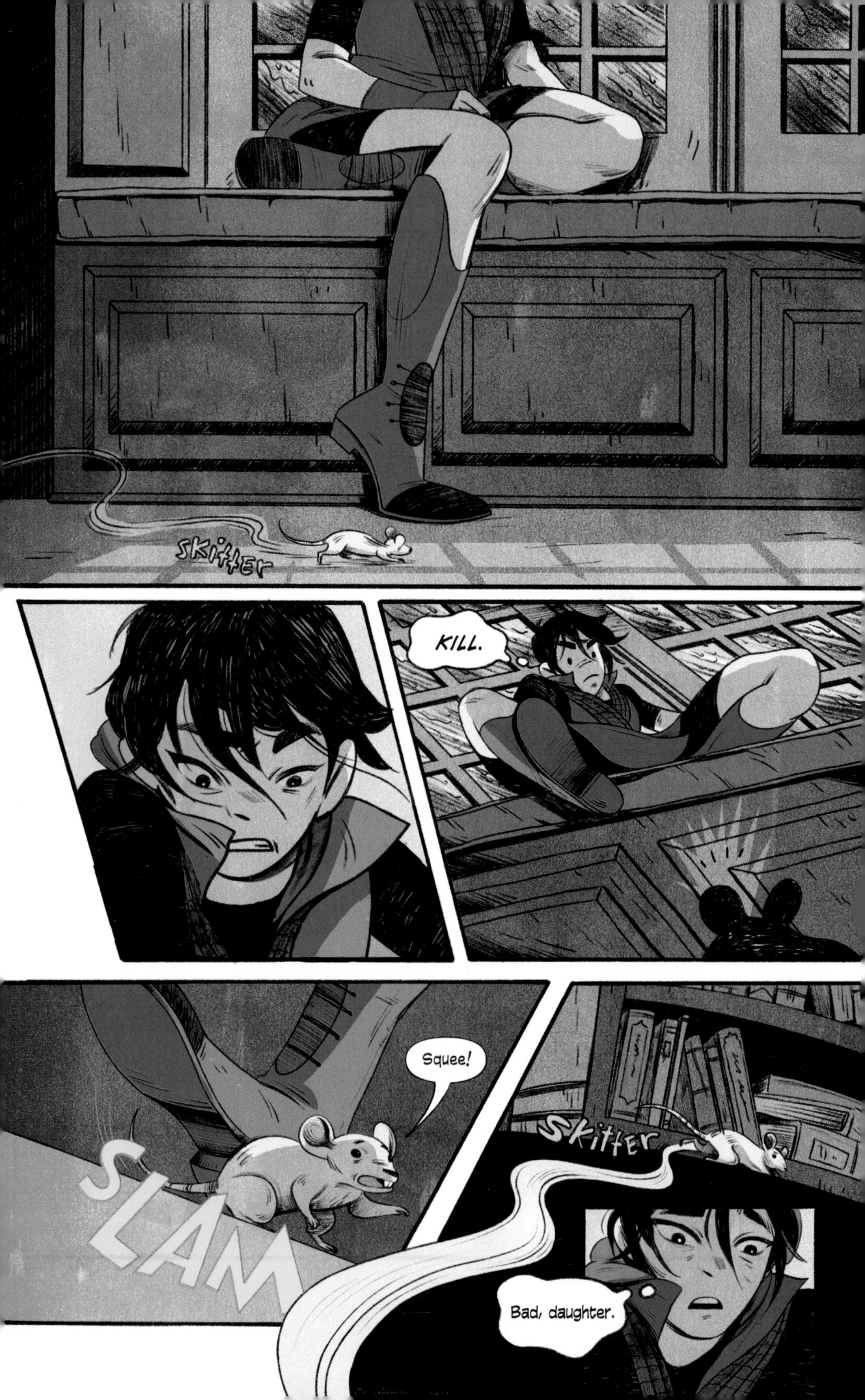
SKITTER
KILL.
Squee!
SLAM
SKITTER
Bad, daughter.

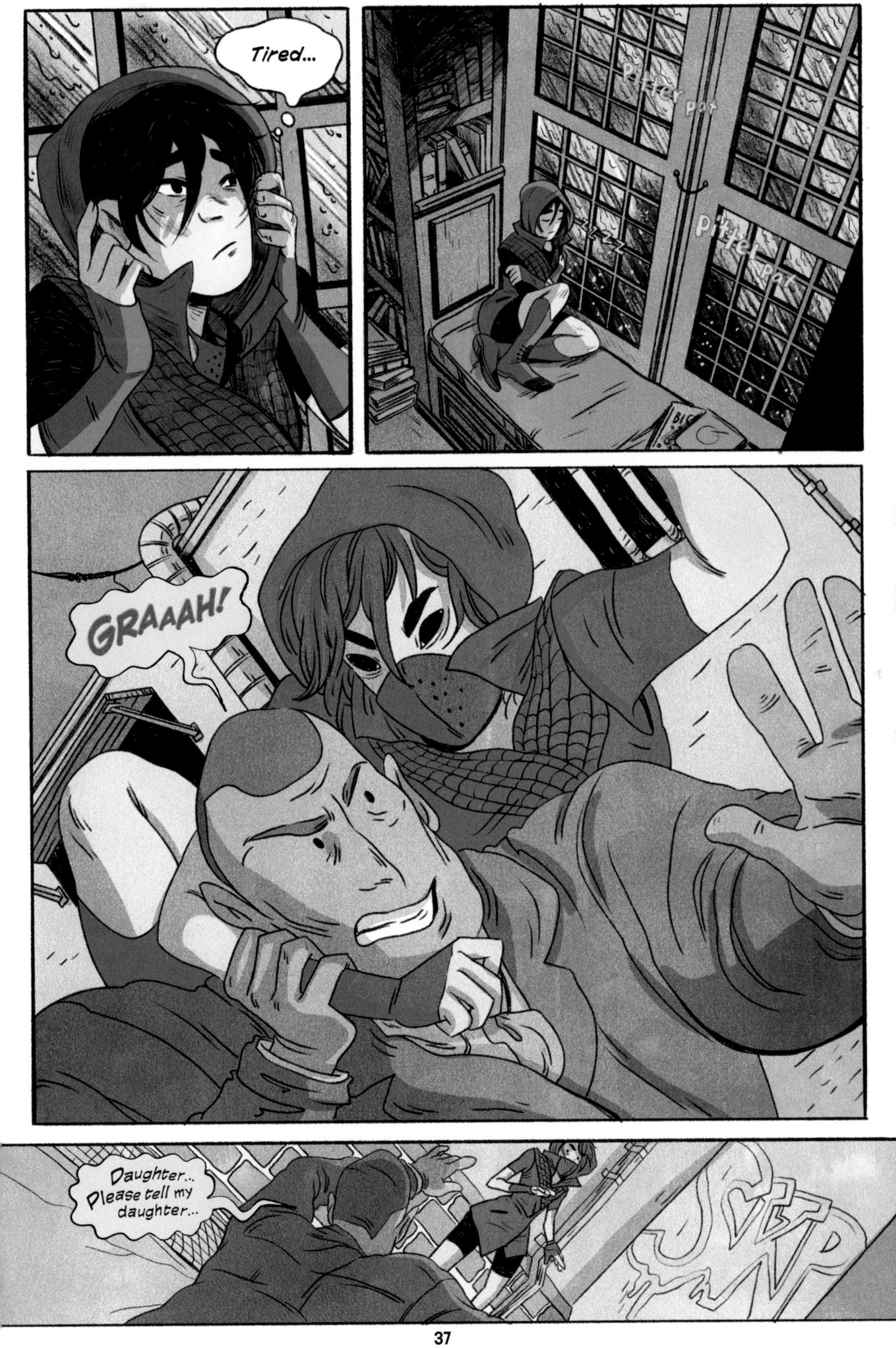
Tired...
Pitter pat
Pitter pat
GRAAAH!
Daughter... Please tell my daughter...

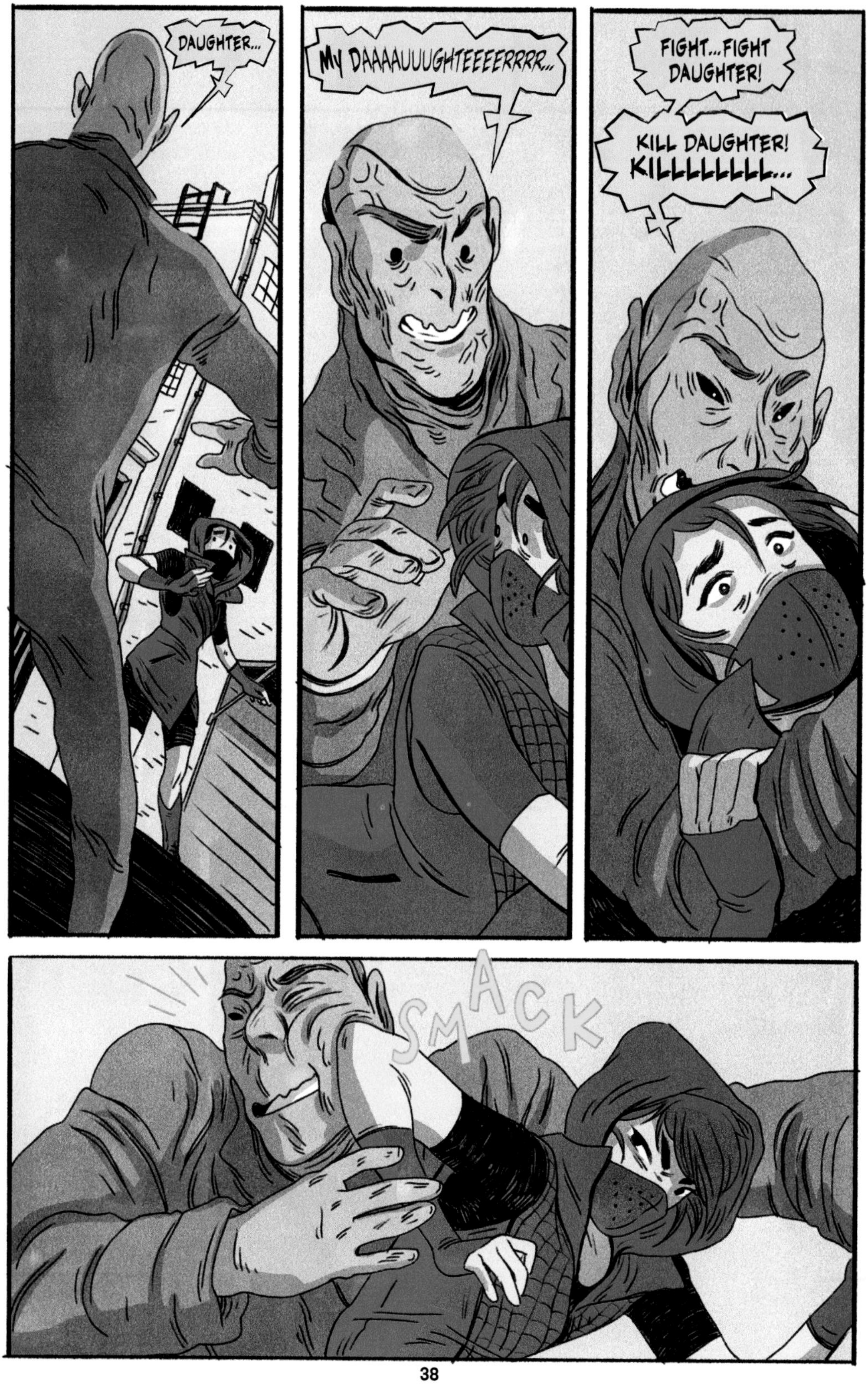
DAUGHTER...
MY DAAAAUUUGHTEEEERRRR...
FIGHT...FIGHT DAUGHTER!
KILL DAUGHTER! KILLLLLLLL...
SMACK

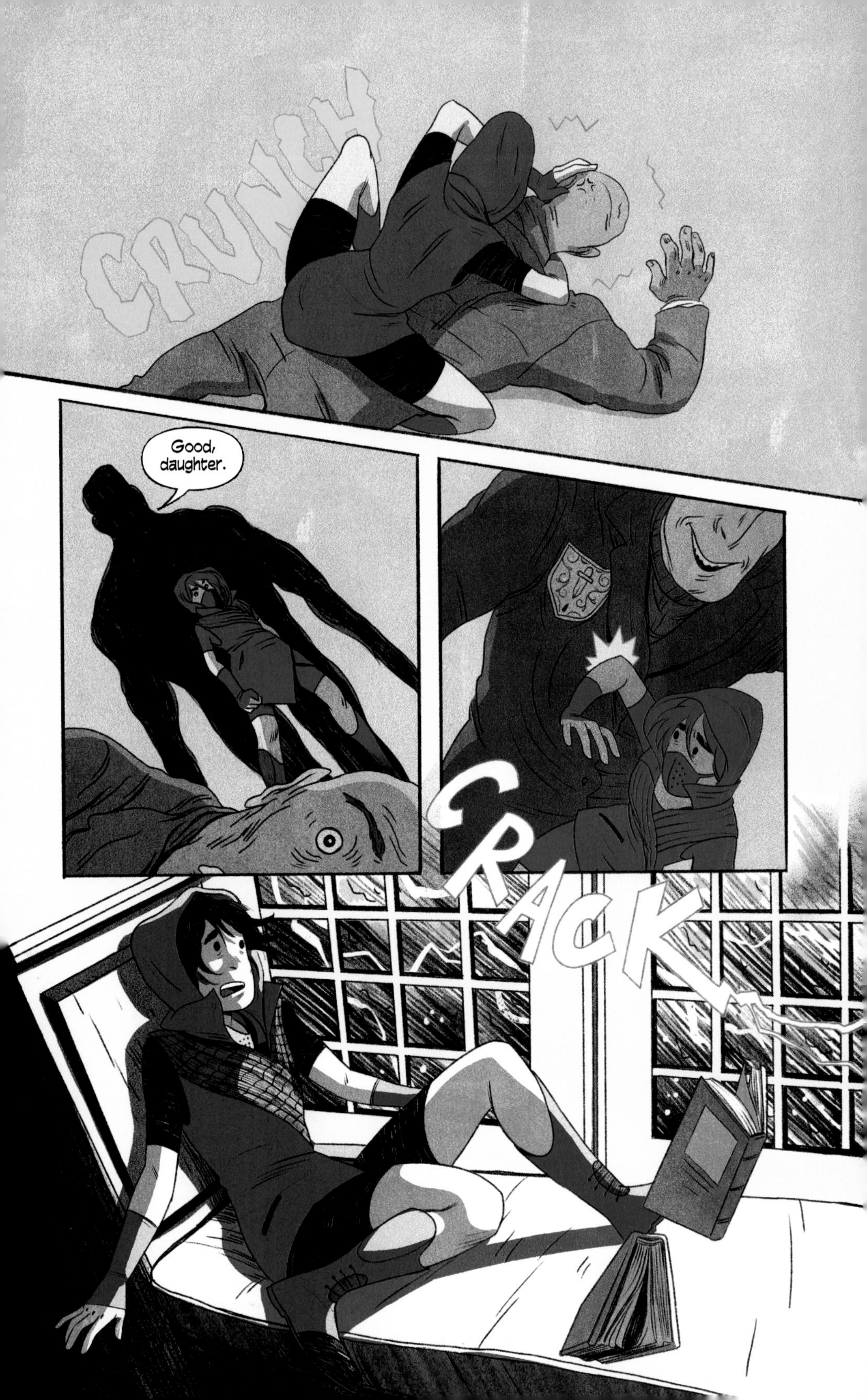
CRUNCH
Good, daughter.
CRACK

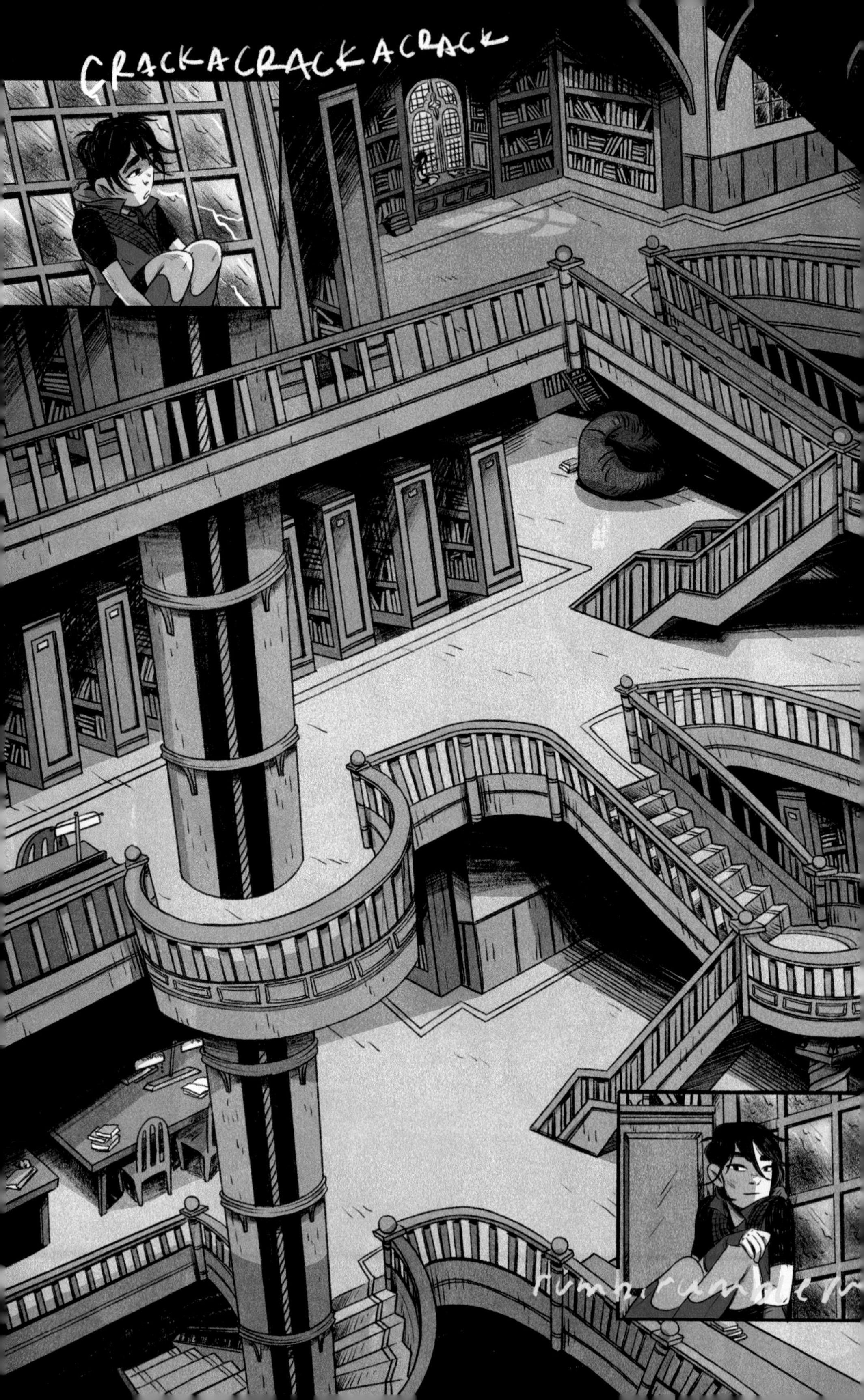
CRACKACRACKACRACK
rumble

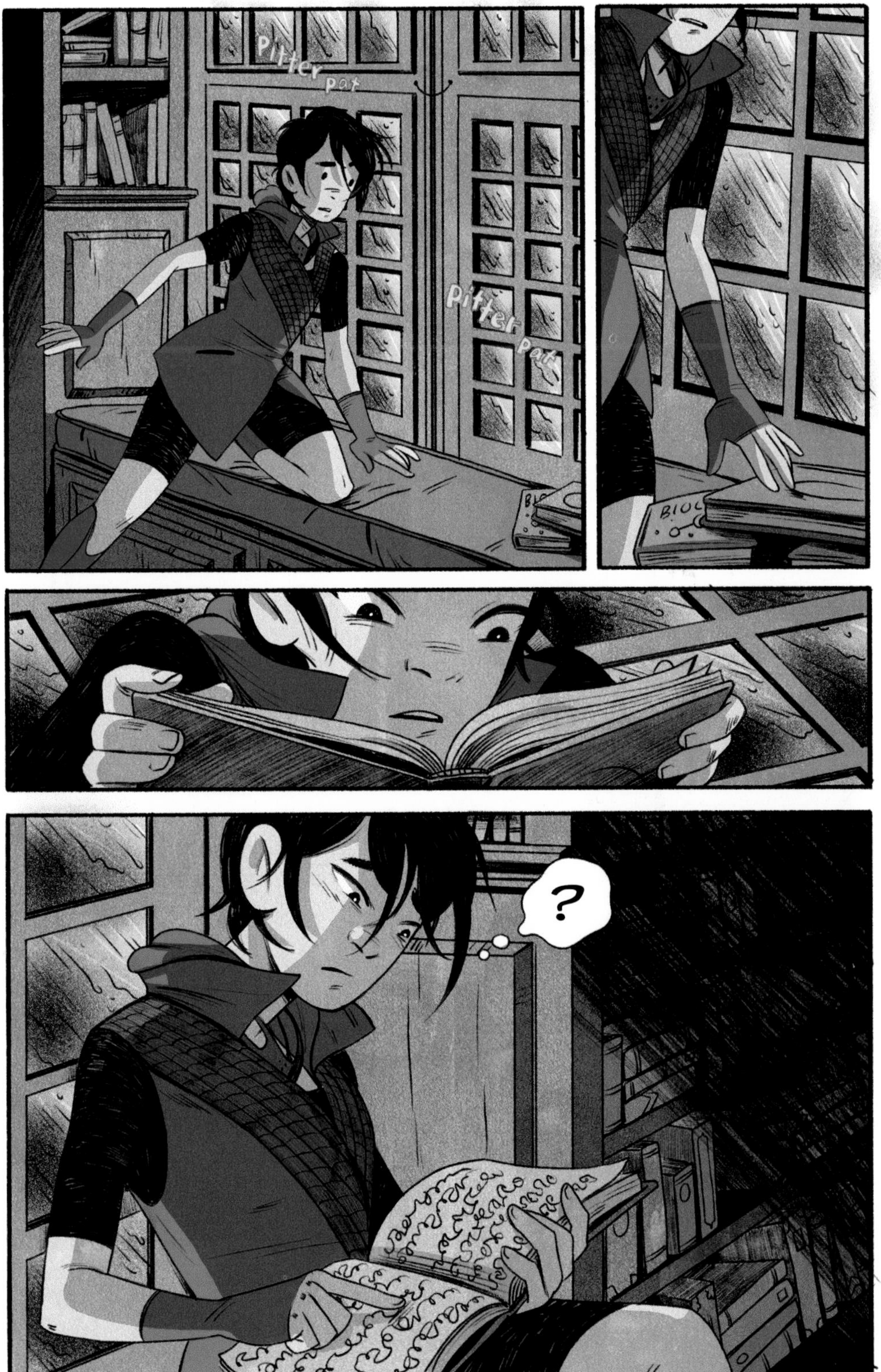
Pitter pat
Pitter pat
?

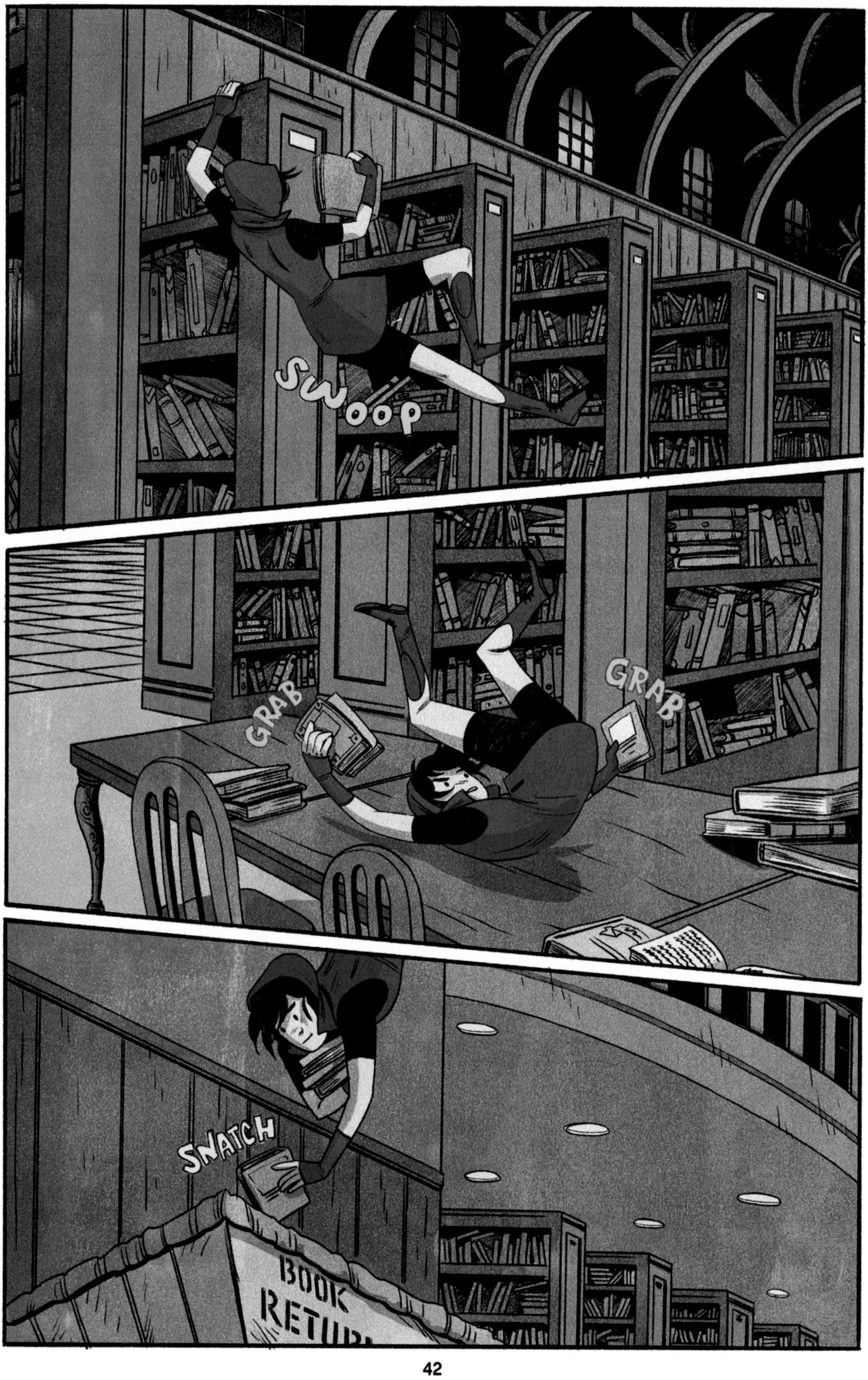
SWOOP
GRAB
GRAB
SNATCH
BOOK
RETUR

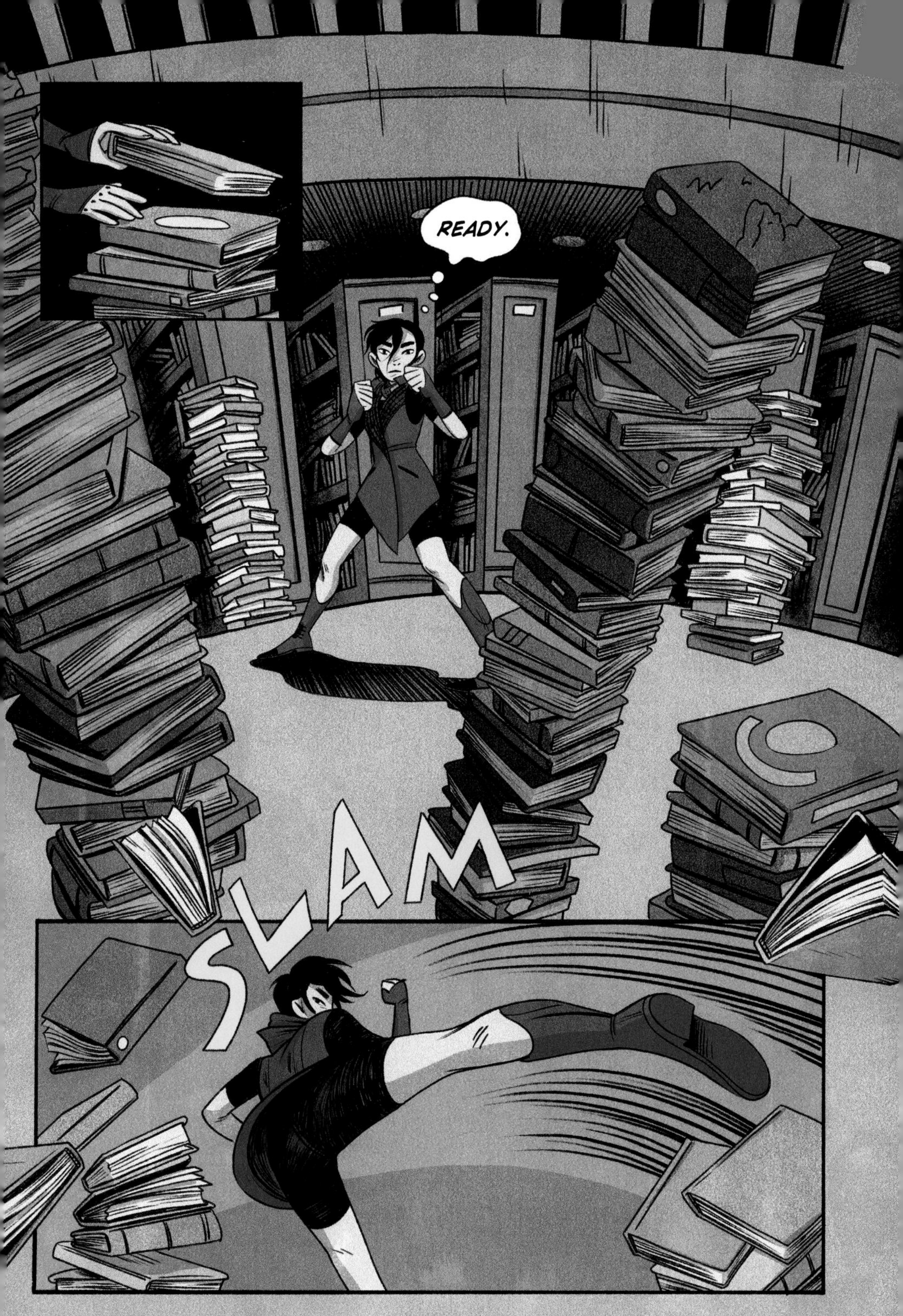
READY.
SLAM

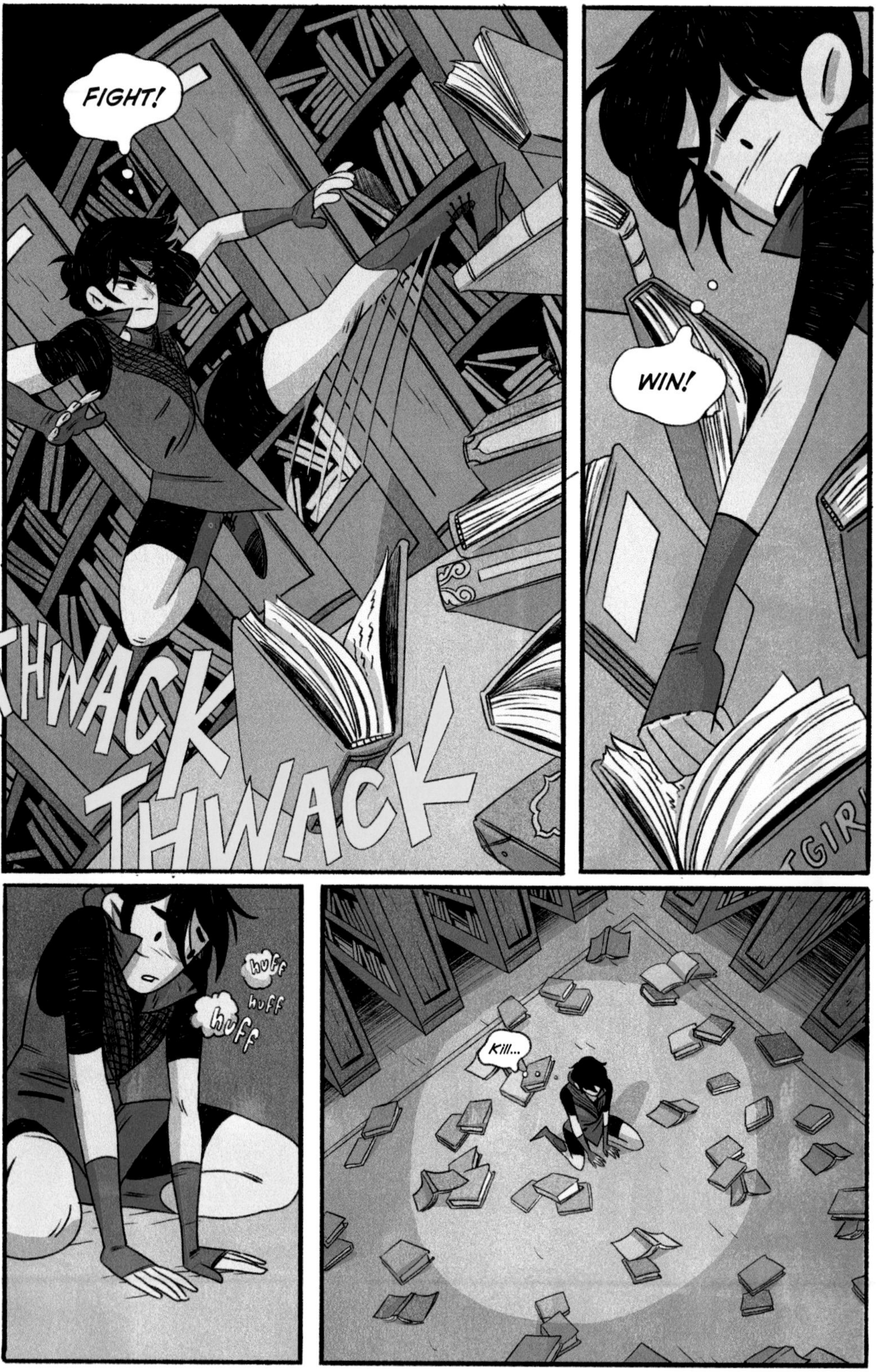
FIGHT!
THWACK
THWACK
WIN!
huff
huff
huff
Kill...

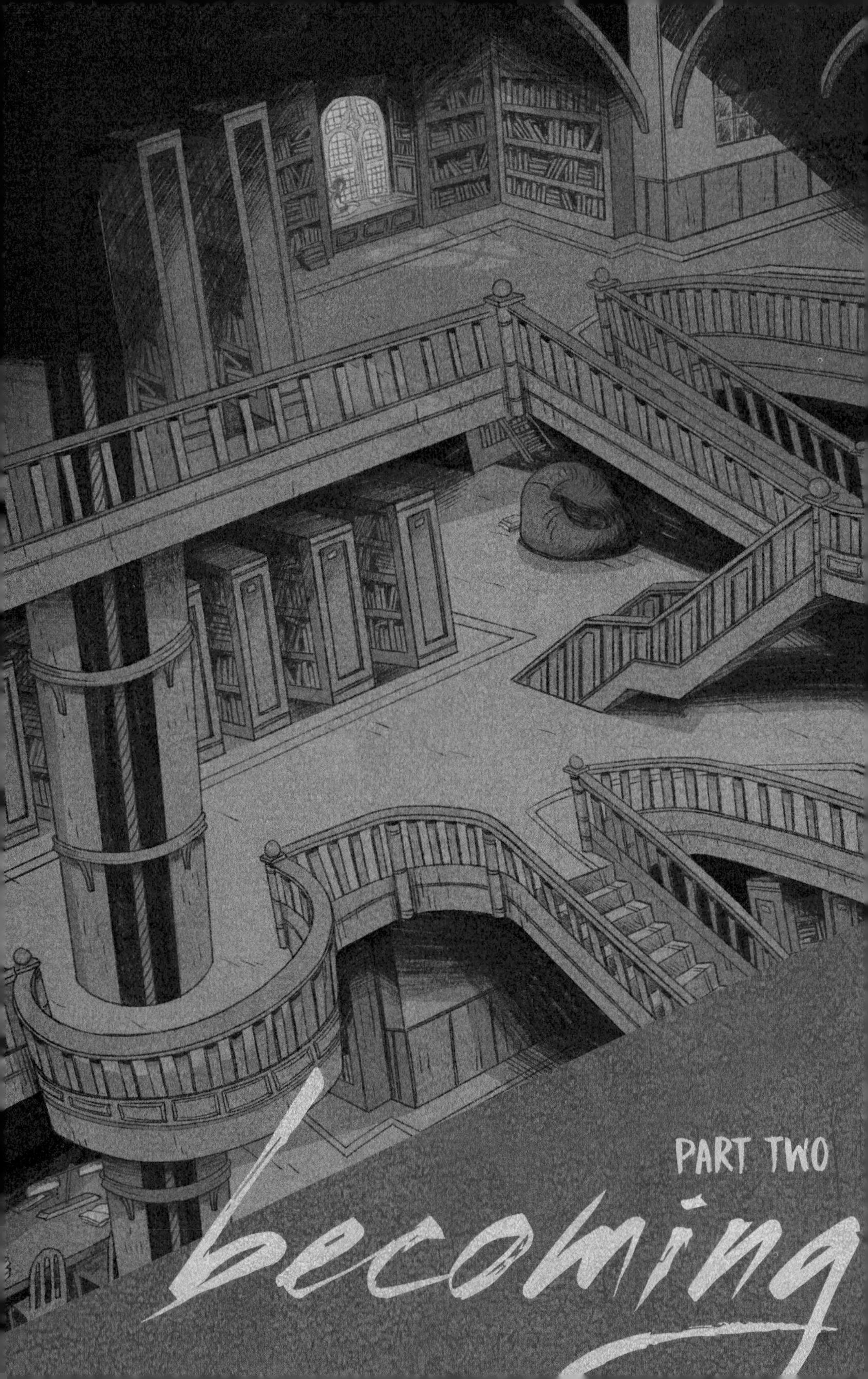
PART TWO
becoming

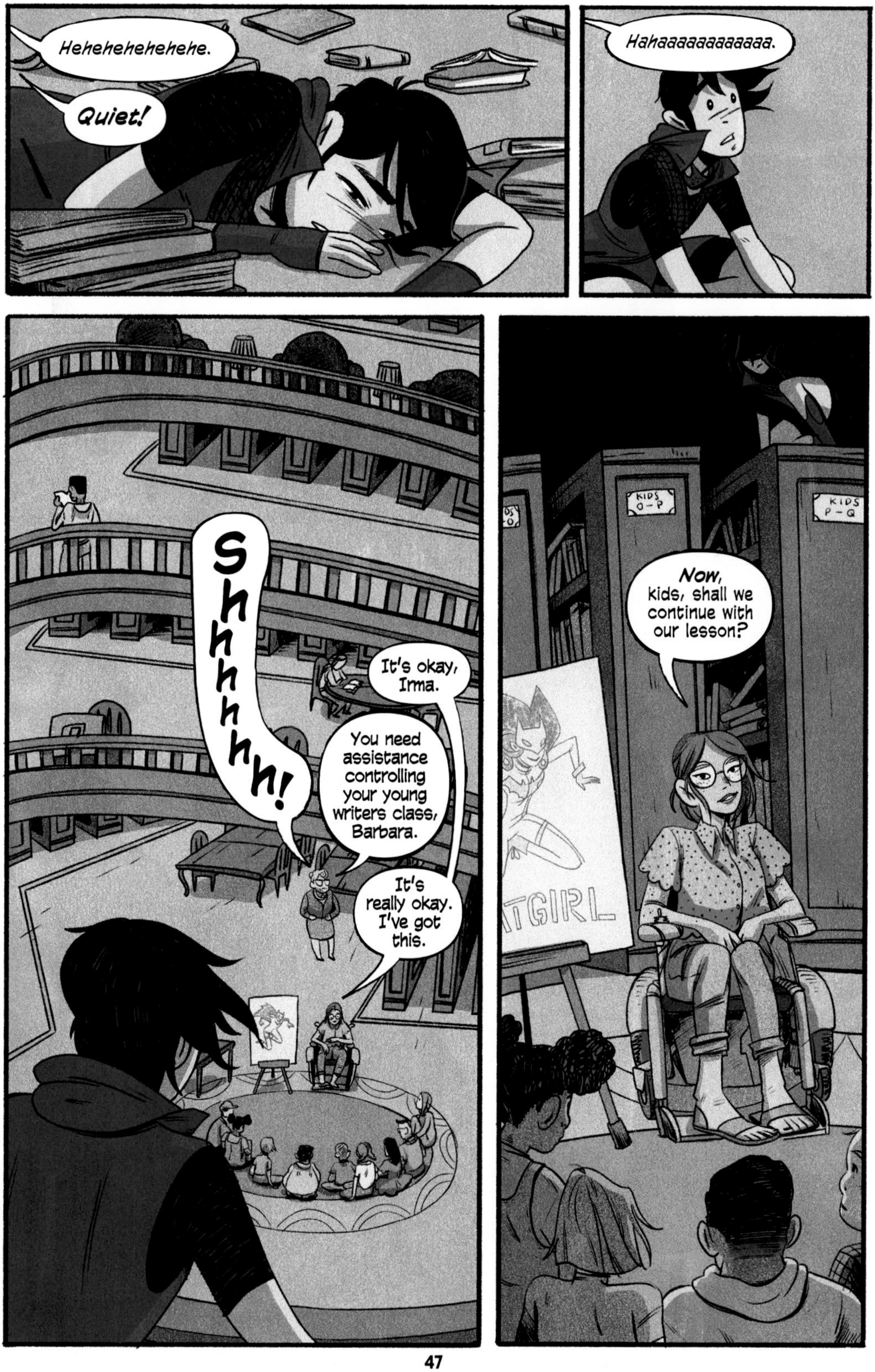
Hehehehehehehe.
Quiet!
Hahaaaaaaaaaaaaa.
Shhhhhh!
It's okay, Irma.
You need assistance controlling your young writers class, Barbara.
It's really okay. I've got this.
Now, kids, shall we continue with our lesson?
KIDS O-P
KIDS P-Q
ATGIRL

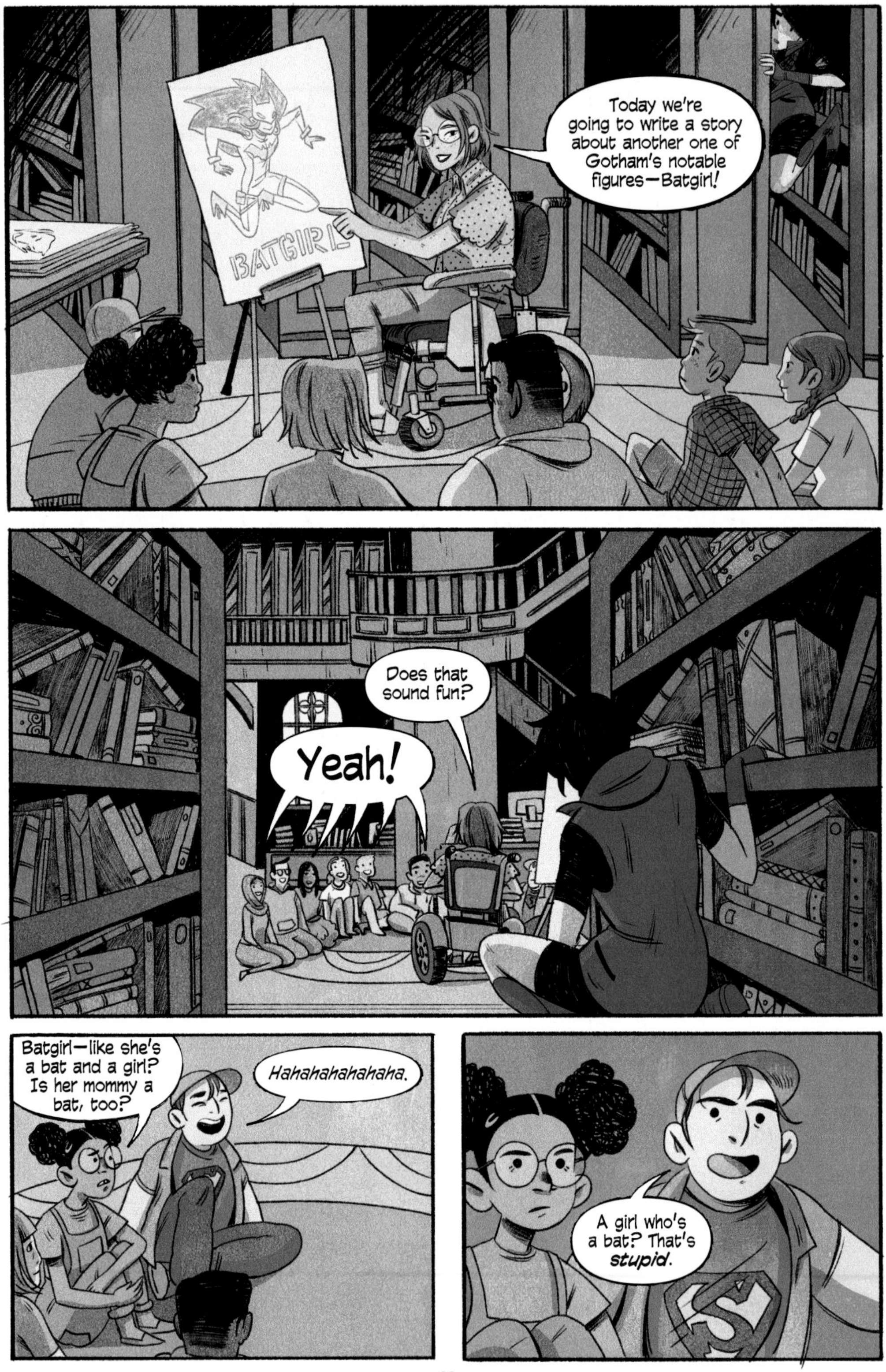
BATGIRL
Today we're going to write a story about another one of Gotham's notable figures—Batgirl!
Does that sound fun?
Yeah!
Batgirl—like she's a bat and a girl? Is her mommy a bat, too?
Hahahahahahaha.
A girl who's a bat? That's *stupid*.

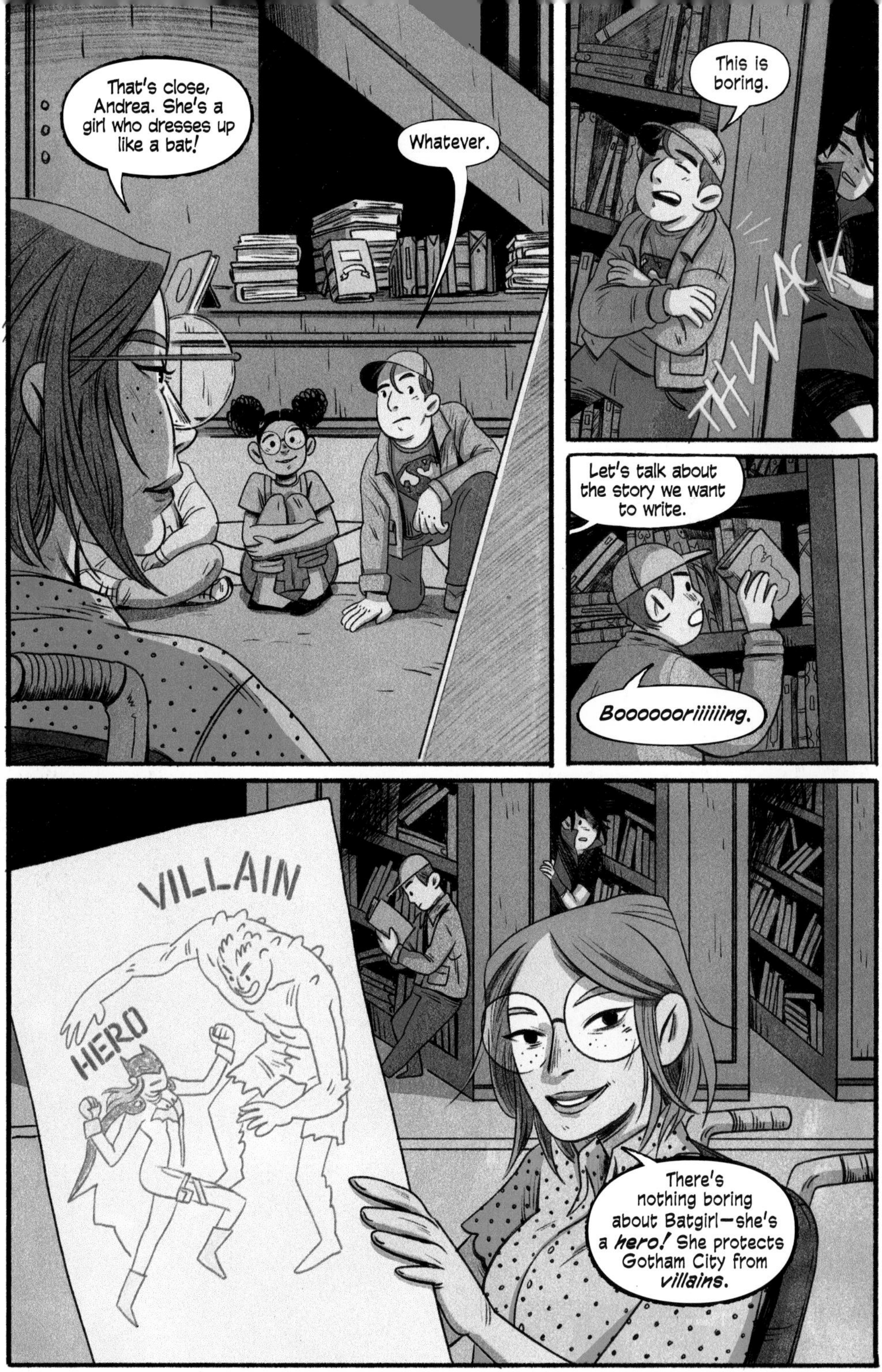
That's close, Andrea. She's a girl who dresses up like a bat!
Whatever.
This is boring.
THWACK
Let's talk about the story we want to write.
Booooooriiiiiing.
VILLAIN
HERO
There's nothing boring about Batgirl—she's a *hero!* She protects Gotham City from *villains*.

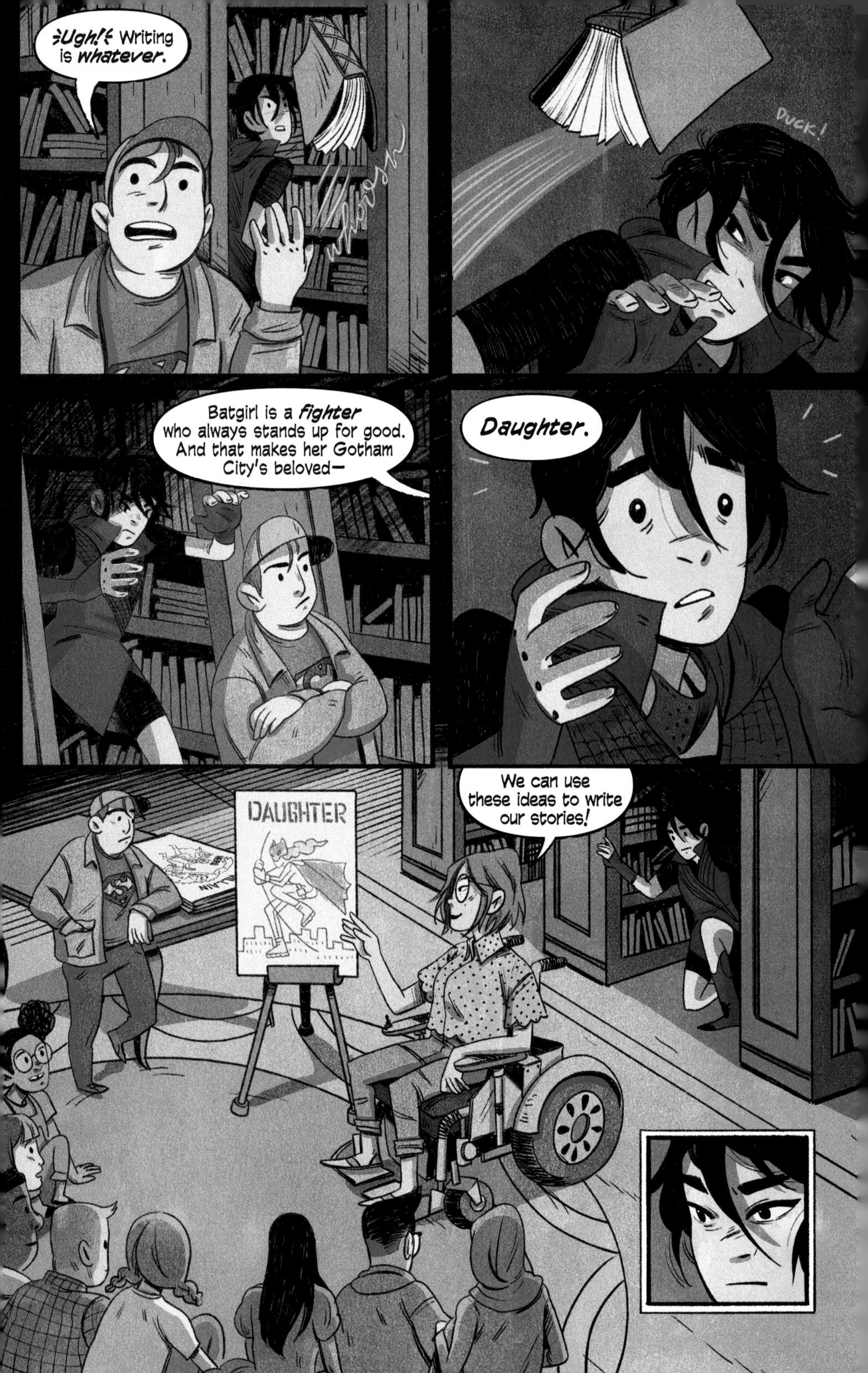
Ugh! Writing is whatever.
DUCK!
Batgirl is a fighter who always stands up for good. And that makes her Gotham City's beloved—
Daughter.
DAUGHTER
We can use these ideas to write our stories!

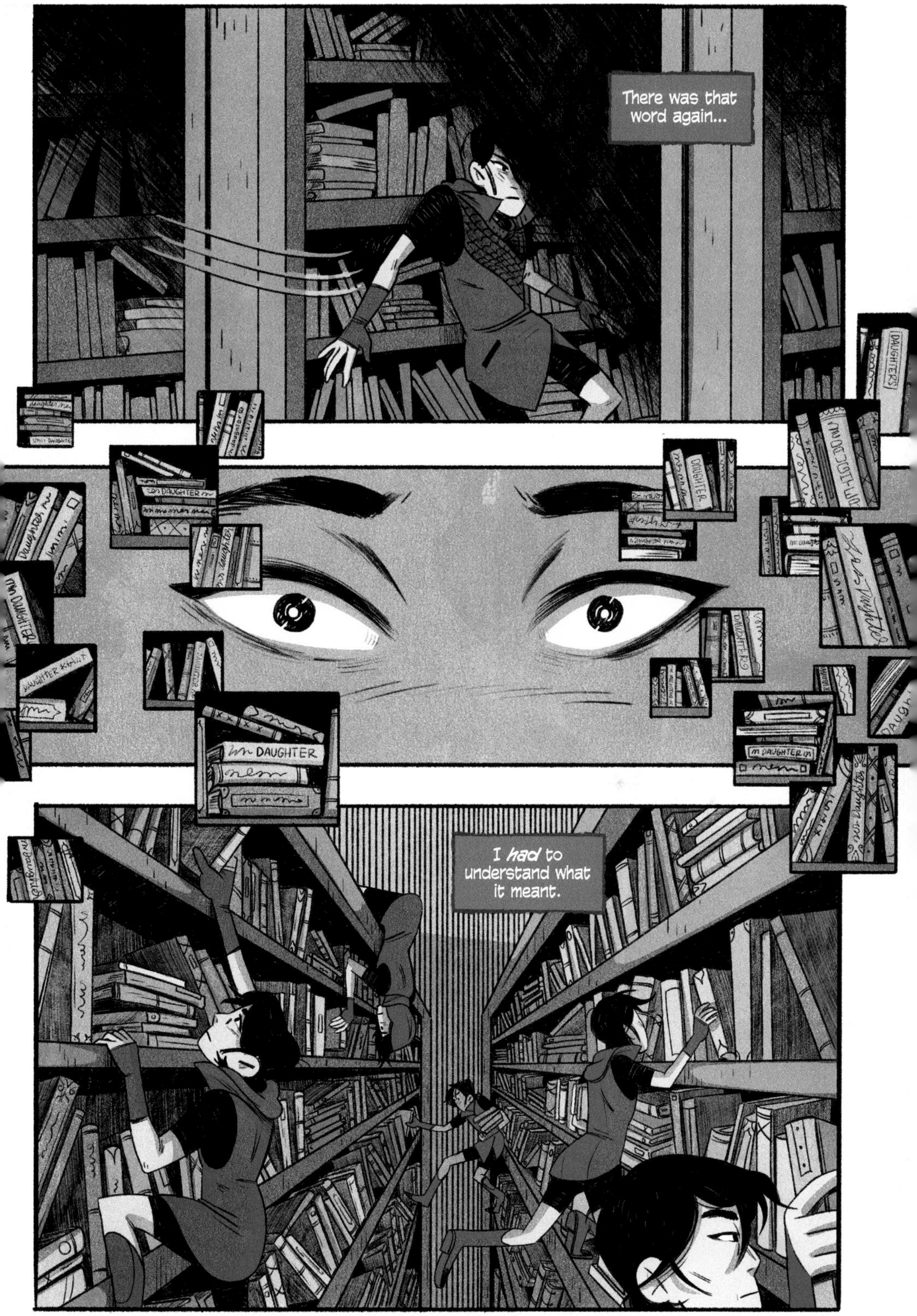
There was that word again...
I *had* to understand what it meant.

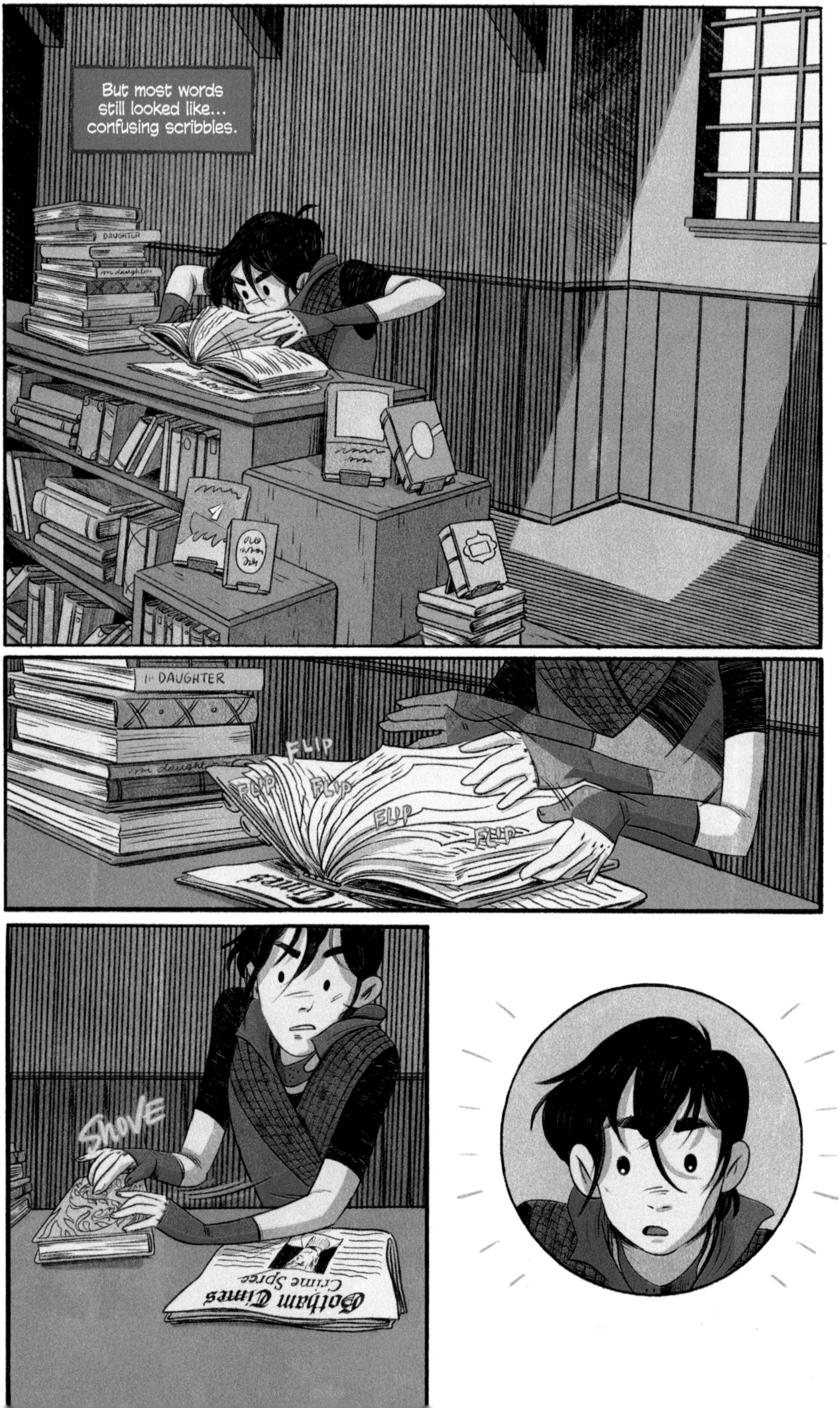

But most words still looked like... confusing scribbles.
DAUGHTER
DAUGHTER
FLIP
FLIP
FLIP
FLIP
FLIP
SHOVE
Gotham Times
Crime Spree

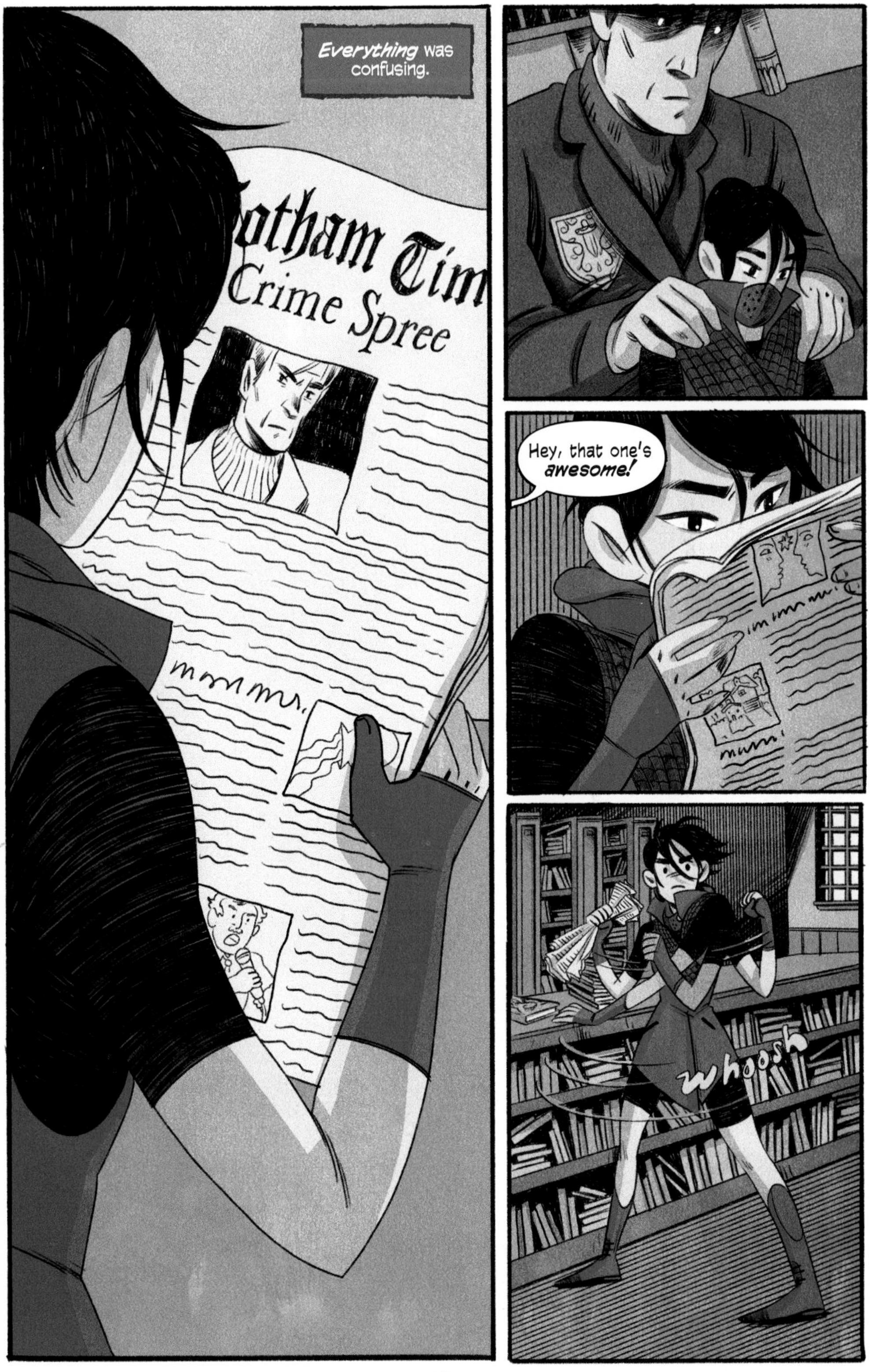
Everything was confusing.
otham Tim
Crime Spree
Hey, that one's *awesome!*
whoosh

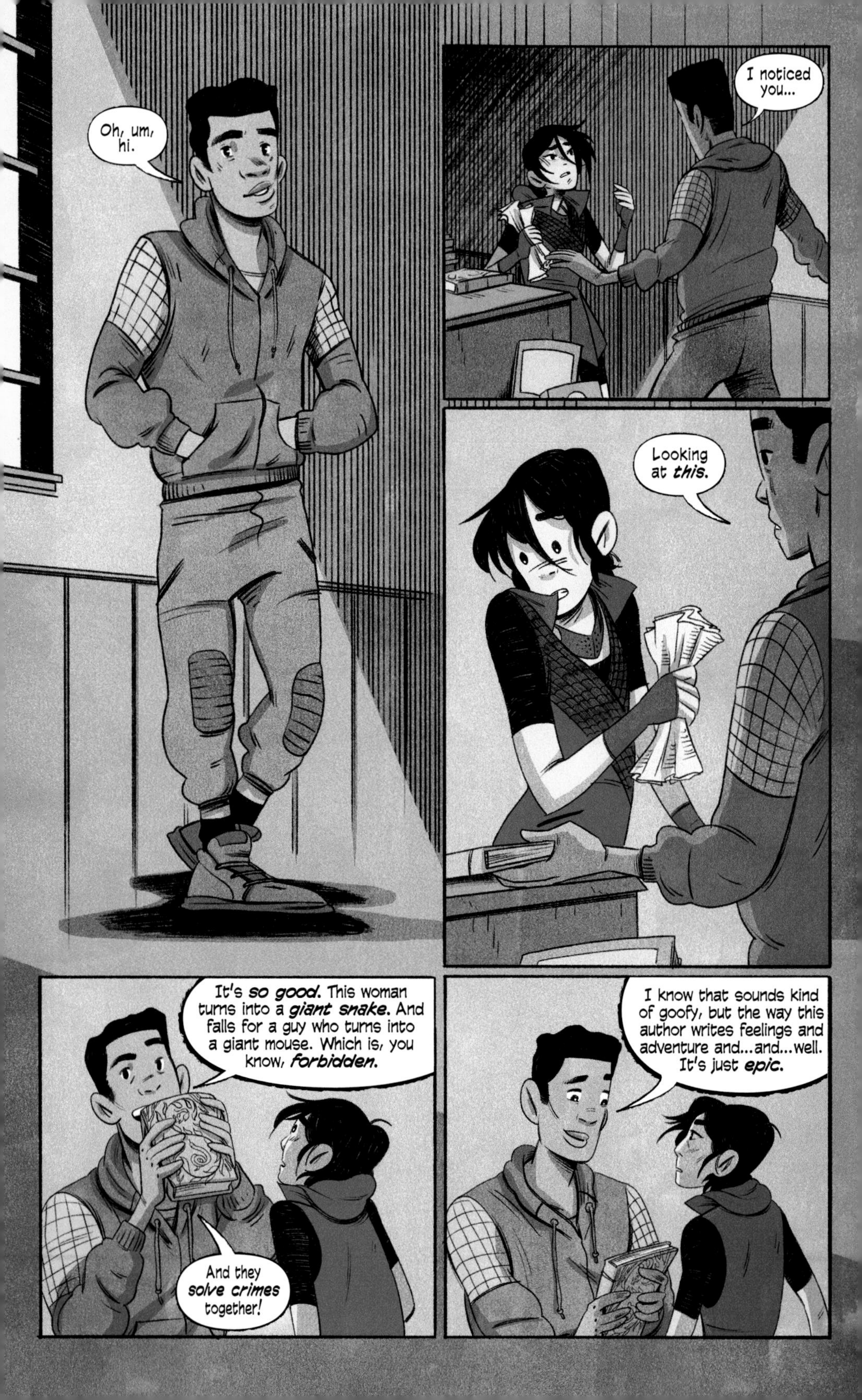
Oh, um, hi.
I noticed you...
Looking at *this*.
It's *so good*. This woman turns into a *giant snake*. And falls for a guy who turns into a giant mouse. Which is, you know, *forbidden*.
And they *solve crimes* together!
I know that sounds kind of goofy, but the way this author writes feelings and adventure and...and...well. It's just *epic*.

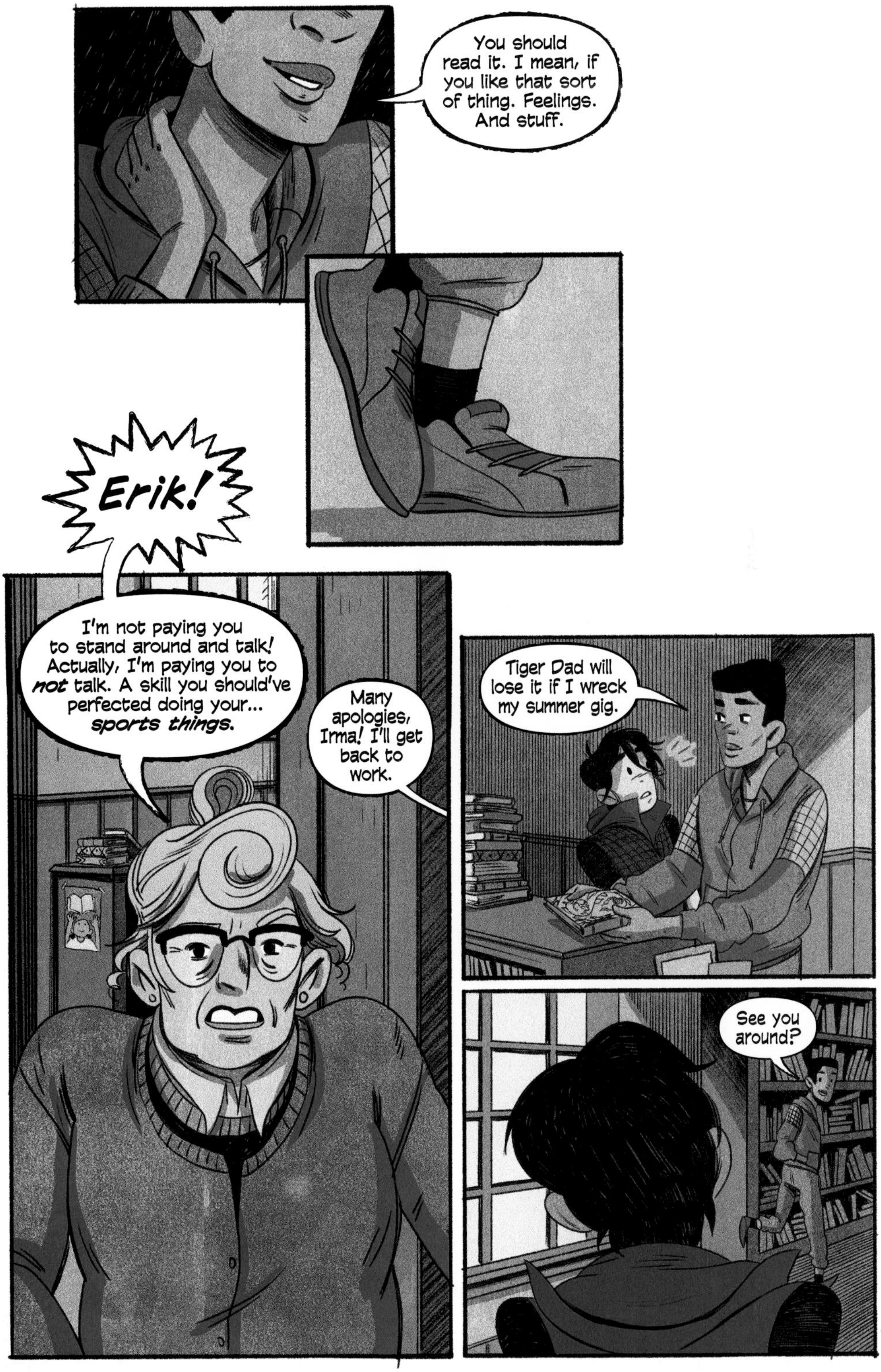
You should read it. I mean, if you like that sort of thing. Feelings. And stuff.
Erik!
I'm not paying you to stand around and talk! Actually, I'm paying you to *not* talk. A skill you should've perfected doing your... *sports things*.
Many apologies, Irma! I'll get back to work.
Tiger Dad will lose it if I wreck my summer gig.
See you around?

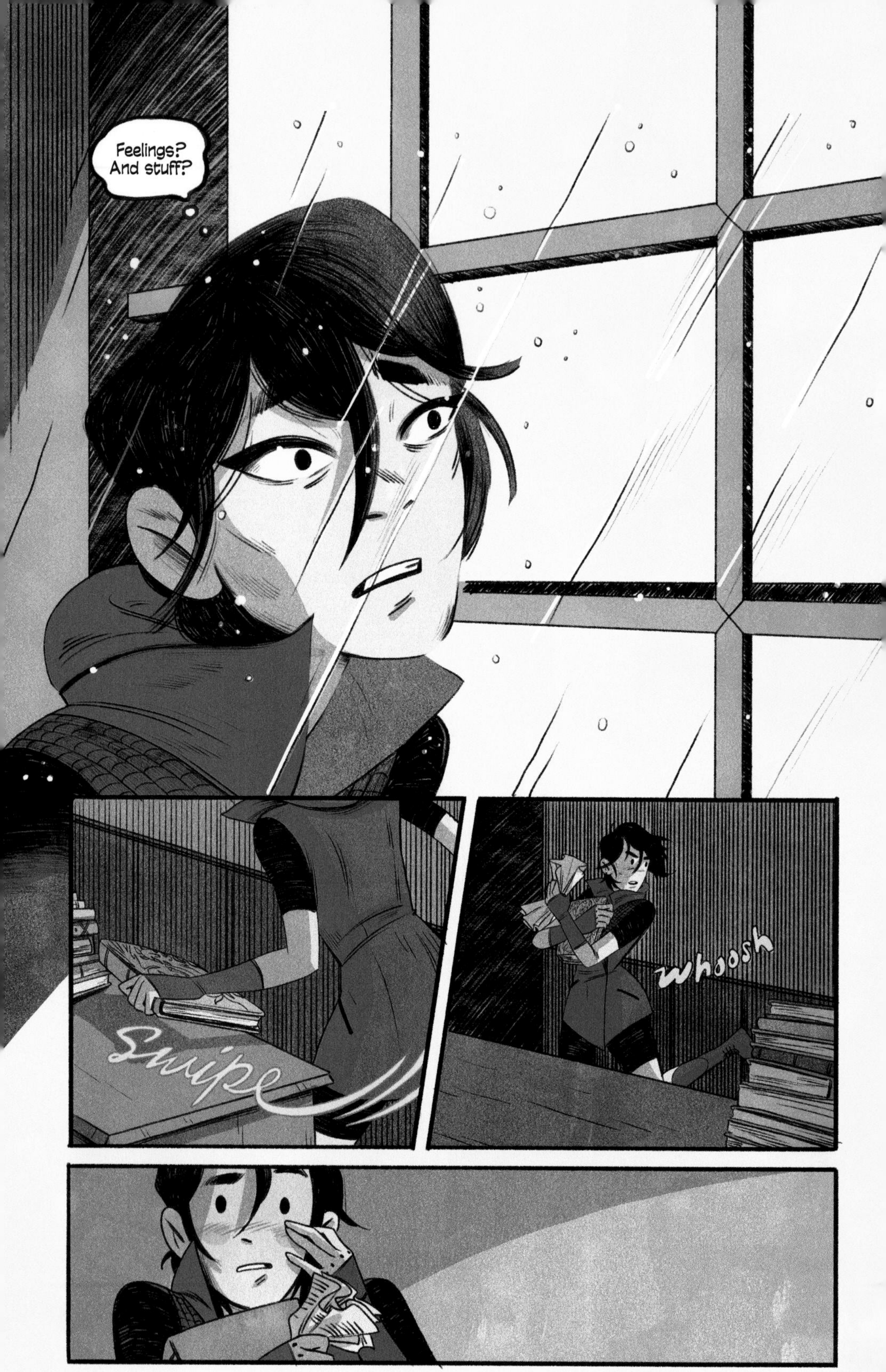
Feelings? And stuff?
Swipe
whoosh

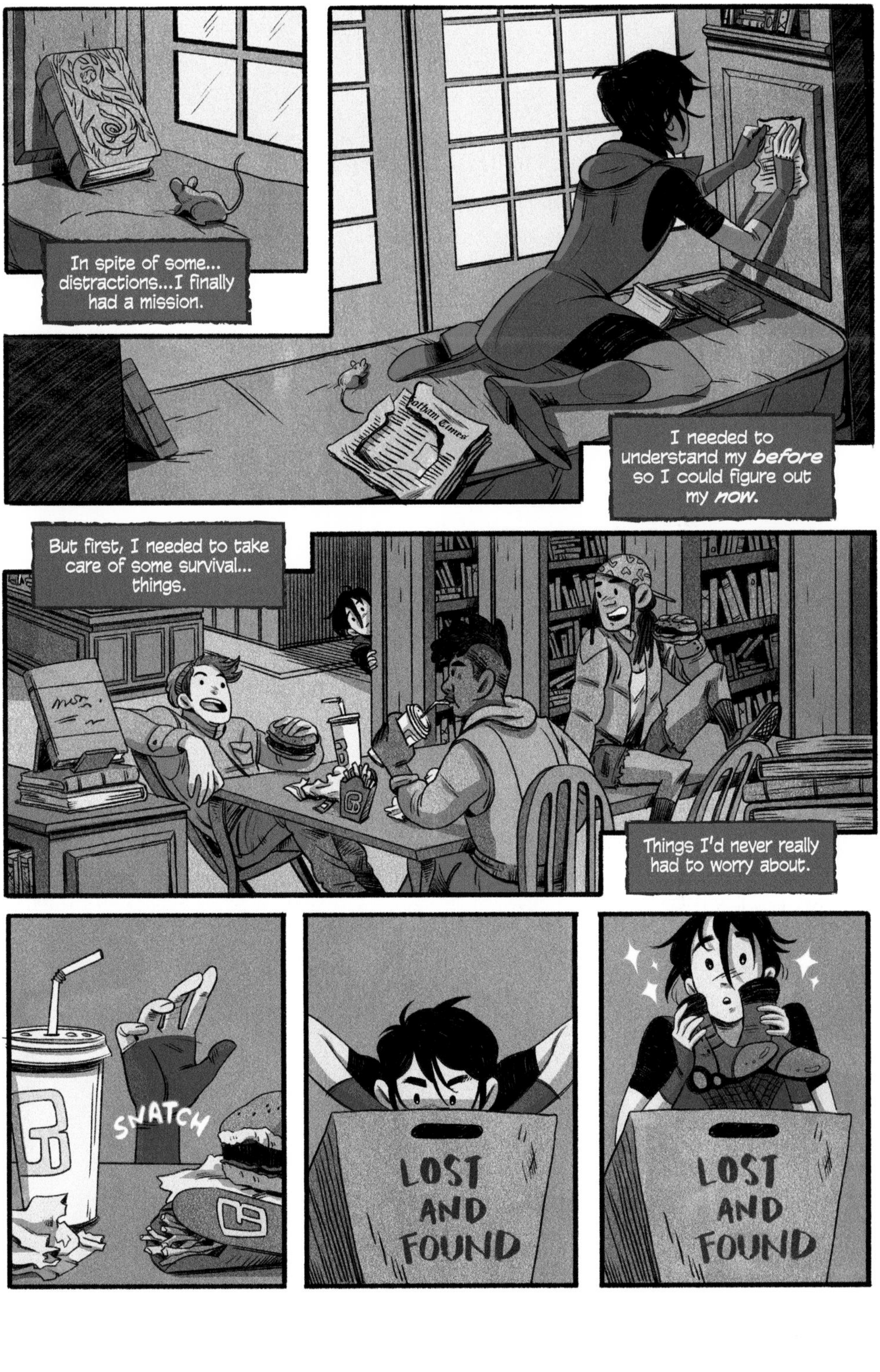
In spite of some... distractions...I finally had a mission.
Gotham Times
I needed to understand my *before* so I could figure out my *now*.
But first, I needed to take care of some survival... things.
Things I'd never really had to worry about.
SNATCH
LOST AND FOUND
LOST AND FOUND

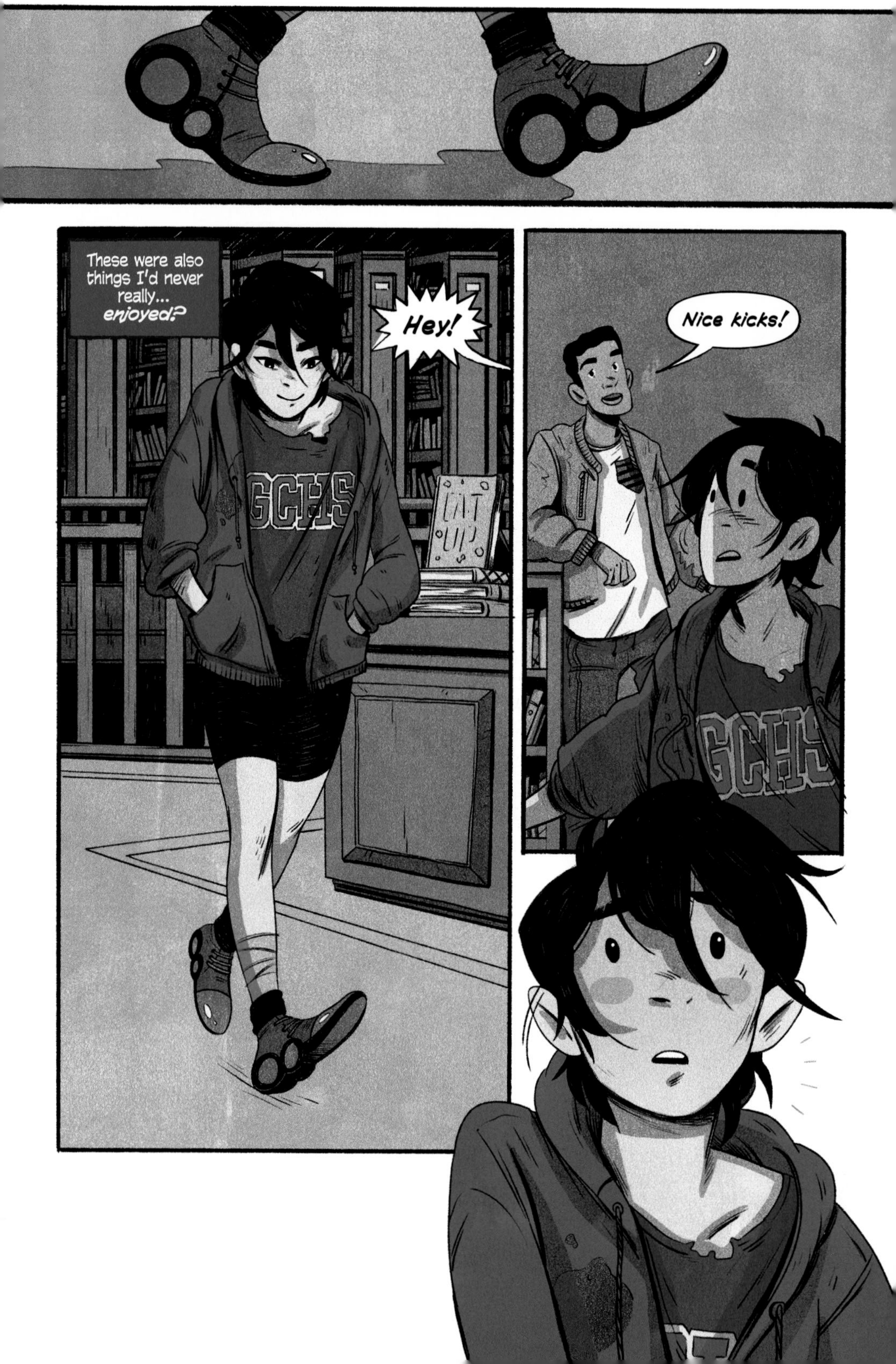
These were also things I'd never really... *enjoyed?*
Hey!
Nice kicks!

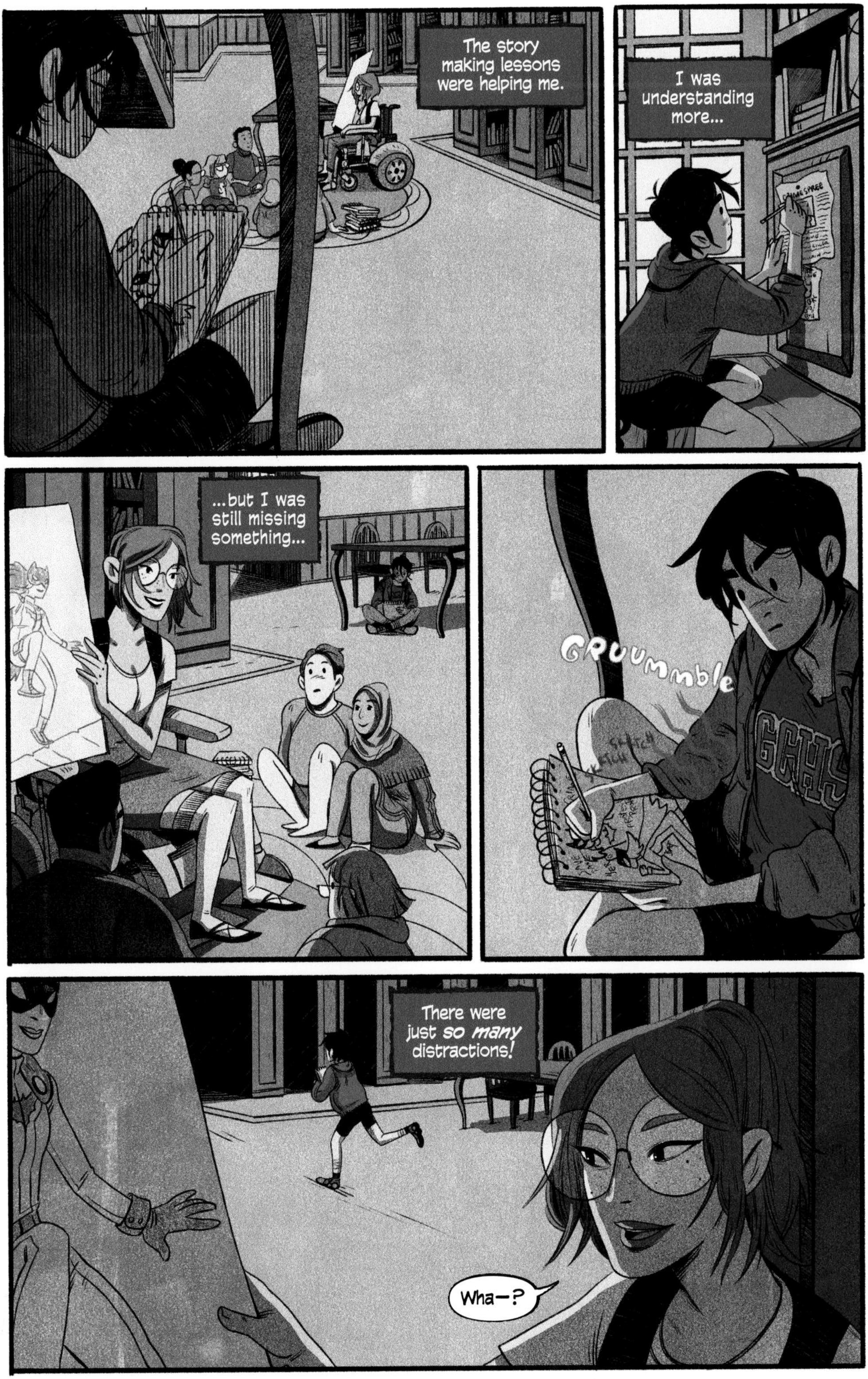
The story making lessons were helping me.
I was understanding more...
...but I was still missing something...
GRUUMMble
There were just *so many* distractions!
Wha—?

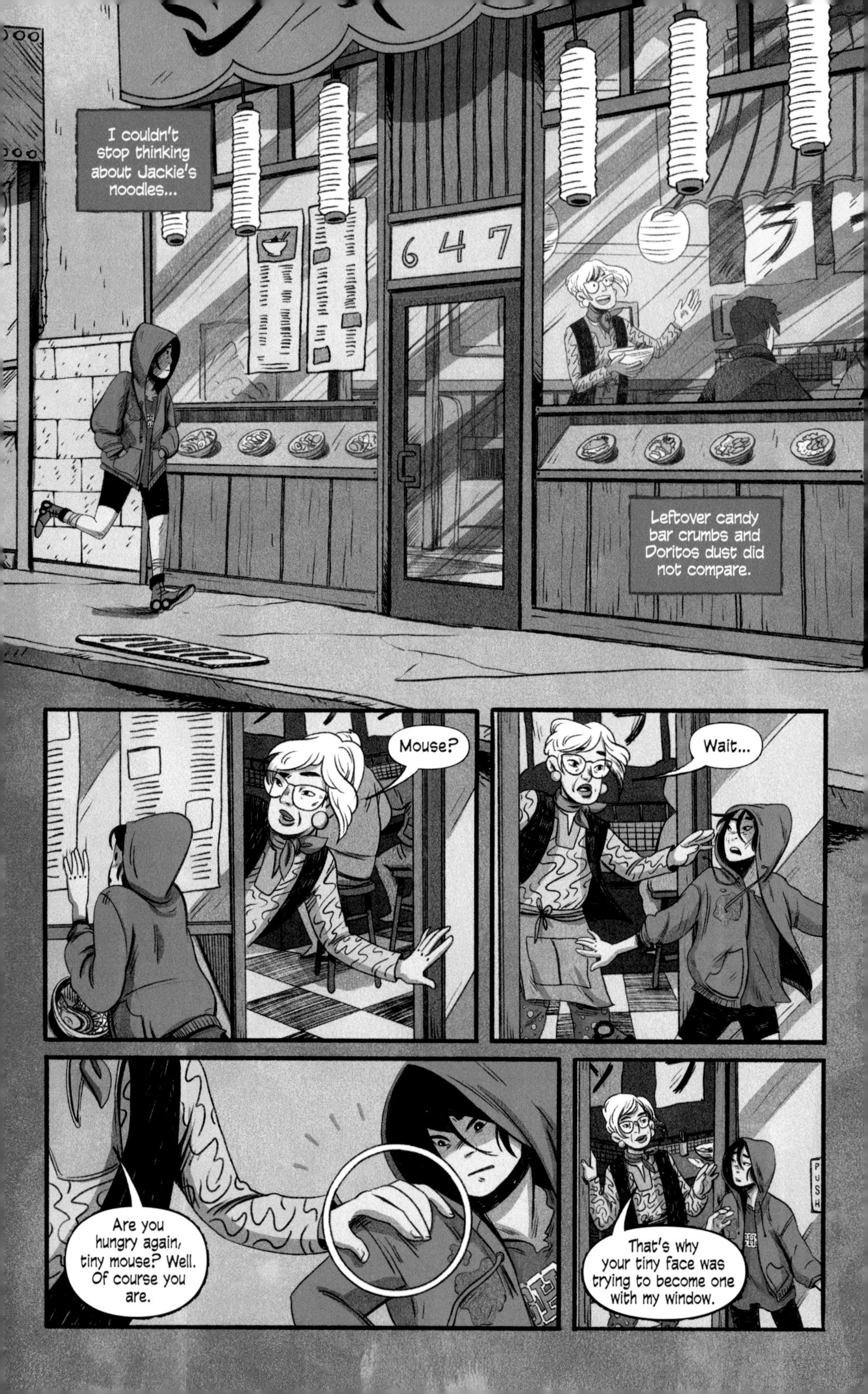

I couldn't stop thinking about Jackie's noodles...
647
Leftover candy bar crumbs and Doritos dust did not compare.
Mouse?
Wait...
Are you hungry again, tiny mouse? Well. Of course you are.
That's why your tiny face was trying to become one with my window.
PUSH

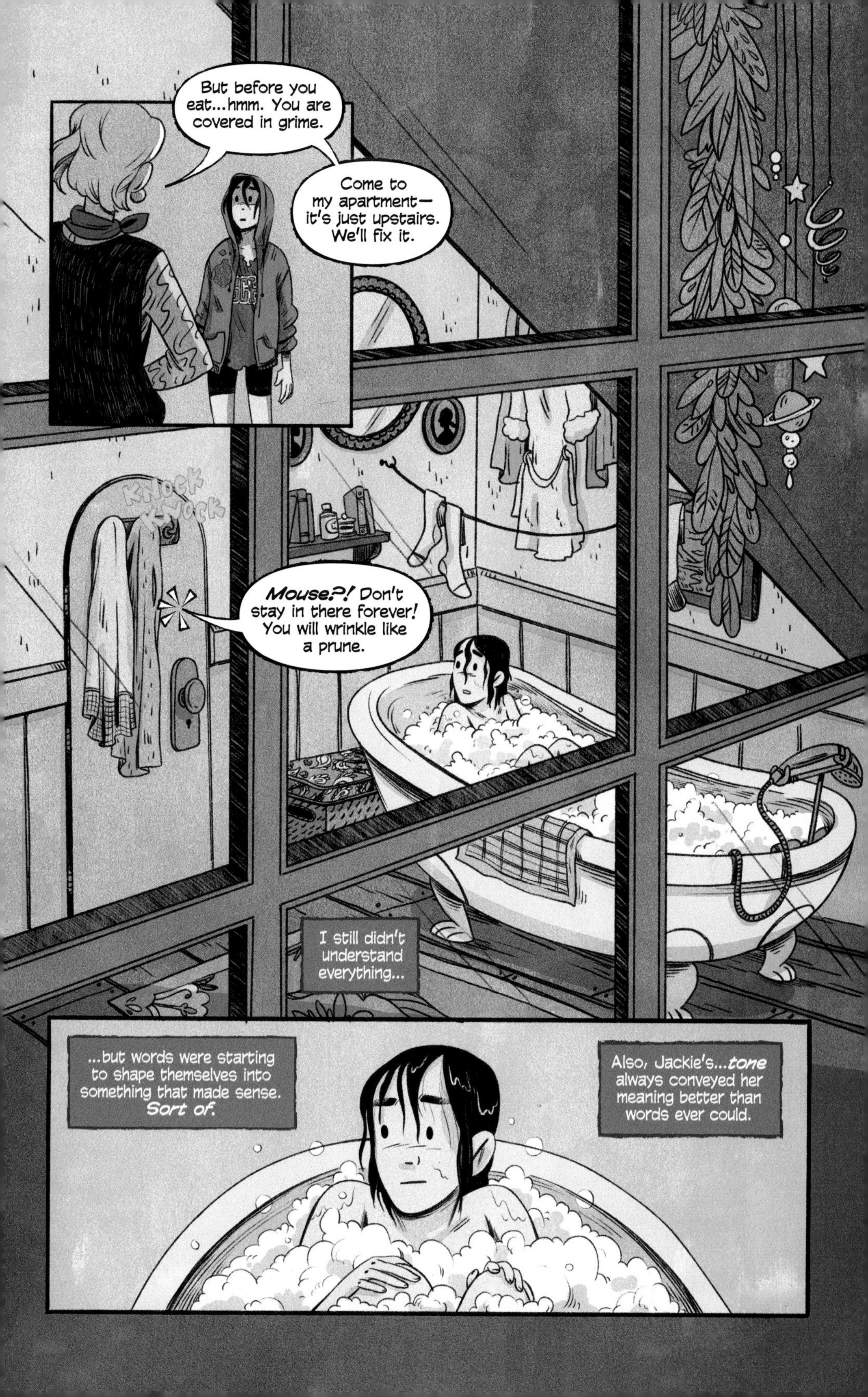
But before you eat...hmm. You are covered in grime.
Come to my apartment— it's just upstairs. We'll fix it.
KNOCK KNOCK
Mouse?! Don't stay in there forever! You will wrinkle like a prune.
I still didn't understand everything...
...but words were starting to shape themselves into something that made sense. *Sort of.*
Also, Jackie's...*tone* always conveyed her meaning better than words ever could.

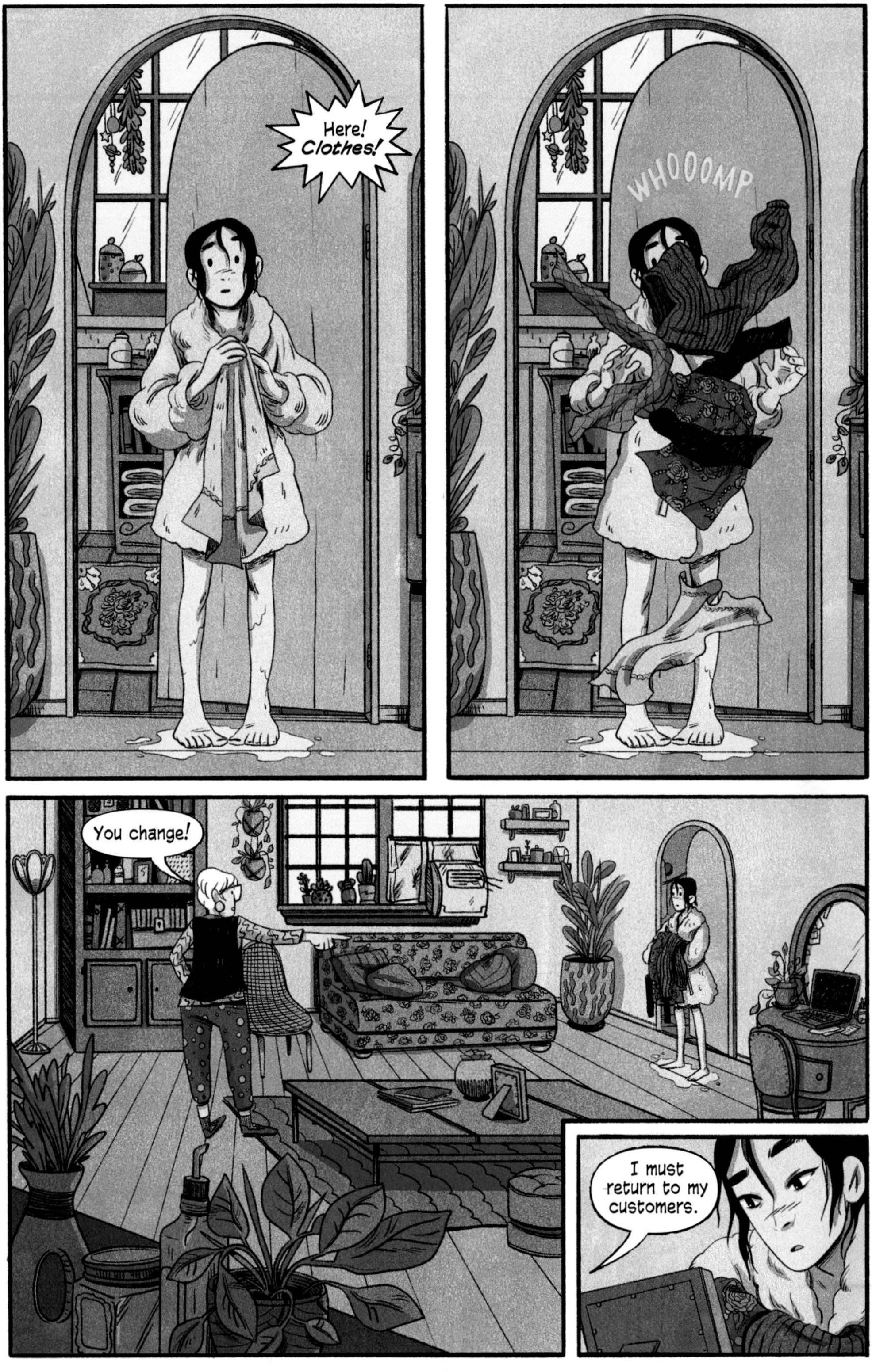
Here! Clothes!
WHOOOMP
You change!
I must return to my customers.

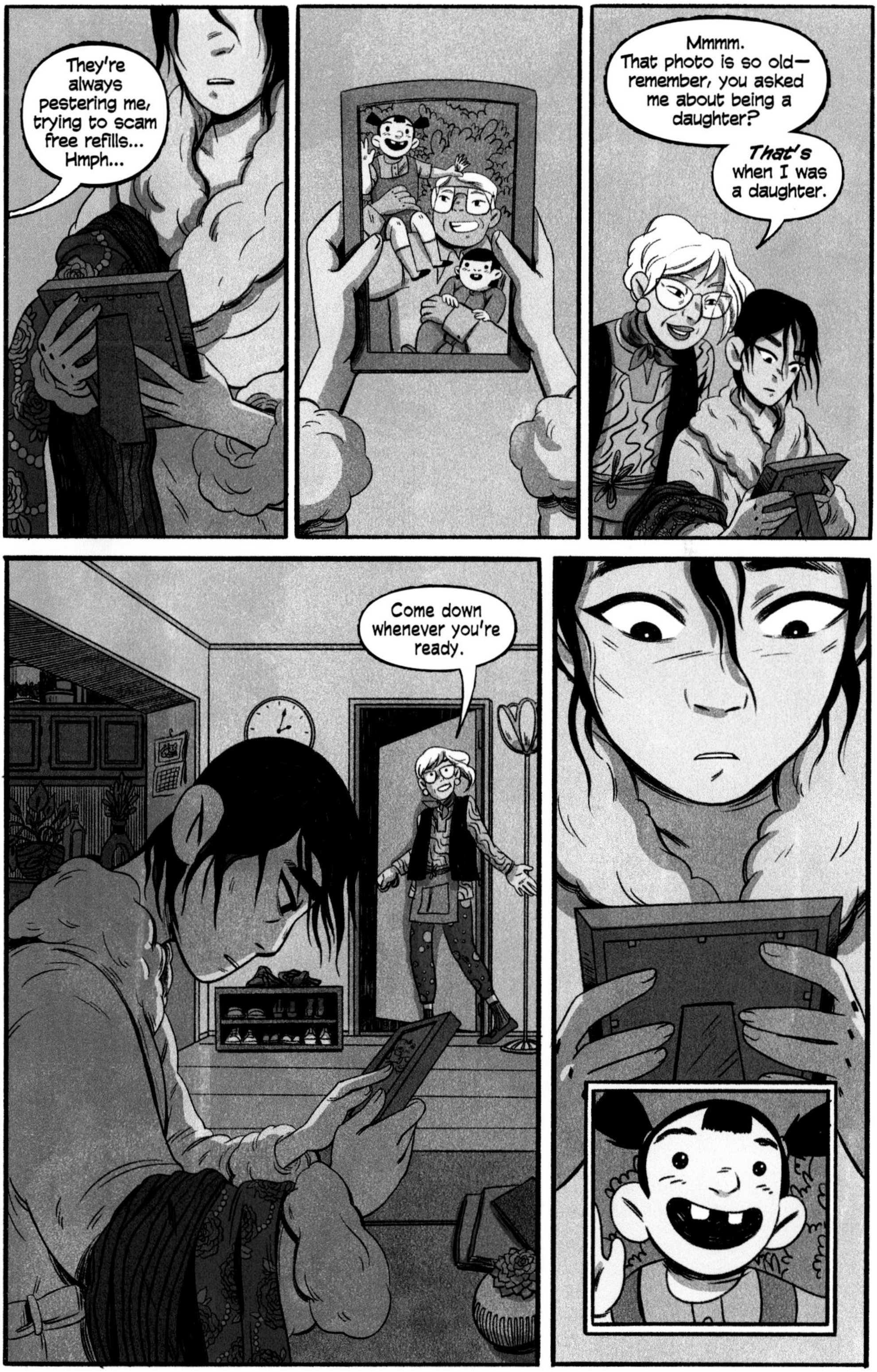
They're always pestering me, trying to scam free refills... Hmph...
Mmmm. That photo is so old— remember, you asked me about being a daughter?
That's when I was a daughter.
Come down whenever you're ready.

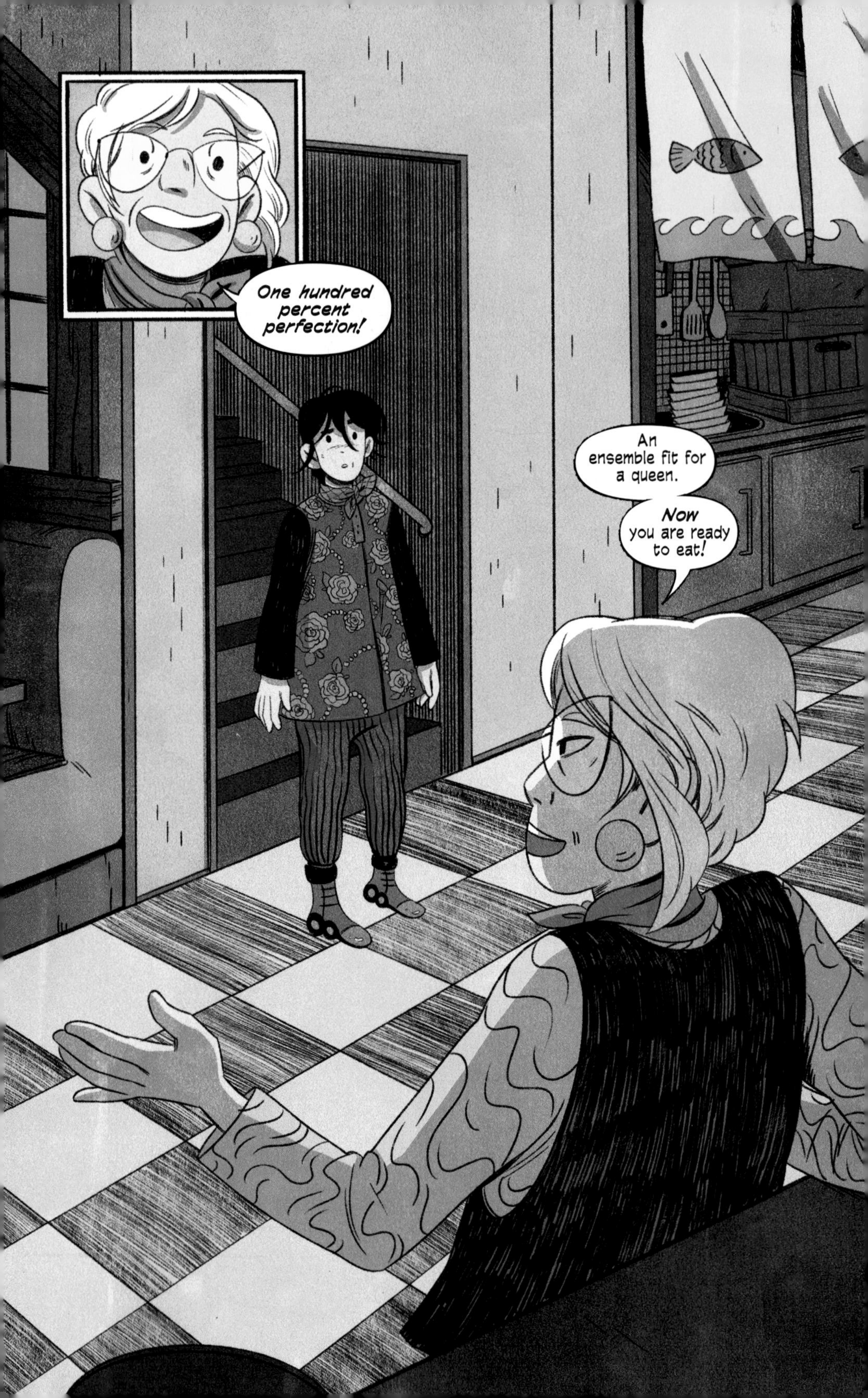

One hundred percent perfection!
An ensemble fit for a queen.
Now you are ready to eat!

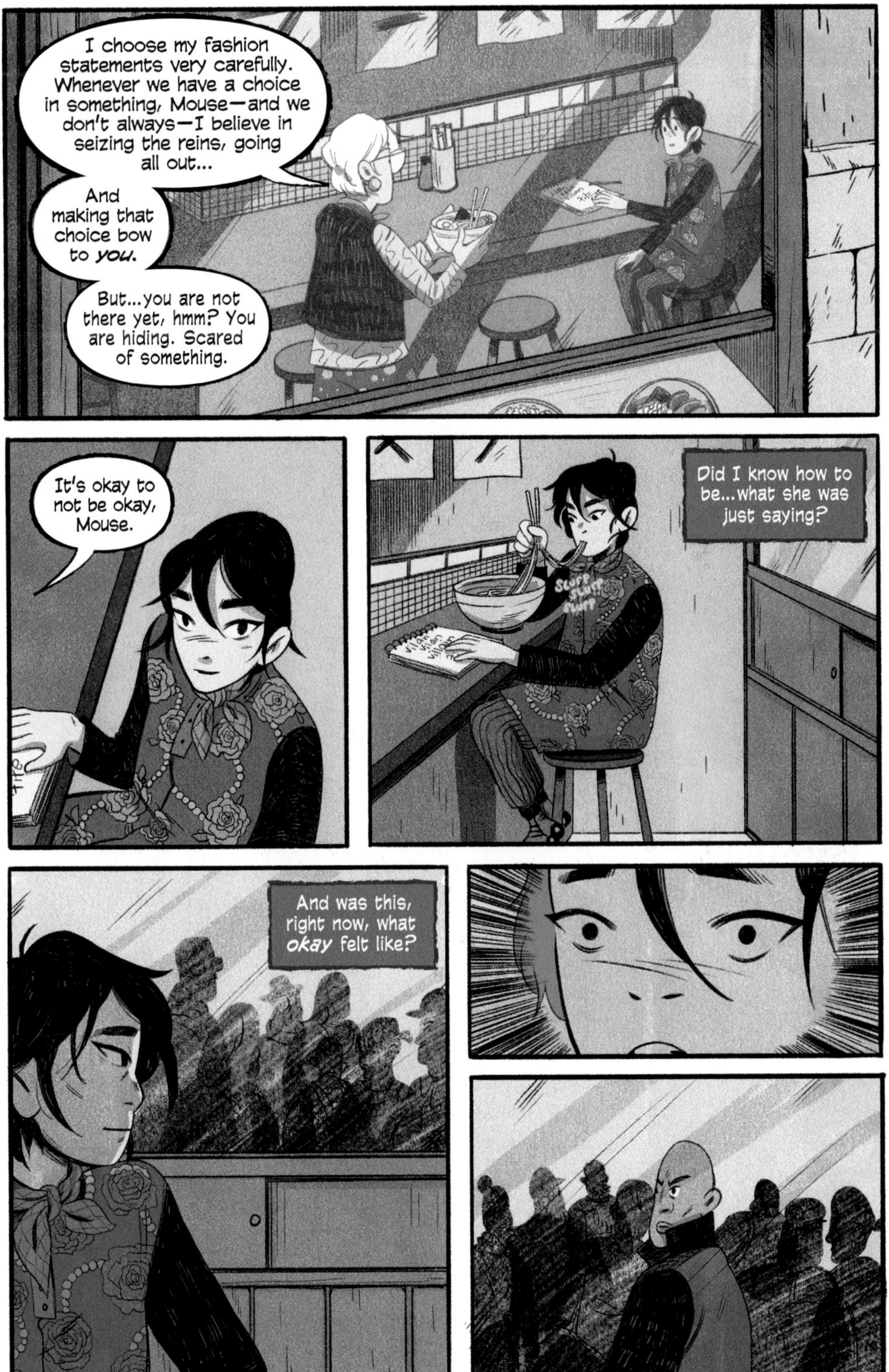
I choose my fashion statements very carefully. Whenever we have a choice in something, Mouse—and we don't always—I believe in seizing the reins, going all out...
And making that choice bow to *you.*
But...you are not there yet, hmm? You are hiding. Scared of something.
It's okay to not be okay, Mouse.
Did I know how to be...what she was just saying?
And was this, right now, what *okay* felt like?

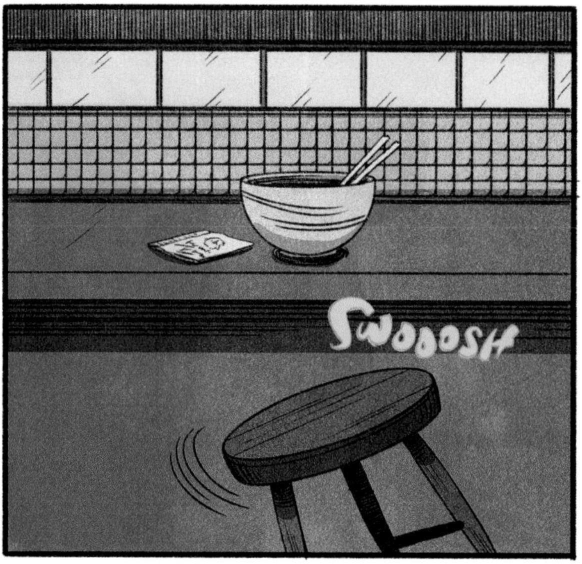
SWOOSH

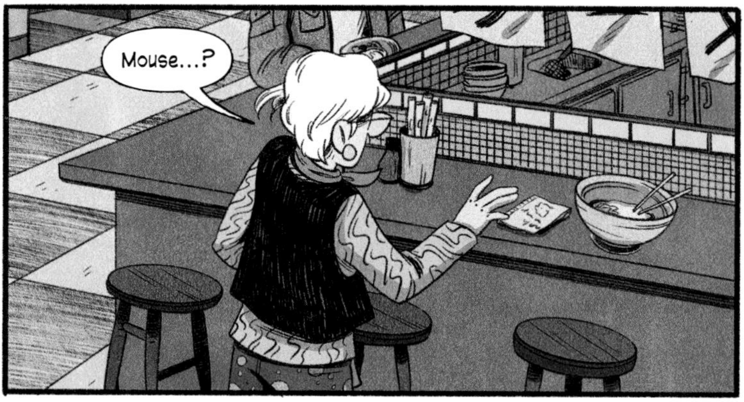
Mouse...?

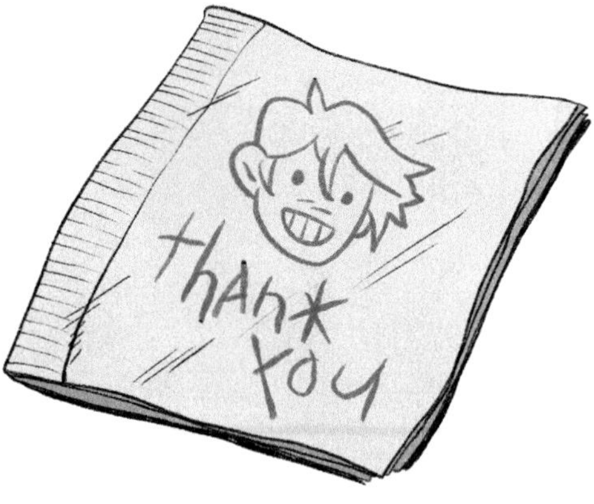
thank you

I should have known...

Even when *now* starts to feel okay...

...*before* never goes away.

But I was starting to understand why that man's words...*word*... had changed me.

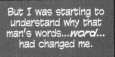

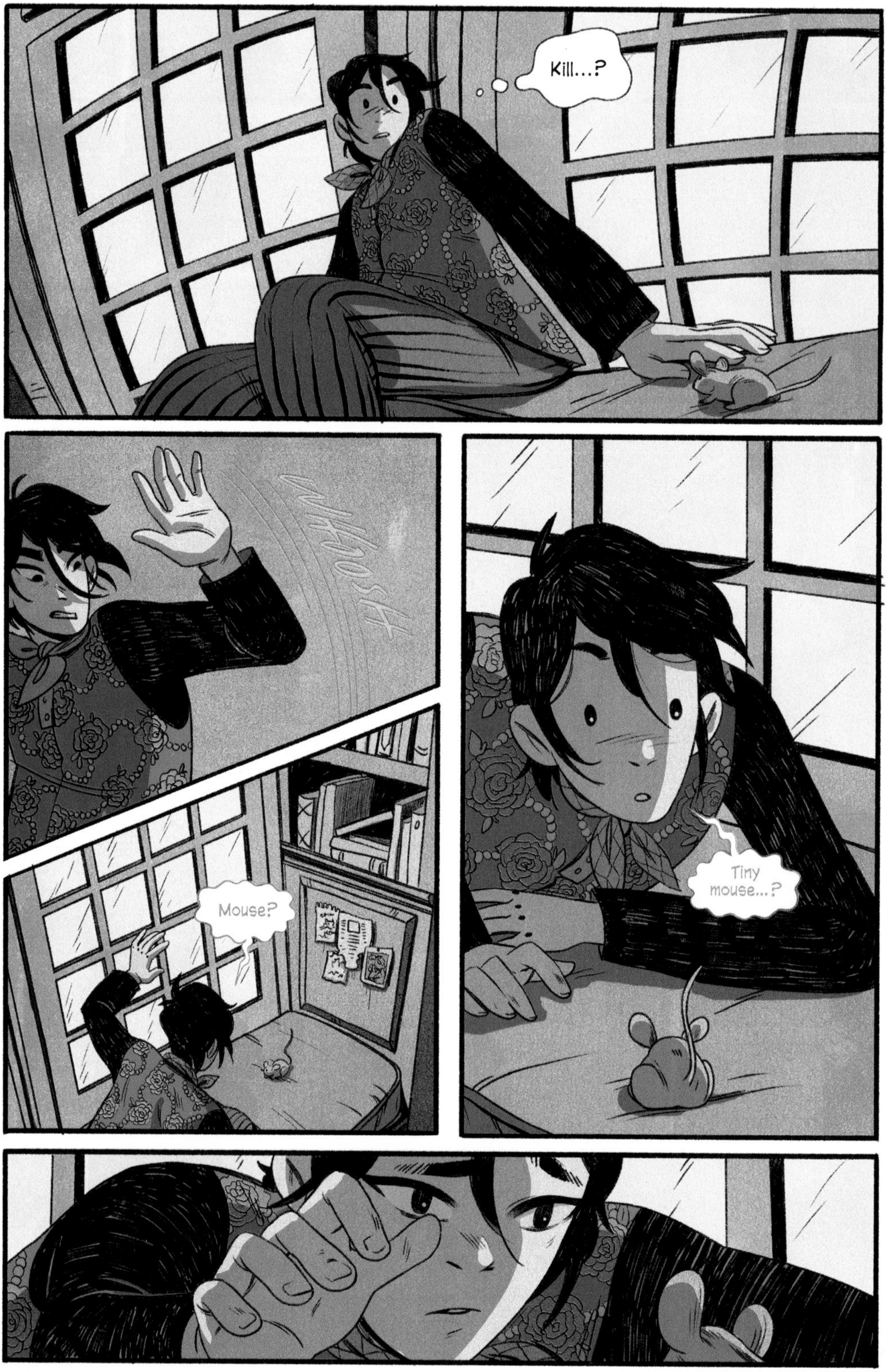
Kill...?
WHOOSH
Mouse?
Tiny mouse...?

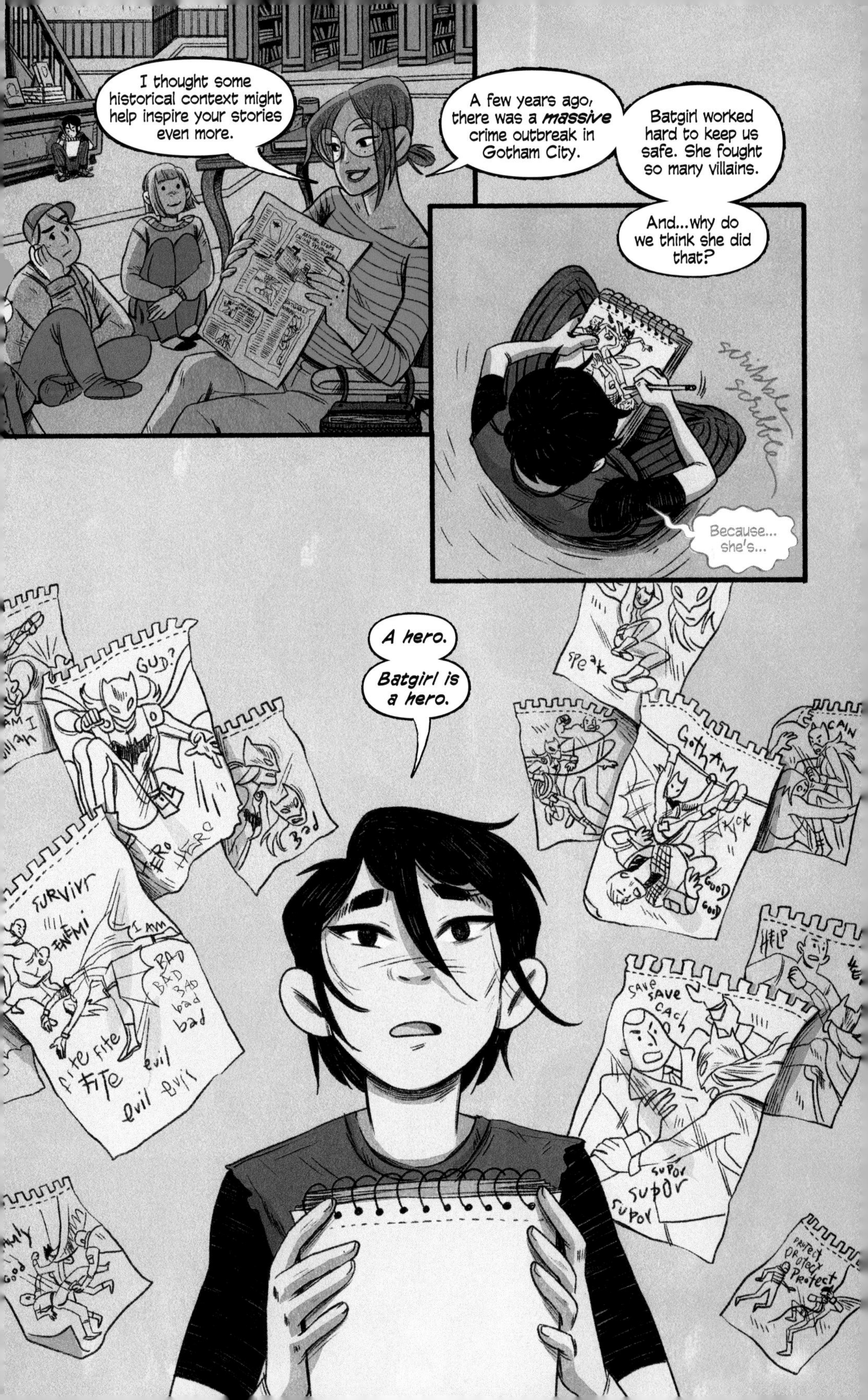

I thought some historical context might help inspire your stories even more.
A few years ago, there was a ***massive*** crime outbreak in Gotham City.
Batgirl worked hard to keep us safe. She fought so many villains.
And...why do we think she did that?
scribble scribble
Because... she's...
A hero.
Batgirl is a hero.

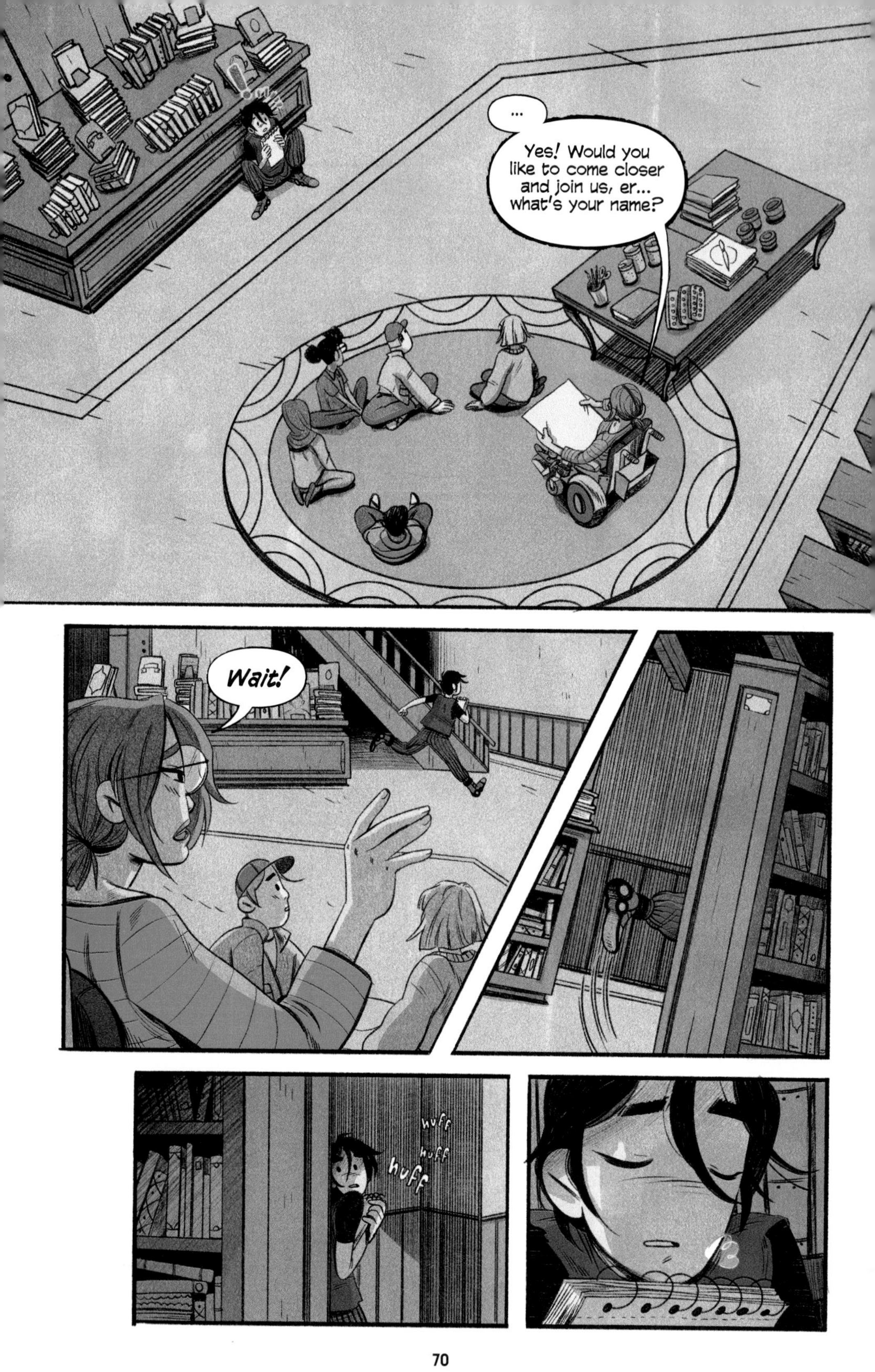
...
Yes! Would you like to come closer and join us, er... what's your name?
Wait!
huff
huff
huff

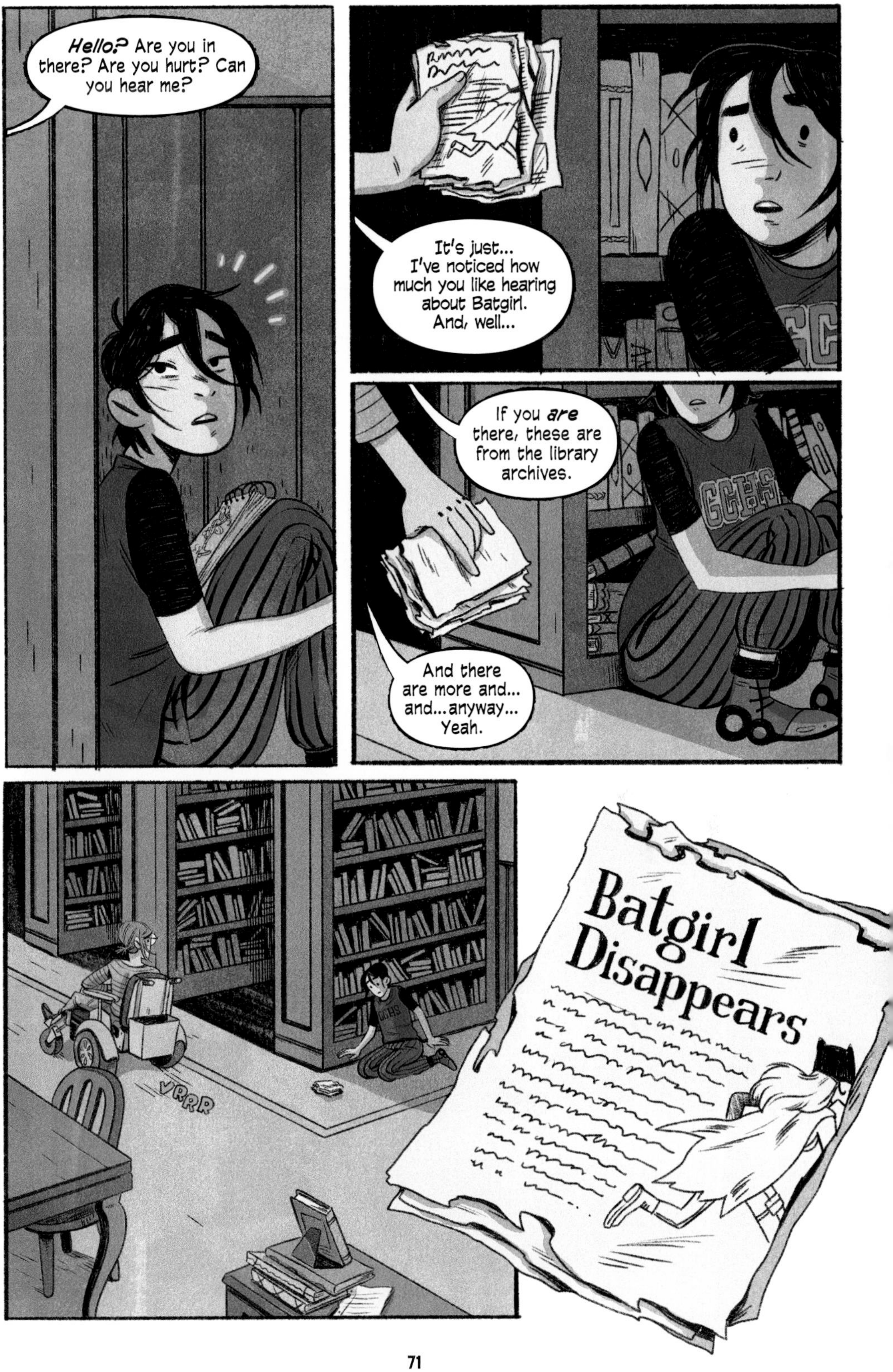

Hello? Are you in there? Are you hurt? Can you hear me?
It's just... I've noticed how much you like hearing about Batgirl. And, well...
If you *are* there, these are from the library archives.
And there are more and... and...anyway... Yeah.
VRRR
Batgirl Disappears

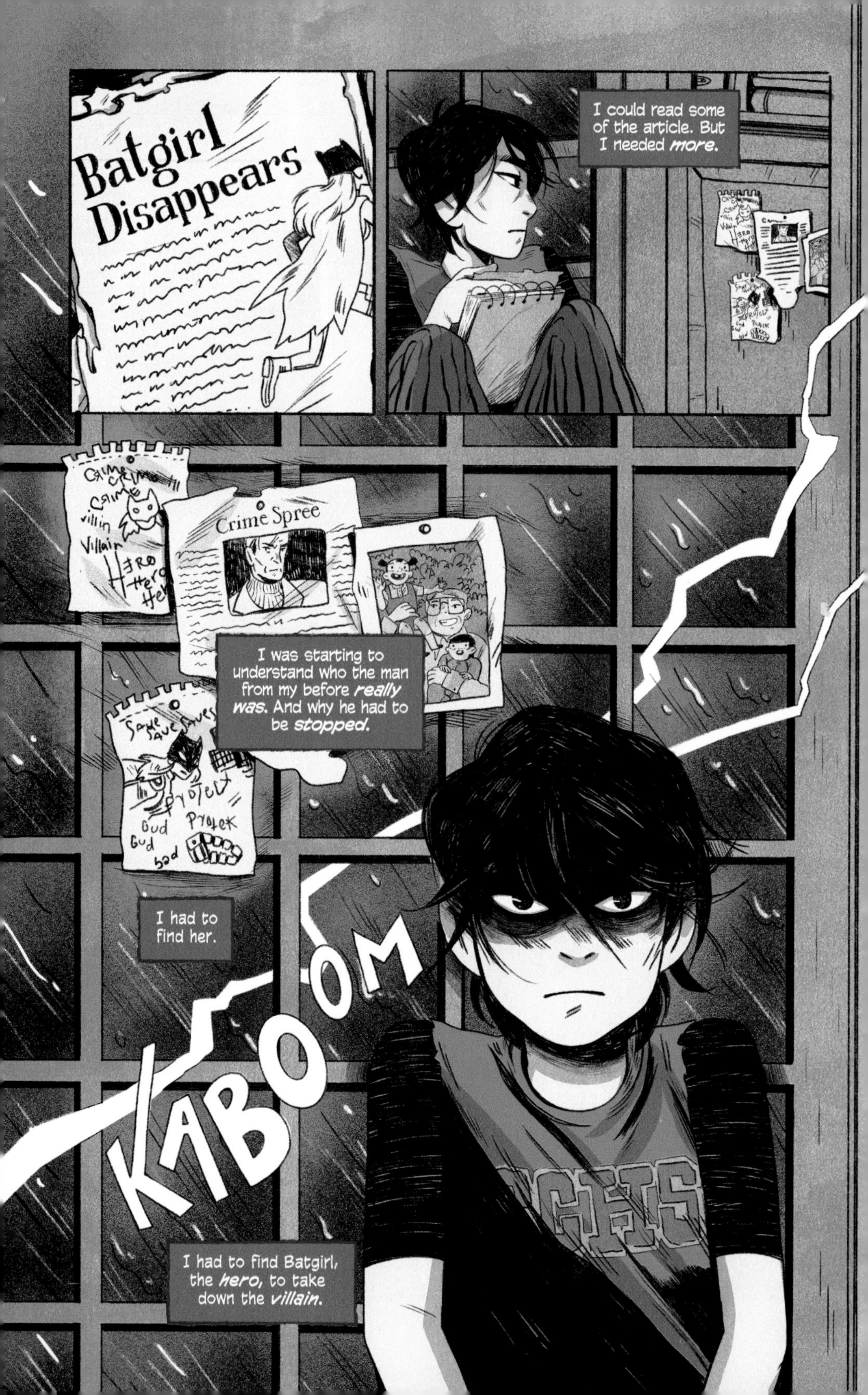

Batgirl Disappears
I could read some of the article. But I needed *more*.
Crime Spree
I was starting to understand who the man from my before *really was*. And why he had to be *stopped*.
I had to find her.
KABOOM
I had to find Batgirl, the *hero*, to take down the *villain*.

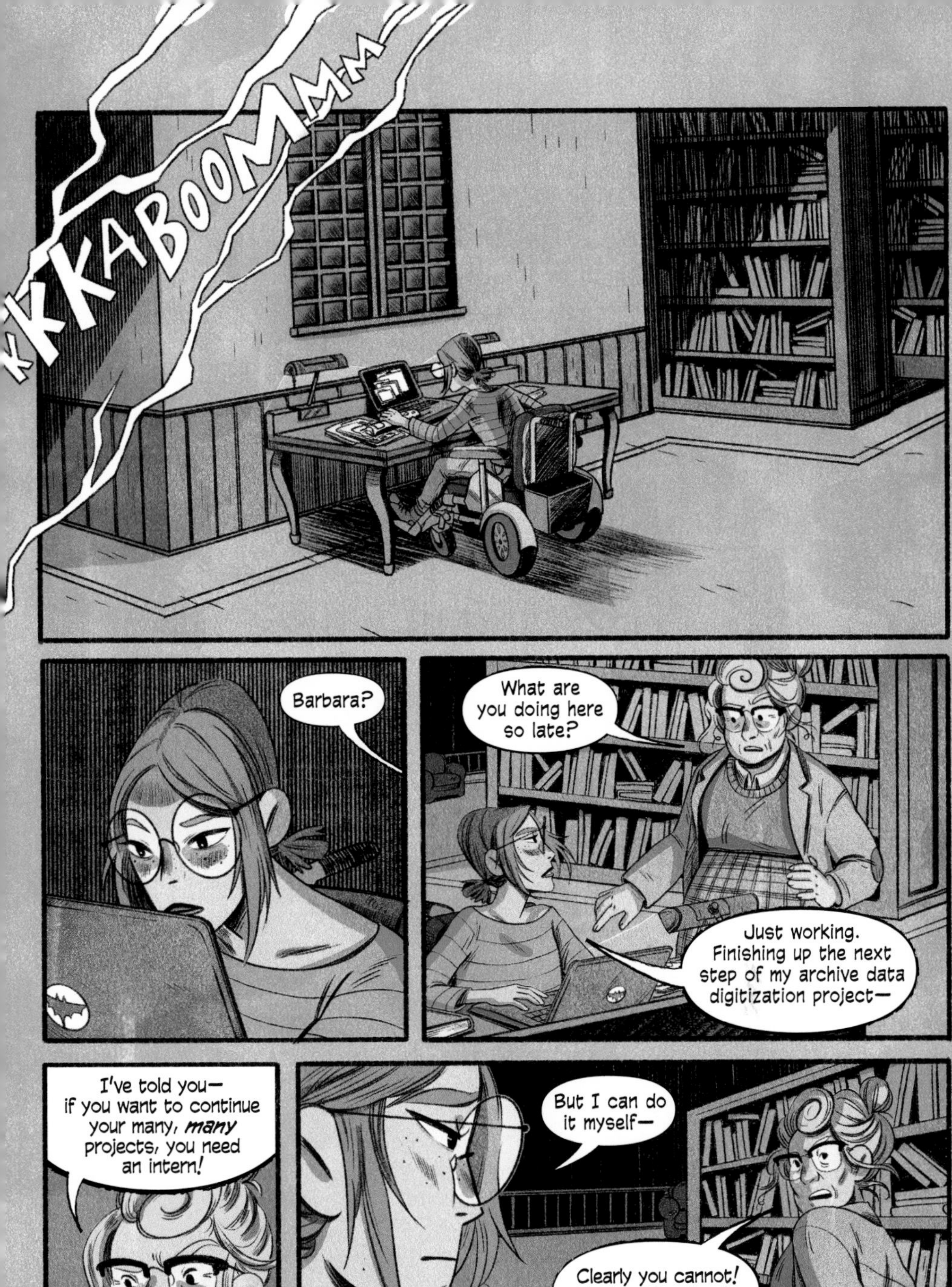
KKABOOMMM
Barbara?
What are you doing here so late?
Just working. Finishing up the next step of my archive data digitization project—
I've told you— if you want to continue your many, *many* projects, you need an intern!
But I can do it myself—
Clearly you cannot! The hour is *simply ghastly!*
Find an intern, Barbara— one of the fine young minds of Gotham we're supposed to be educating!

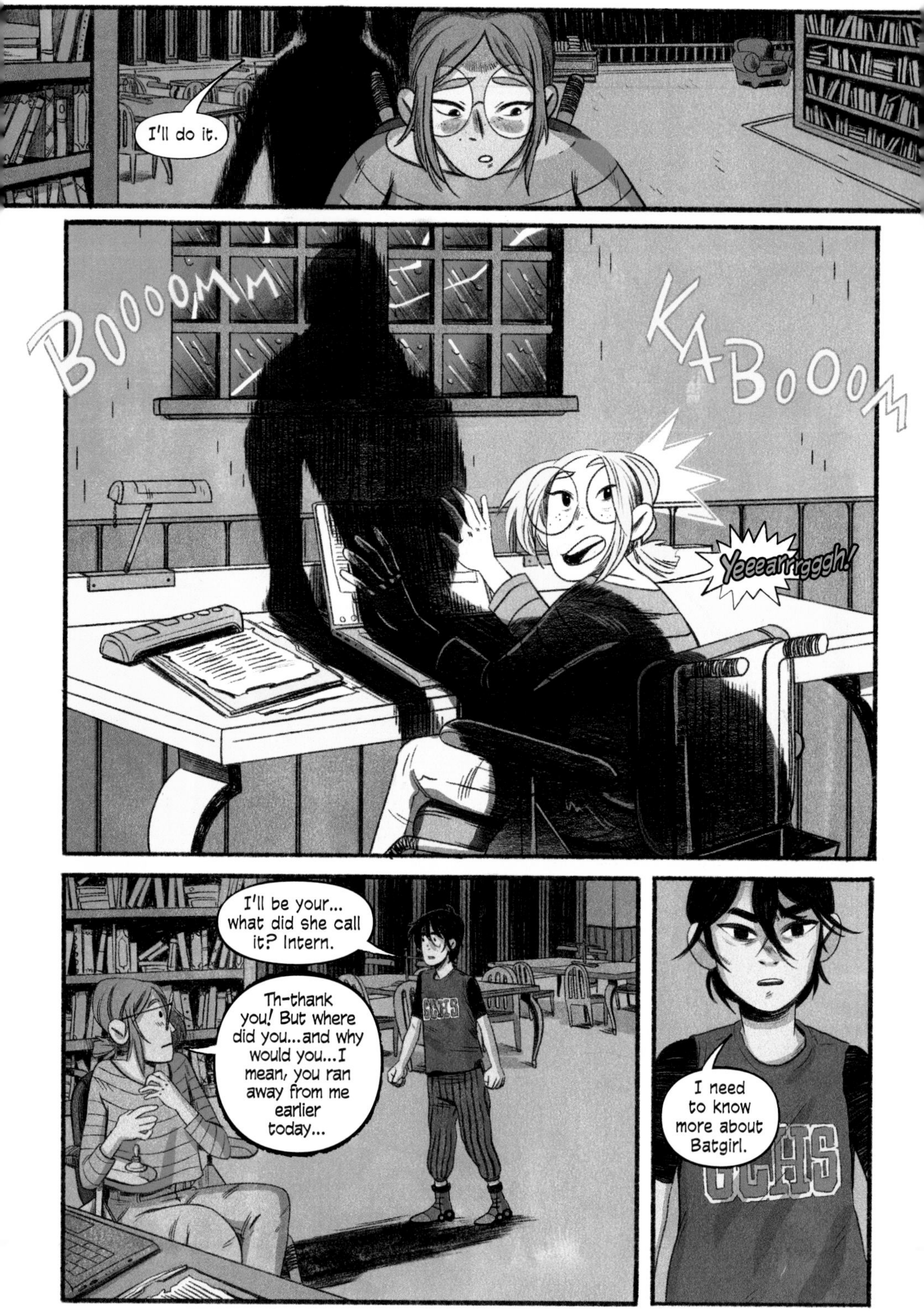
I'll do it.
BOOOOMM
KABOOOM
Yeeeanrrgggh!
I'll be your... what did she call it? Intern.
Th-thank you! But where did you...and why would you...I mean, you ran away from me earlier today...
I need to know more about Batgirl.

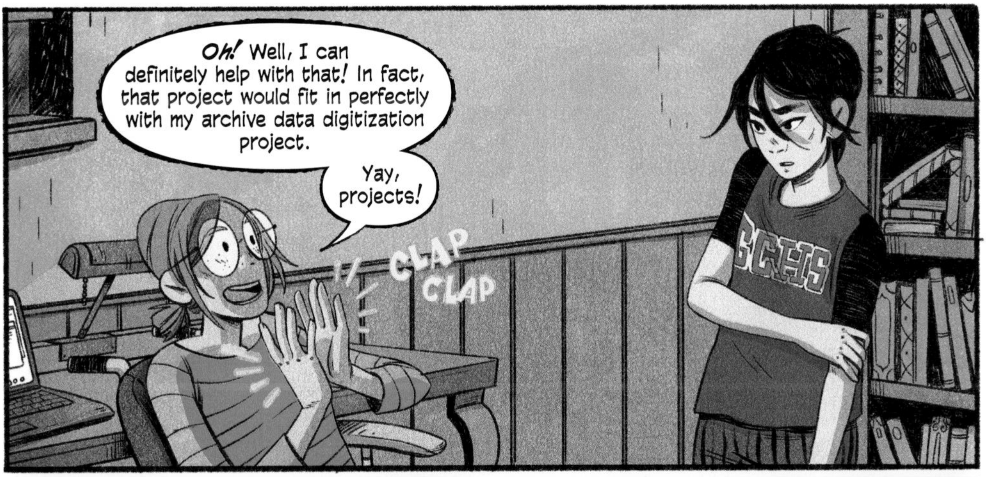
Oh! Well, I can definitely help with that! In fact, that project would fit in perfectly with my archive data digitization project.
Yay, projects!
CLAP CLAP
GCHS

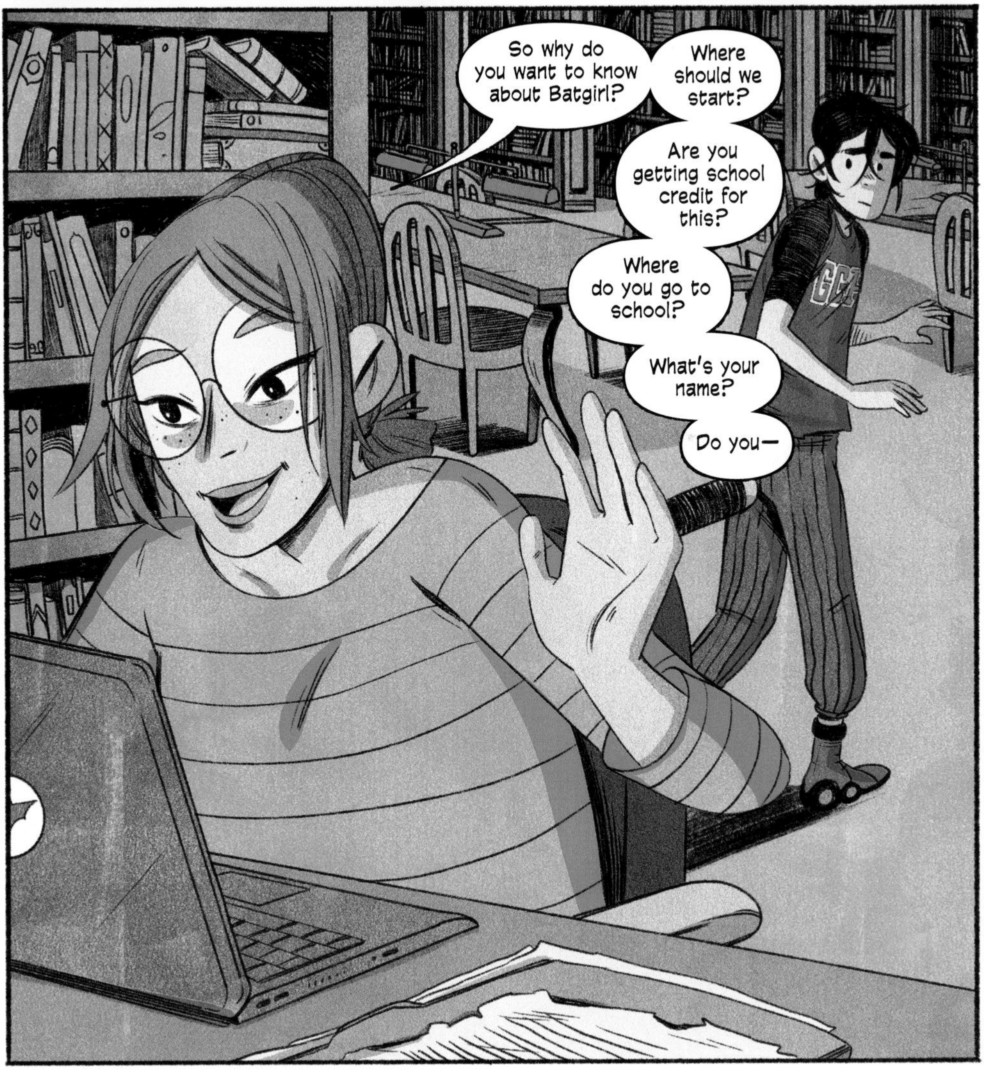
So why do you want to know about Batgirl?
Where should we start?
Are you getting school credit for this?
Where do you go to school?
What's your name?
Do you—

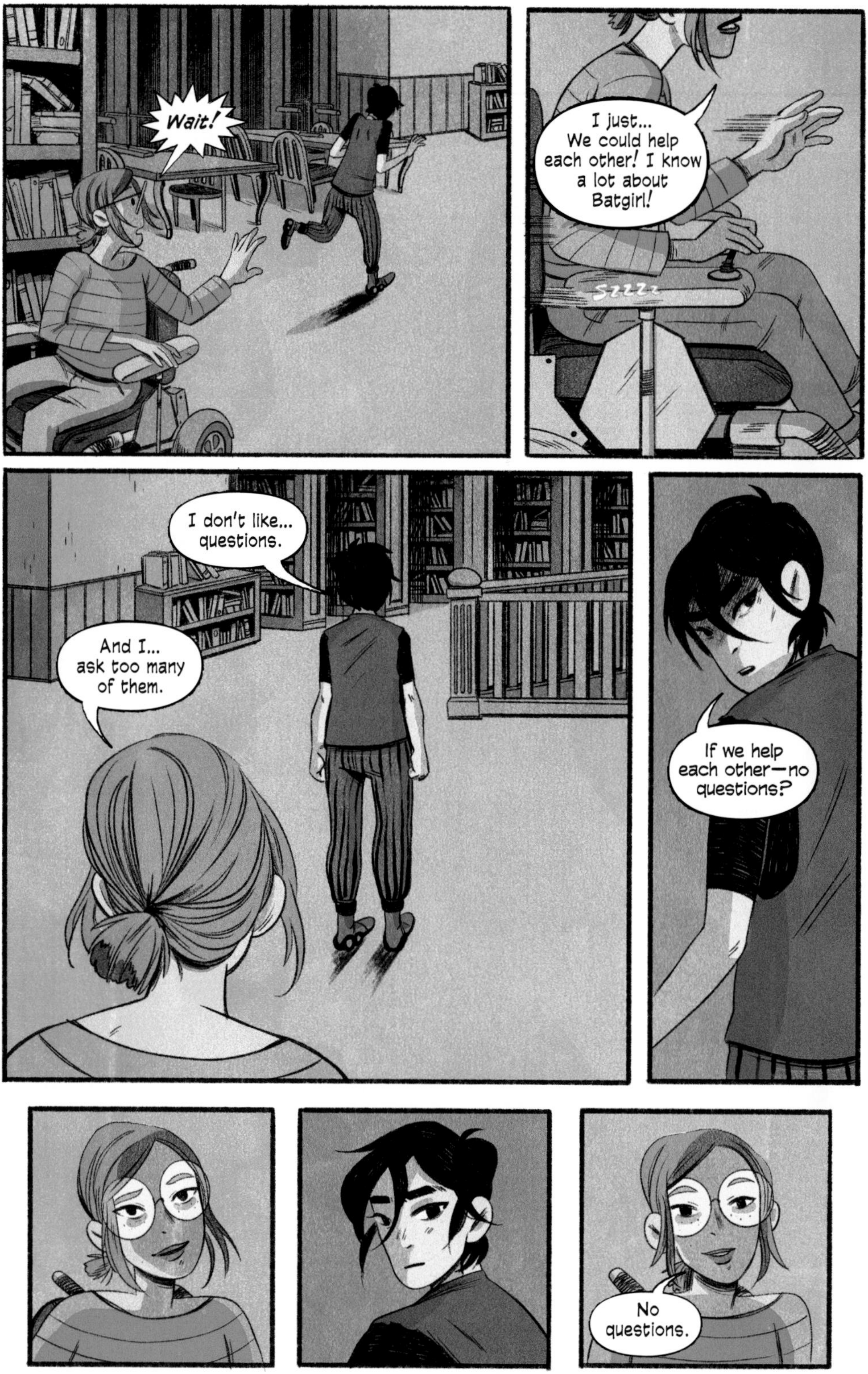
Wait!
I just... We could help each other! I know a lot about Batgirl!
Szzzz
I don't like... questions.
And I... ask too many of them.
If we help each other—no questions?
No questions.

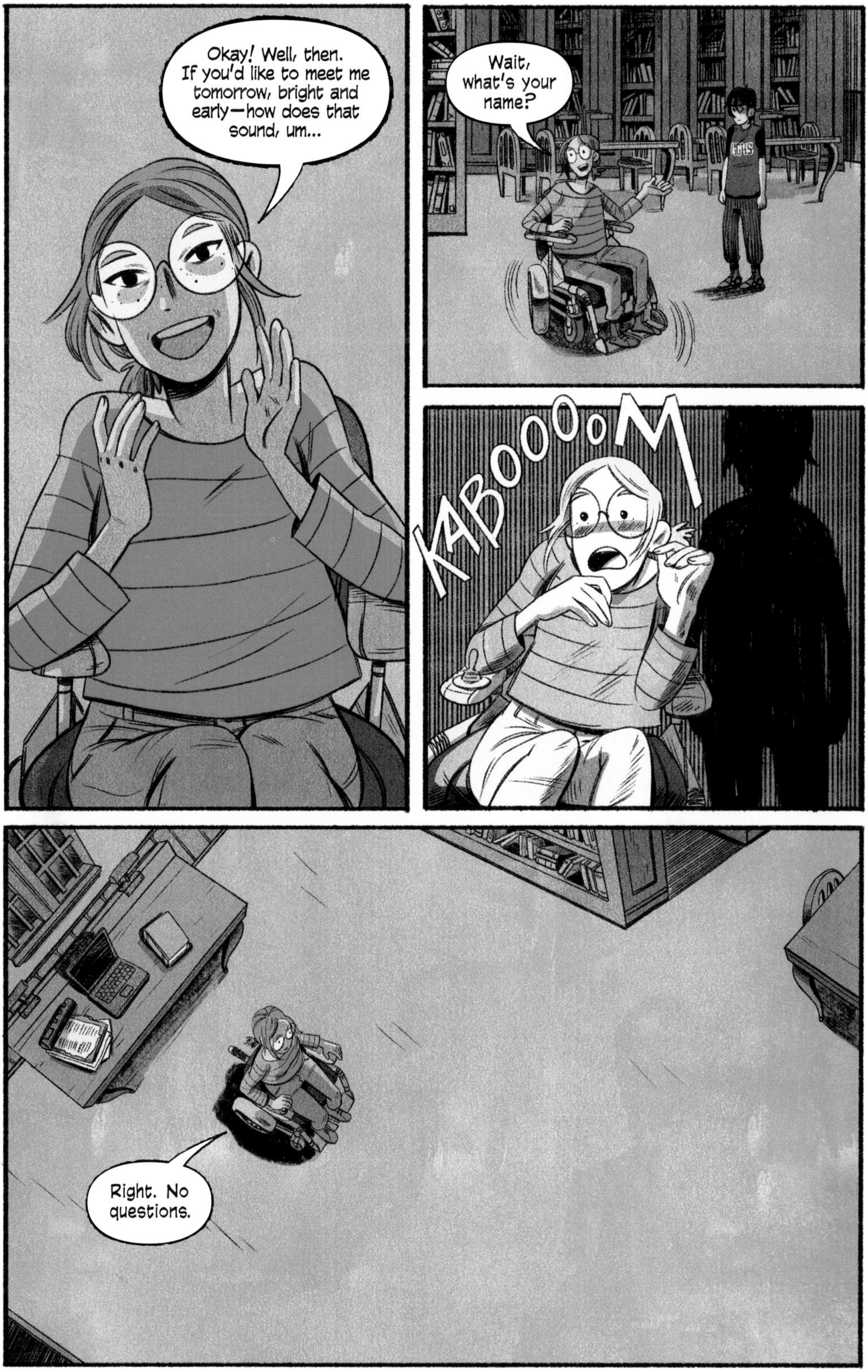
Okay! Well, then. If you'd like to meet me tomorrow, bright and early—how does that sound, um...
Wait, what's your name?
KABOOOOM
Right. No questions.

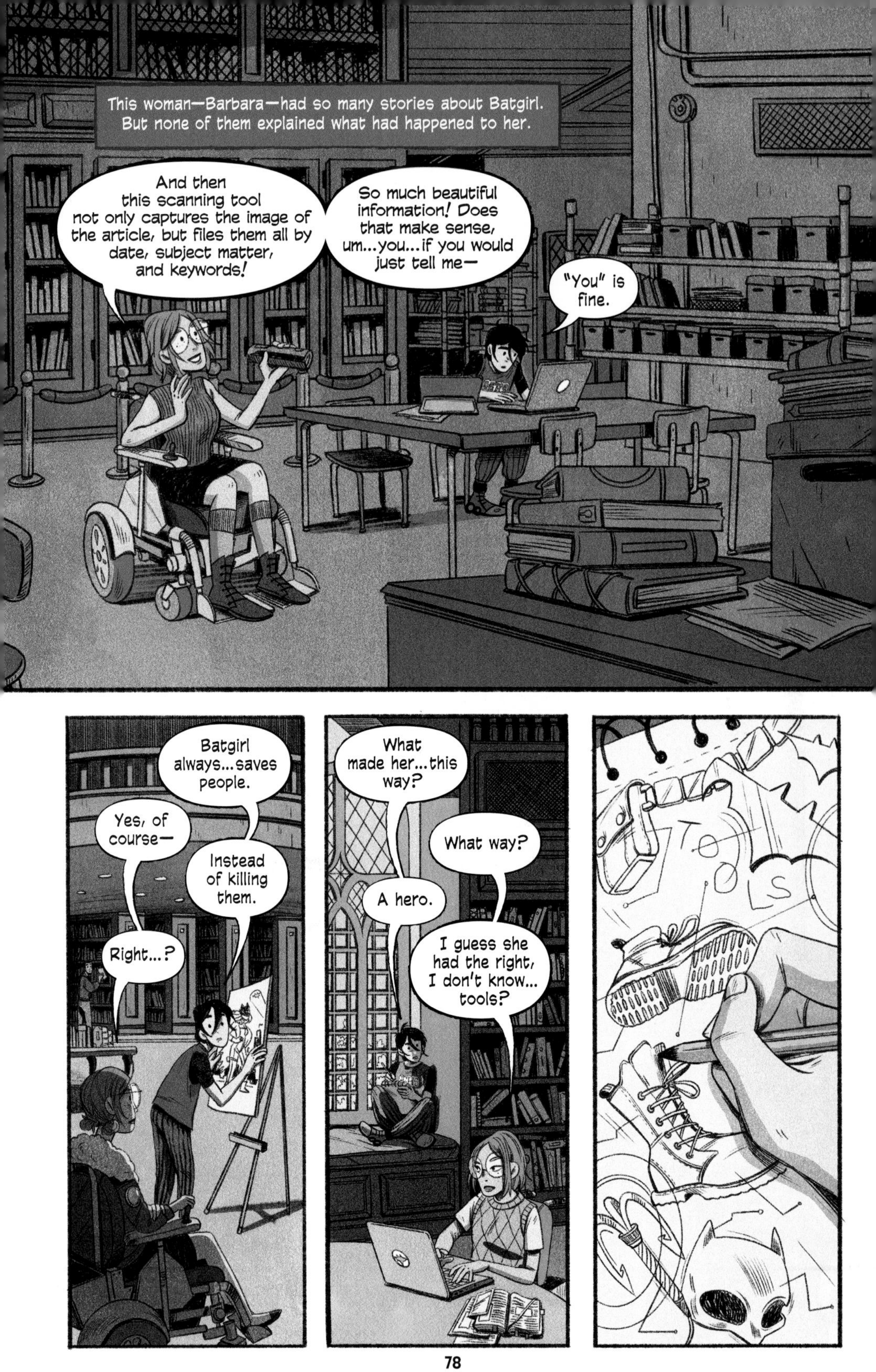
This woman—Barbara—had so many stories about Batgirl. But none of them explained what had happened to her.
And then this scanning tool not only captures the image of the article, but files them all by date, subject matter, and keywords!
So much beautiful information! Does that make sense, um...you...if you would just tell me—
"You" is fine.
Batgirl always...saves people.
Yes, of course—
Instead of killing them.
Right...?
What made her...this way?
What way?
A hero.
I guess she had the right, I don't know... tools?
TOOLS

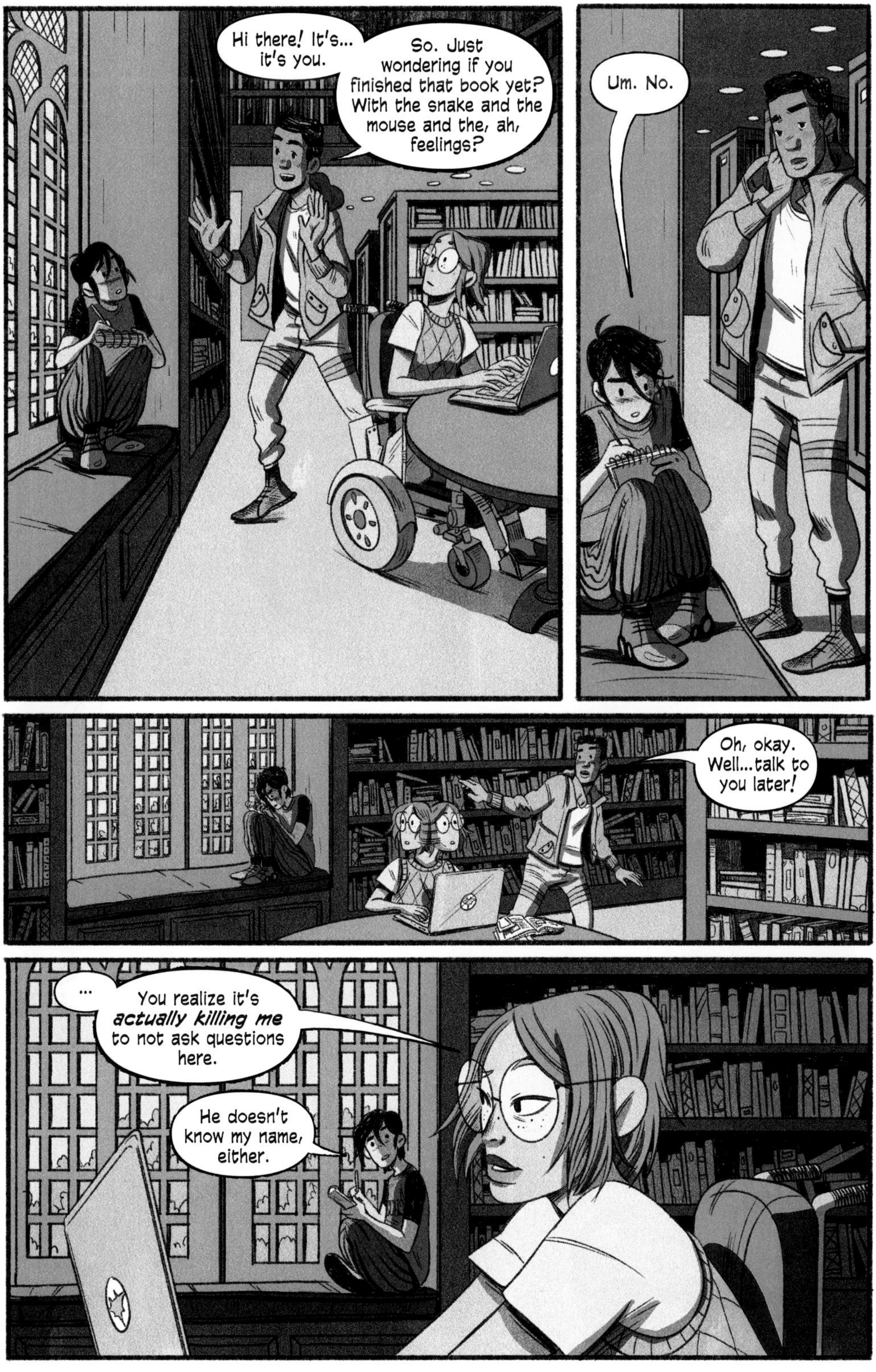
Hi there! It's... it's you.
So. Just wondering if you finished that book yet? With the snake and the mouse and the, ah, feelings?
Um. No.
Oh, okay. Well...talk to you later!
...
You realize it's ***actually killing me*** to not ask questions here.
He doesn't know my name, either.

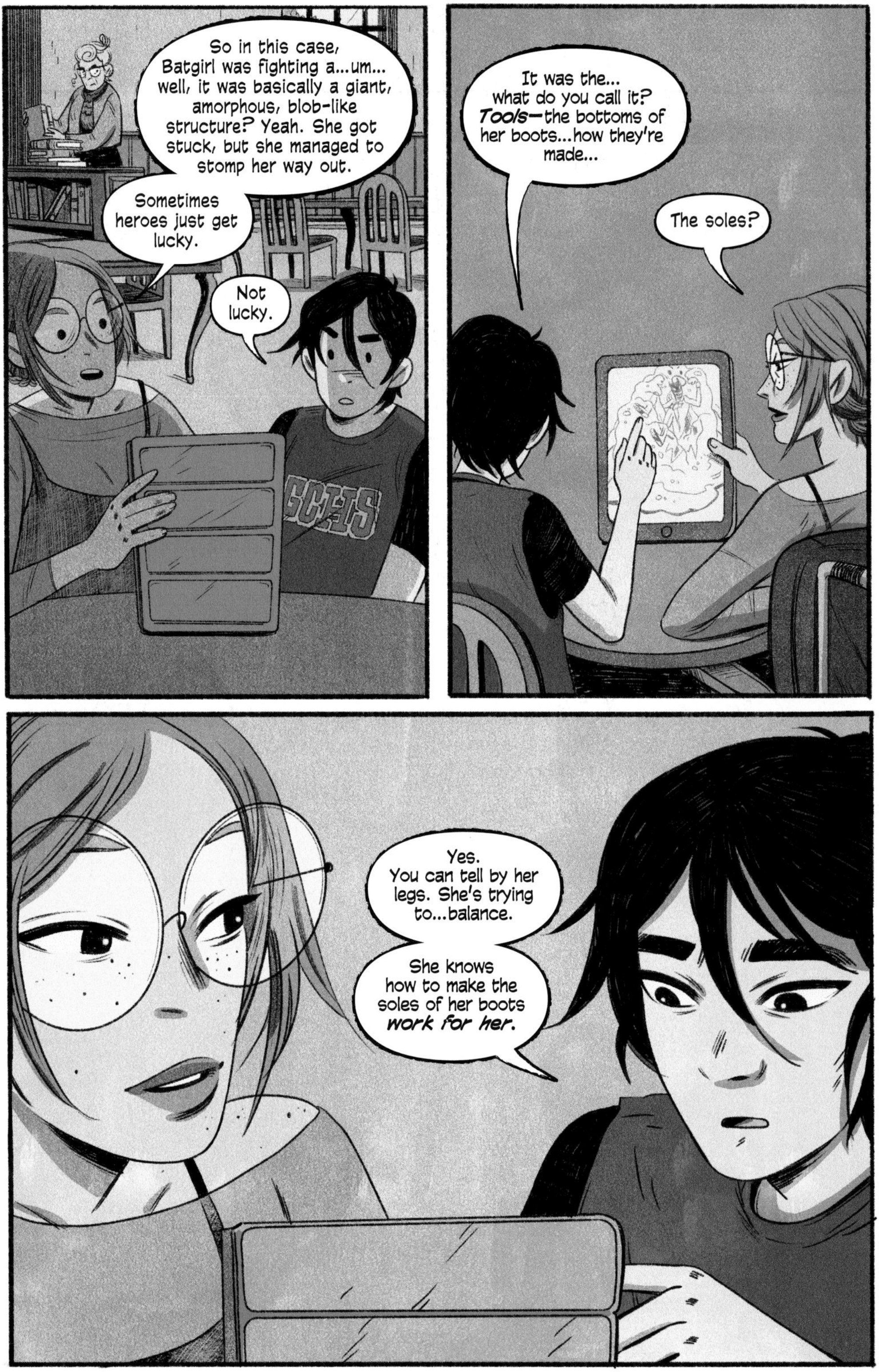
So in this case, Batgirl was fighting a...um... well, it was basically a giant, amorphous, blob-like structure? Yeah. She got stuck, but she managed to stomp her way out.
Sometimes heroes just get lucky.
Not lucky.
It was the... what do you call it? *Tools*—the bottoms of her boots...how they're made...
The soles?
Yes. You can tell by her legs. She's trying to...balance.
She knows how to make the soles of her boots *work for her*.

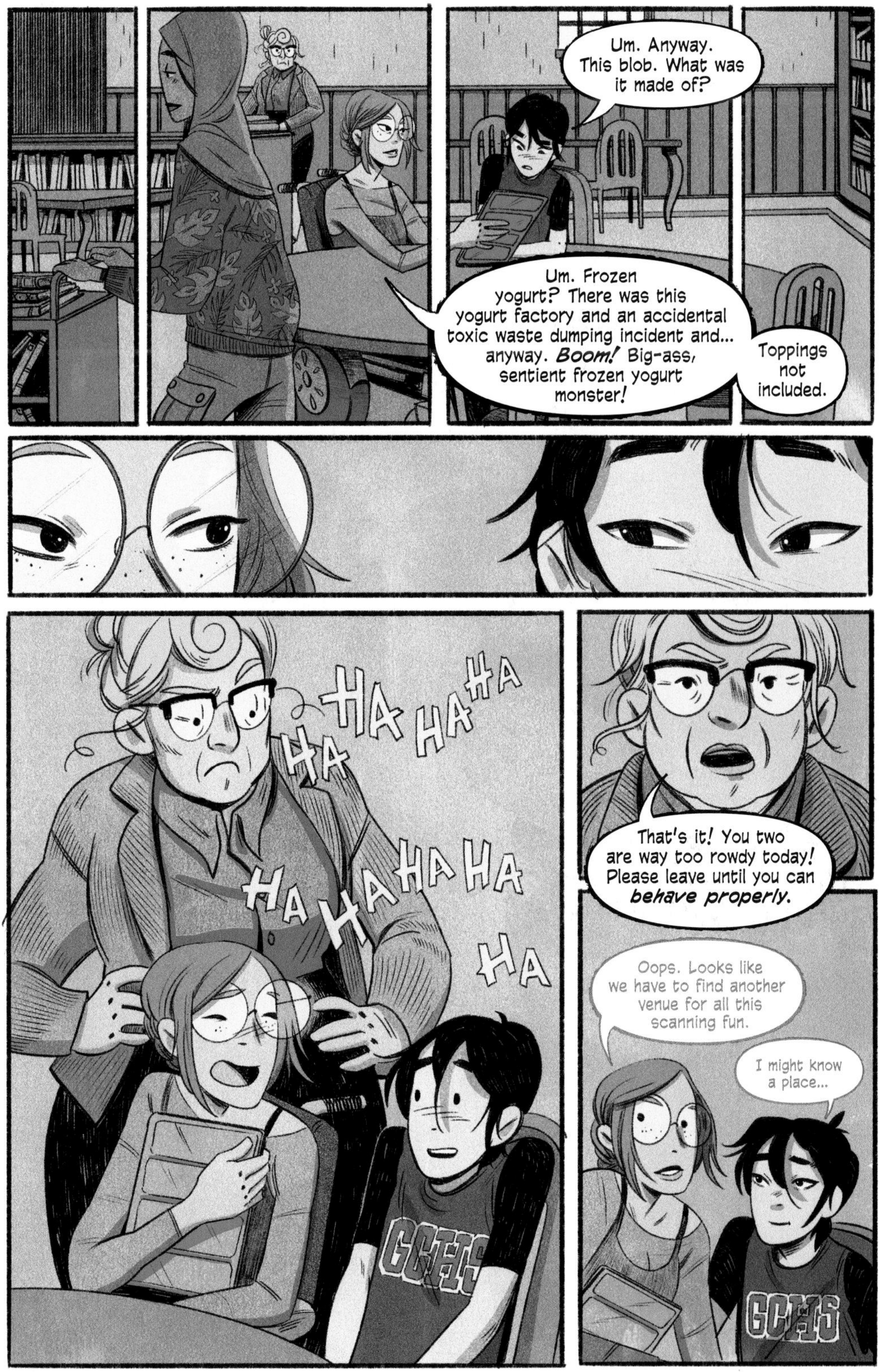
Um. Anyway.
This blob. What was it made of?
Um. Frozen yogurt? There was this yogurt factory and an accidental toxic waste dumping incident and... anyway. *Boom!* Big-ass, sentient frozen yogurt monster!
Toppings not included.
HA HA HA HA HA
HA HA HA HA HA
HA
That's it! You two are way too rowdy today! Please leave until you can **behave properly.**
Oops. Looks like we have to find another venue for all this scanning fun.
I might know a place...

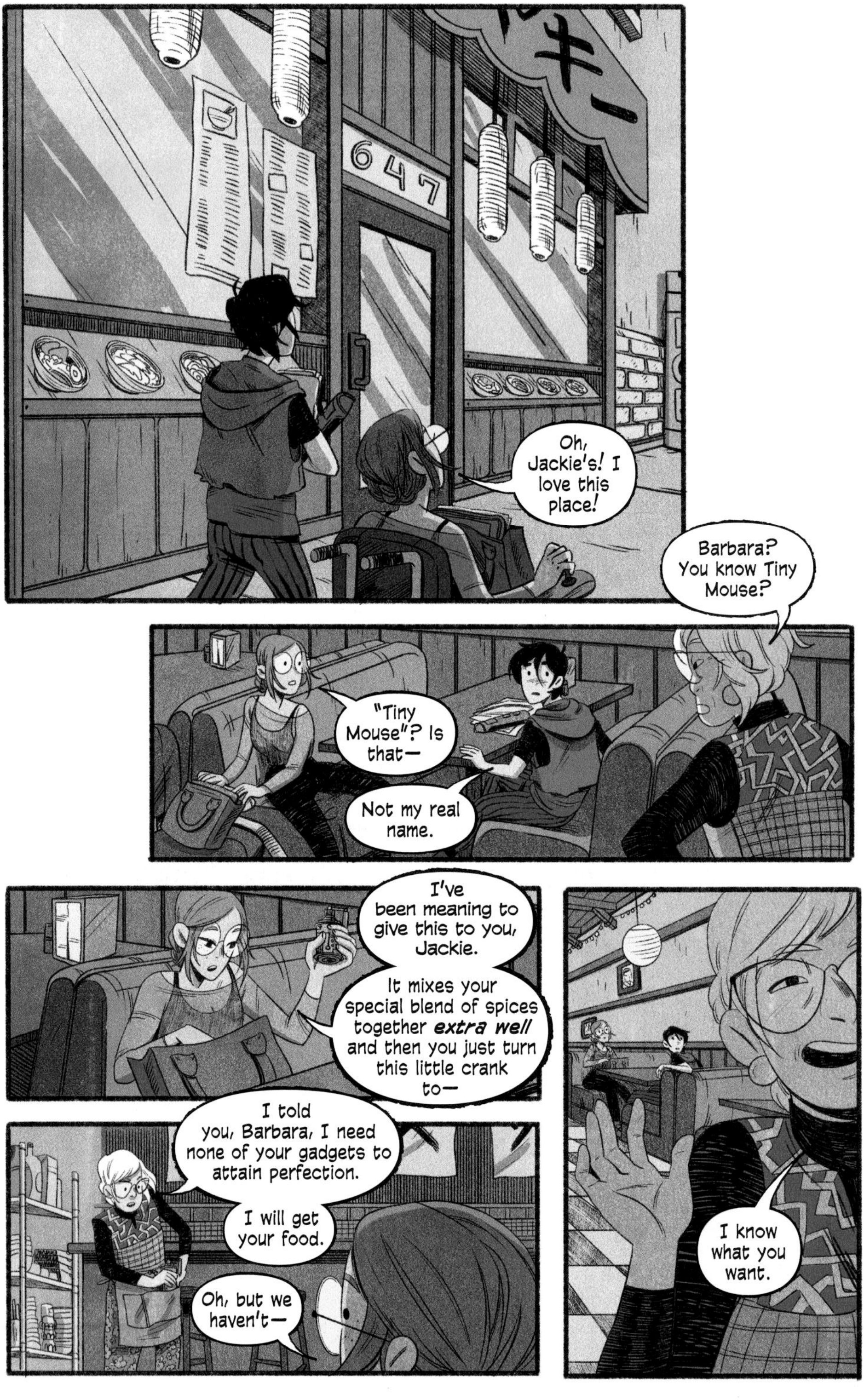

Oh, Jackie's! I love this place!
Barbara? You know Tiny Mouse?
"Tiny Mouse"? Is that—
Not my real name.
I've been meaning to give this to you, Jackie.
It mixes your special blend of spices together *extra well* and then you just turn this little crank to—
I know what you want.
I told you, Barbara, I need none of your gadgets to attain perfection.
I will get your food.
Oh, but we haven't—

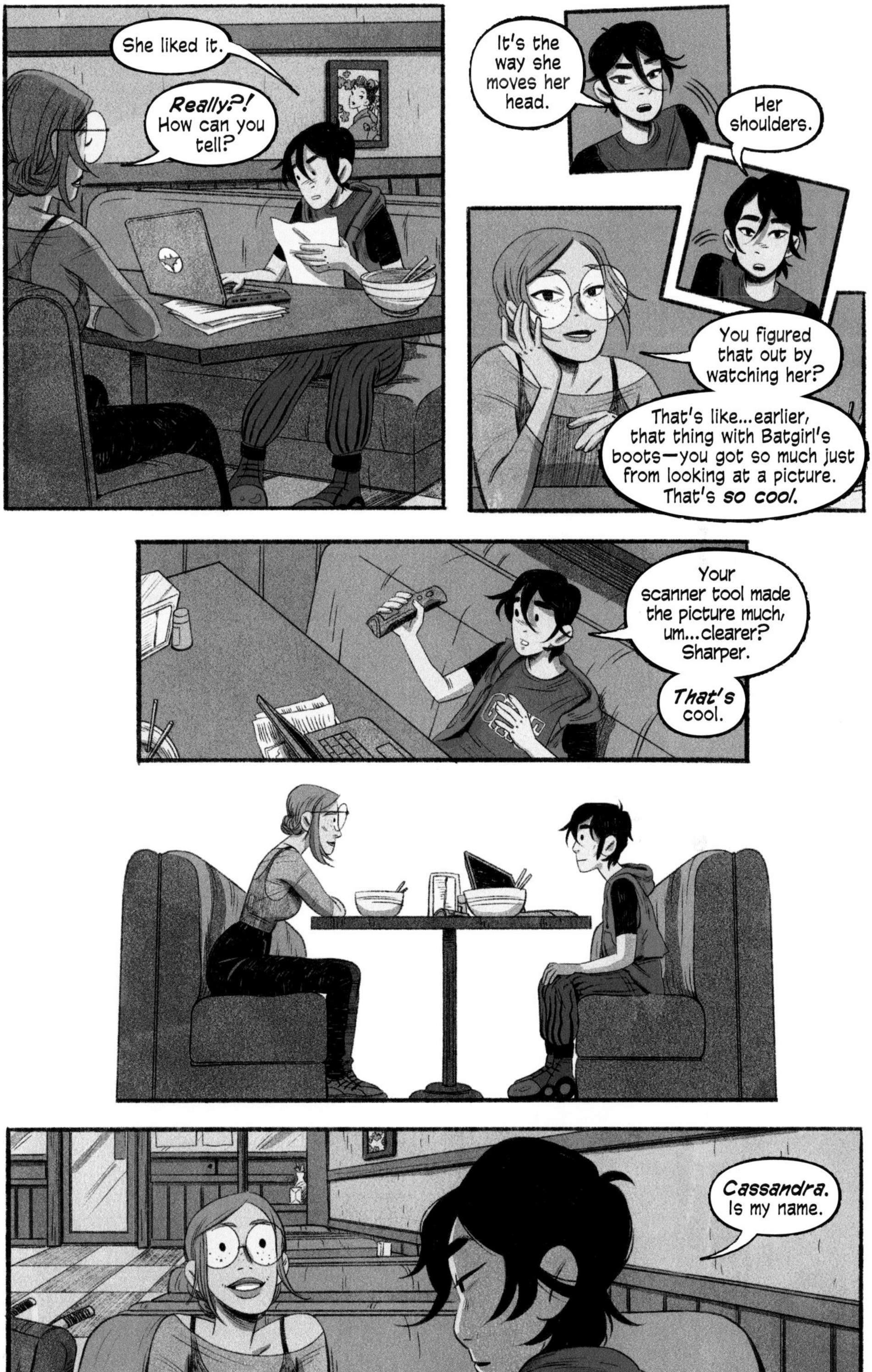
She liked it.
Really?! How can you tell?
It's the way she moves her head.
Her shoulders.
You figured that out by watching her?
That's like...earlier, that thing with Batgirl's boots—you got so much just from looking at a picture. That's *so cool.*
Your scanner tool made the picture much, um...clearer? Sharper.
That's cool.
Cassandra. Is my name.

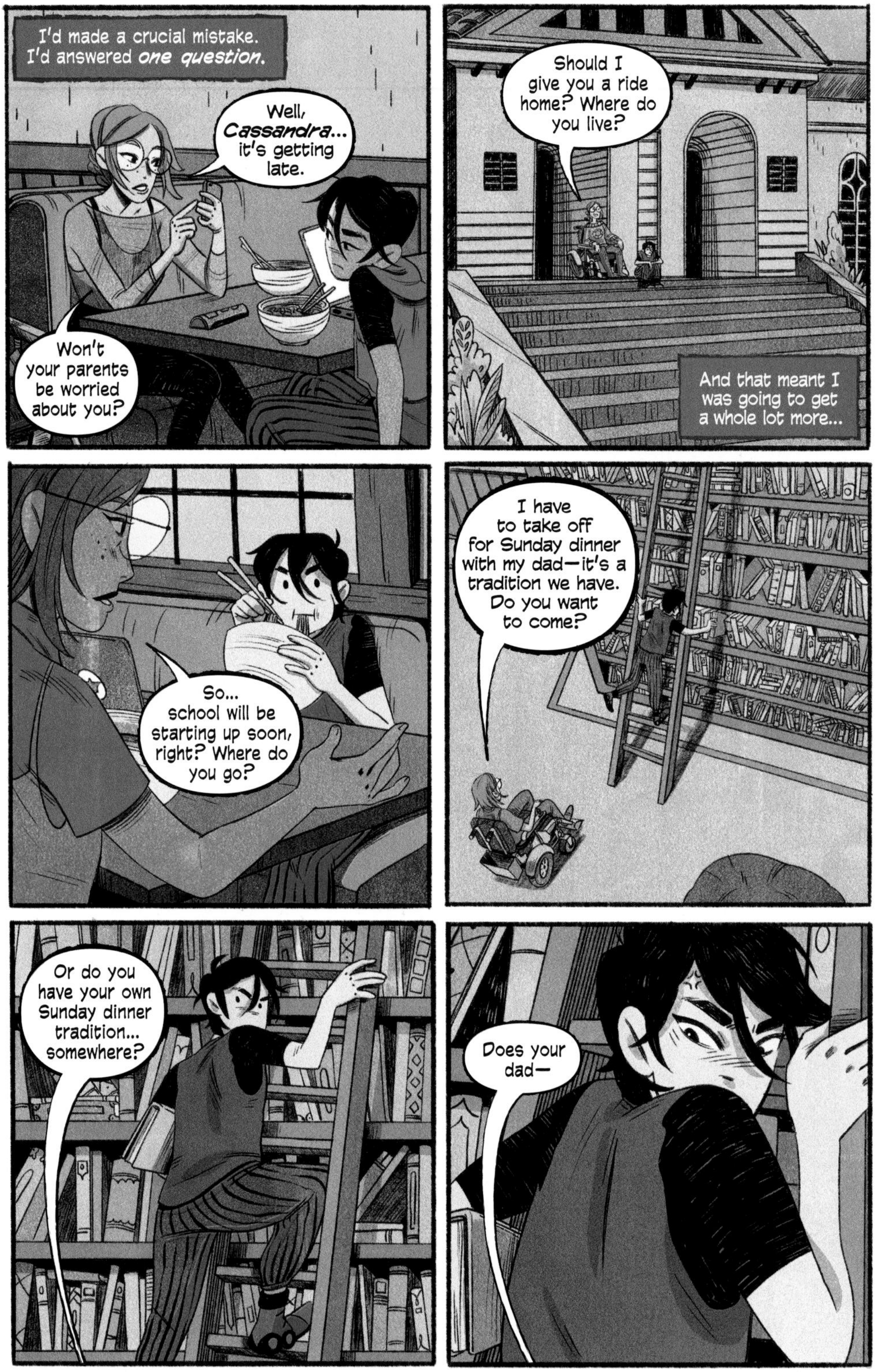
I'd made a crucial mistake. I'd answered *one question*.
Well, *Cassandra*... it's getting late.
Won't your parents be worried about you?
Should I give you a ride home? Where do you live?
And that meant I was going to get a whole lot more...
So... school will be starting up soon, right? Where do you go?
I have to take off for Sunday dinner with my dad—it's a tradition we have. Do you want to come?
Or do you have your own Sunday dinner tradition... somewhere?
Does your dad—

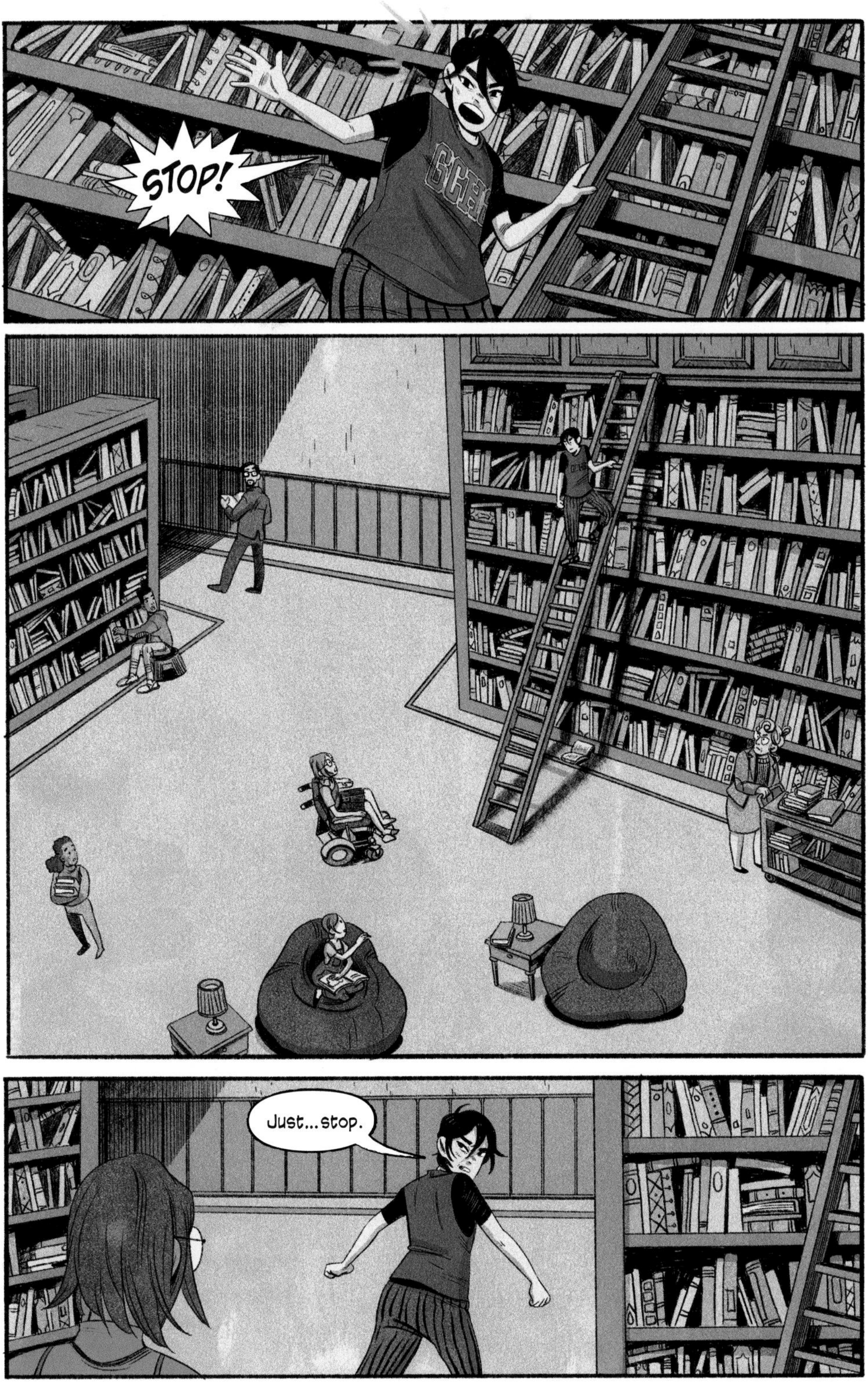
STOP!
Just...stop.

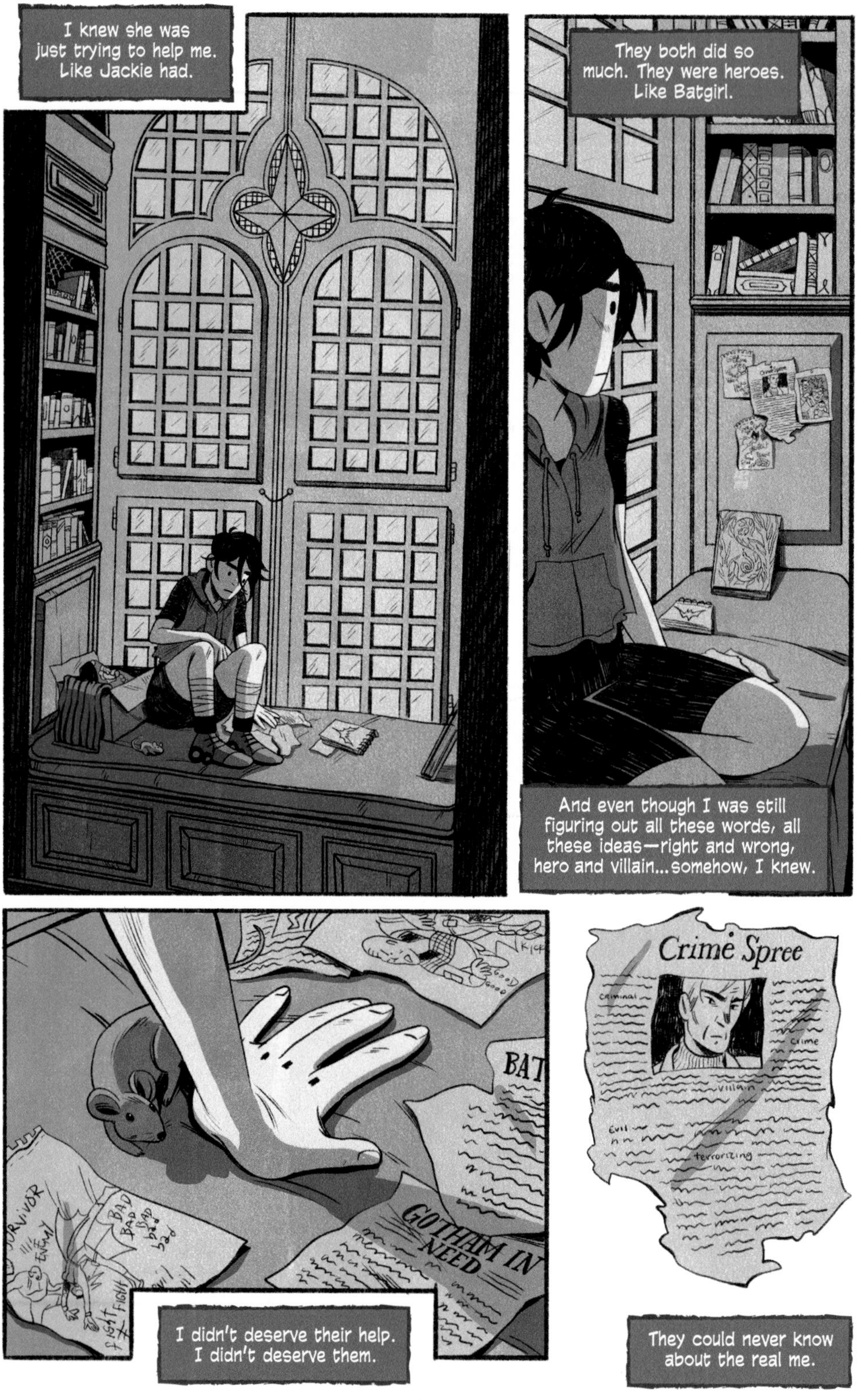
I knew she was just trying to help me. Like Jackie had.
They both did so much. They were heroes. Like Batgirl.
And even though I was still figuring out all these words, all these ideas—right and wrong, hero and villain...somehow, I knew.
BAT
GOTHAM IN NEED
BAD BAD bad bad
SURVIVOR
FIGHT FIGHT
I didn't deserve their help. I didn't deserve them.
Crime Spree
criminal
crime
villain
Evil
terrorizing
They could never know about the real me.

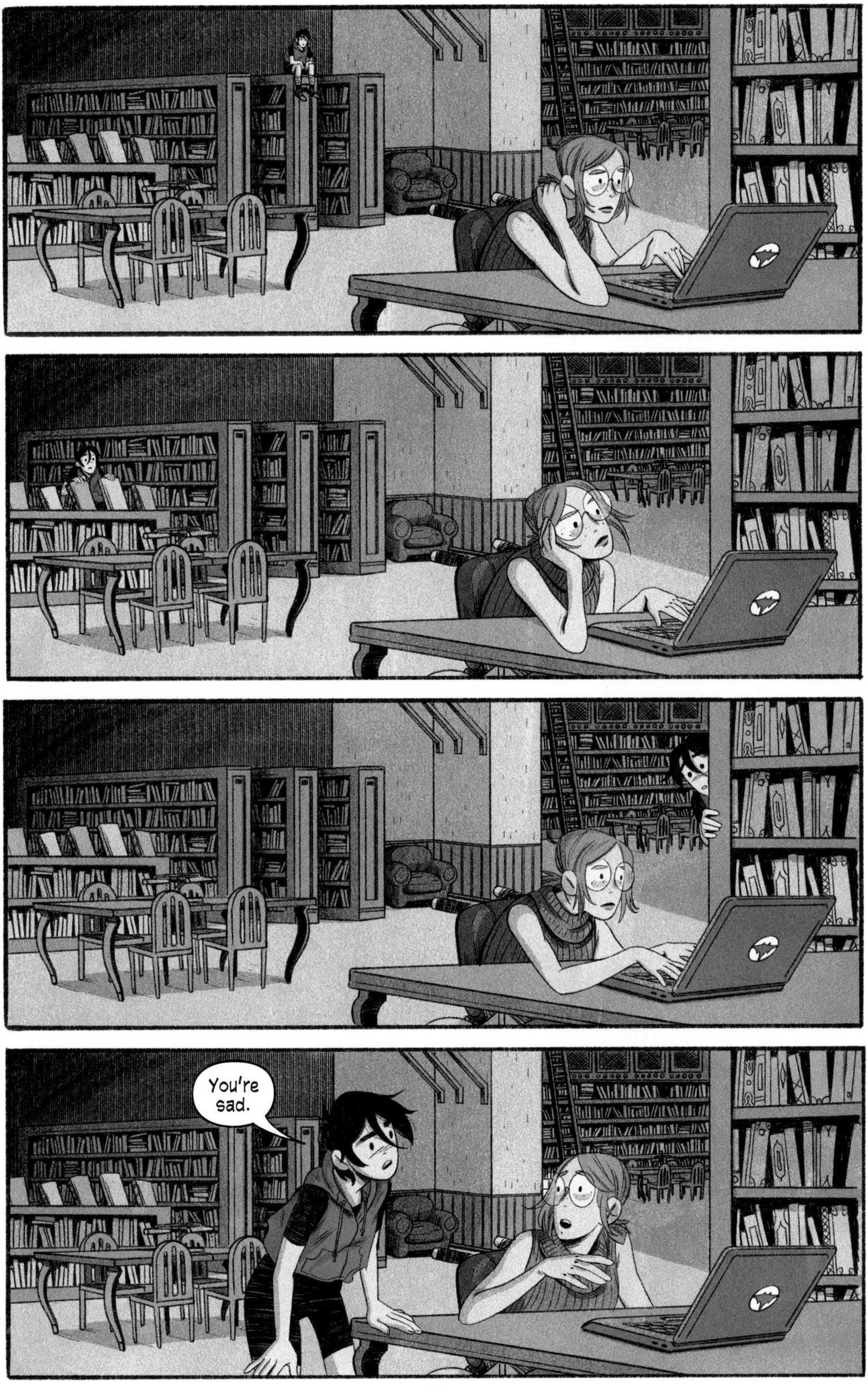
You're sad.

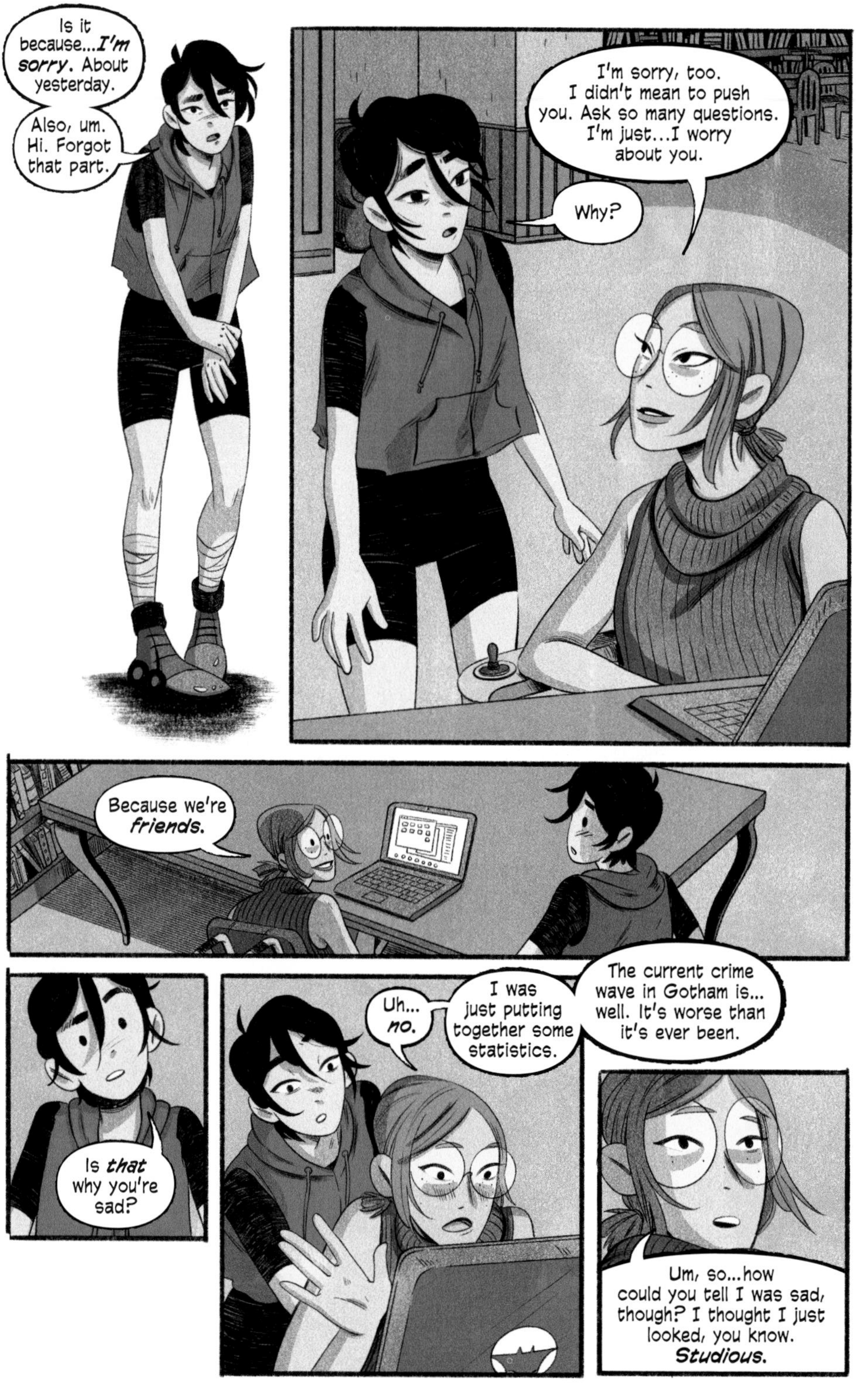
Is it because...*I'm sorry*. About yesterday.
Also, um. Hi. Forgot that part.
I'm sorry, too. I didn't mean to push you. Ask so many questions. I'm just...I worry about you.
Why?
Because we're *friends*.
Is *that* why you're sad?
Uh... *no*.
I was just putting together some statistics.
The current crime wave in Gotham is... well. It's worse than it's ever been.
Um, so...how could you tell I was sad, though? I thought I just looked, you know. *Studious*.

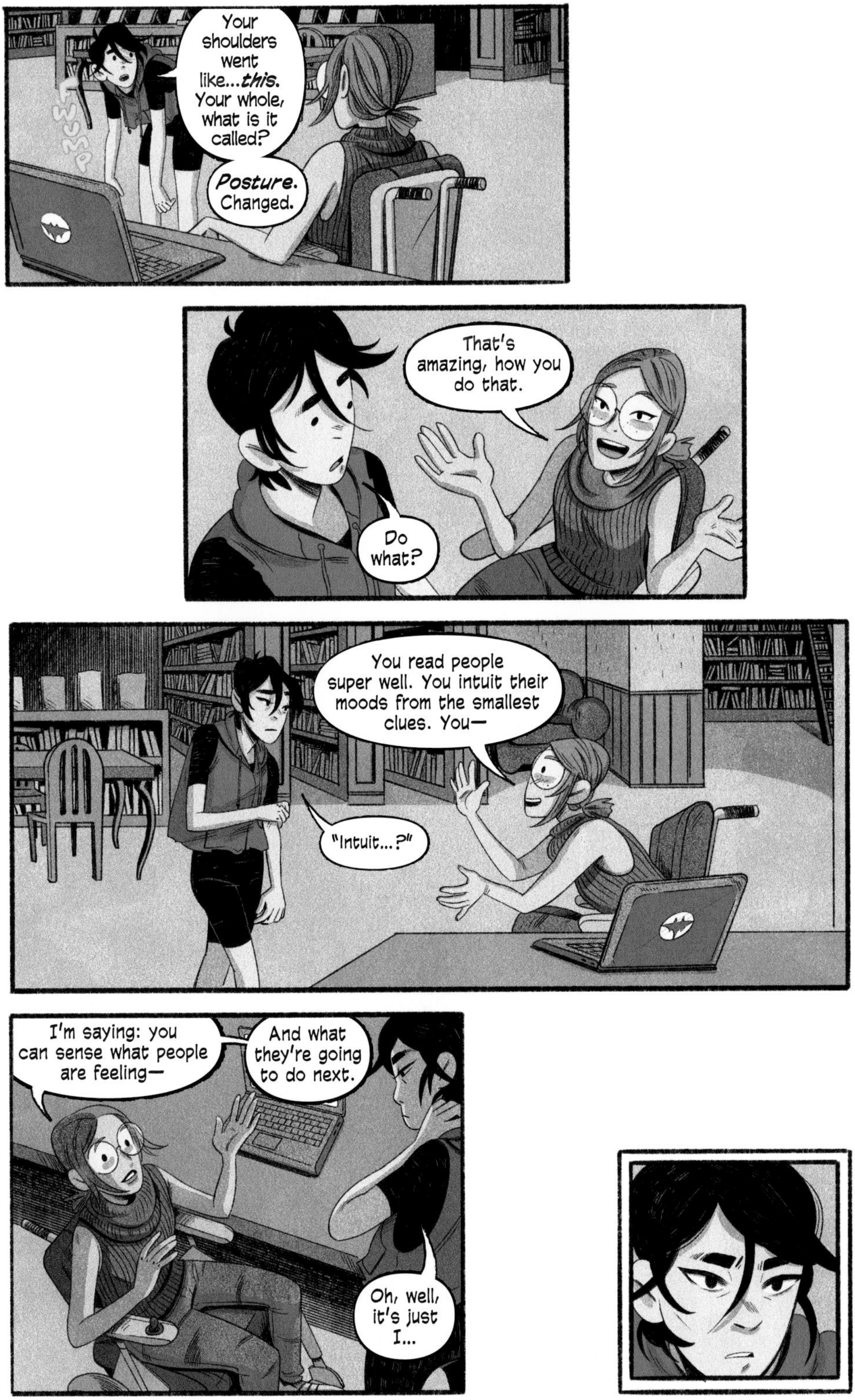
FWUMP
Your shoulders went like...*this*. Your whole, what is it called?
Posture. Changed.
That's amazing, how you do that.
Do what?
You read people super well. You intuit their moods from the smallest clues. You—
"Intuit...?"
I'm saying: you can sense what people are feeling—
And what they're going to do next.
Oh, well, it's just I...

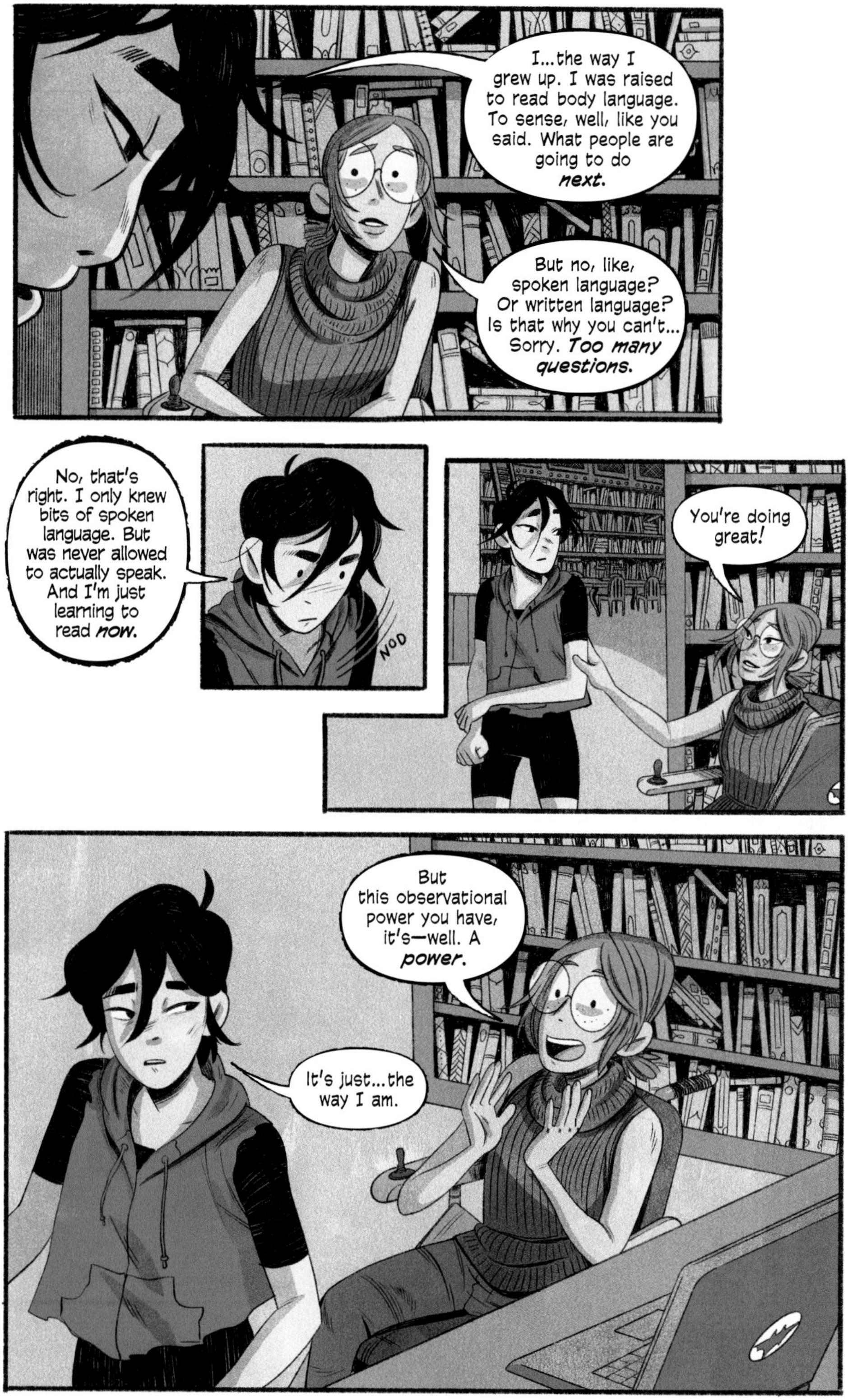
I...the way I grew up. I was raised to read body language. To sense, well, like you said. What people are going to do *next*.
But no, like, spoken language? Or written language? Is that why you can't... Sorry. *Too many questions*.
No, that's right. I only knew bits of spoken language. But was never allowed to actually speak. And I'm just learning to read *now*.
NOD
You're doing great!
But this observational power you have, it's—well. A *power*.
It's just...the way I am.

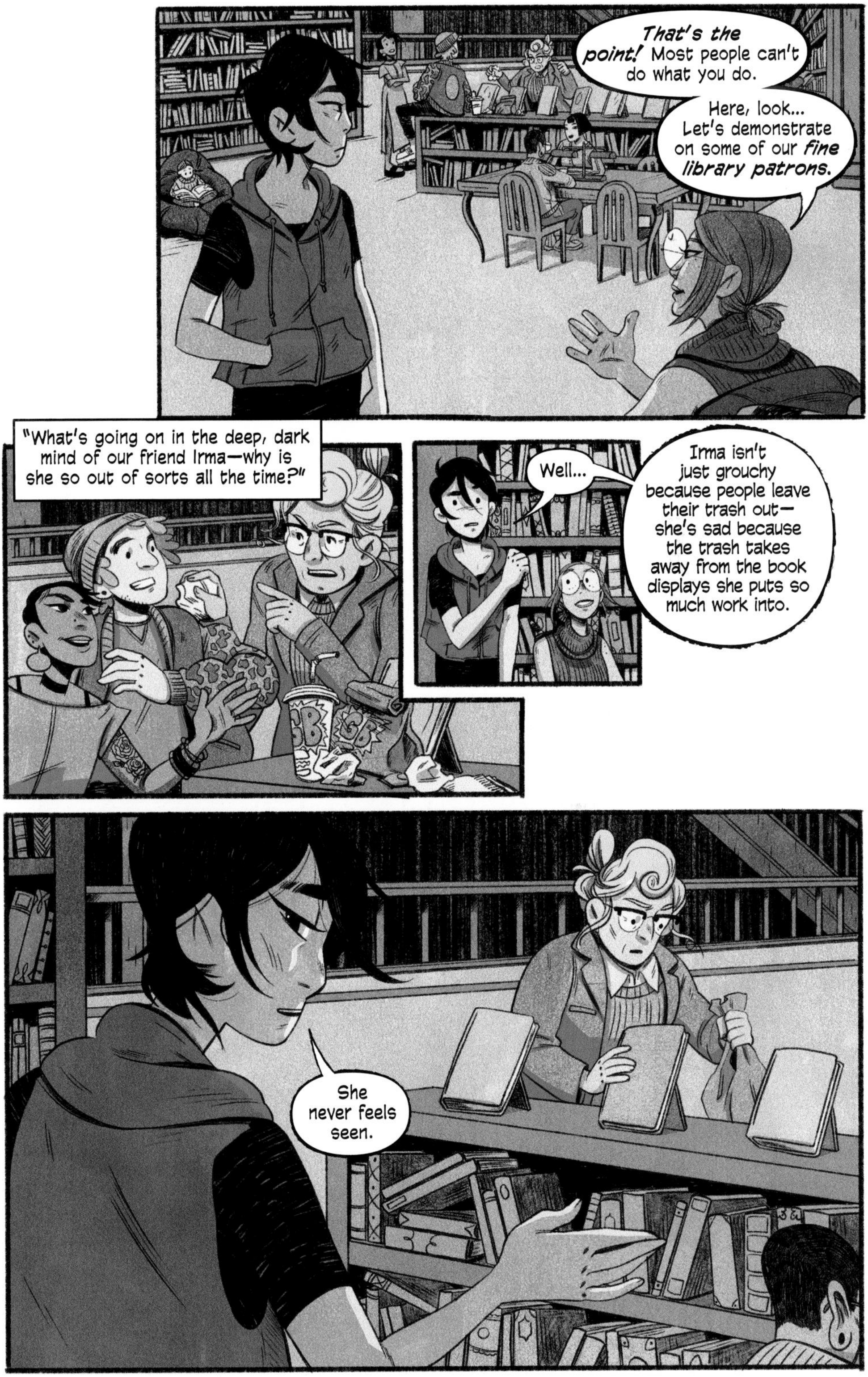
That's the point! Most people can't do what you do.
Here, look... Let's demonstrate on some of our fine library patrons.
"What's going on in the deep, dark mind of our friend Irma—why is she so out of sorts all the time?"
Well...
Irma isn't just grouchy because people leave their trash out—she's sad because the trash takes away from the book displays she puts so much work into.
She never feels seen.

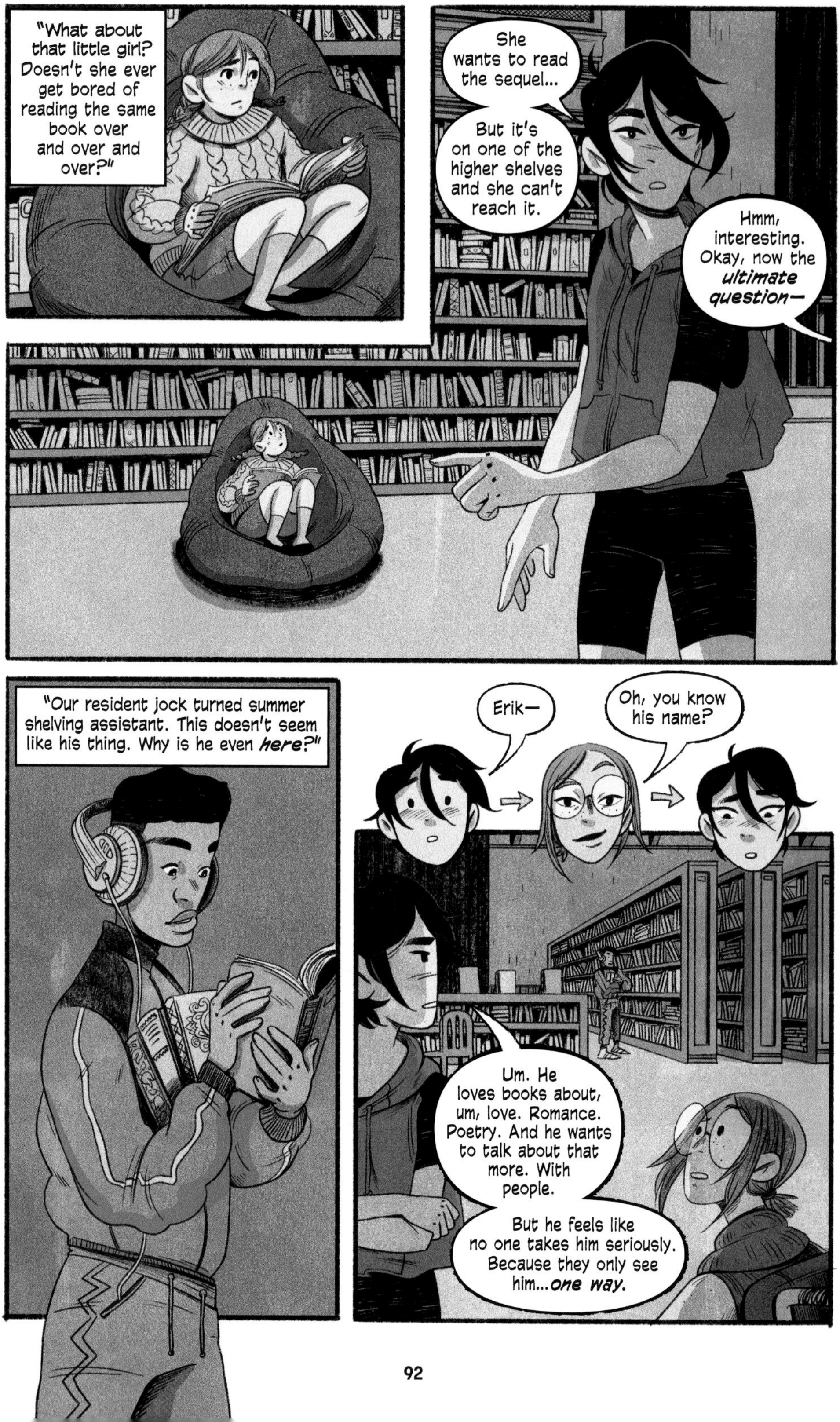
"What about that little girl? Doesn't she ever get bored of reading the same book over and over and over?"
She wants to read the sequel...
But it's on one of the higher shelves and she can't reach it.
Hmm, interesting. Okay, now the *ultimate question—*
"Our resident jock turned summer shelving assistant. This doesn't seem like his thing. Why is he even *here?*"
Erik—
Oh, you know his name?
Um. He loves books about, um, love. Romance. Poetry. And he wants to talk about that more. With people.
But he feels like no one takes him seriously. Because they only see him...*one way.*

Okay, probably back to me asking too many questions, *but*—how are you getting all that from him?

I mean, he *does* seem kind of like one thing. Like a handsome, shallow jock, no?

It's...well. He has these little, um, *movements?*

Like...you don't notice them at first, because he's taught himself to *control* them.

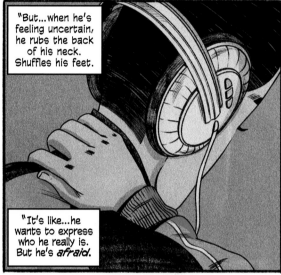

"But...when he's feeling uncertain, he rubs the back of his neck. Shuffles his feet.

"It's like...he wants to express who he really is. But he's *afraid.*

I *understand* that.

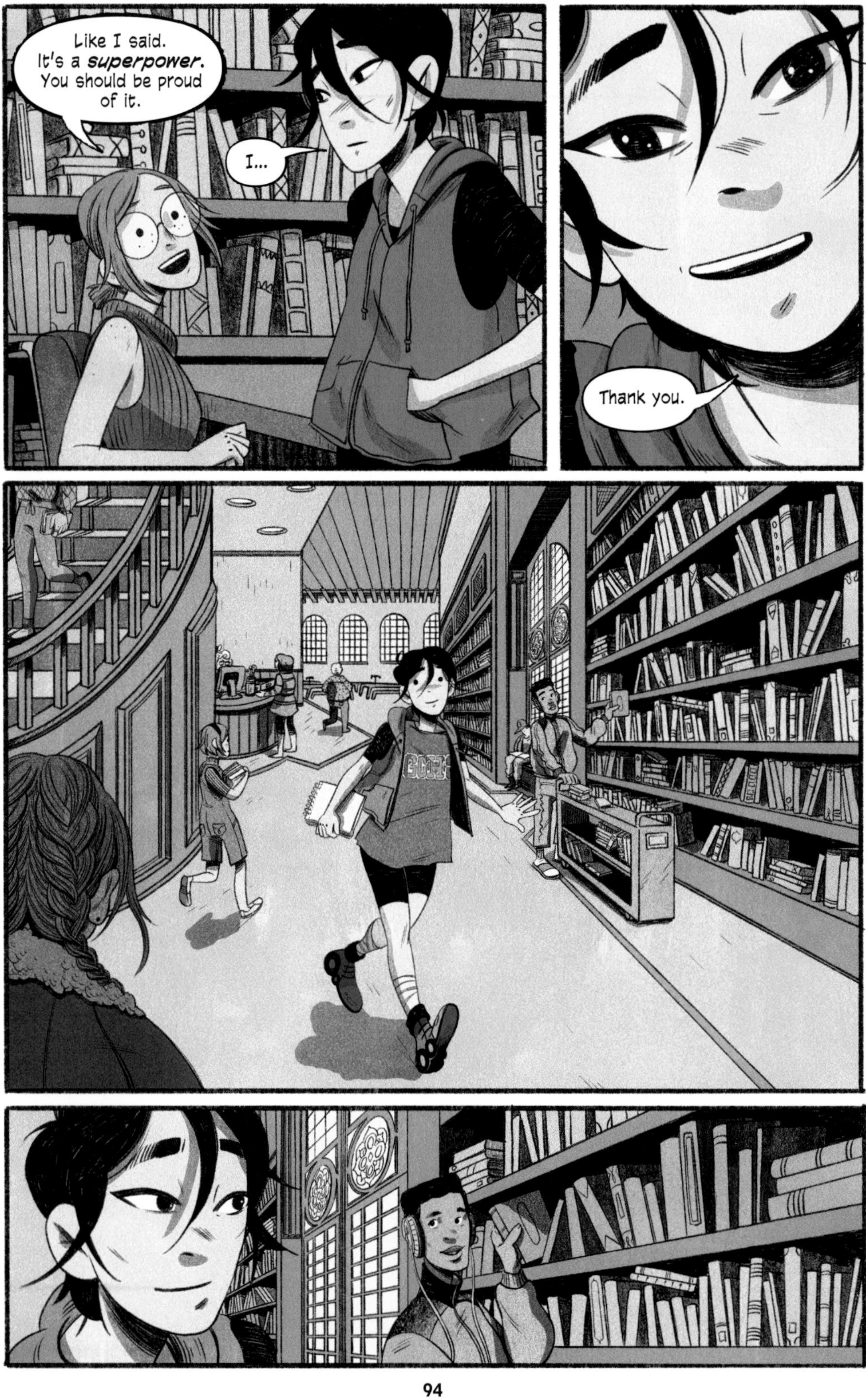
Like I said. It's a ***superpower***. You should be proud of it.
I...
Thank you.

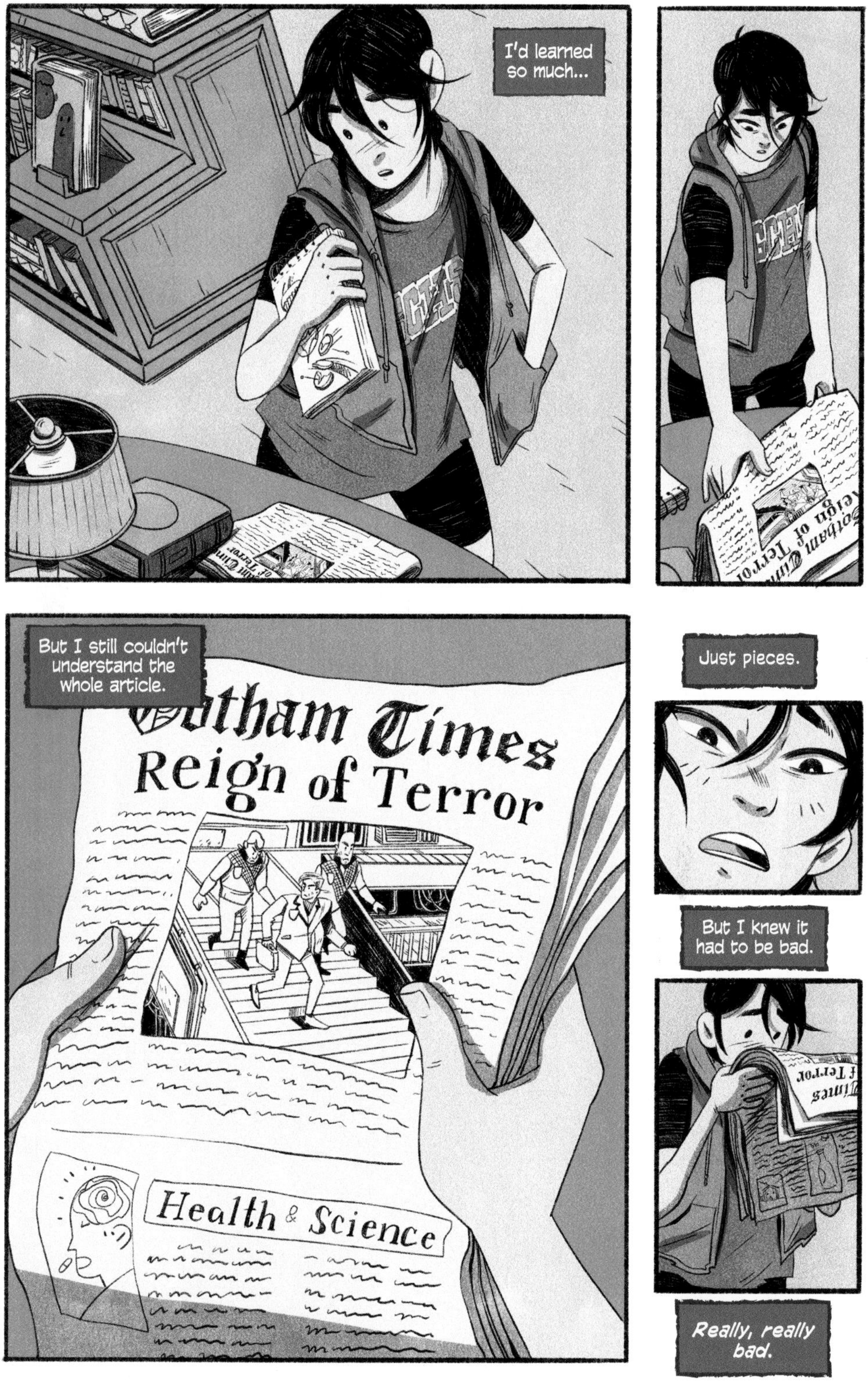
I'd learned so much...
But I still couldn't understand the whole article.
Gotham Times
Reign of Terror
Health & Science
Just pieces.
But I knew it had to be bad.
Really, really bad.

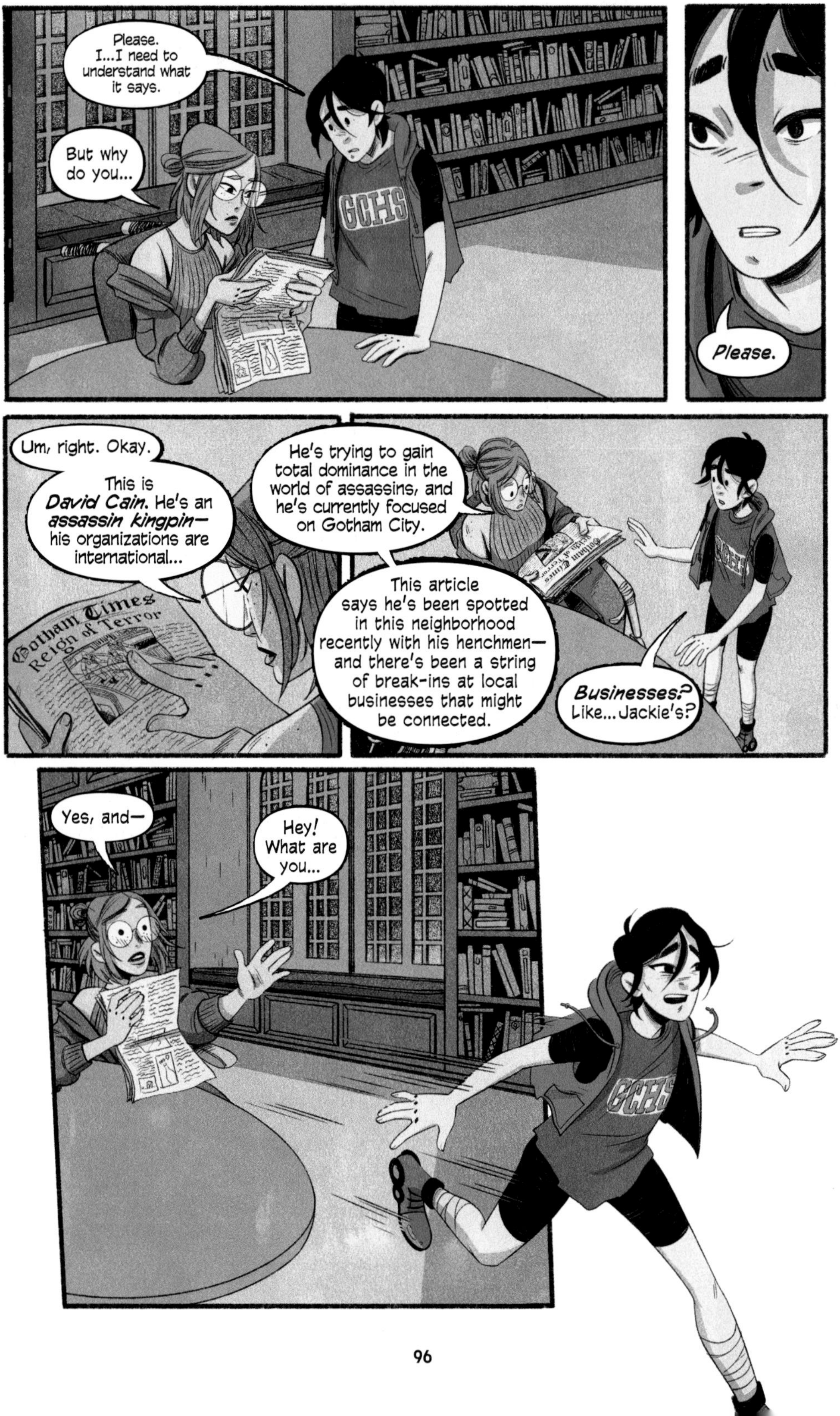
Please.
I...I need to understand what it says.
But why do you...
Please.
Um, right. Okay.
This is David Cain. He's an assassin kingpin—his organizations are international...
Gotham Times
Reign of Terror
He's trying to gain total dominance in the world of assassins, and he's currently focused on Gotham City.
This article says he's been spotted in this neighborhood recently with his henchmen—and there's been a string of break-ins at local businesses that might be connected.
Businesses? Like...Jackie's?
Yes, and—
Hey! What are you...
GCHS

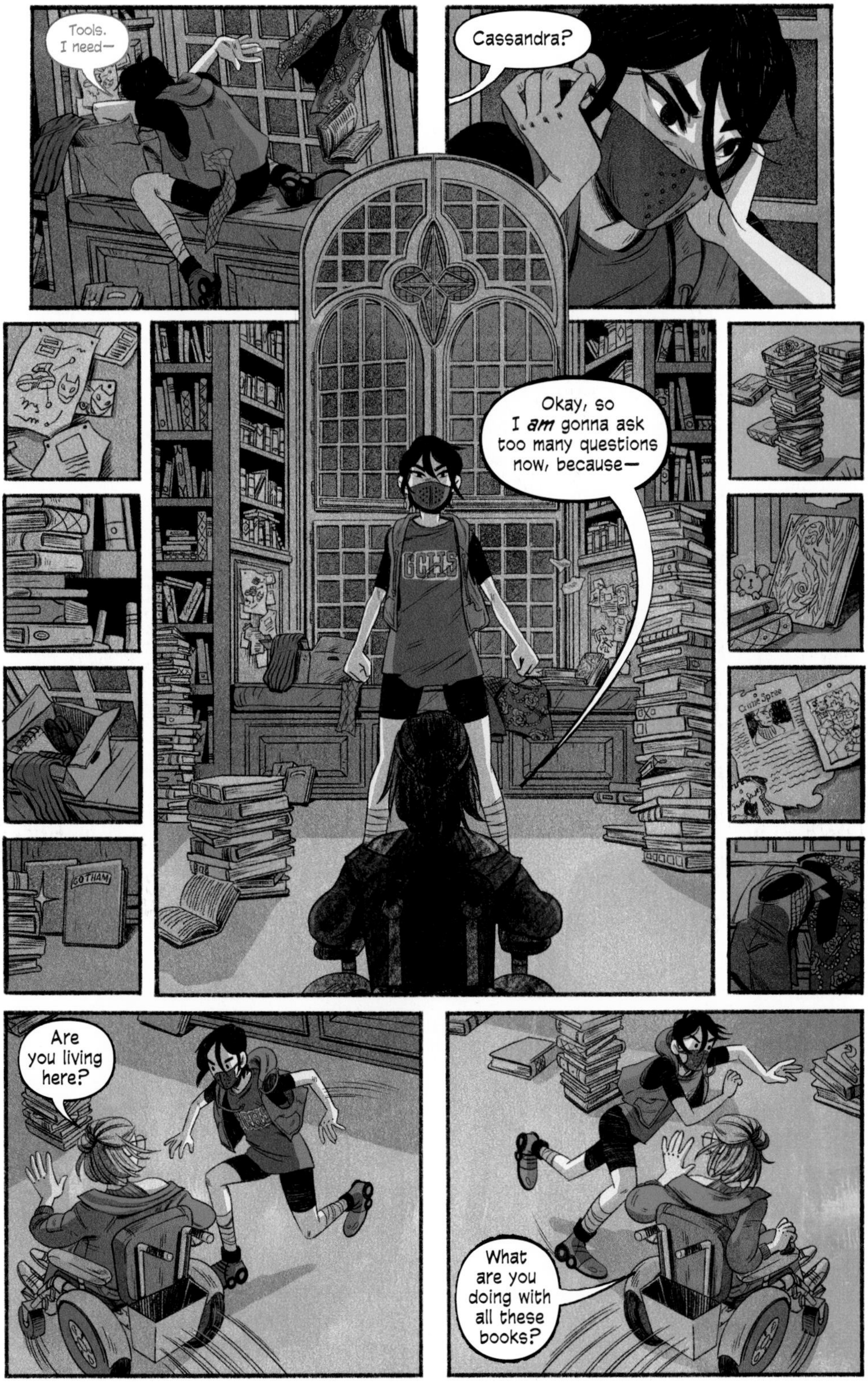
Tools. I need—
Cassandra?
Okay, so I *am* gonna ask too many questions now, because—
GCHS
GOTHAM
Are you living here?
What are you doing with all these books?

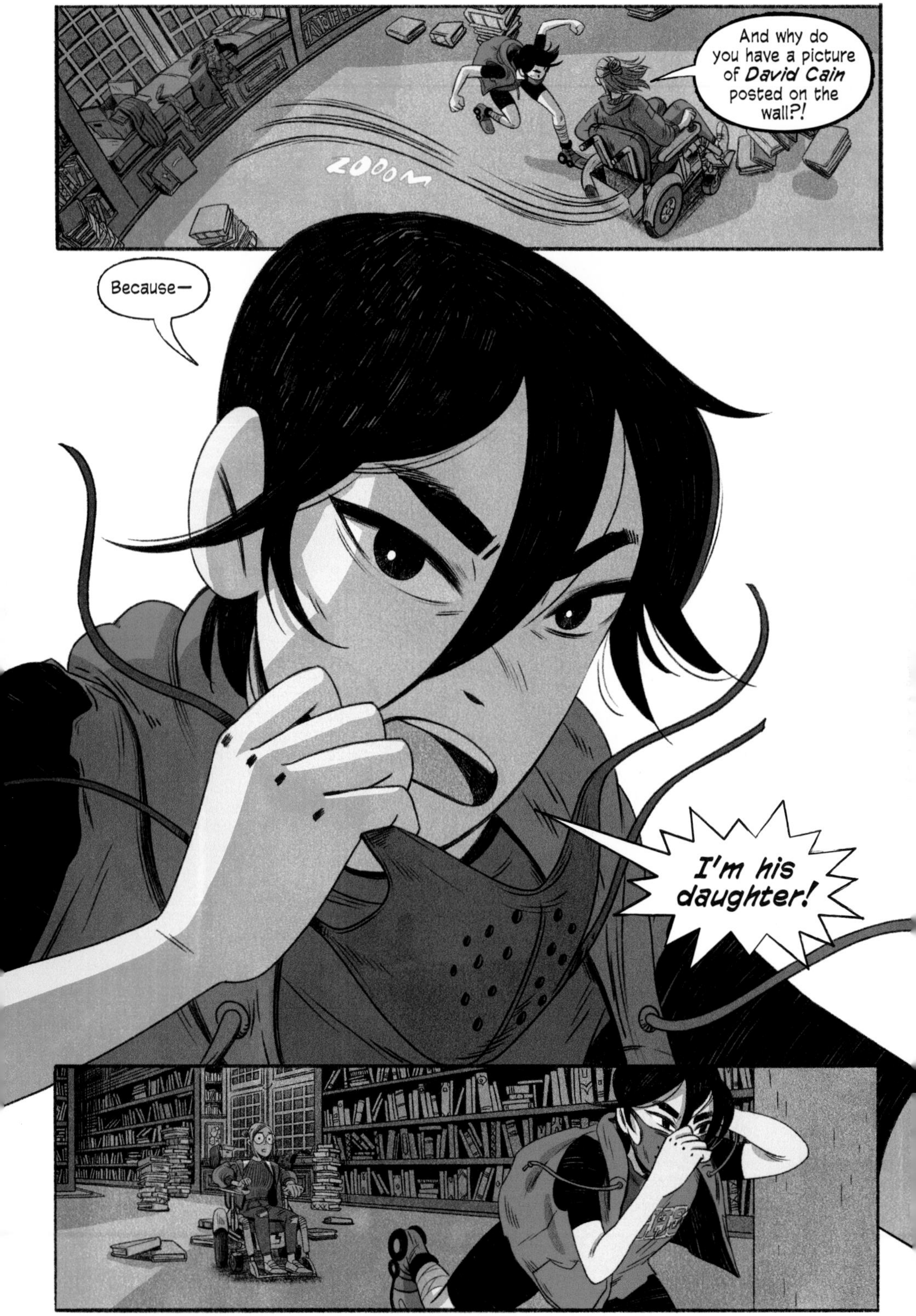
And why do you have a picture of David Cain posted on the wall?!
ZOOOM
Because—
I'm his daughter!

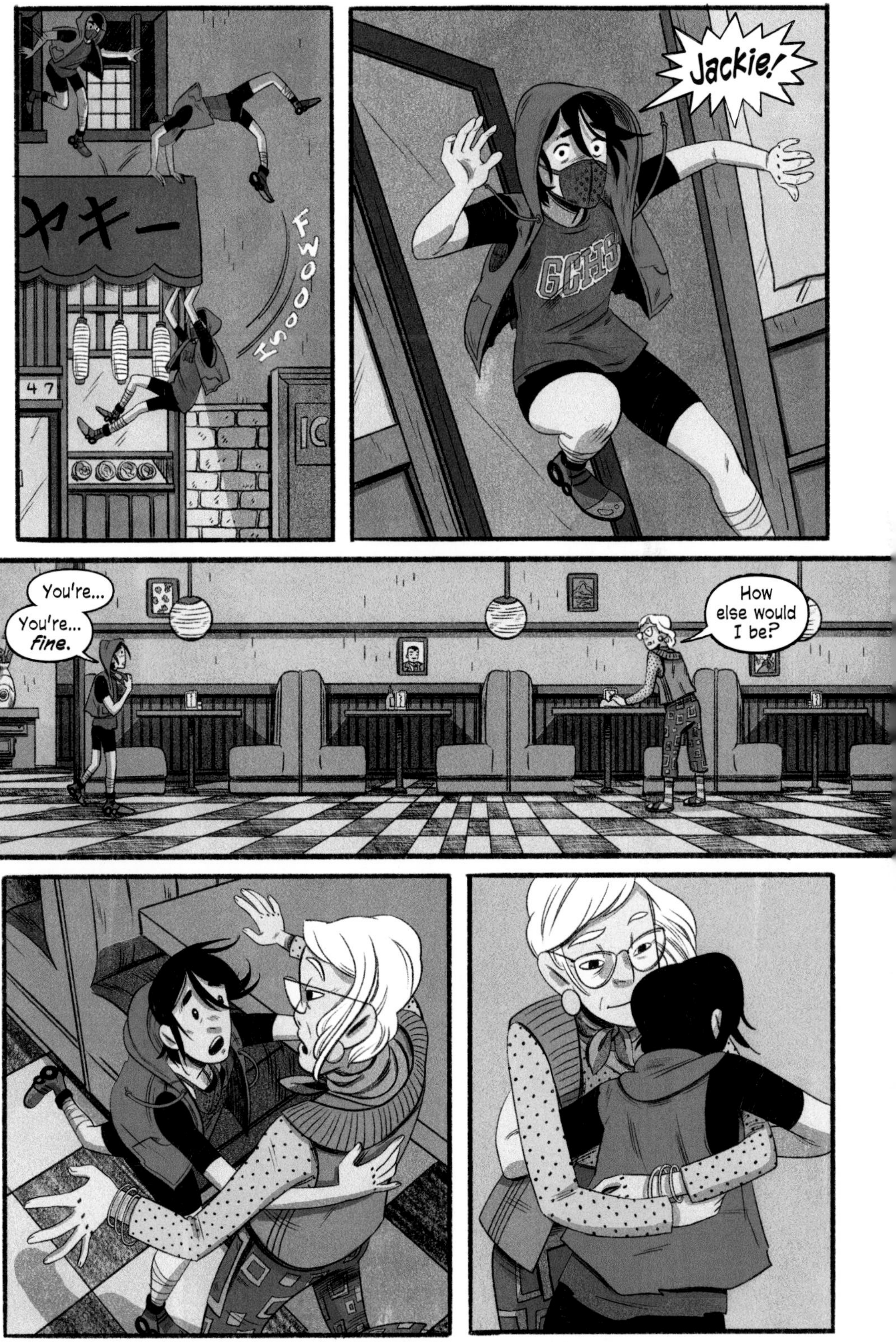

ヤキー
FWOOOSH
47
Jackie!
You're...
You're... *fine.*
How else would I be?

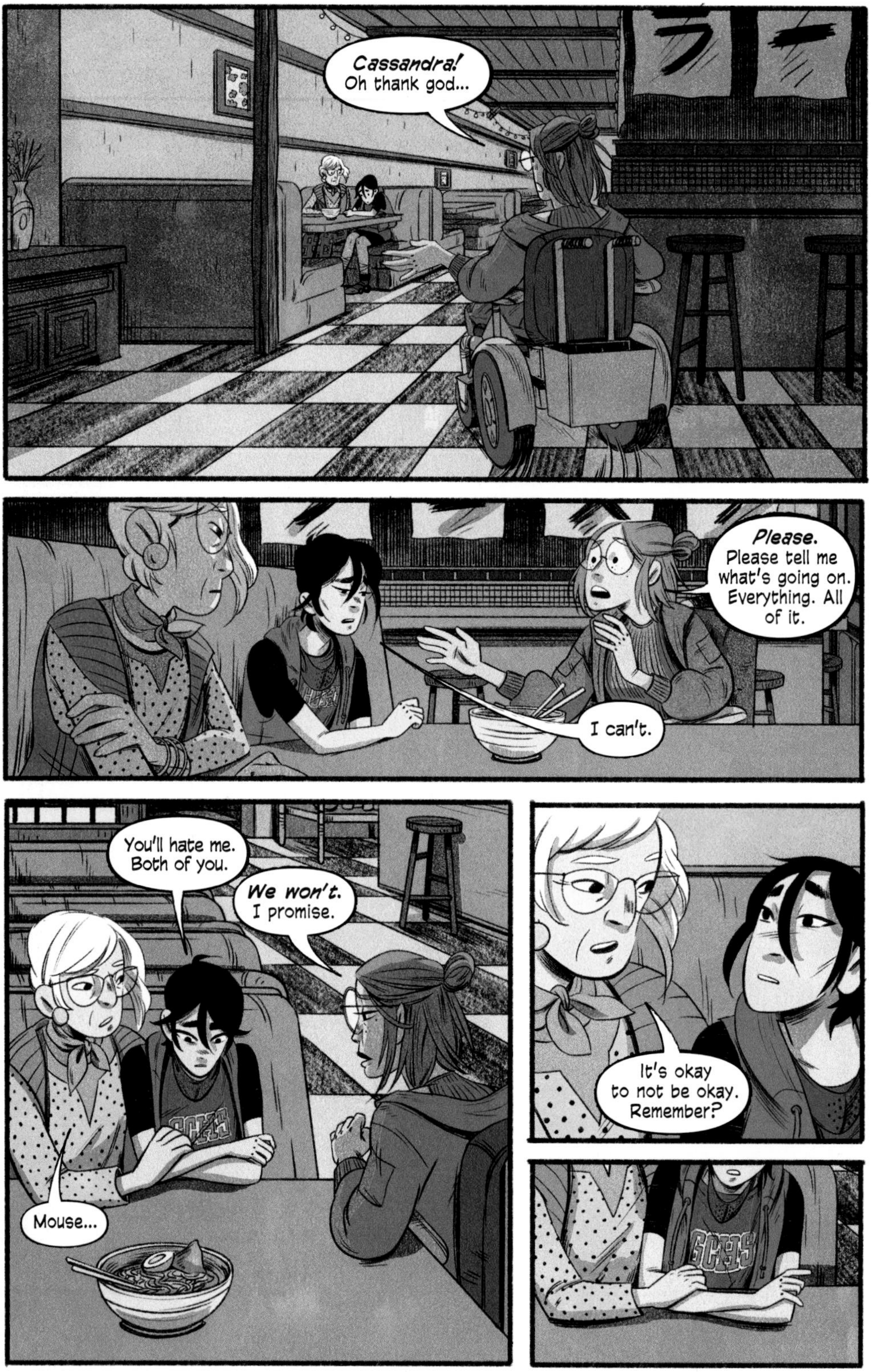

Cassandra! Oh thank god...
Please. Please tell me what's going on. Everything. All of it.
I can't.
You'll hate me. Both of you.
We won't. I promise.
Mouse...
It's okay to not be okay. Remember?

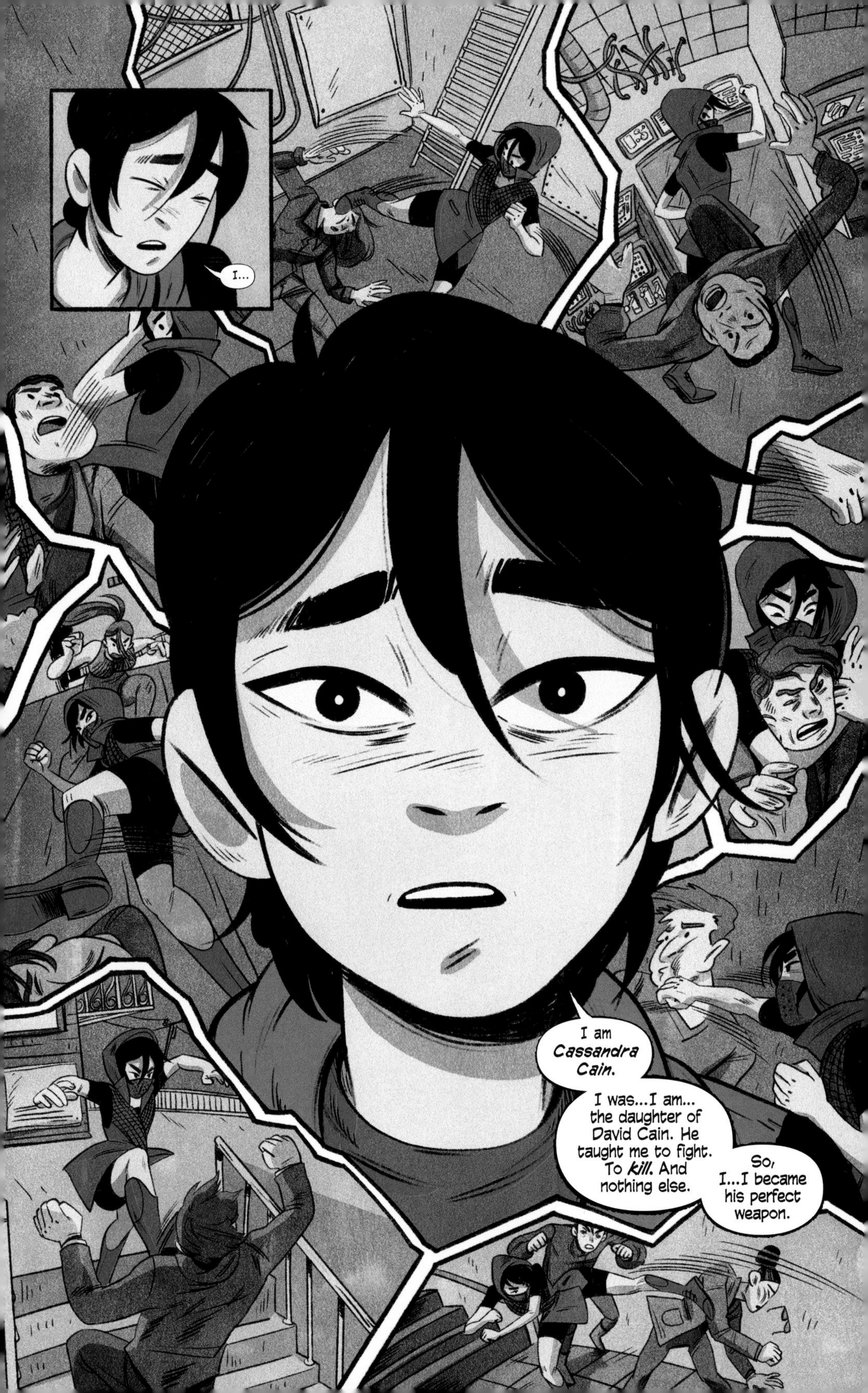
I...
I am *Cassandra Cain.*
I was...I am... the daughter of David Cain. He taught me to fight. To ***kill.*** And nothing else.
So, I...I became his perfect weapon.

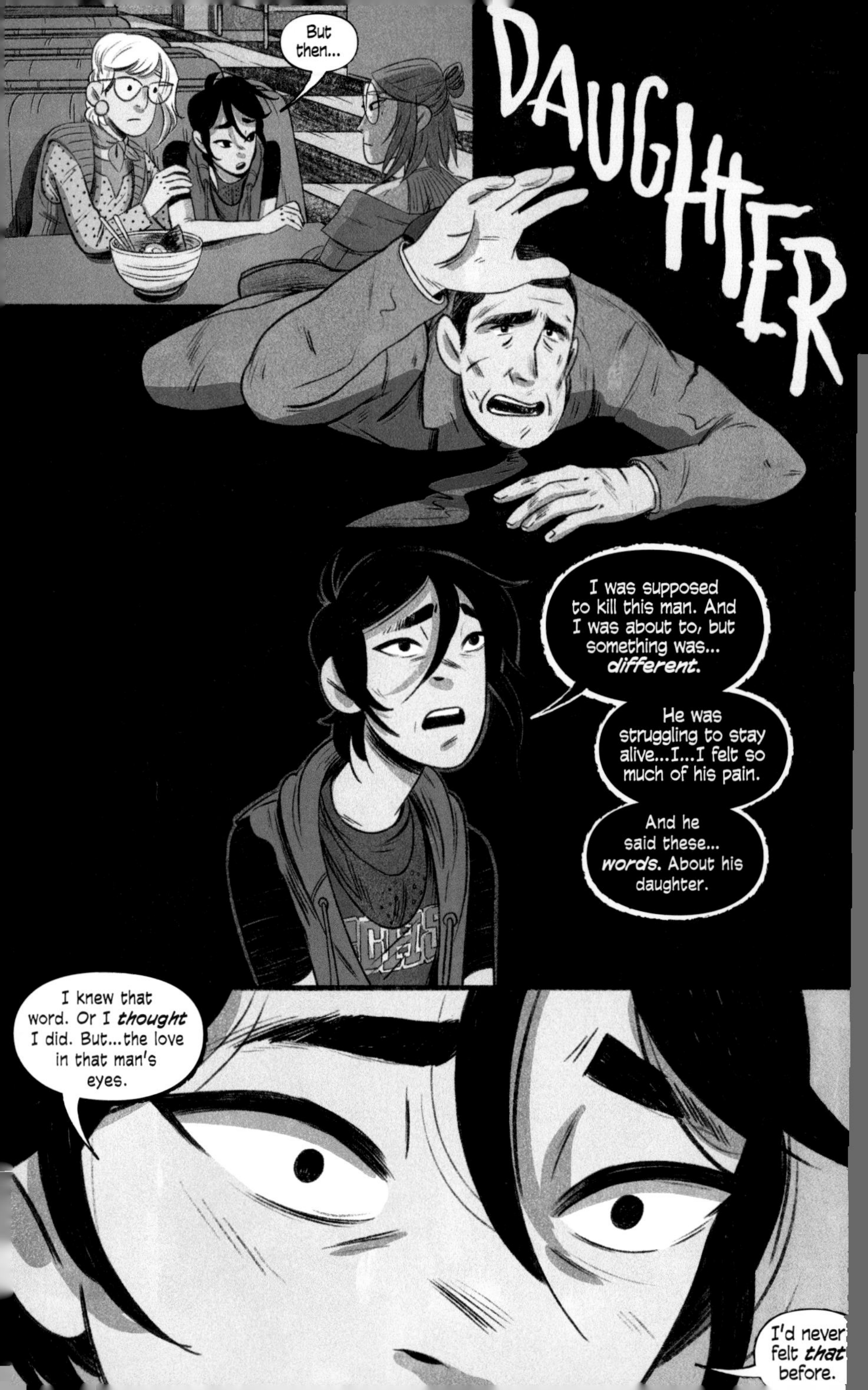
But then...
DAUGHTER
I was supposed to kill this man. And I was about to, but something was... *different*.
He was struggling to stay alive...I...I felt so much of his pain.
And he said these... *words*. About his daughter.
I knew that word. Or I *thought* I did. But...the love in that man's eyes.
I'd never felt *that* before.

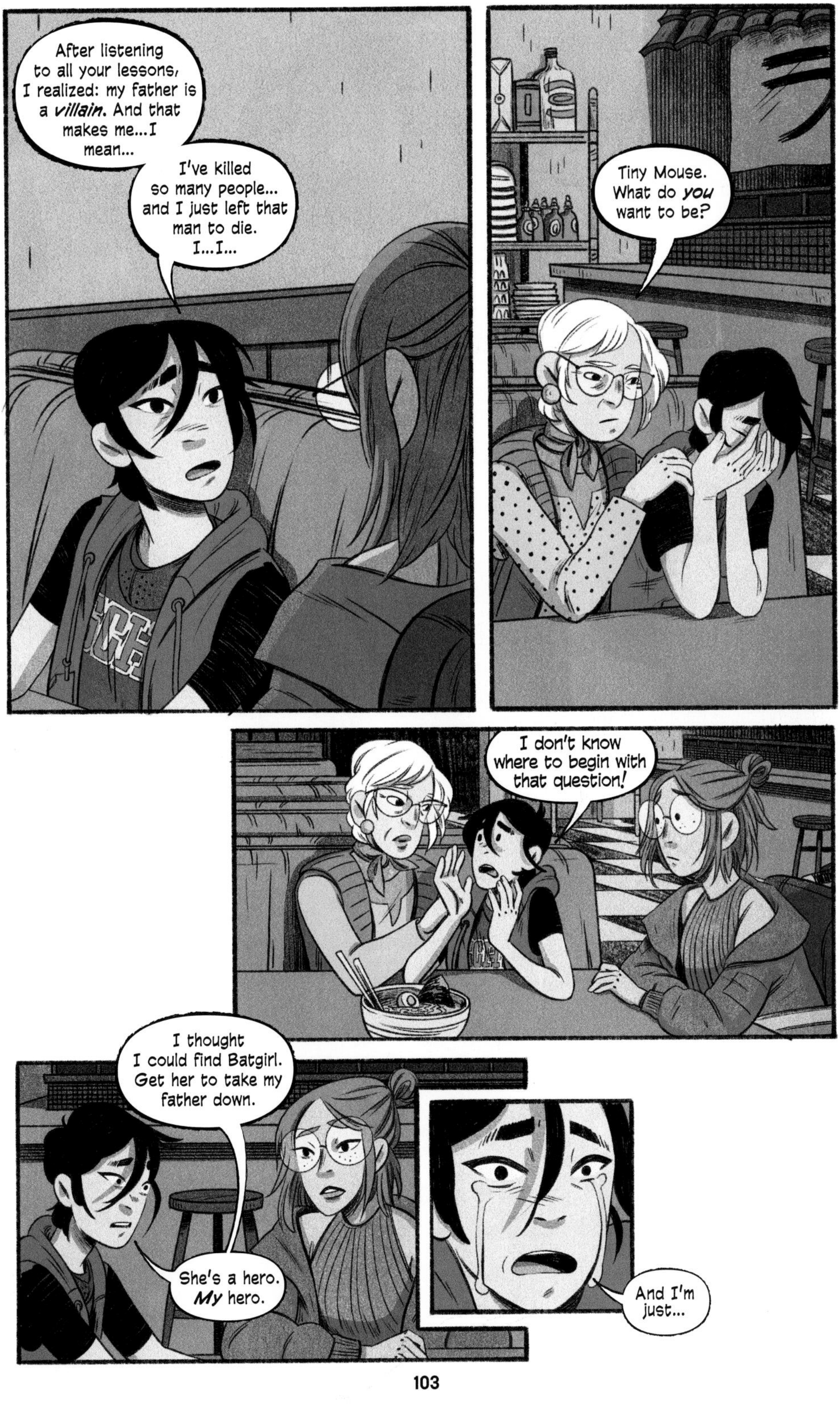
After listening to all your lessons, I realized: my father is a *villain.* And that makes me...I mean...
I've killed so many people... and I just left that man to die. I...I...
Tiny Mouse. What do *you* want to be?
I don't know where to begin with that question!
I thought I could find Batgirl. Get her to take my father down.
She's a hero. ***My*** hero.
And I'm just...

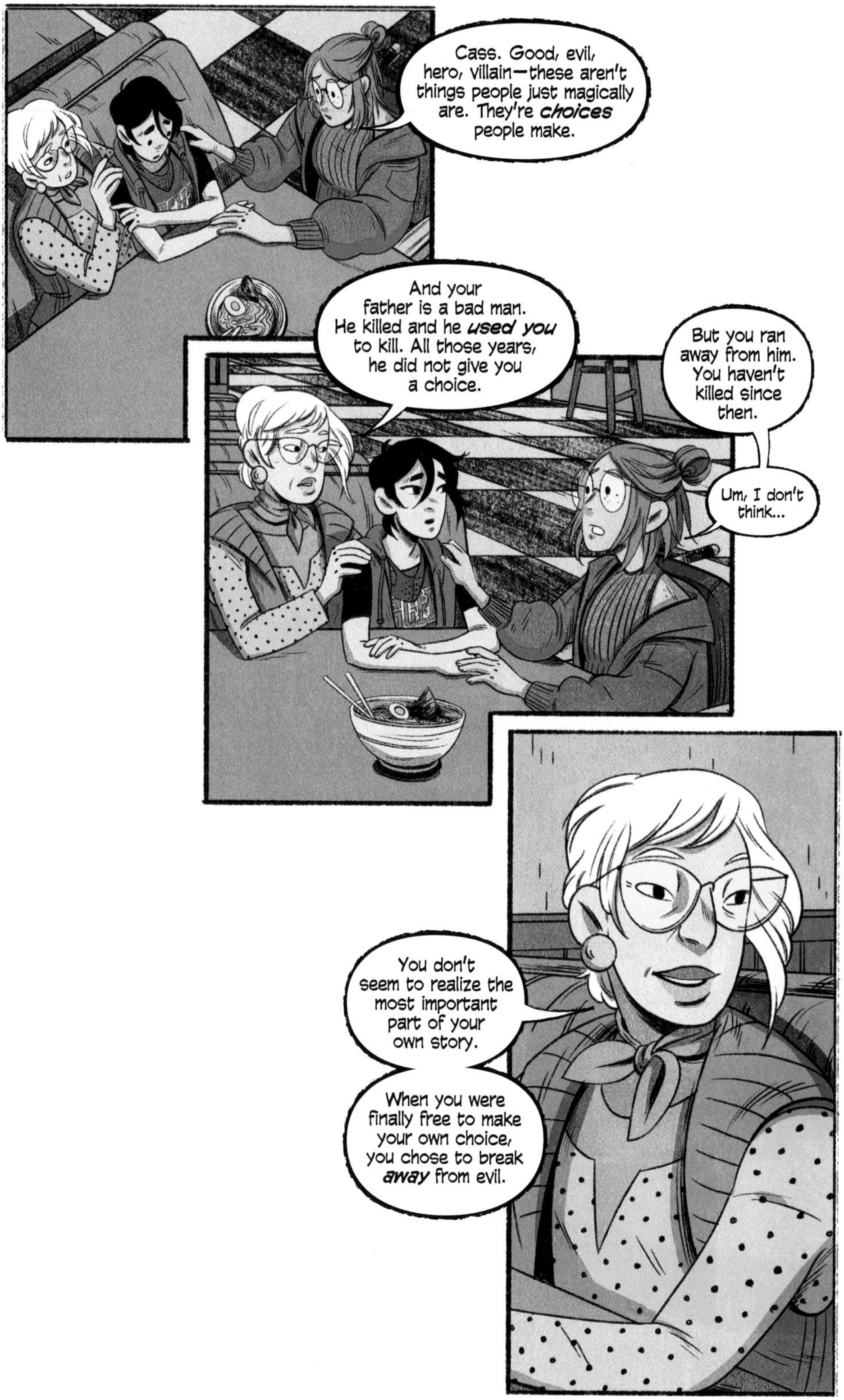
Cass. Good, evil, hero, villain—these aren't things people just magically are. They're *choices* people make.
And your father is a bad man. He killed and he *used you* to kill. All those years, he did not give you a choice.
But you ran away from him. You haven't killed since then.
Um, I don't think...
You don't seem to realize the most important part of your own story.
When you were finally free to make your own choice, you chose to break *away* from evil.

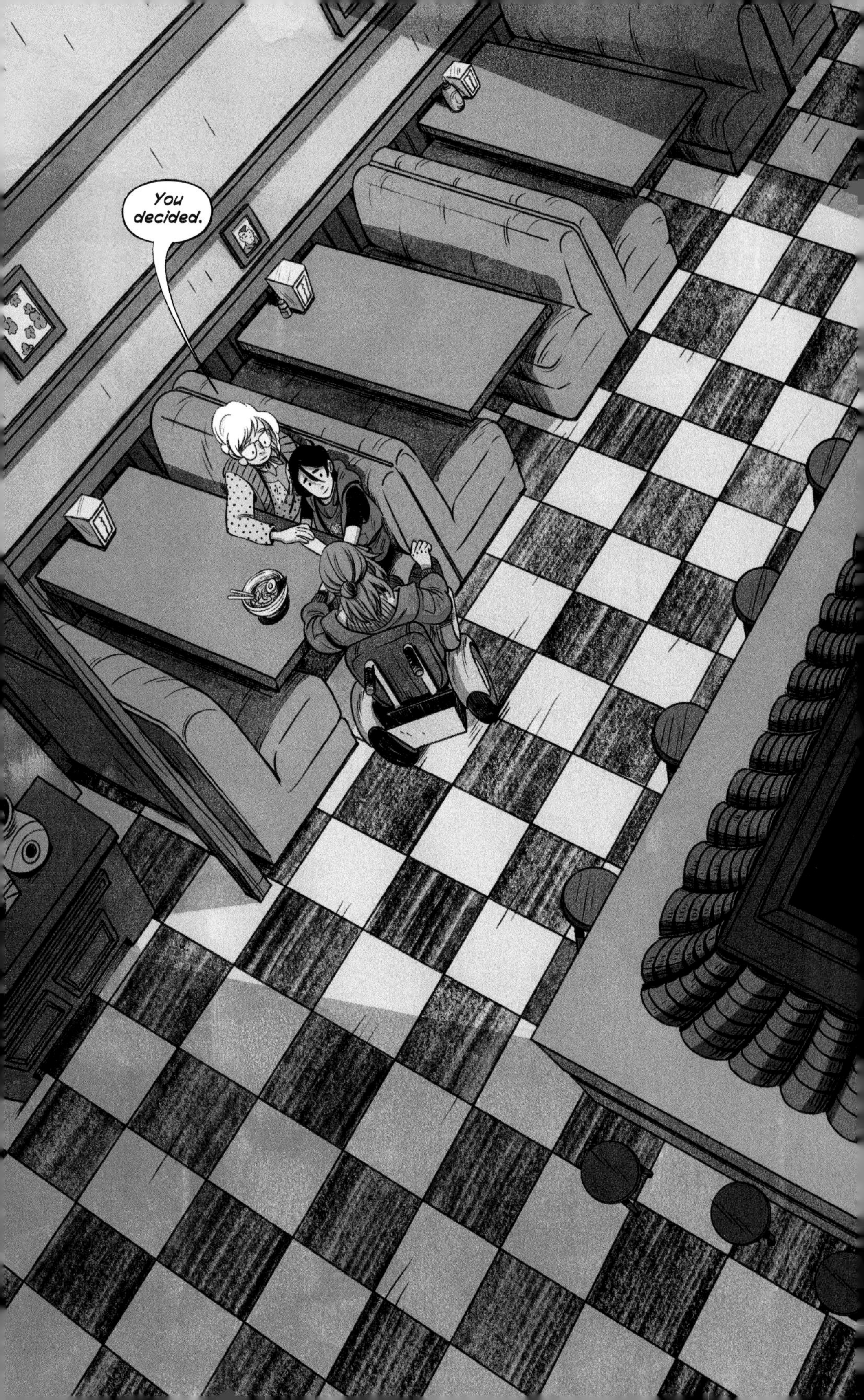
You decided.

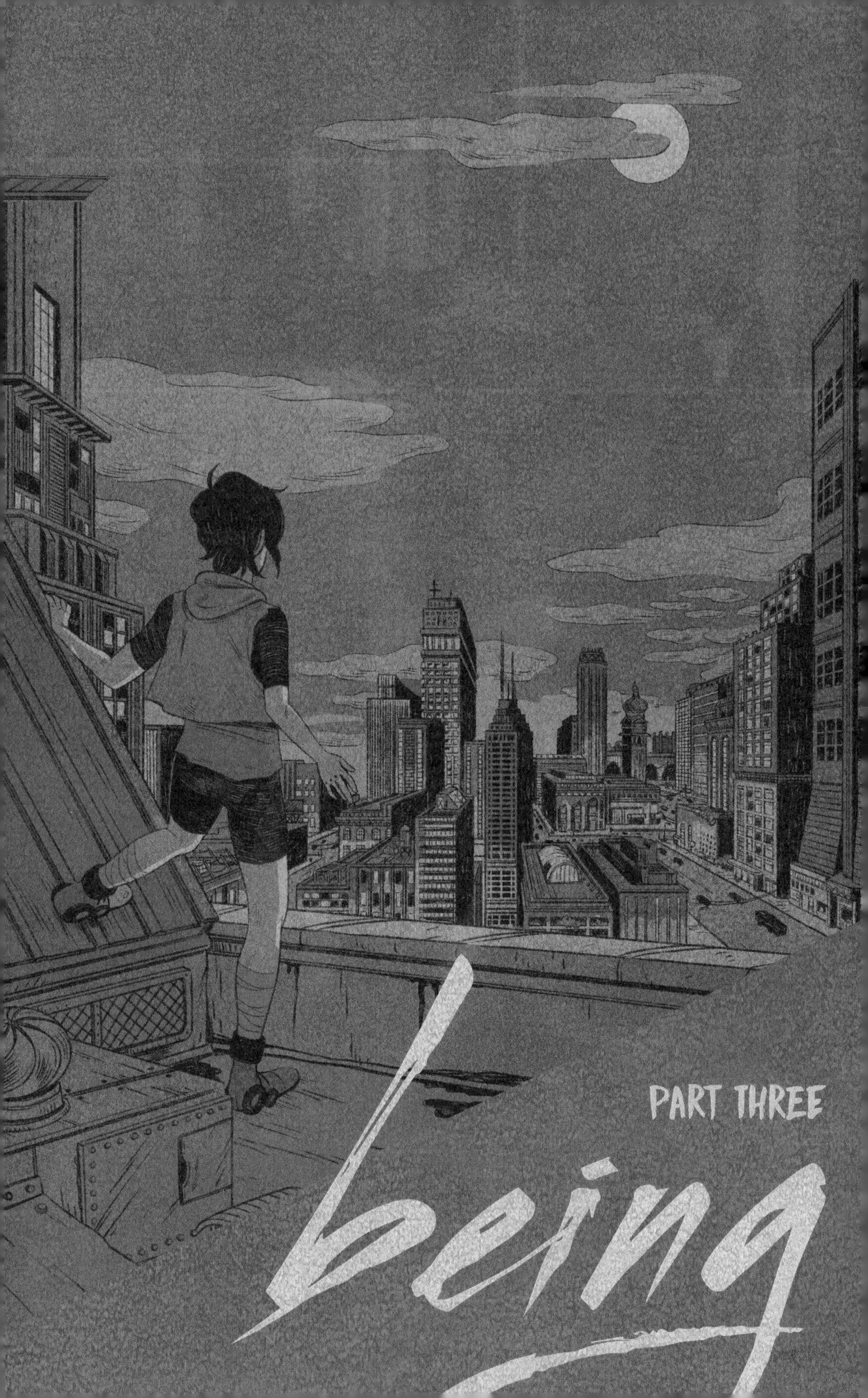
PART THREE
being

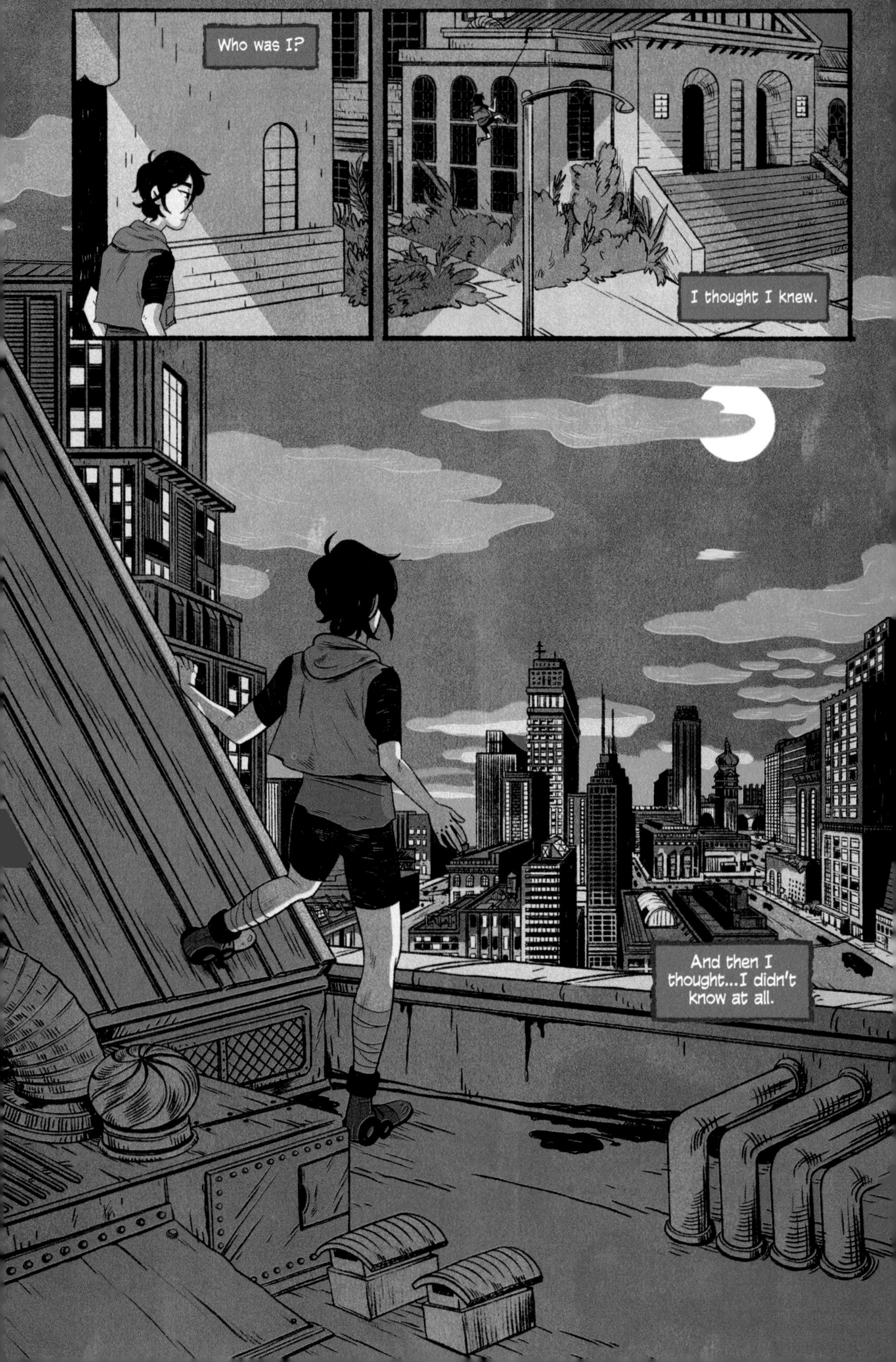
Who was I?
I thought I knew.
And then I thought...I didn't know at all.

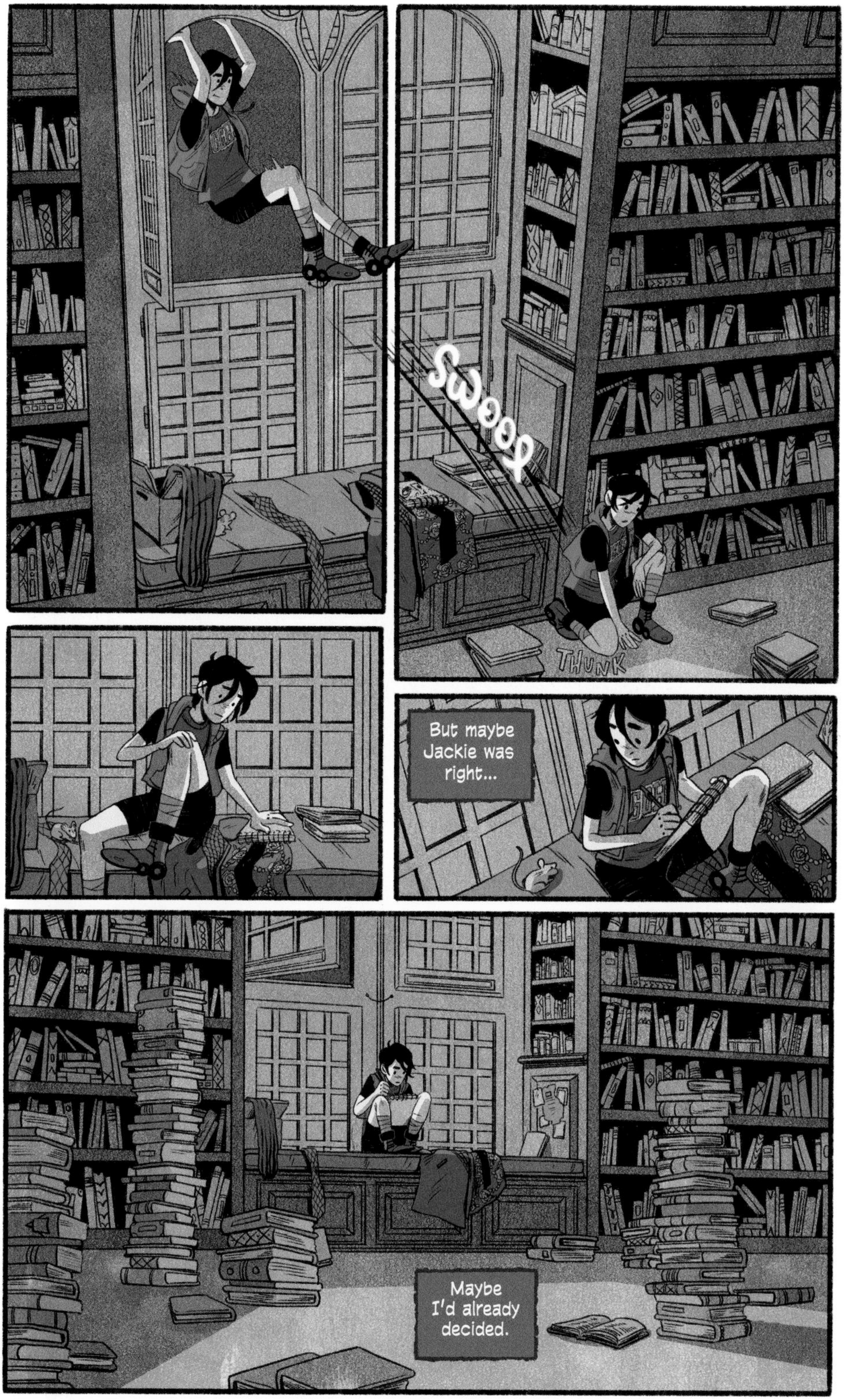
SWOOP
THUNK
But maybe Jackie was right...
Maybe I'd already decided.

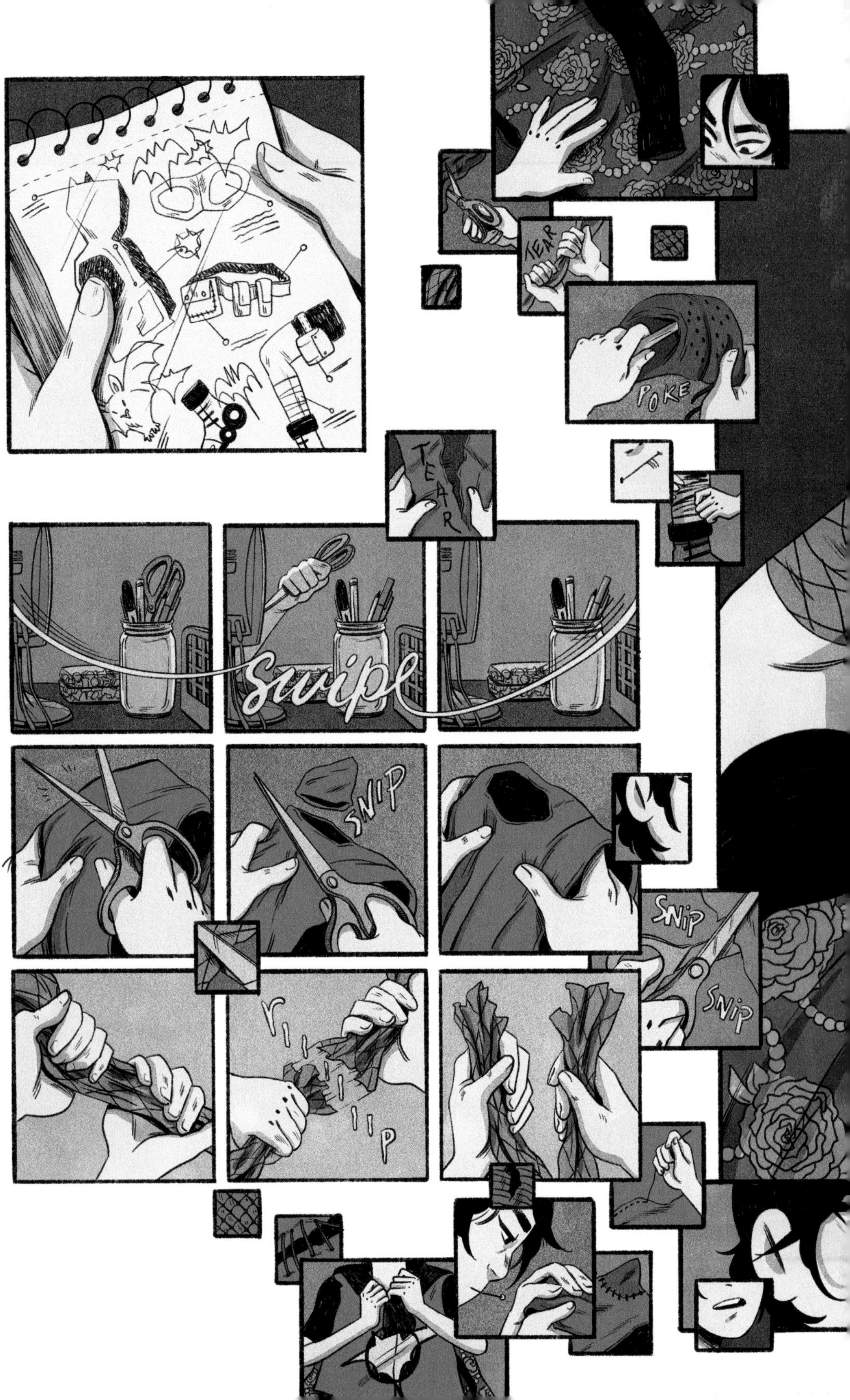
TEAR
POKE
TEAR
swipe
SNIP
SNIP
SNIP
rIIIIIIP

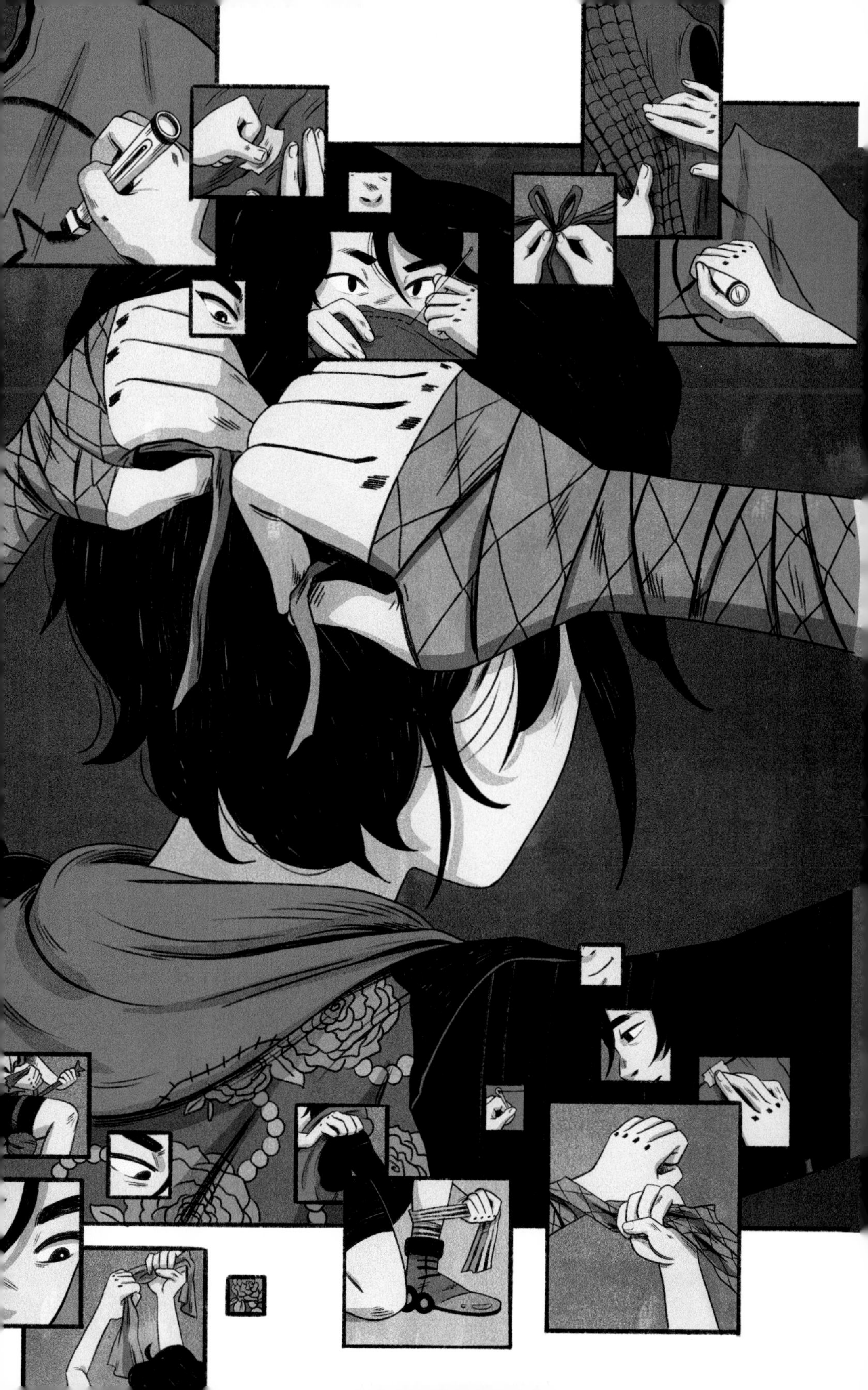

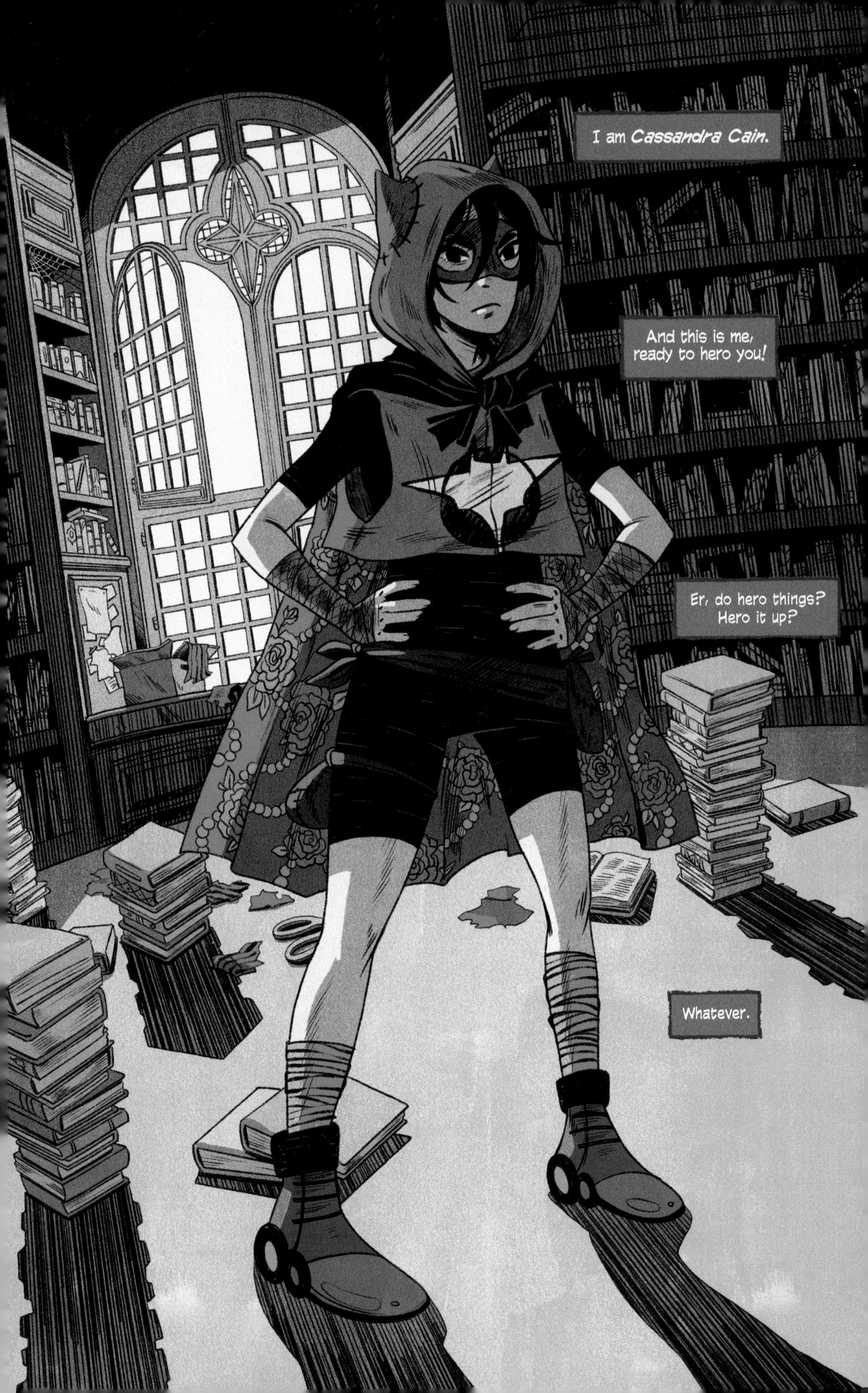
I am Cassandra Cain.
And this is me, ready to hero you!
Er, do hero things? Hero it up?
Whatever.

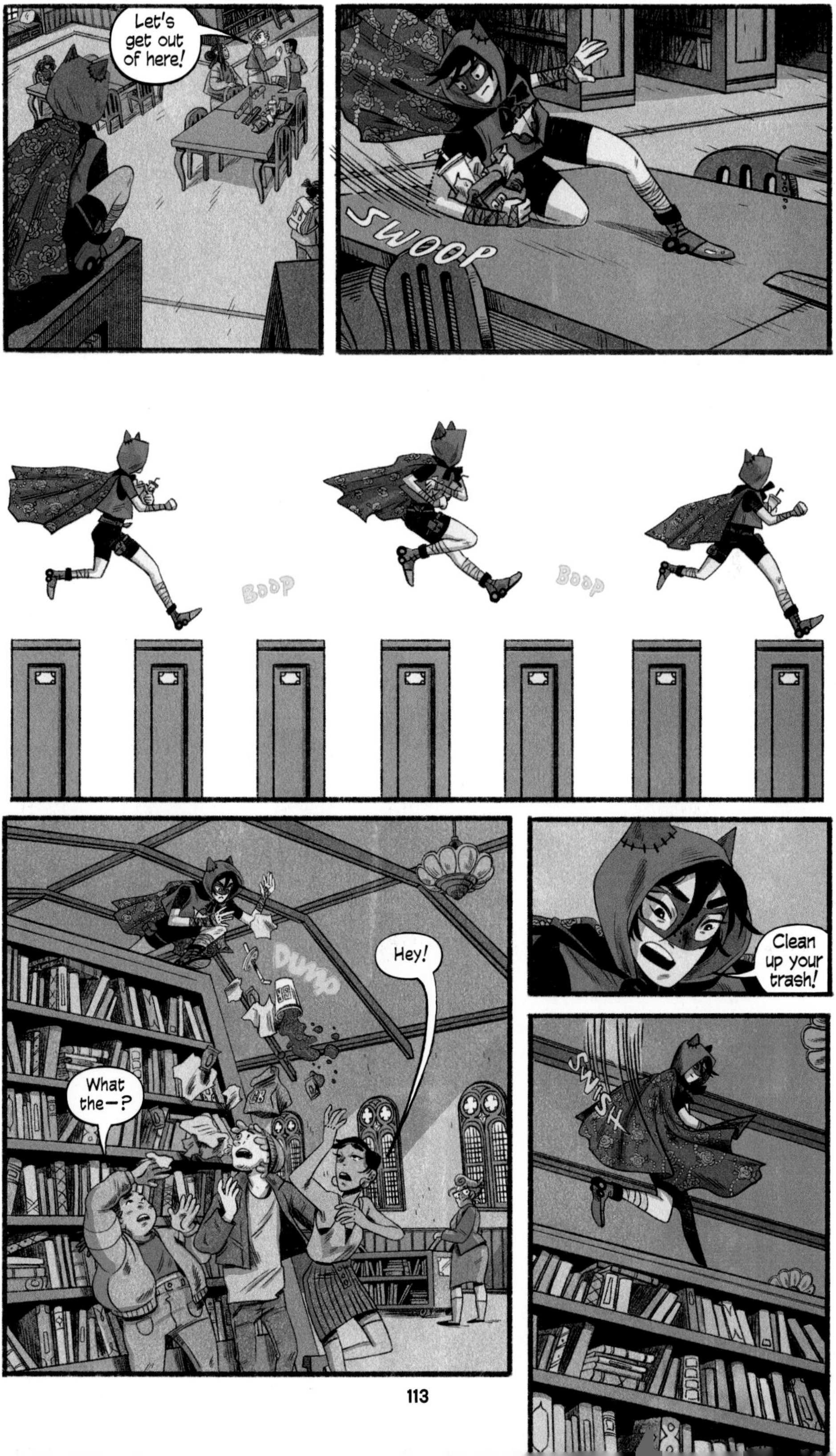
Let's get out of here!
SWOOP
BOOP
BOOP
DUMP
Hey!
What the—?
Clean up your trash!
SWISH

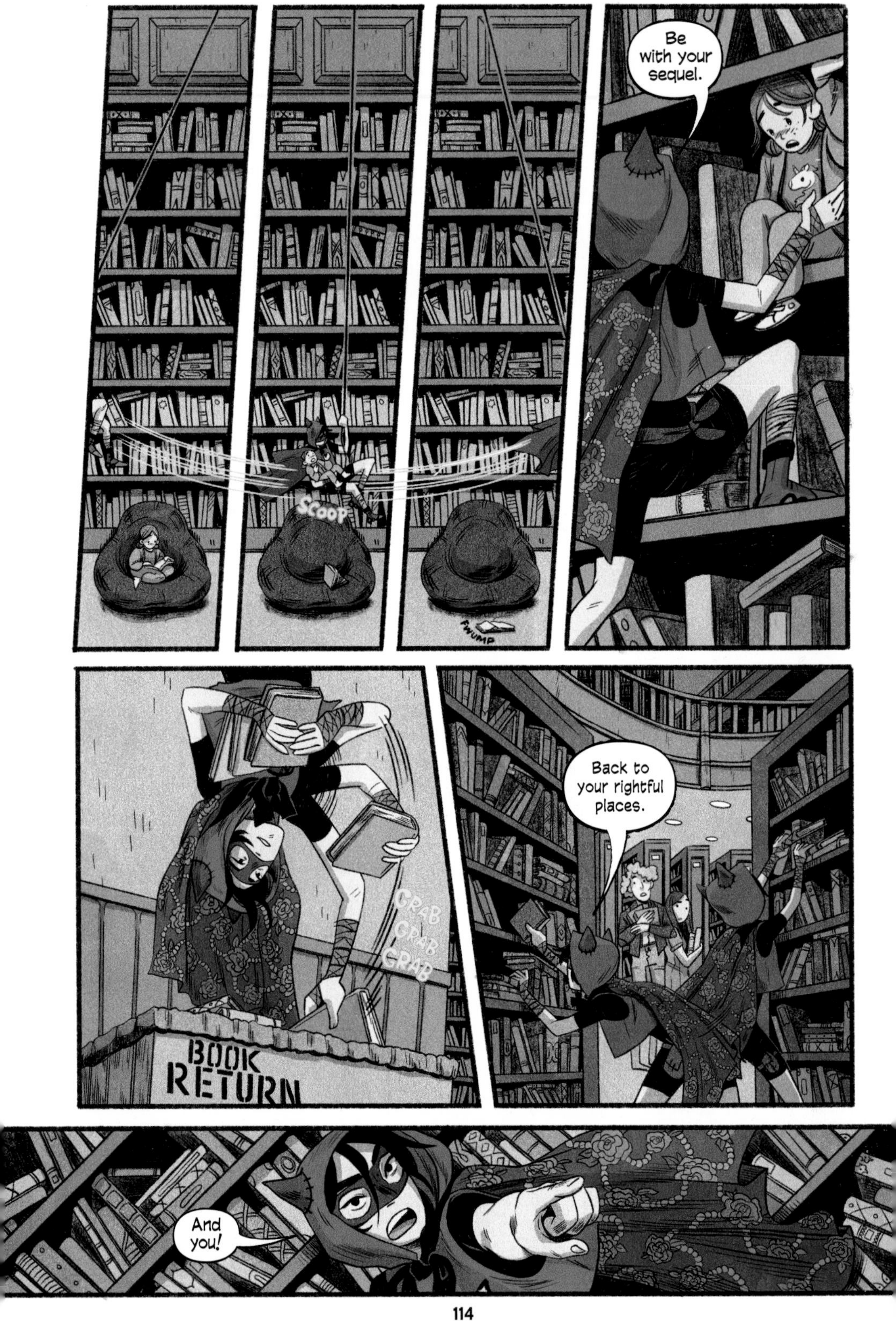
SCOOP
FWUMP
Be with your sequel.
GRAB GRAB GRAB
BOOK RETURN
Back to your rightful places.
And you!

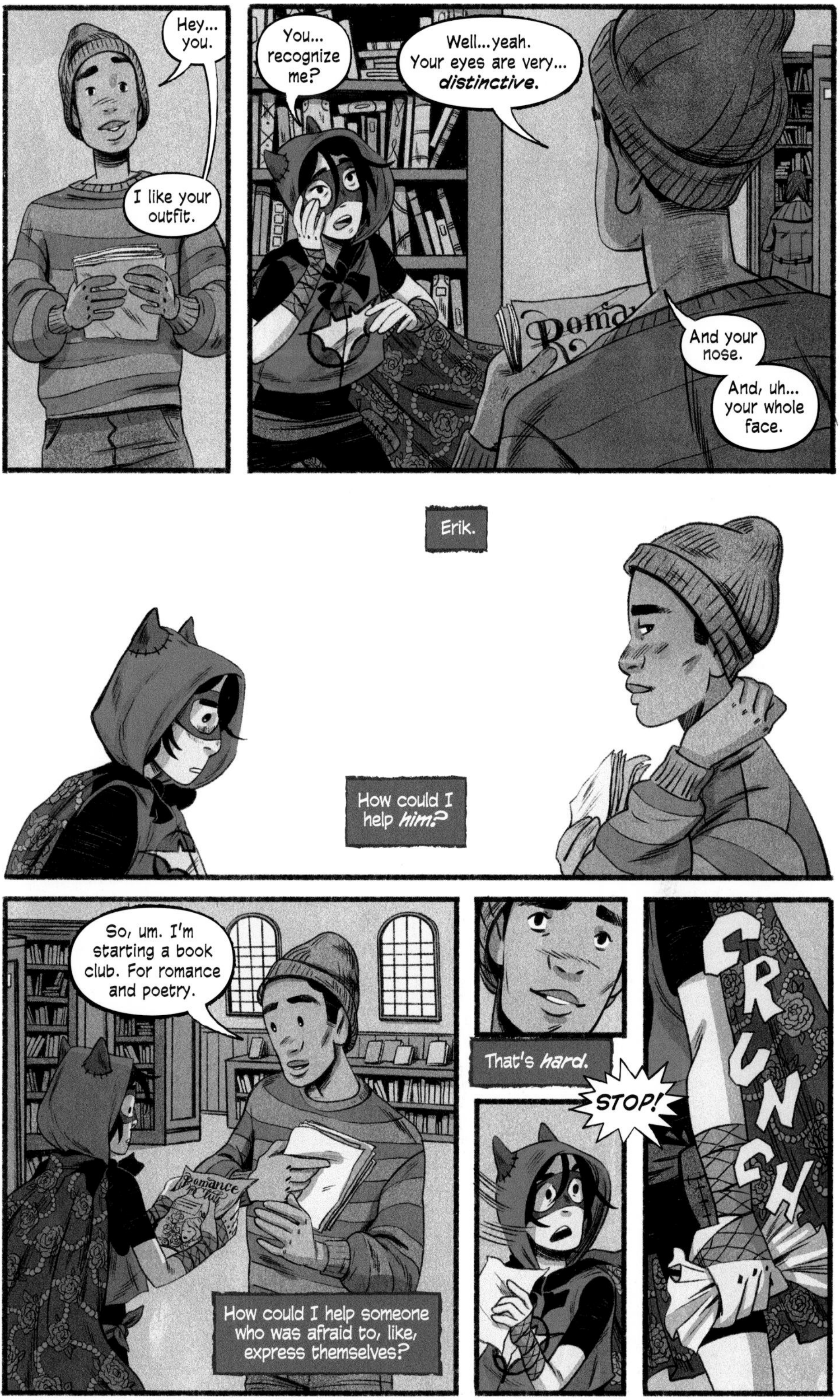
Hey... you.
I like your outfit.
You... recognize me?
Well...yeah. Your eyes are very... *distinctive*.
And your nose.
And, uh... your whole face.
Erik.
How could I help *him?*
So, um. I'm starting a book club. For romance and poetry.
How could I help someone who was afraid to, like, express themselves?
That's *hard*.
STOP!
CRUNCH

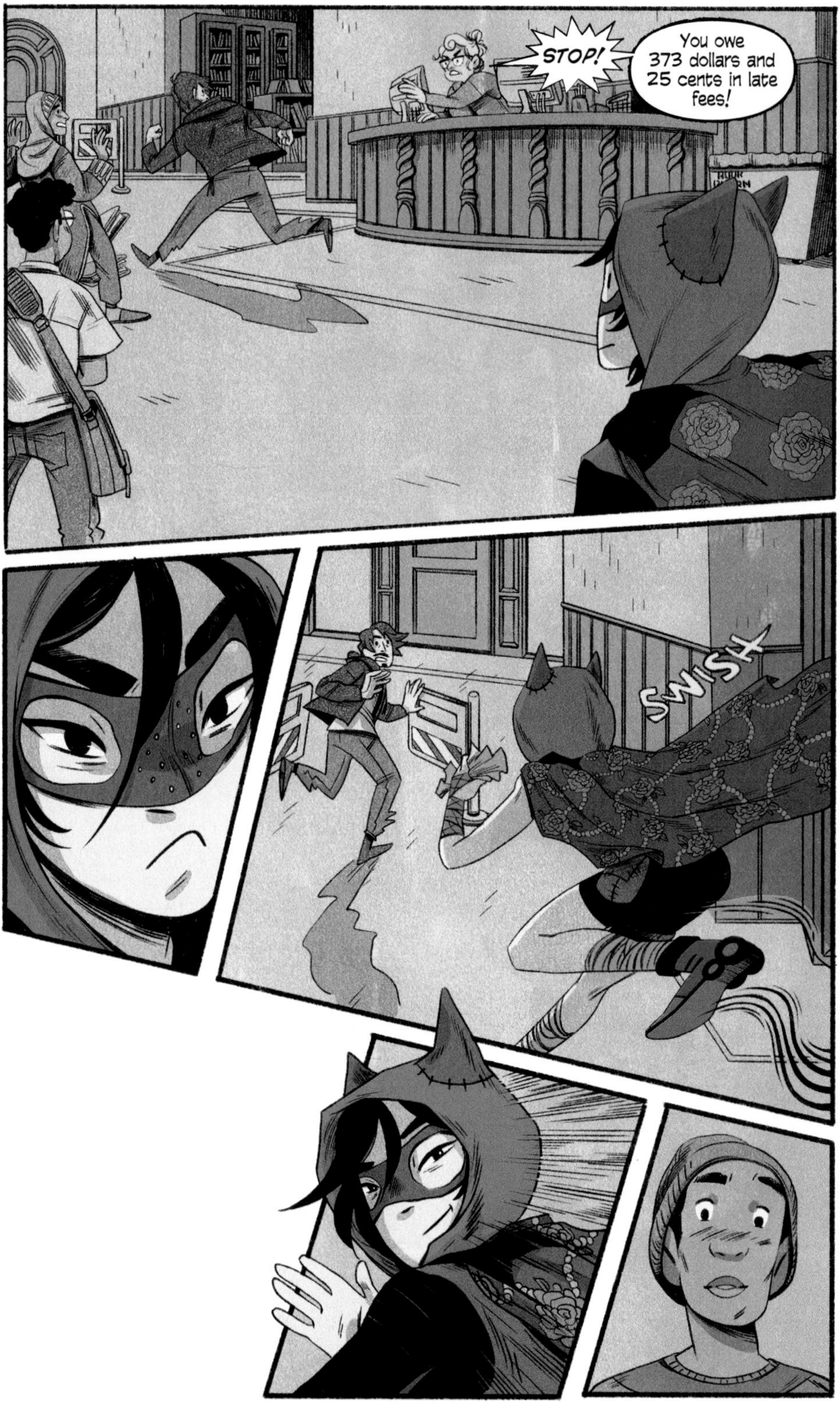
STOP!
You owe 373 dollars and 25 cents in late fees!
SWISH

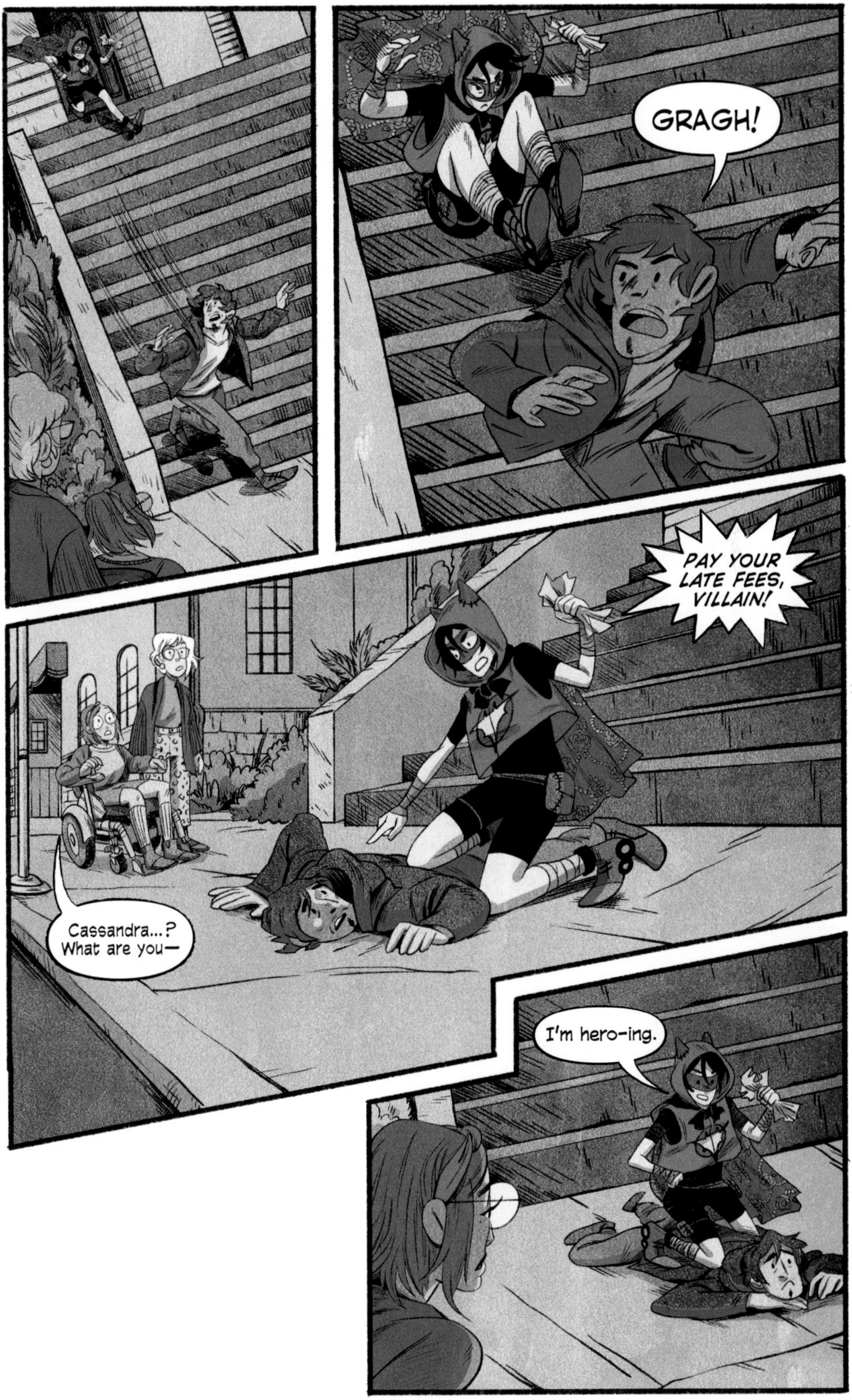
GRAGH!
PAY YOUR LATE FEES, VILLAIN!
Cassandra...? What are you—
I'm hero-ing.

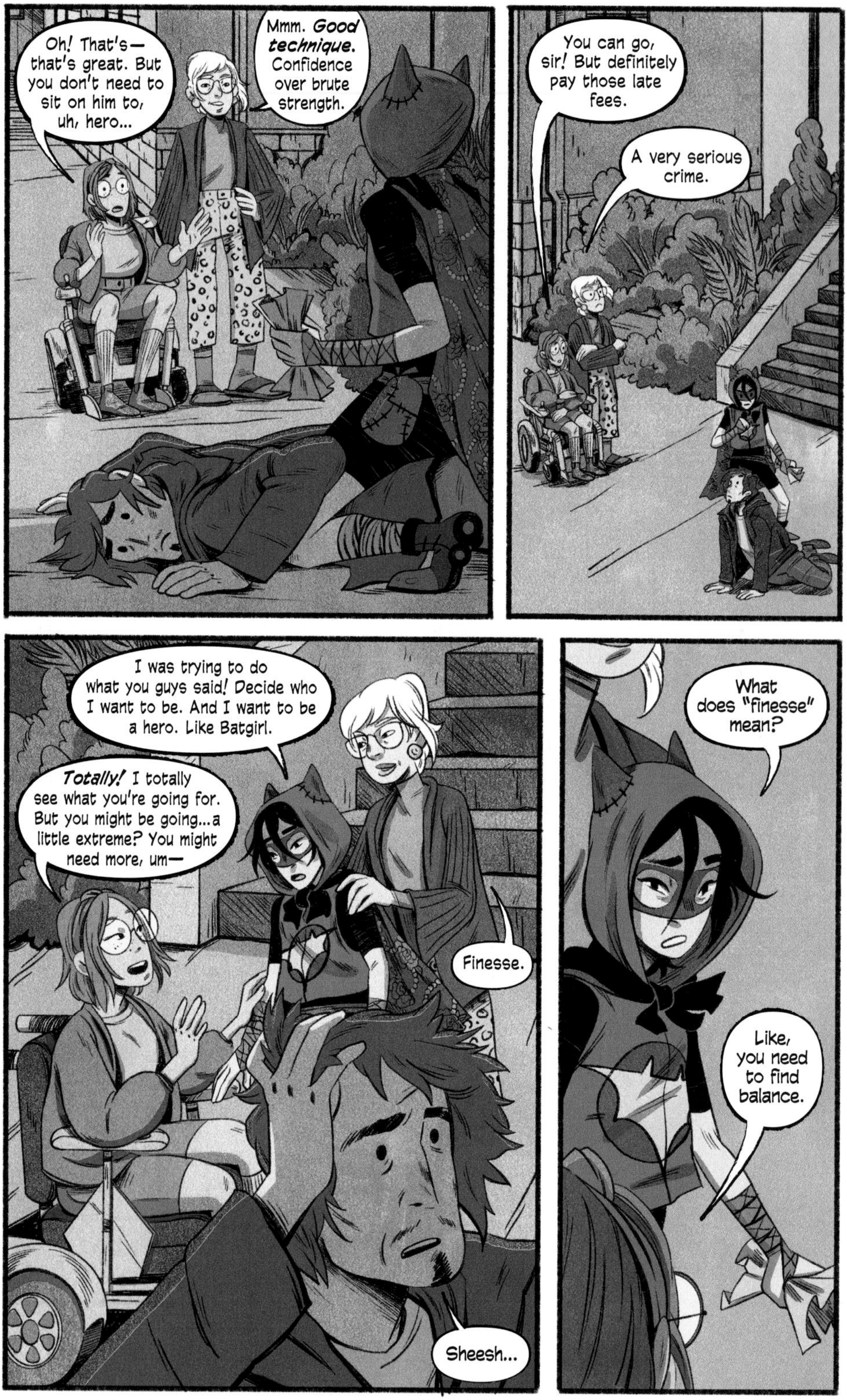

Oh! That's— that's great. But you don't need to sit on him to, uh, hero...
Mmm. *Good technique.* Confidence over brute strength.
You can go, sir! But definitely pay those late fees.
A very serious crime.
I was trying to do what you guys said! Decide who I want to be. And I want to be a hero. Like Batgirl.
Totally! I totally see what you're going for. But you might be going...a little extreme? You might need more, um—
Finesse.
Sheesh...
What does "finesse" mean?
Like, you need to find balance.

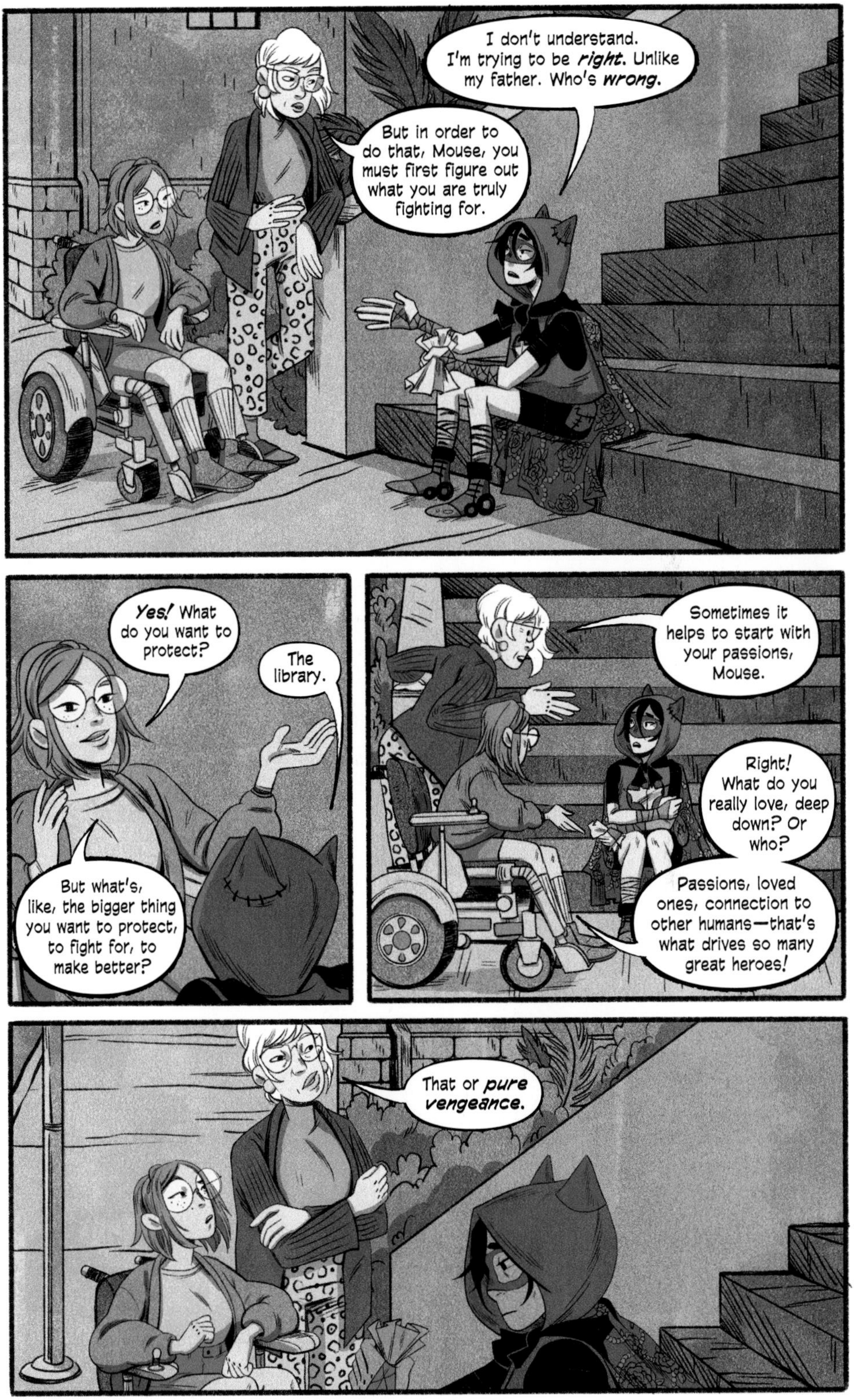
I don't understand. I'm trying to be *right*. Unlike my father. Who's *wrong*.
But in order to do that, Mouse, you must first figure out what you are truly fighting for.
Yes! What do you want to protect?
The library.
But what's, like, the bigger thing you want to protect, to fight for, to make better?
Sometimes it helps to start with your passions, Mouse.
Right! What do you really love, deep down? Or who?
Passions, loved ones, connection to other humans—that's what drives so many great heroes!
That or *pure vengeance*.

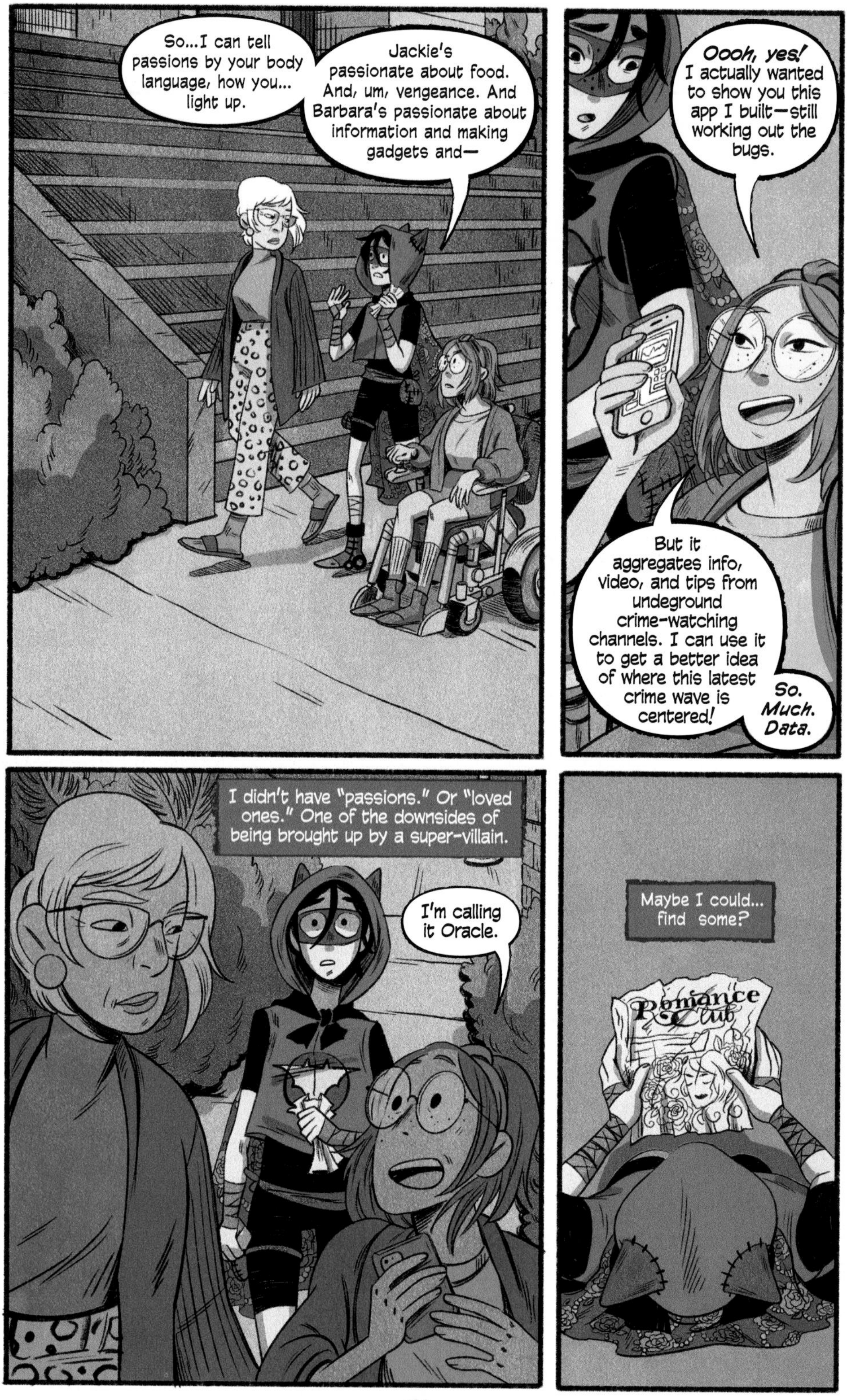
So...I can tell passions by your body language, how you... light up.
Jackie's passionate about food. And, um, vengeance. And Barbara's passionate about information and making gadgets and—
Oooh, yes! I actually wanted to show you this app I built—still working out the bugs.
But it aggregates info, video, and tips from undeground crime-watching channels. I can use it to get a better idea of where this latest crime wave is centered!
So. Much. Data.
I didn't have "passions." Or "loved ones." One of the downsides of being brought up by a super-villain.
I'm calling it Oracle.
Maybe I could... find some?
Romance Club

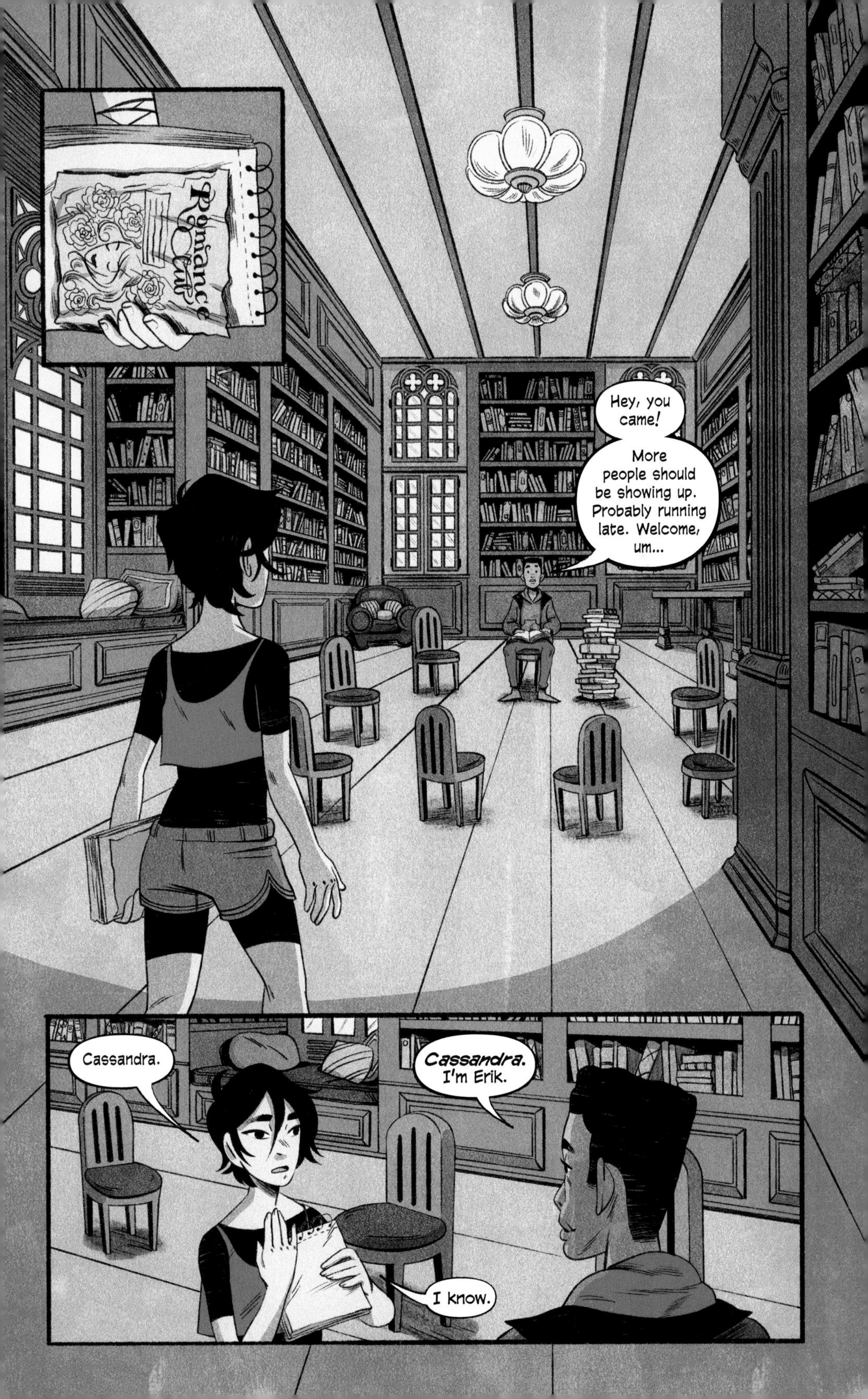
Romance Cult
Hey, you came!
More people should be showing up. Probably running late. Welcome, um...
Cassandra.
Cassandra. I'm Erik.
I know.

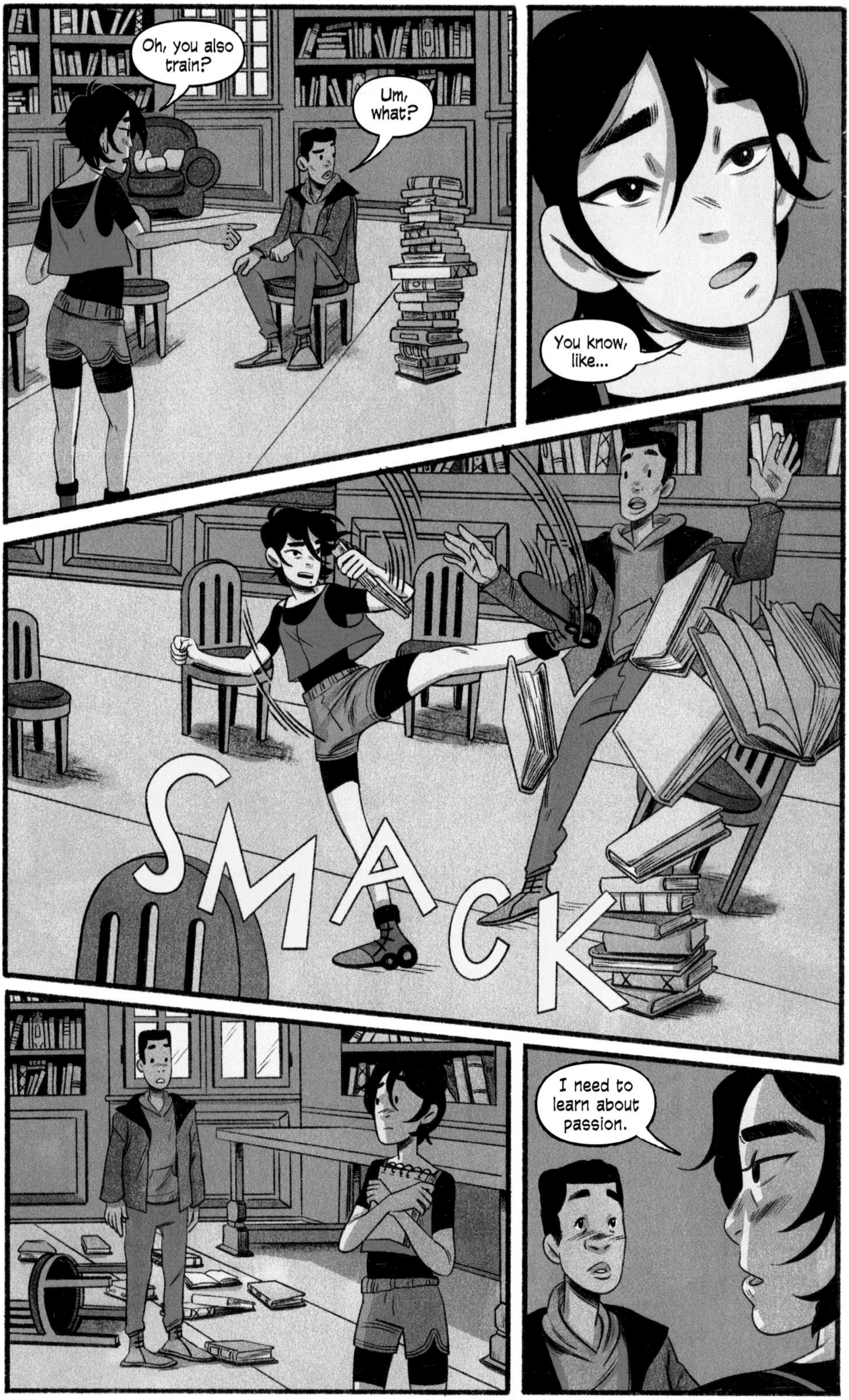
Oh, you also train?
Um, what?
You know, like...
SMACK
I need to learn about passion.

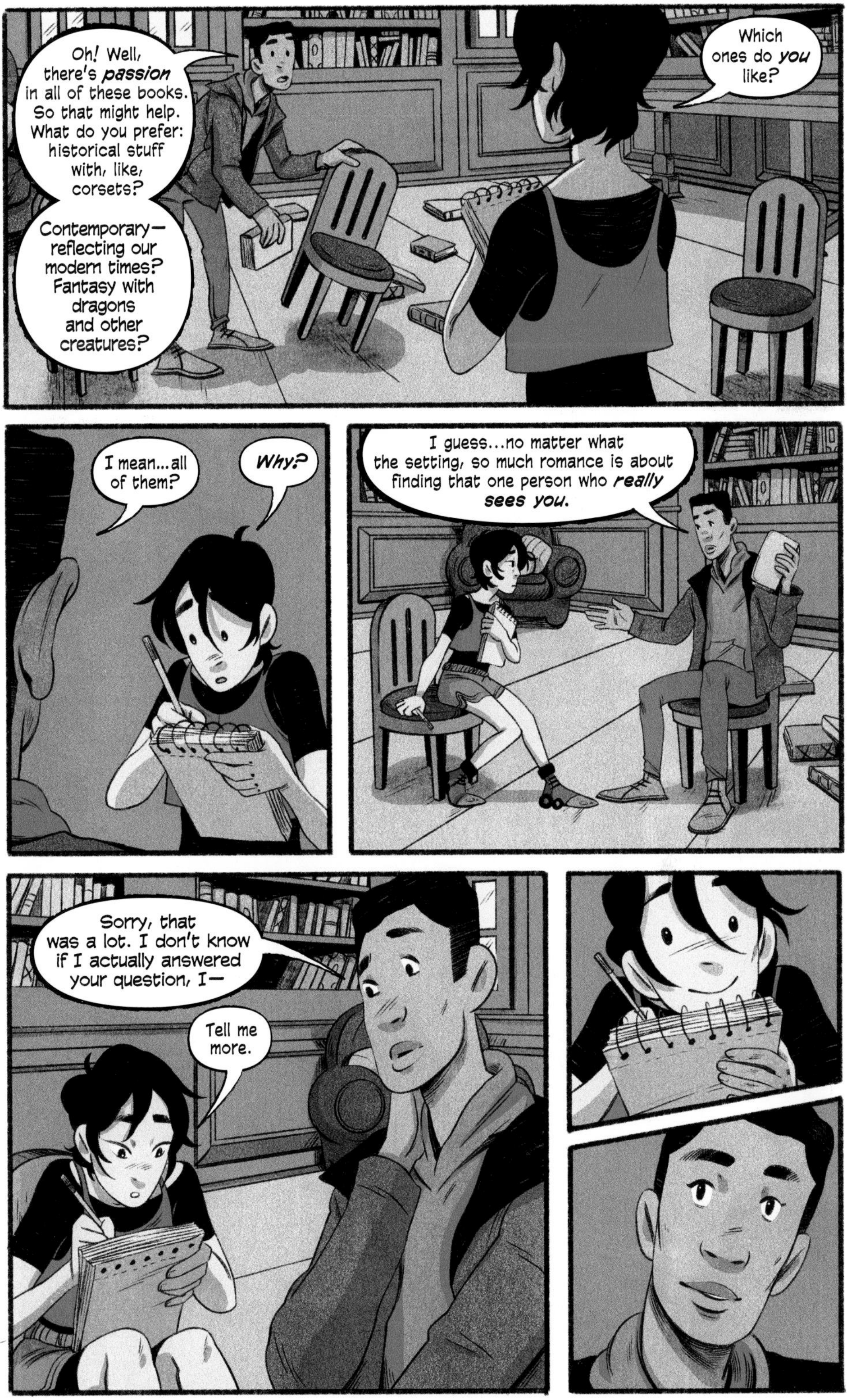

Oh! Well, there's *passion* in all of these books. So that might help. What do you prefer: historical stuff with, like, corsets?
Contemporary—reflecting our modern times? Fantasy with dragons and other creatures?
Which ones do *you* like?
I mean...all of them?
Why?
I guess...no matter what the setting, so much romance is about finding that one person who *really sees you*.
Sorry, that was a lot. I don't know if I actually answered your question, I—
Tell me more.

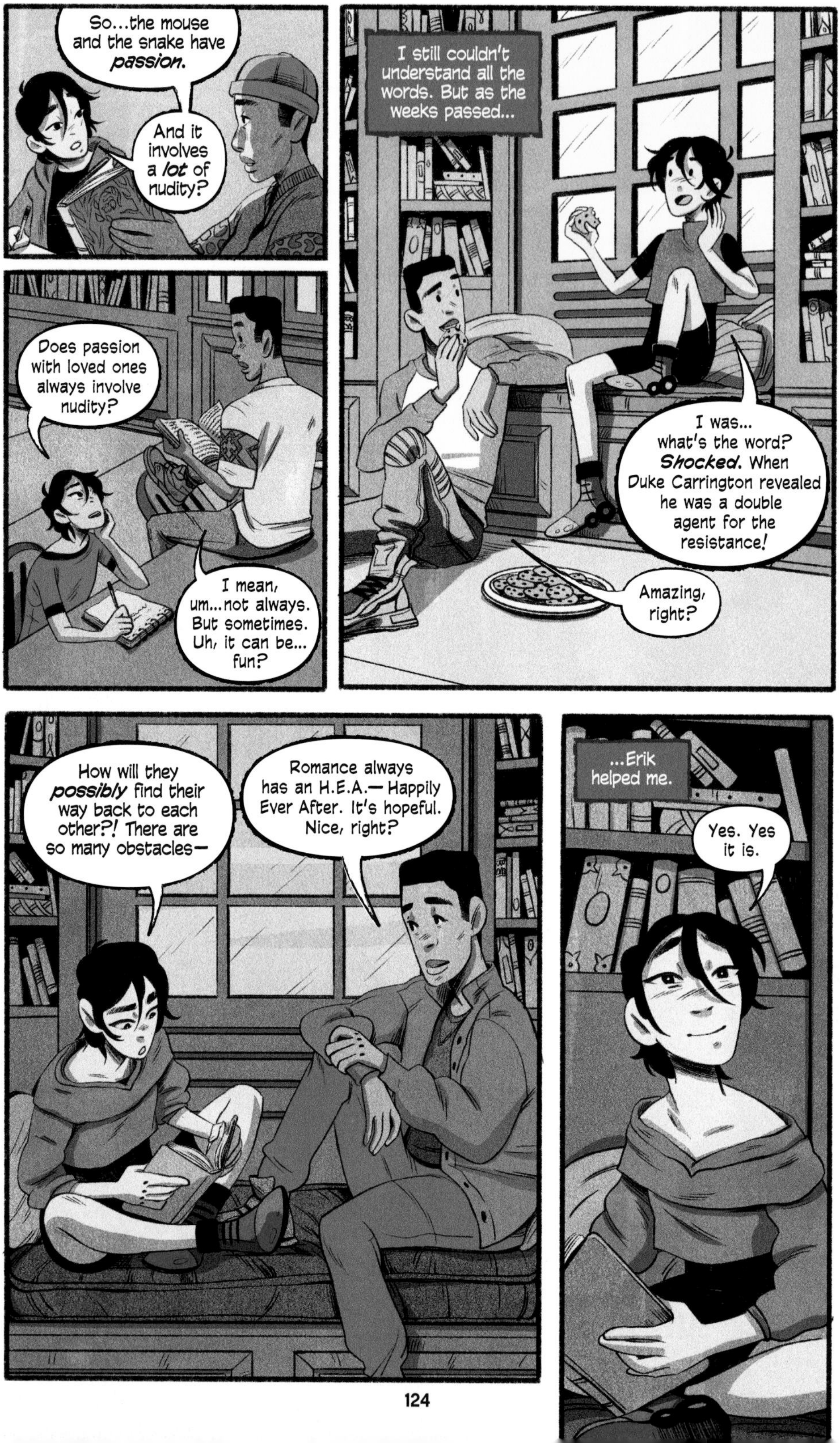
So...the mouse and the snake have *passion*.
And it involves a *lot* of nudity?
I still couldn't understand all the words. But as the weeks passed...
Does passion with loved ones always involve nudity?
I mean, um...not always. But sometimes. Uh, it can be... fun?
I was... what's the word? *Shocked*. When Duke Carrington revealed he was a double agent for the resistance!
Amazing, right?
How will they *possibly* find their way back to each other?! There are so many obstacles—
Romance always has an H.E.A.—Happily Ever After. It's hopeful. Nice, right?
...Erik helped me.
Yes. Yes it is.

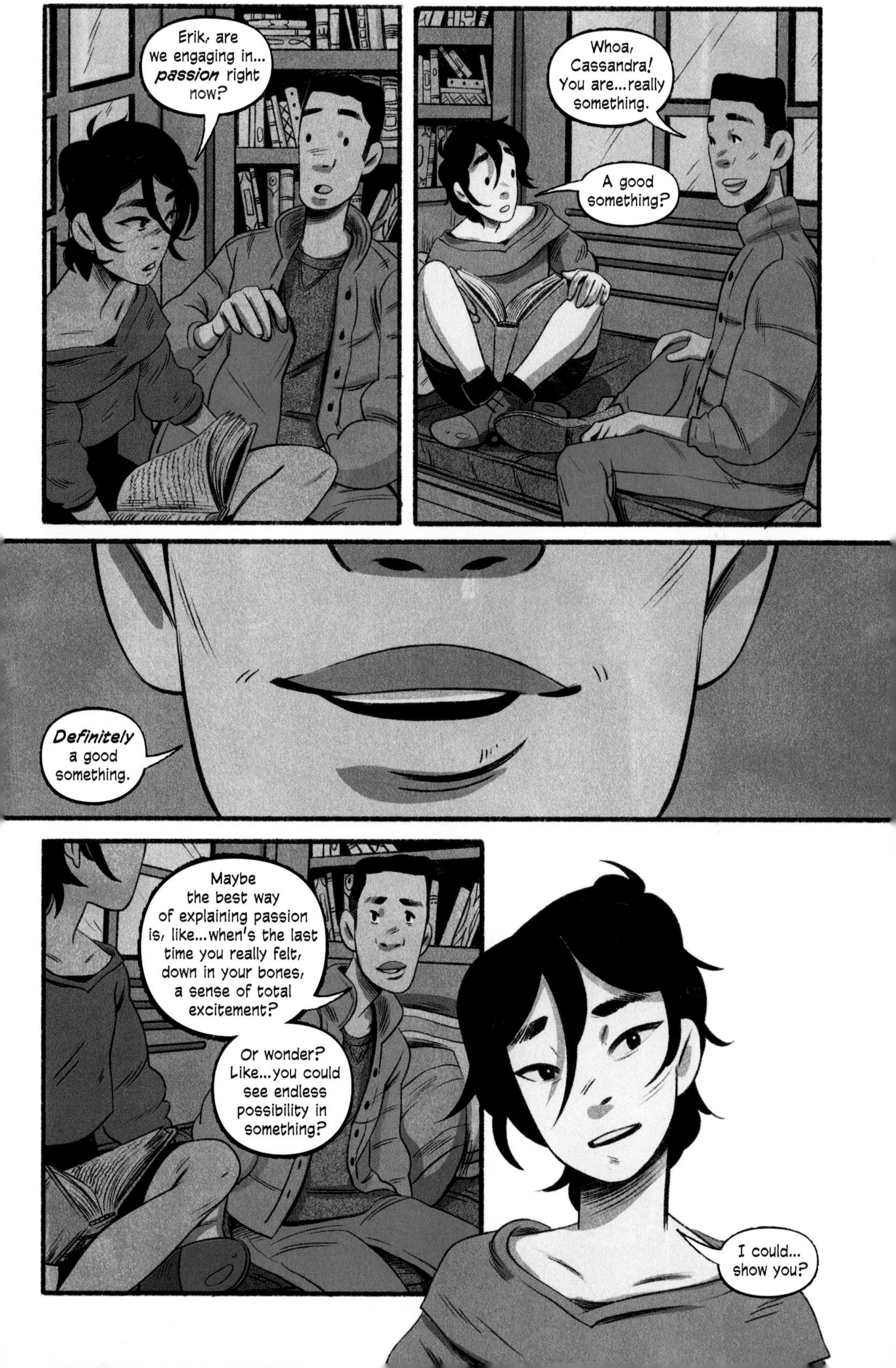
Erik, are we engaging in... *passion* right now?
Whoa, Cassandra! You are...really something.
A good something?
Definitely a good something.
Maybe the best way of explaining passion is, like...when's the last time you really felt, down in your bones, a sense of total excitement?
Or wonder? Like...you could see endless possibility in something?
I could... show you?

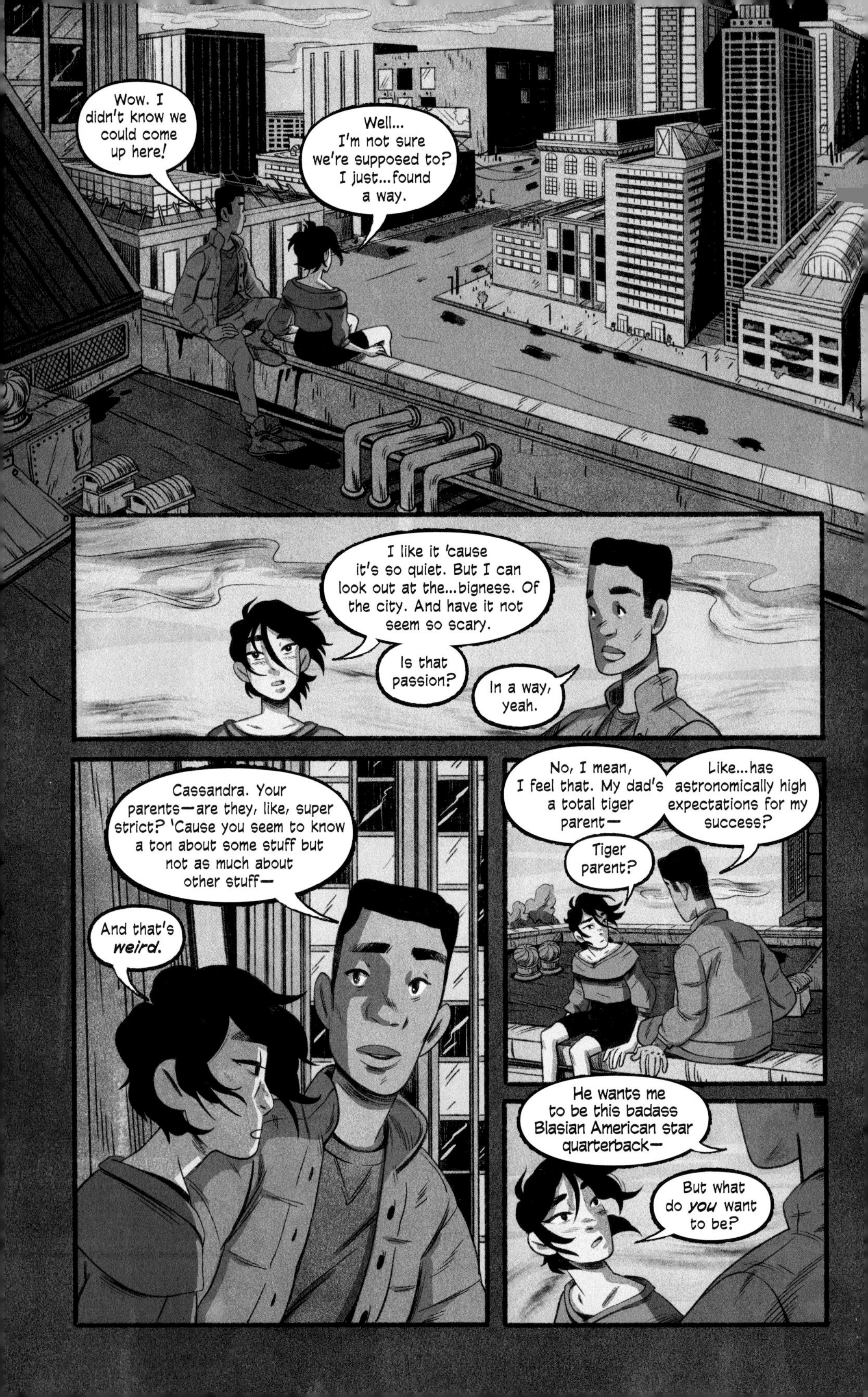

Wow. I didn't know we could come up here!
Well... I'm not sure we're supposed to? I just...found a way.
I like it 'cause it's so quiet. But I can look out at the...bigness. Of the city. And have it not seem so scary.
Is that passion?
In a way, yeah.
Cassandra. Your parents—are they, like, super strict? 'Cause you seem to know a ton about some stuff but not as much about other stuff—
And that's *weird*.
No, I mean, I feel that. My dad's a total tiger parent—
Tiger parent?
Like...has astronomically high expectations for my success?
He wants me to be this badass Blasian American star quarterback—
But what do *you* want to be?

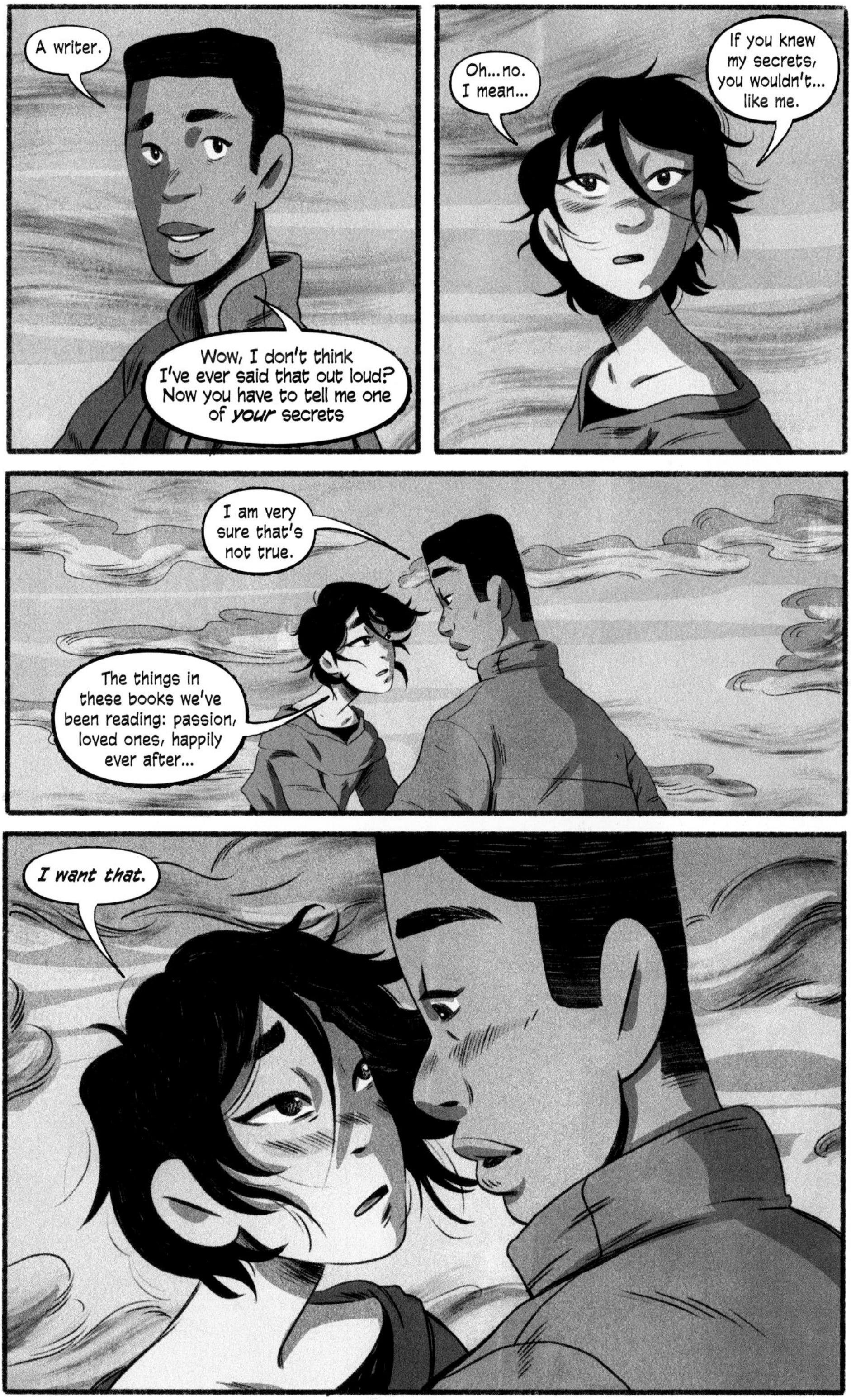
A writer.
Wow, I don't think I've ever said that out loud? Now you have to tell me one of *your* secrets
Oh...no. I mean...
If you knew my secrets, you wouldn't... like me.
I am very sure that's not true.
The things in these books we've been reading: passion, loved ones, happily ever after...
I want that.

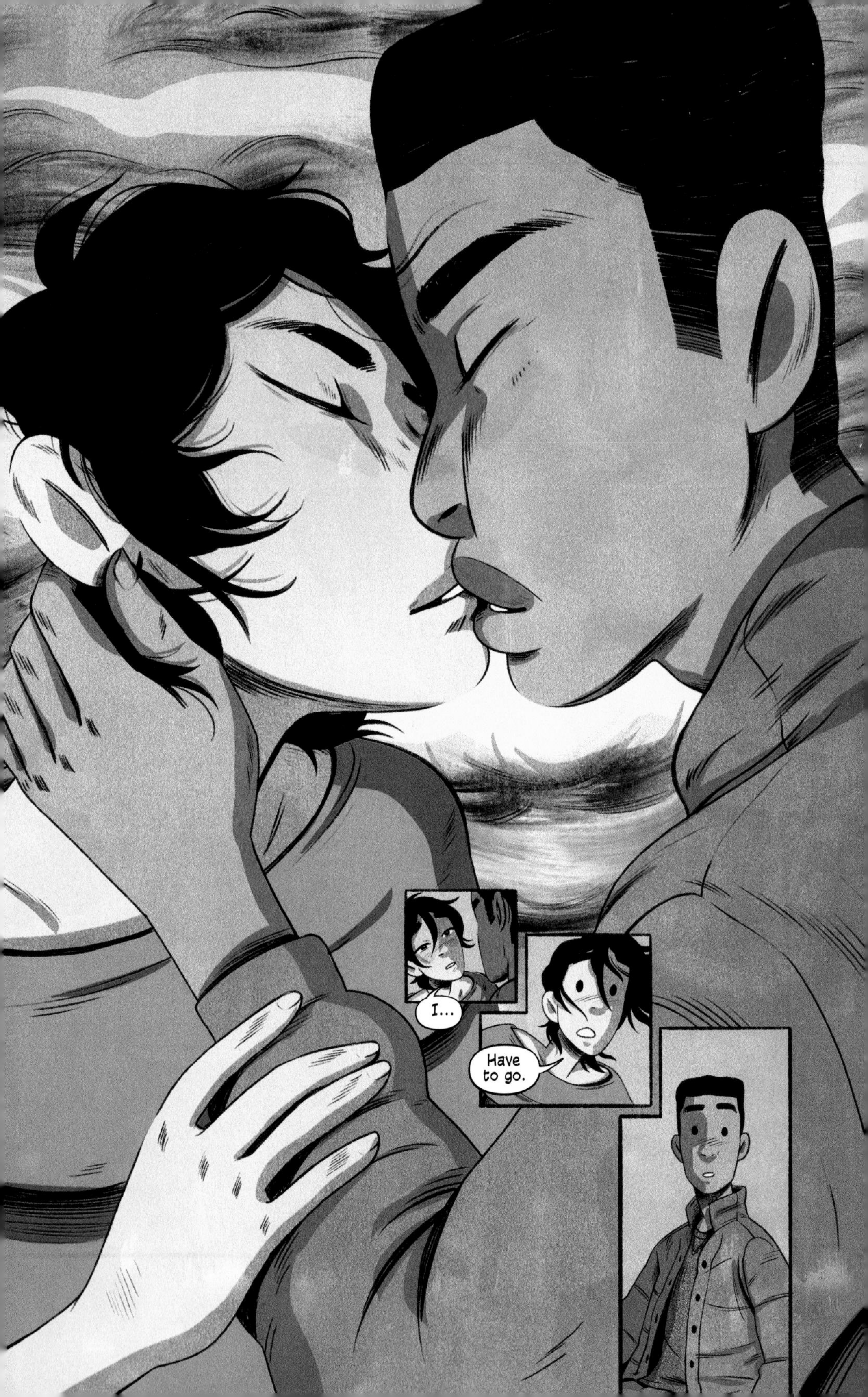

I...
Have to go.

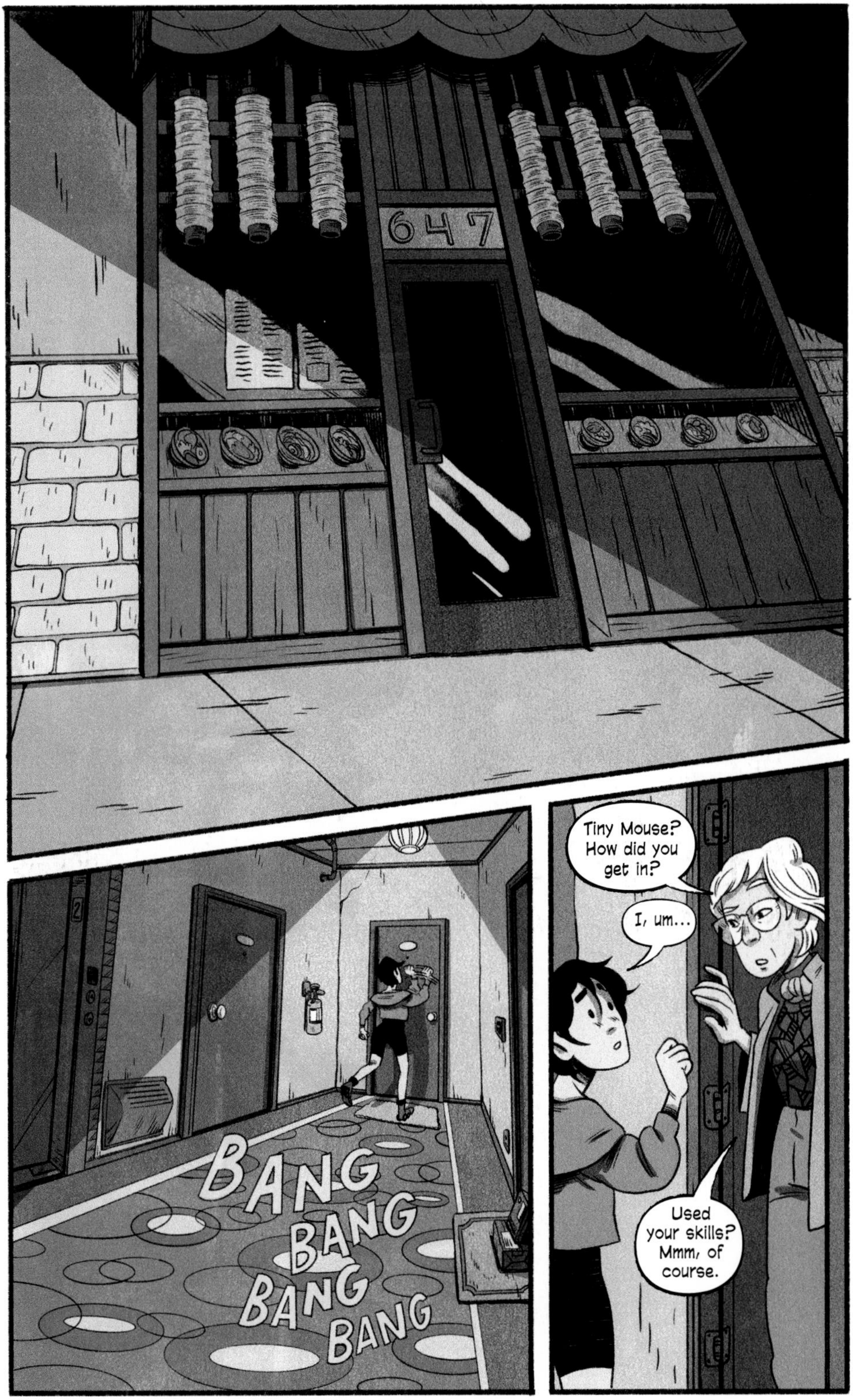
647
BANG
BANG
BANG
BANG
Tiny Mouse? How did you get in?
I, um...
Used your skills? Mmm, of course.

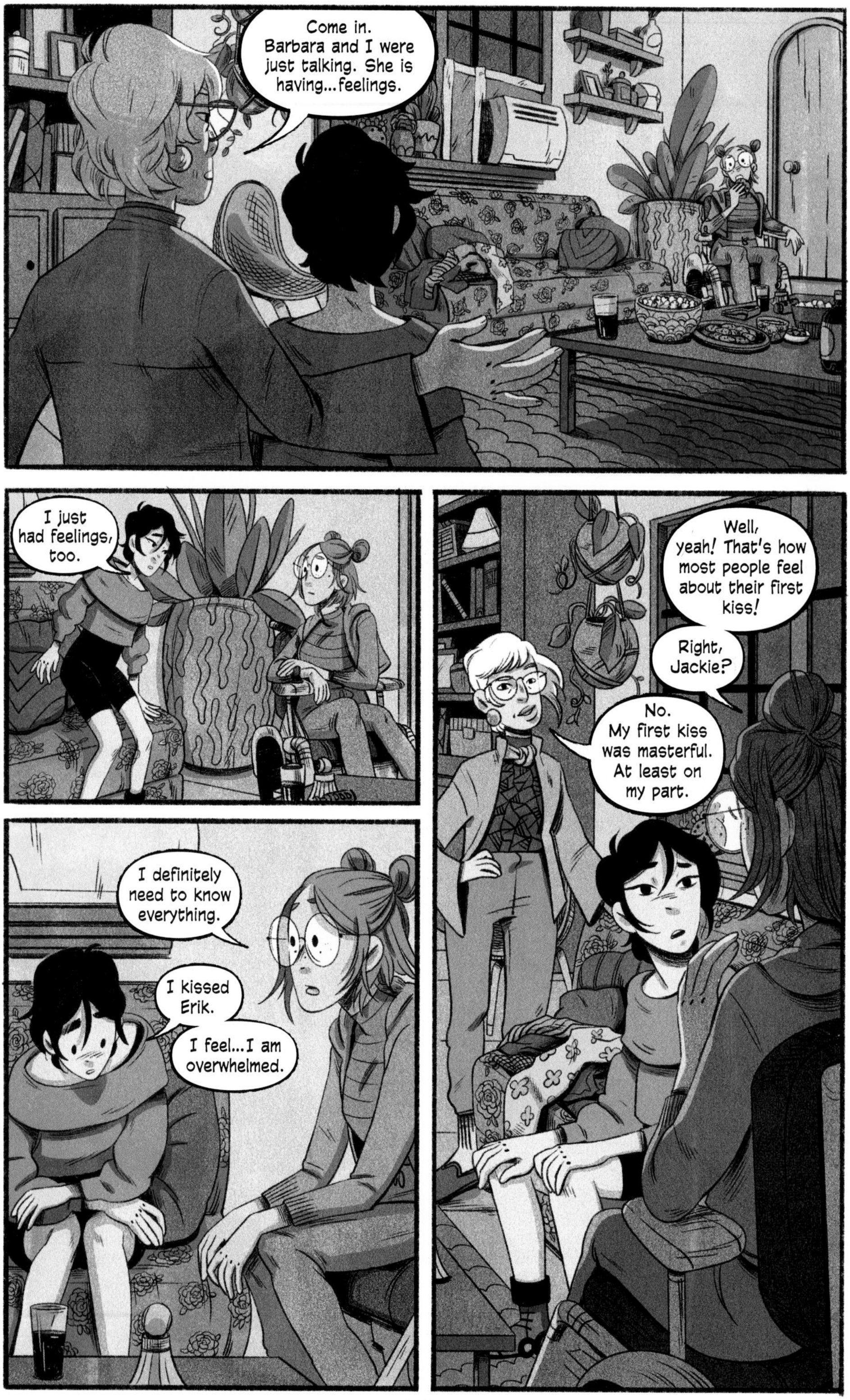
Come in. Barbara and I were just talking. She is having...feelings.
I just had feelings, too.
I definitely need to know everything.
I kissed Erik.
I feel...I am overwhelmed.
Well, yeah! That's how most people feel about their first kiss!
Right, Jackie?
No. My first kiss was masterful. At least on my part.

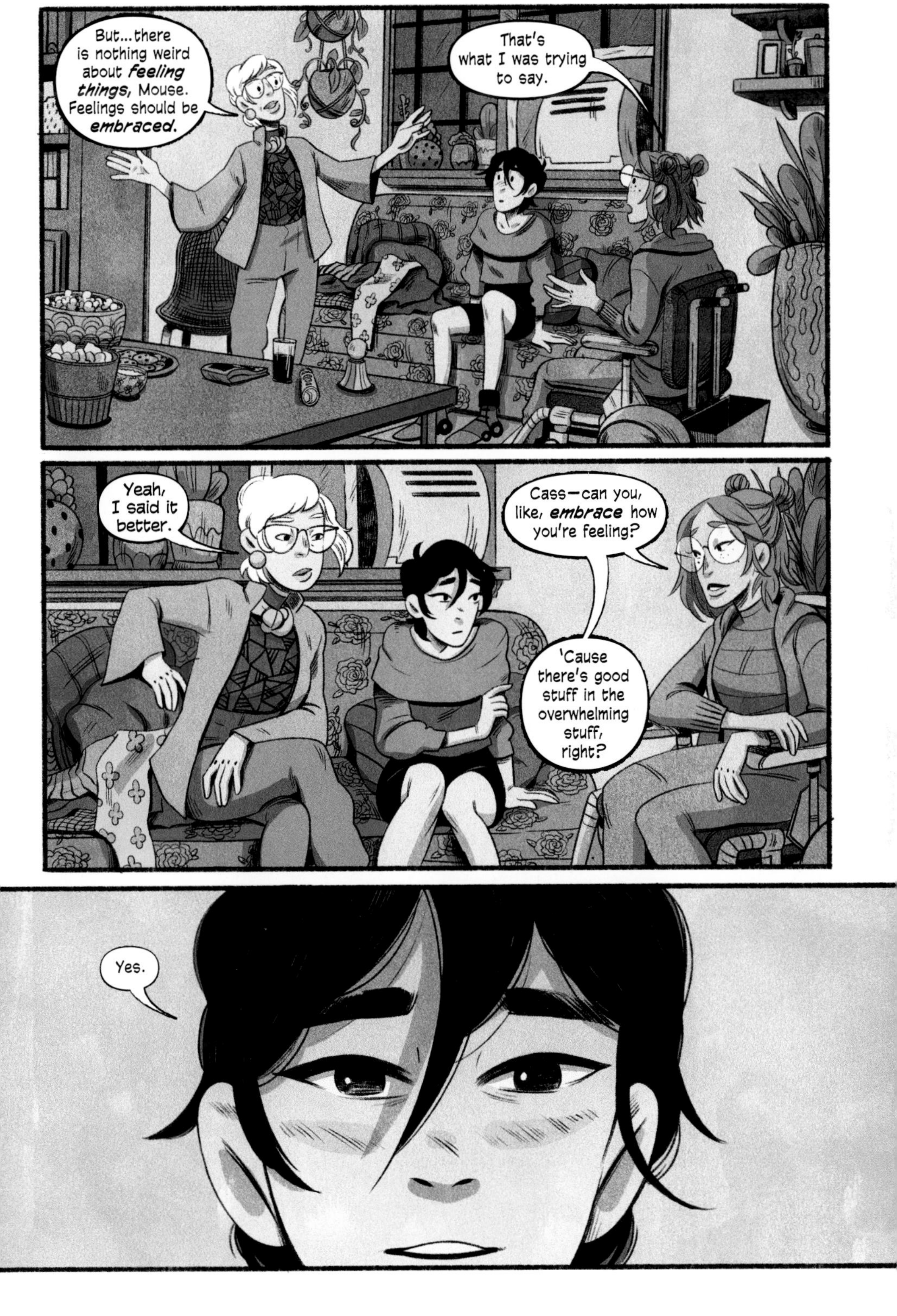
But...there is nothing weird about *feeling things,* Mouse. Feelings should be *embraced.*
That's what I was trying to say.
Yeah, I said it better.
Cass—can you, like, *embrace* how you're feeling?
'Cause there's good stuff in the overwhelming stuff, right?
Yes.

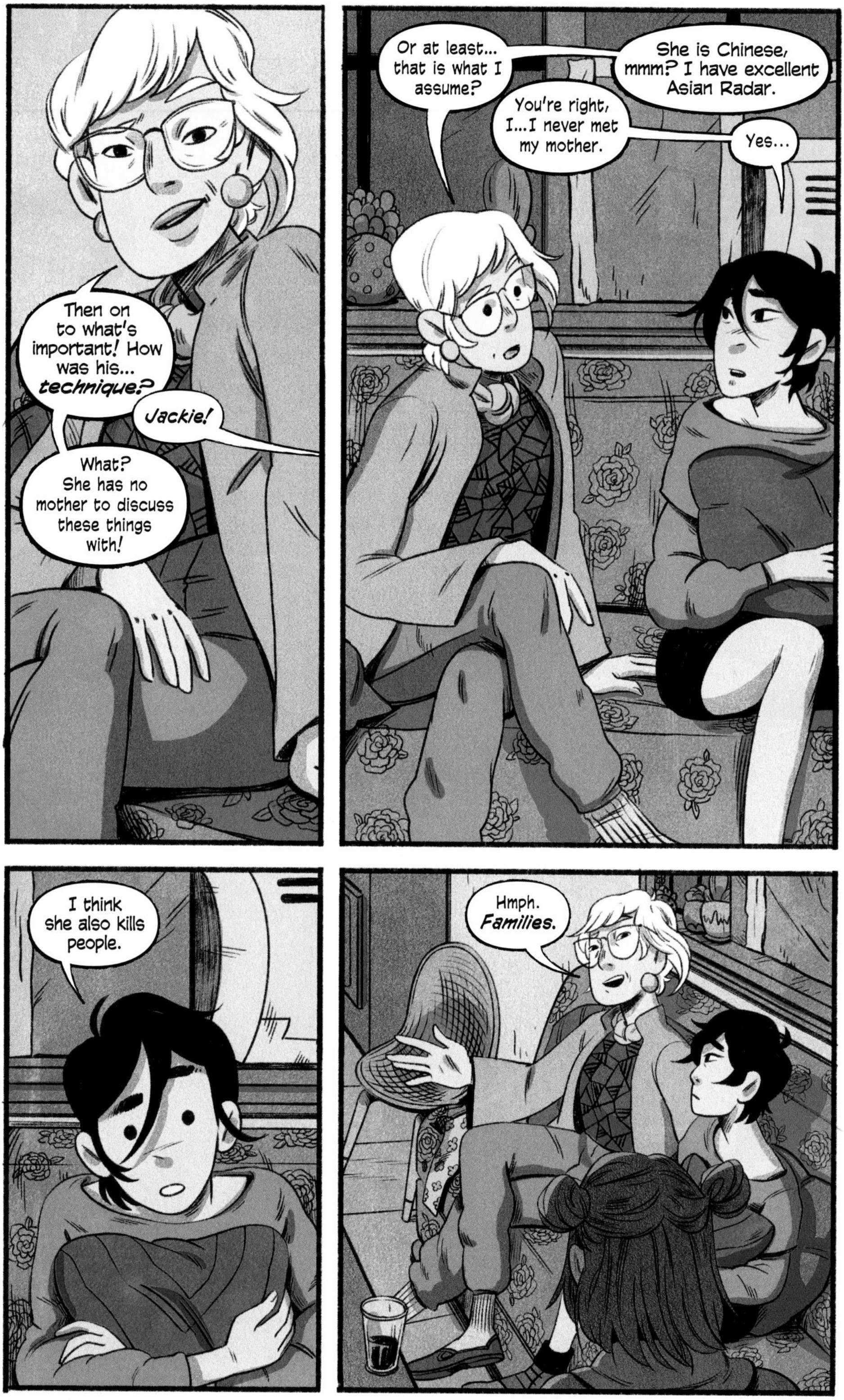
Then on to what's important! How was his... *technique?*
Jackie!
What? She has no mother to discuss these things with!
She is Chinese, mmm? I have excellent Asian Radar.
Or at least... that is what I assume?
Yes...
You're right, I...I never met my mother.
I think she also kills people.
Hmph. *Families.*

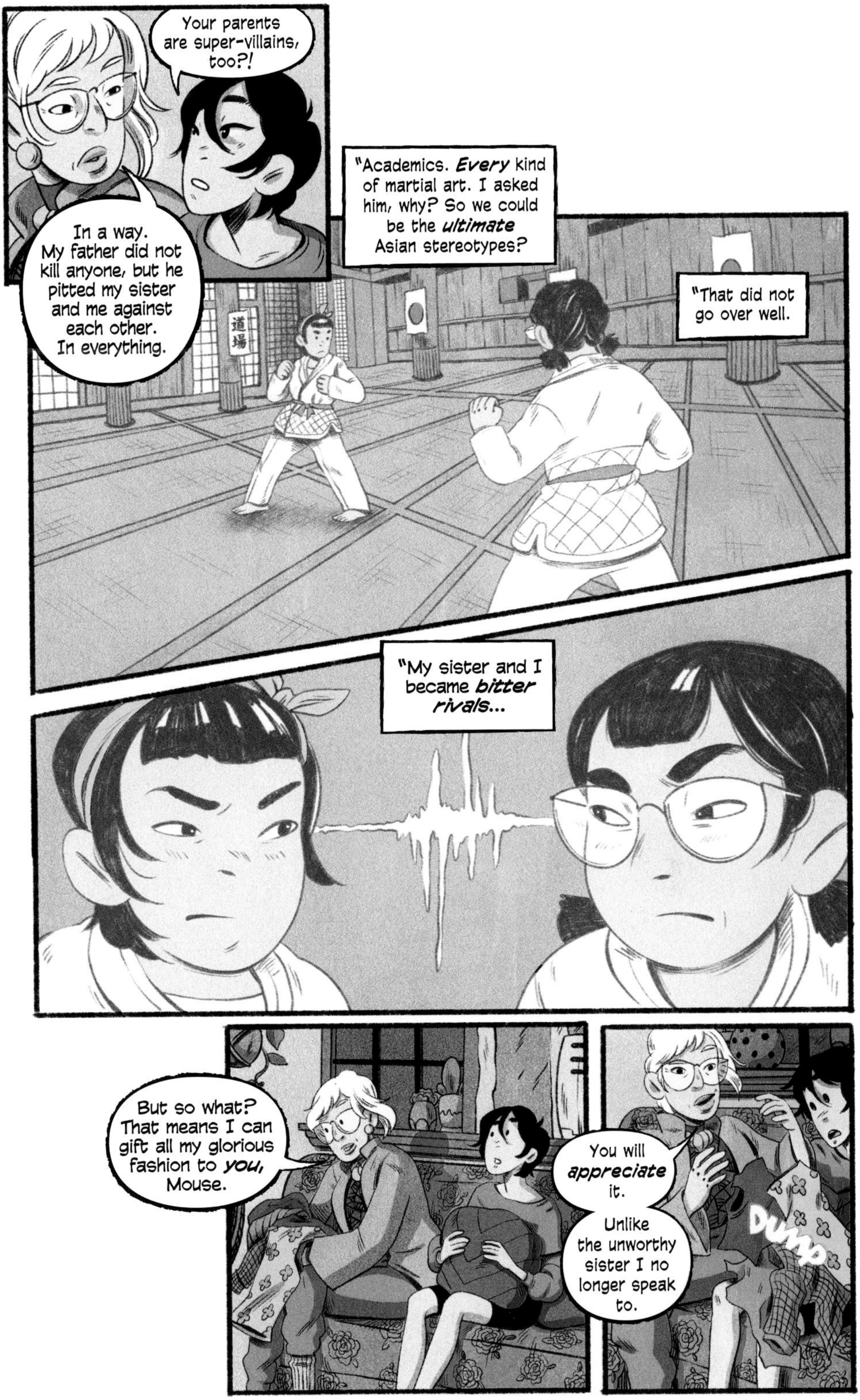
Your parents are super-villains, too?!
In a way. My father did not kill anyone, but he pitted my sister and me against each other. In everything.
"Academics. *Every* kind of martial art. I asked him, why? So we could be the *ultimate* Asian stereotypes?
道場
"That did not go over well.
"My sister and I became *bitter rivals*...
But so what? That means I can gift all my glorious fashion to *you*, Mouse.
You will *appreciate* it.
Unlike the unworthy sister I no longer speak to.
DUMP

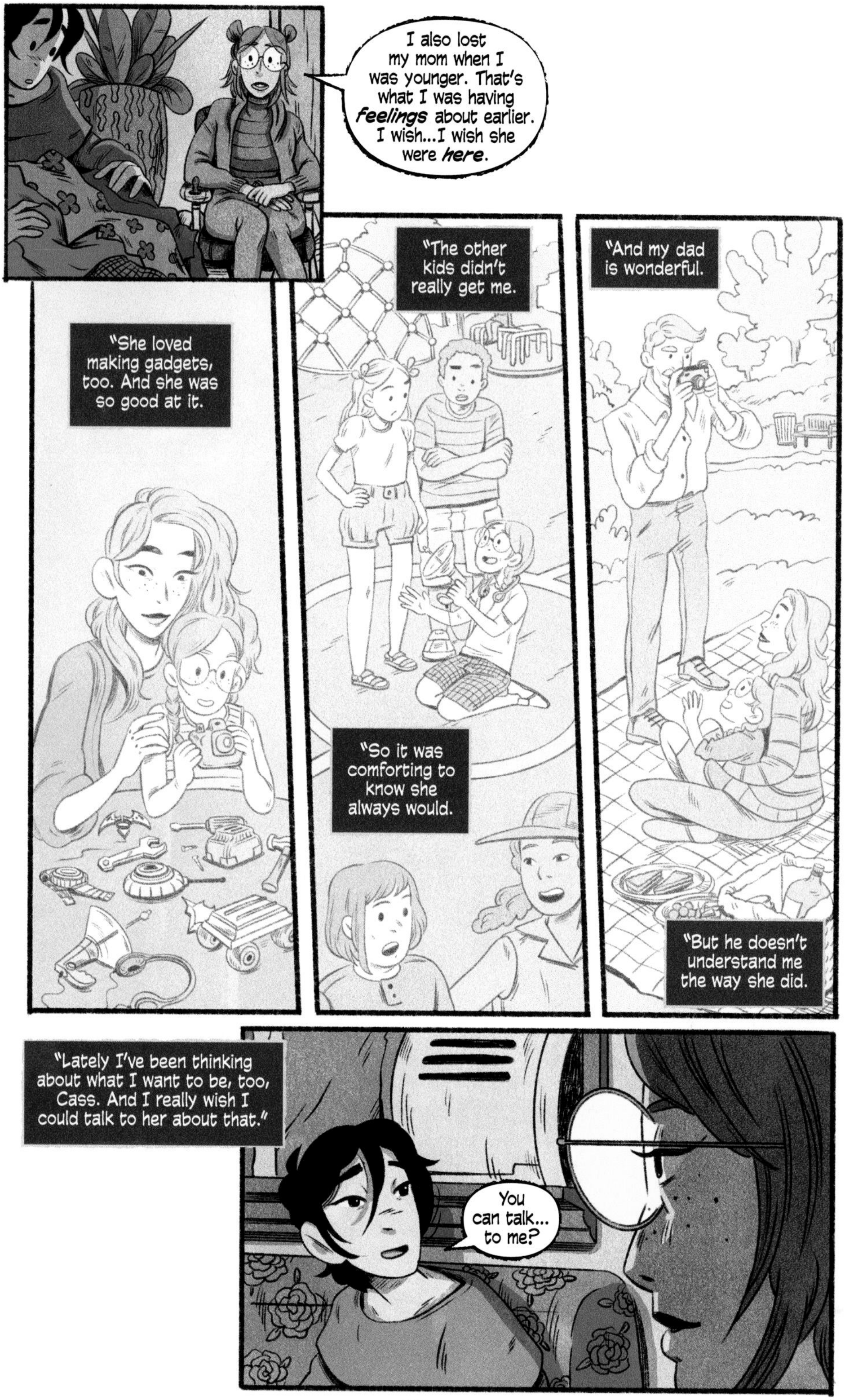
I also lost my mom when I was younger. That's what I was having *feelings* about earlier. I wish...I wish she were *here*.
"She loved making gadgets, too. And she was so good at it.
"The other kids didn't really get me.
"So it was comforting to know she always would.
"And my dad is wonderful.
"But he doesn't understand me the way she did.
"Lately I've been thinking about what I want to be, too, Cass. And I really wish I could talk to her about that."
You can talk... to me?

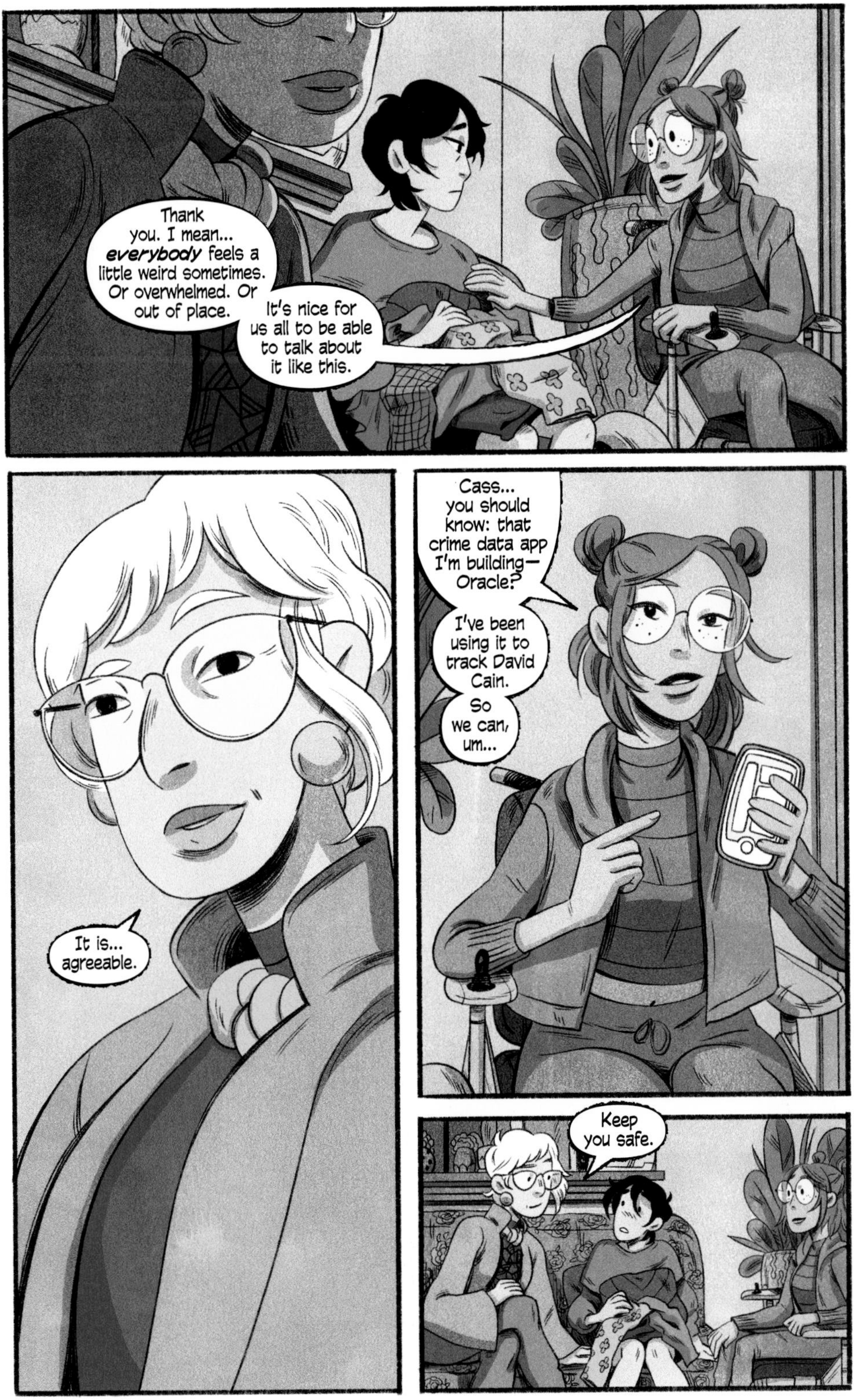
Thank you. I mean... **everybody** feels a little weird sometimes. Or overwhelmed. Or out of place.
It's nice for us all to be able to talk about it like this.
It is... agreeable.
Cass... you should know: that crime data app I'm building—Oracle?
I've been using it to track David Cain.
So we can, um...
Keep you safe.

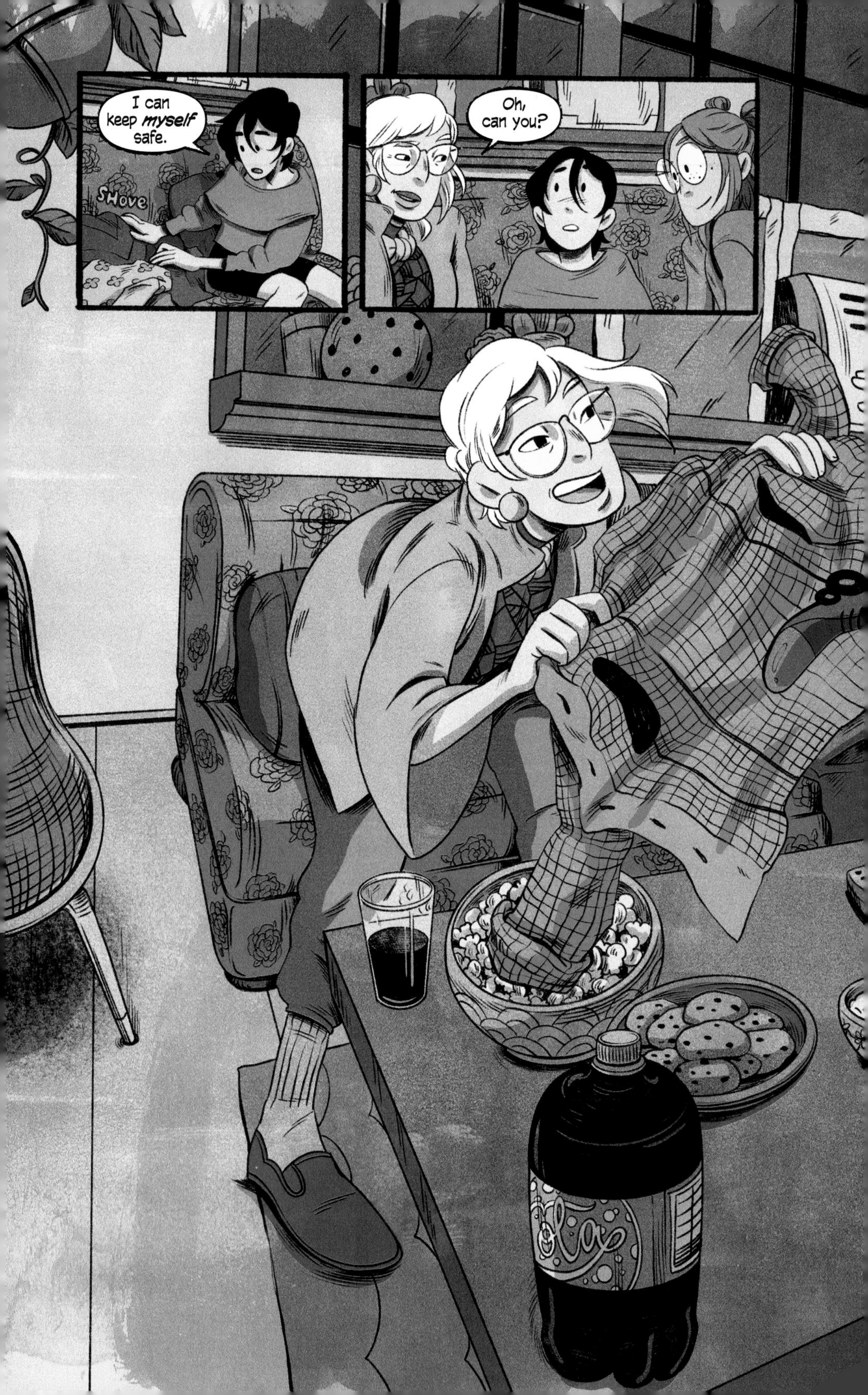
I can keep *myself* safe.
SHOVE
Oh, can you?
Cola

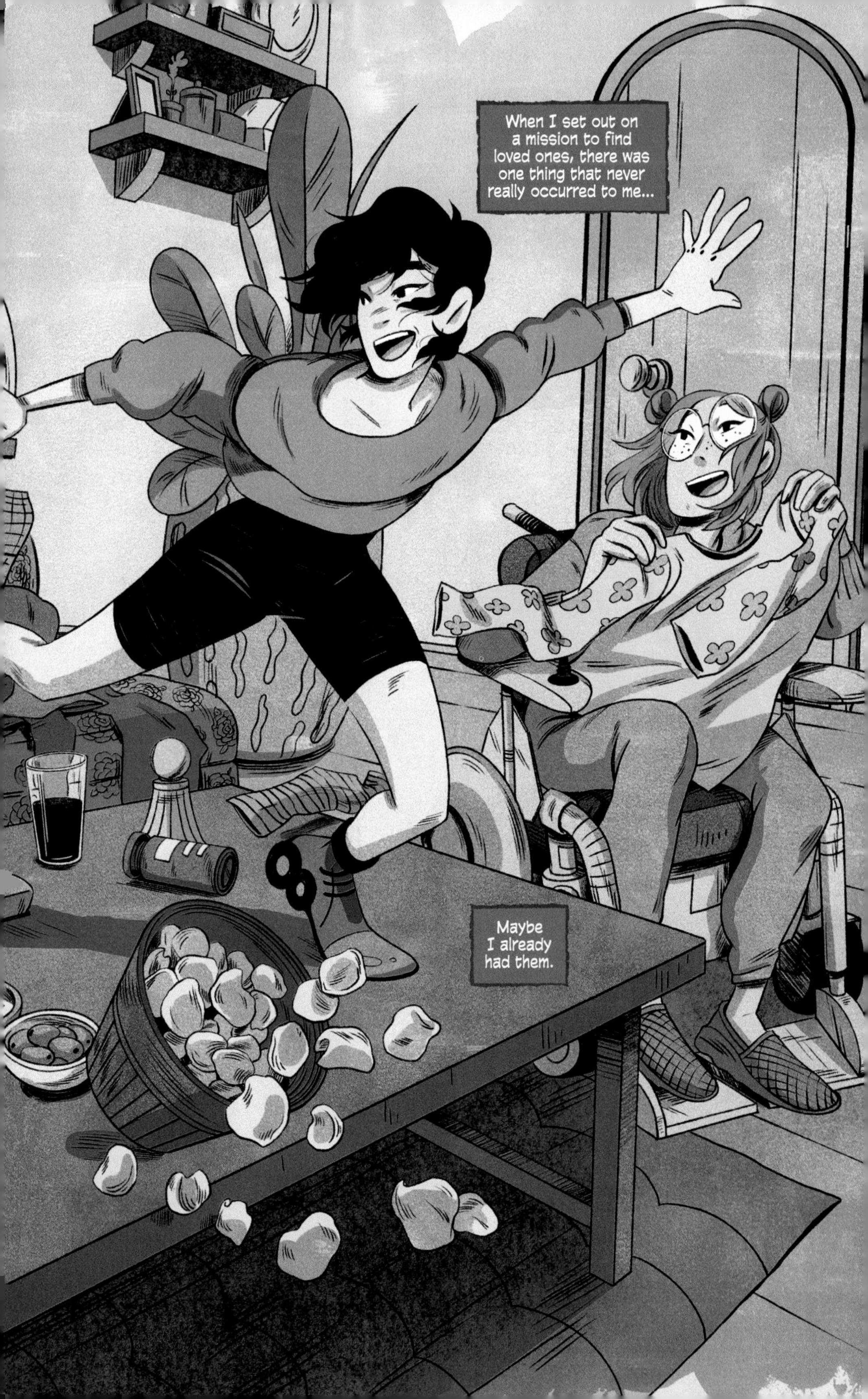
When I set out on a mission to find loved ones, there was one thing that never really occurred to me...
Maybe I already had them.

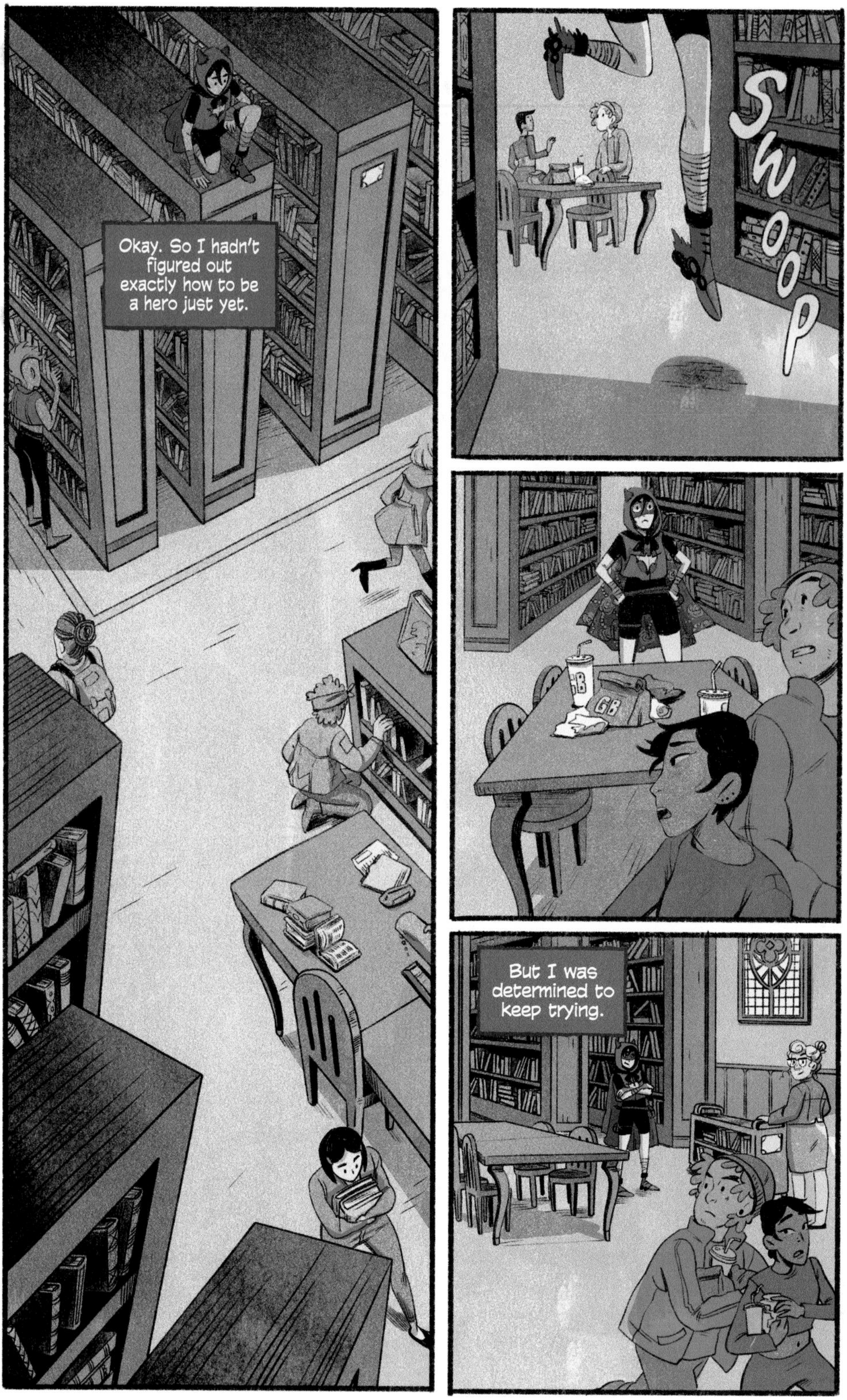
Okay. So I hadn't figured out exactly how to be a hero just yet.
SWOOP
But I was determined to keep trying.

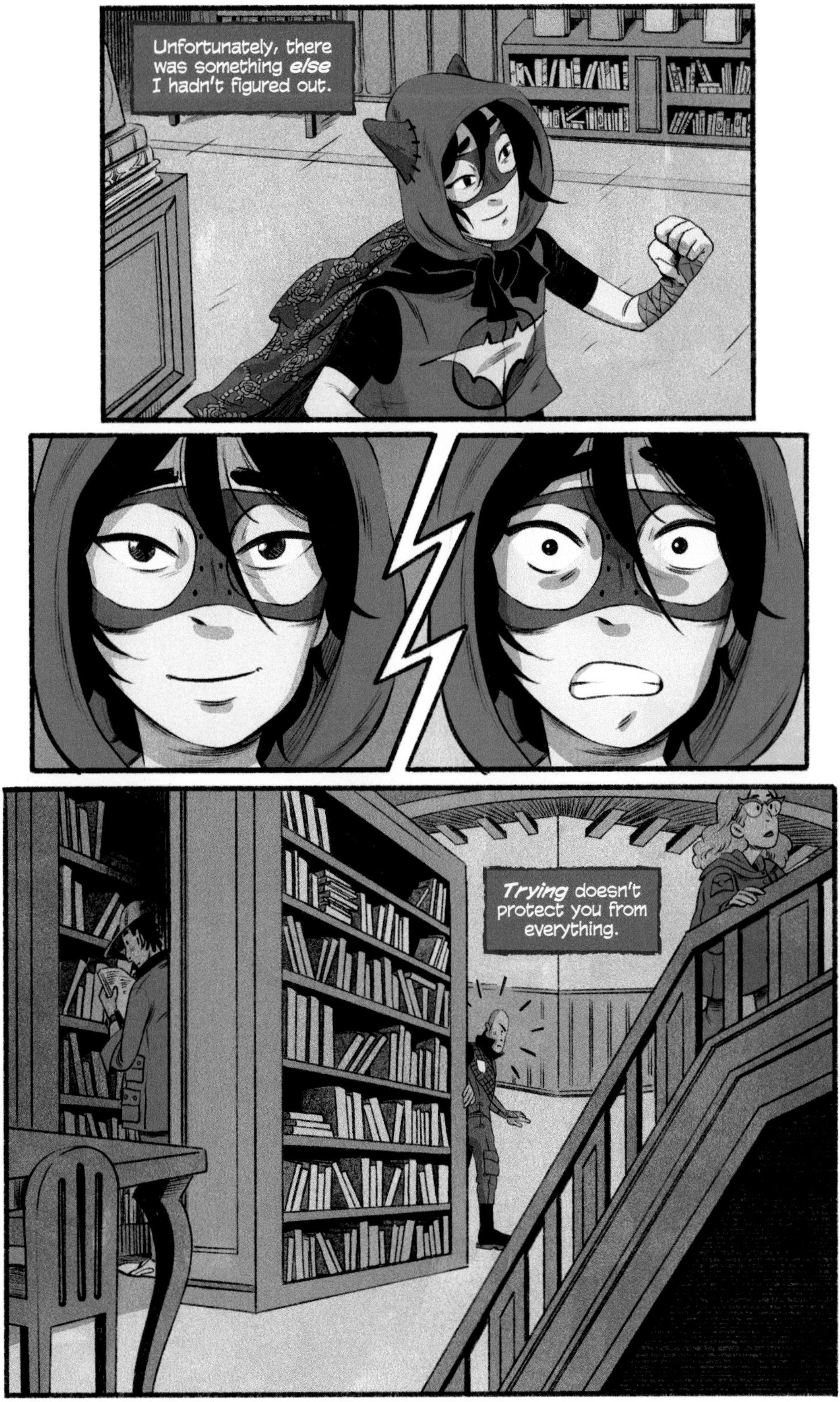
Unfortunately, there was something *else* I hadn't figured out.
Trying doesn't protect you from everything.

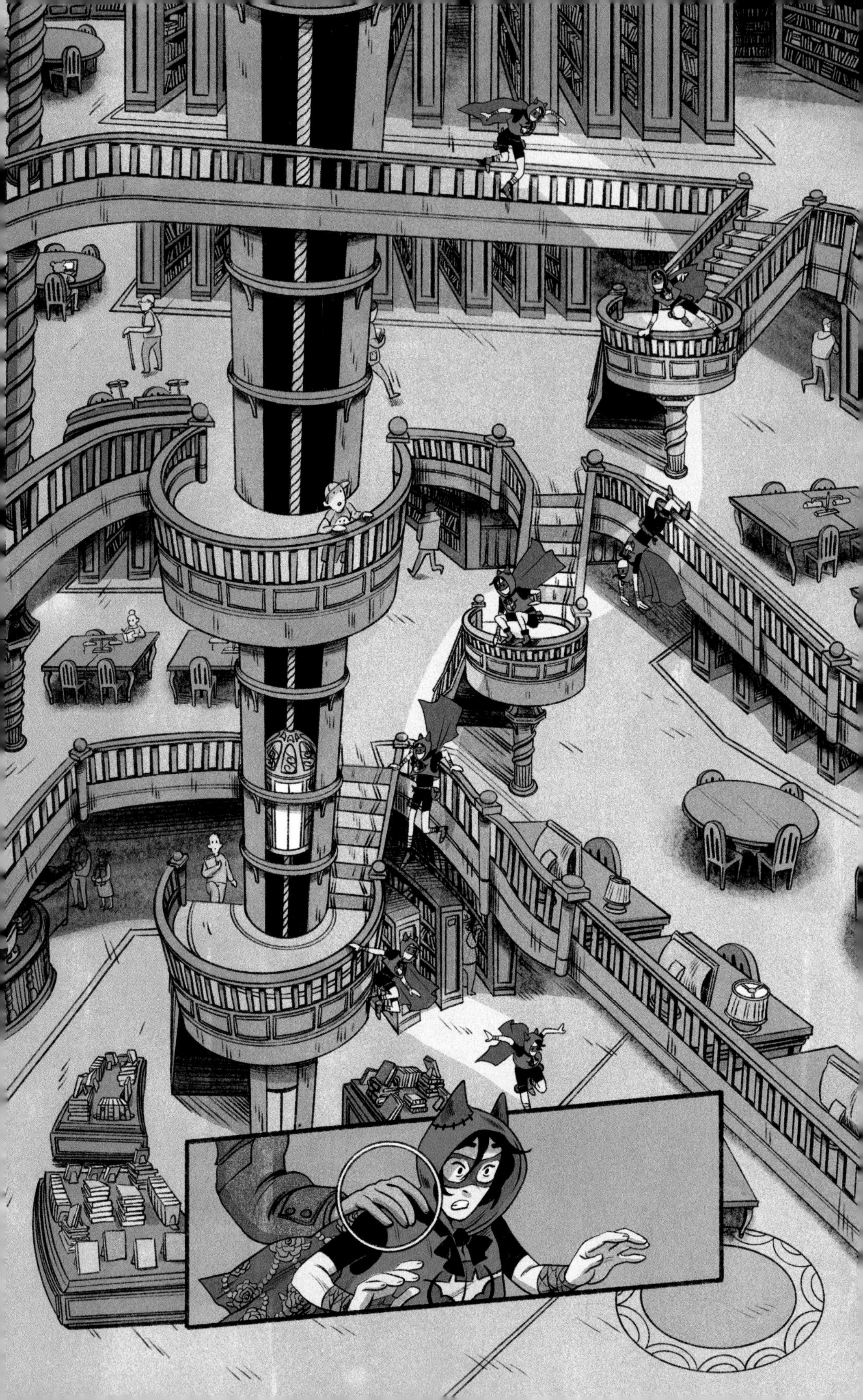

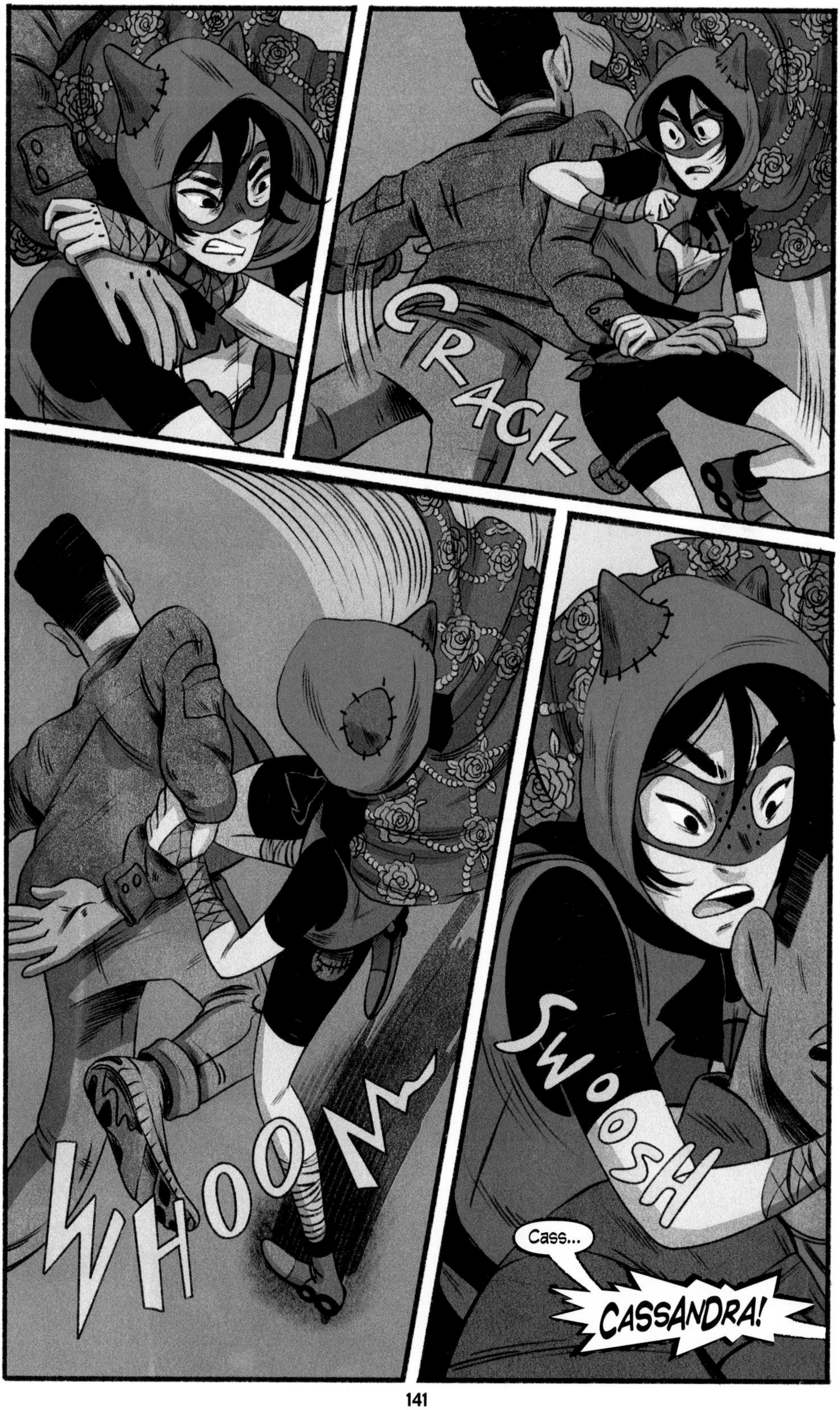
CRACK
WHOOM
SWOOSH
Cass...
CASSANDRA!

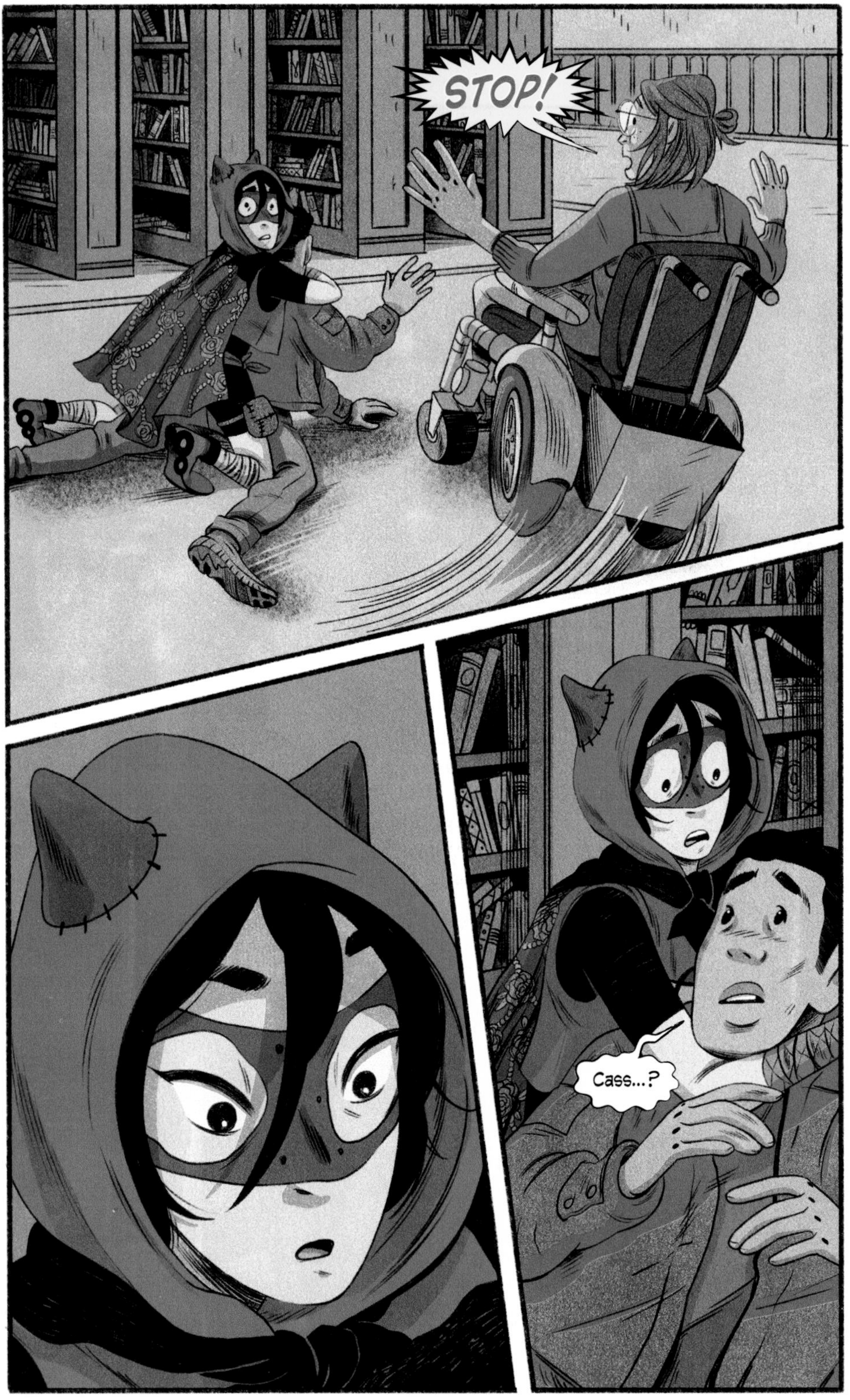
STOP!
Cass...?

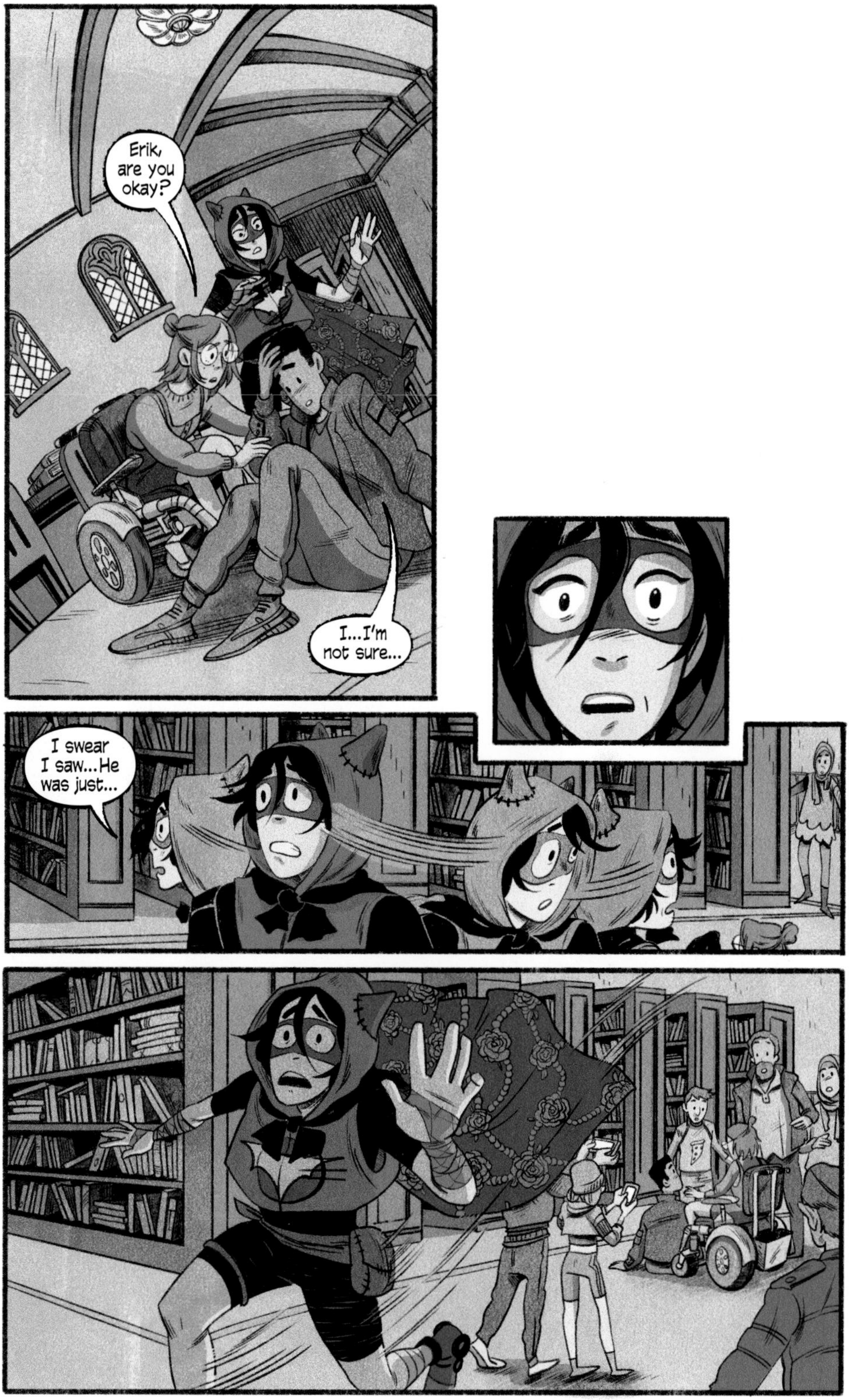
Erik, are you okay?
I...I'm not sure...
I swear I saw...He was just...

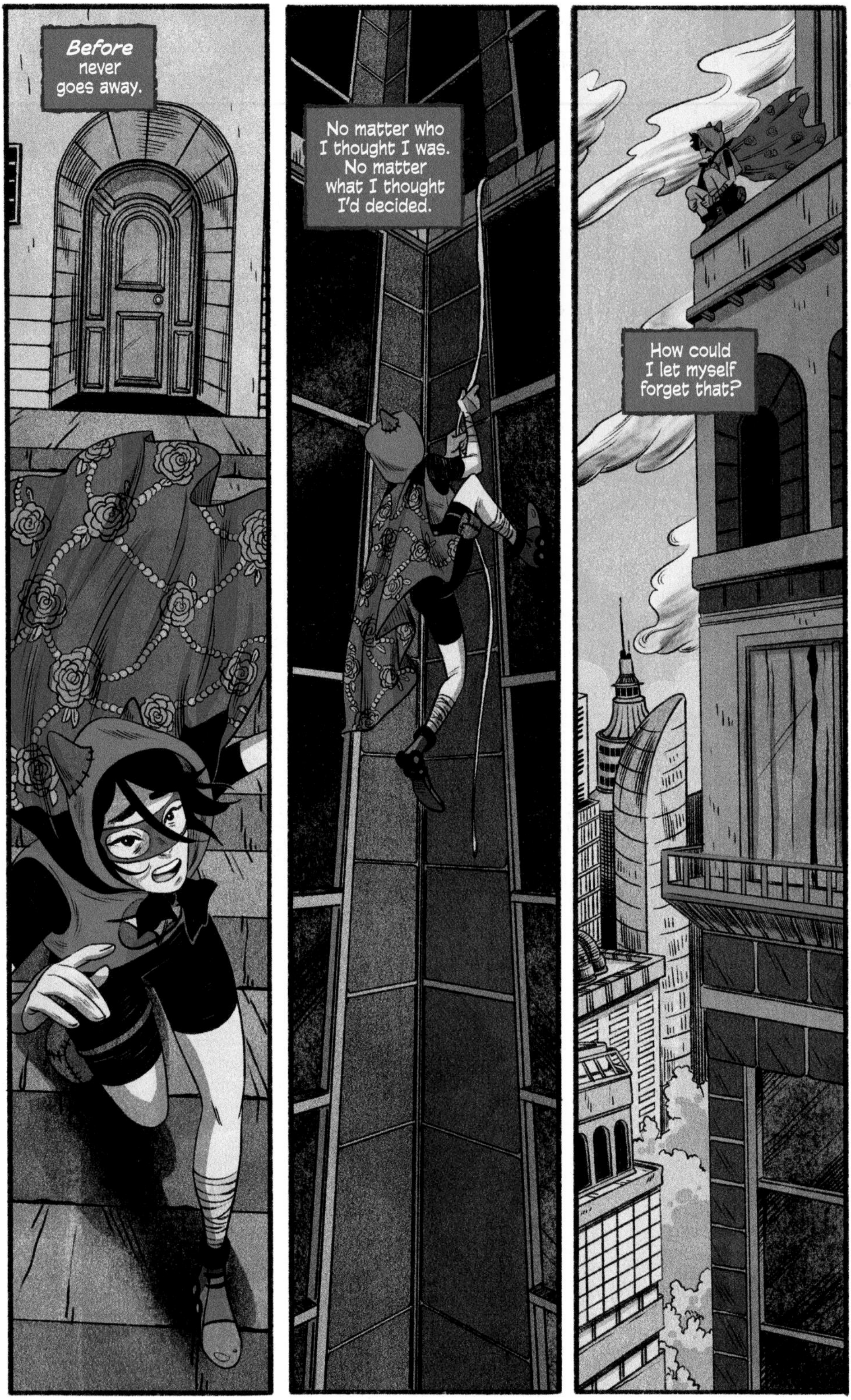
Before never goes away.
No matter who I thought I was. No matter what I thought I'd decided.
How could I let myself forget that?

I couldn't run forever.

And I couldn't stop thinking about Erik.

GOTHAM CITY HOSPITAL

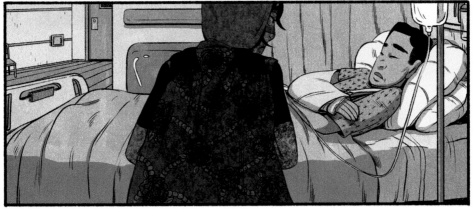

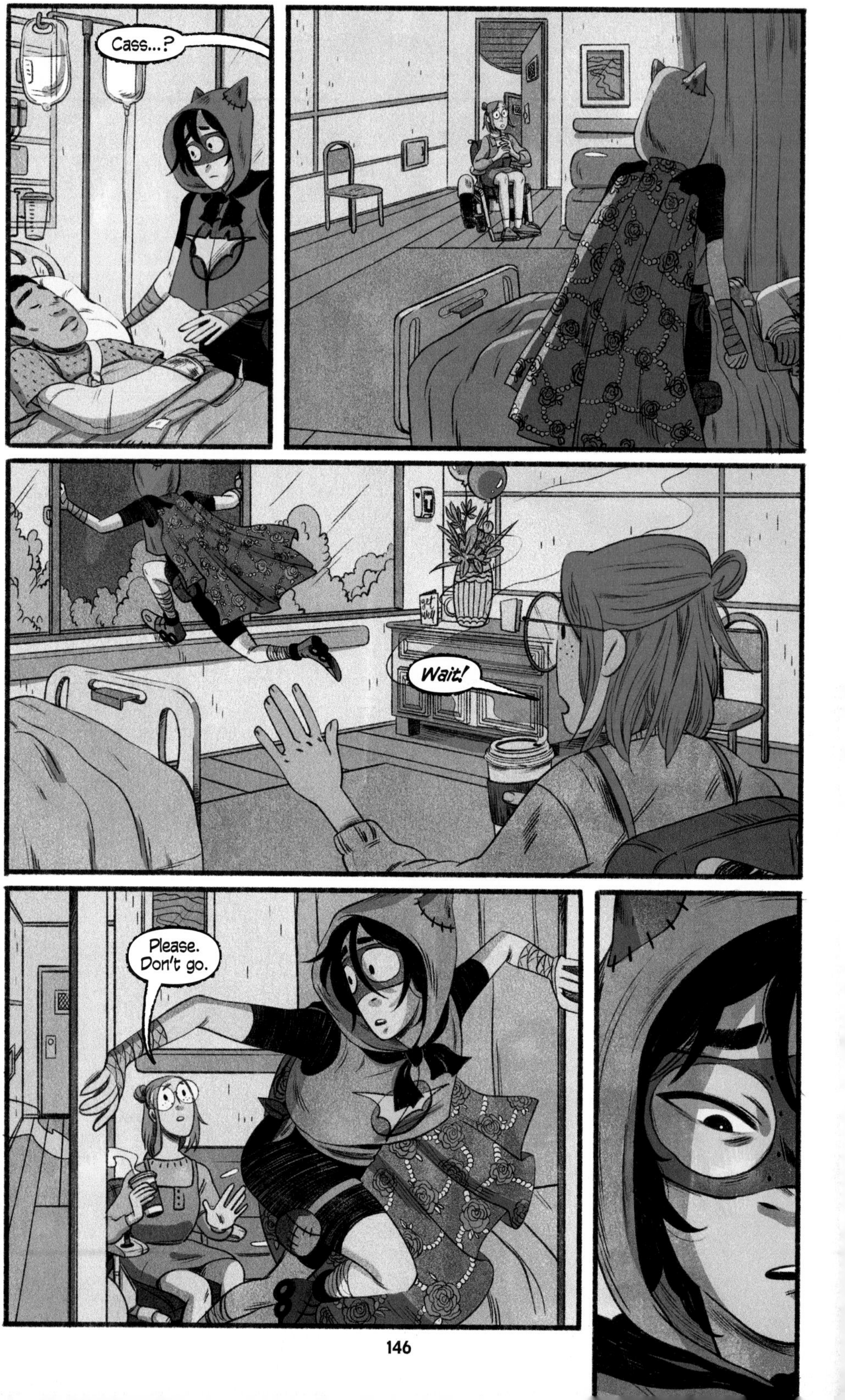
Cass...?
Wait!
Please. Don't go.

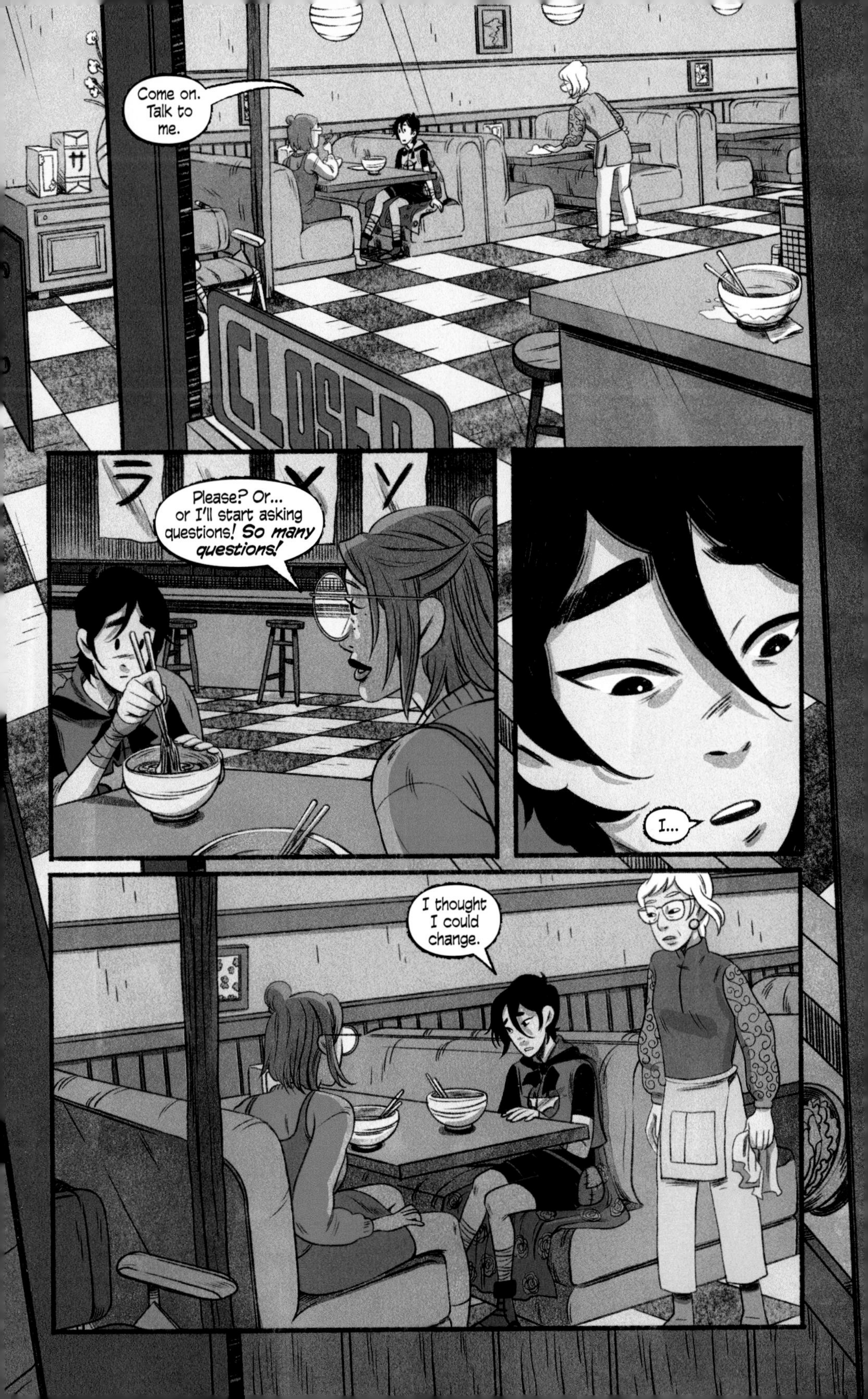
Come on. Talk to me.
CLOSED
Please? Or... or I'll start asking questions! *So many questions!*
I...
I thought I could change.

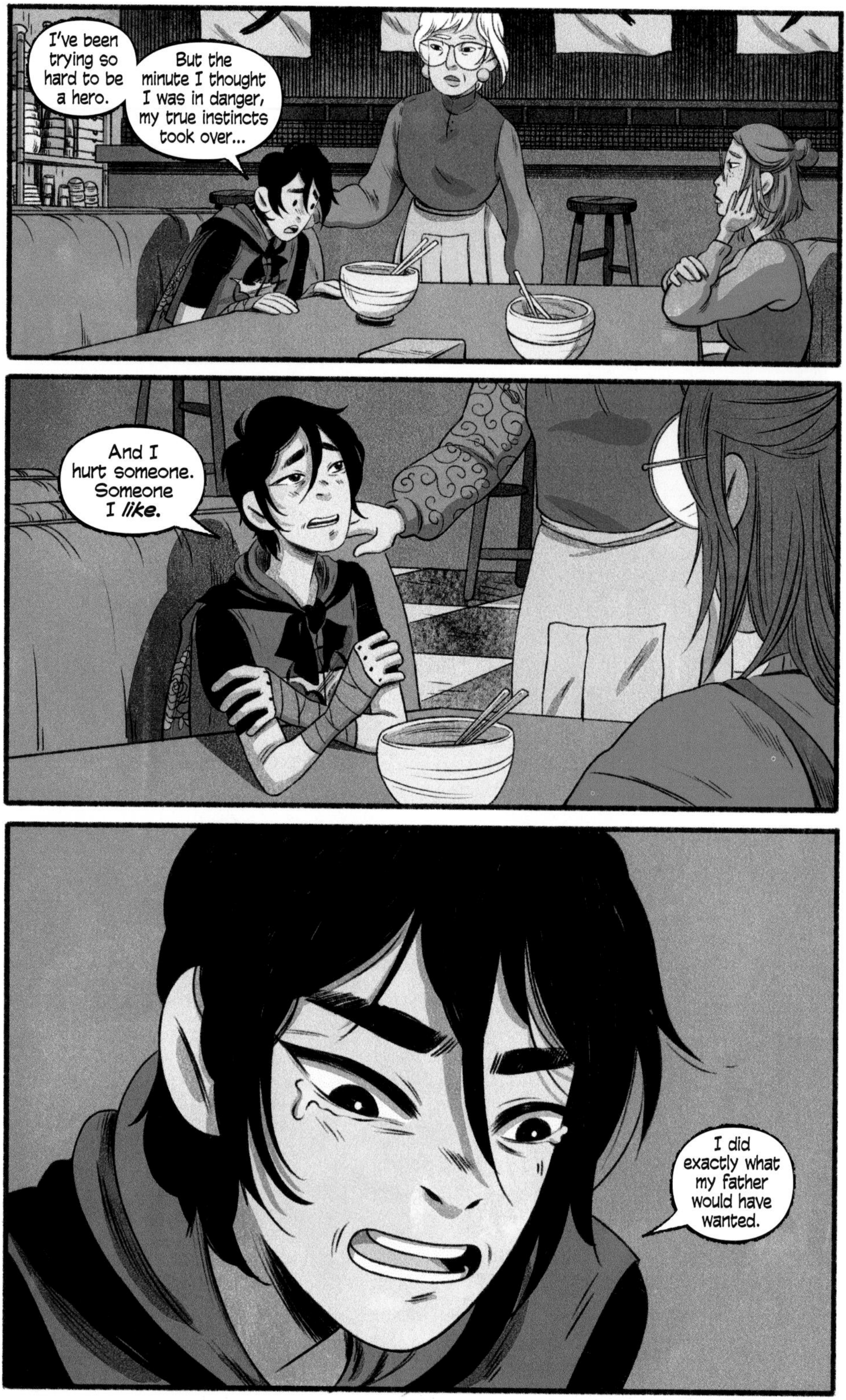
I've been trying so hard to be a hero.
But the minute I thought I was in danger, my true instincts took over...
And I hurt someone. Someone I *like.*
I did exactly what my father would have wanted.

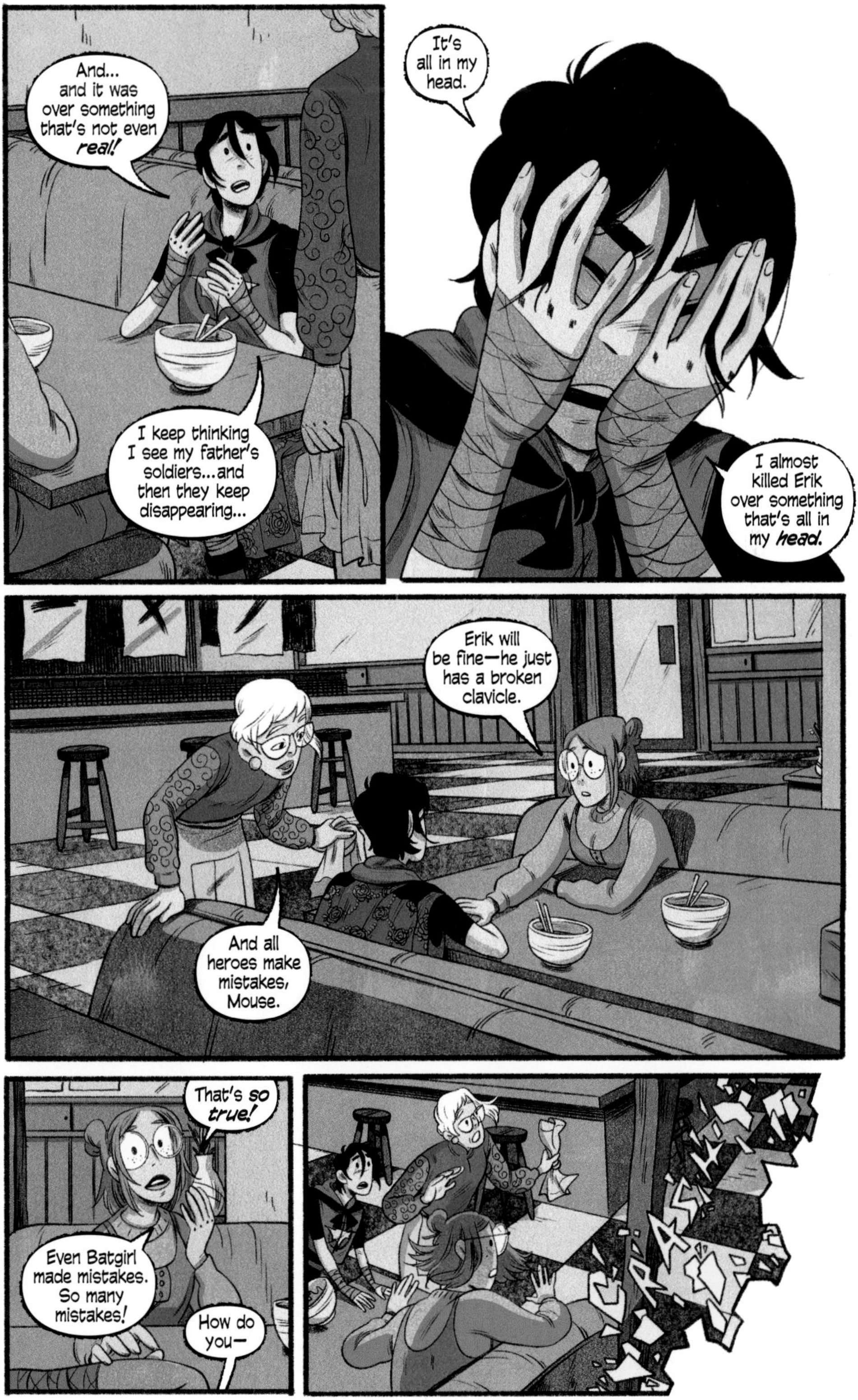
And... and it was over something that's not even *real!*
It's all in my head.
I keep thinking I see my father's soldiers...and then they keep disappearing...
I almost killed Erik over something that's all in my *head.*
Erik will be fine—he just has a broken clavicle.
And all heroes make mistakes, Mouse.
That's *so true!*
Even Batgirl made mistakes. So many mistakes!
How do you—

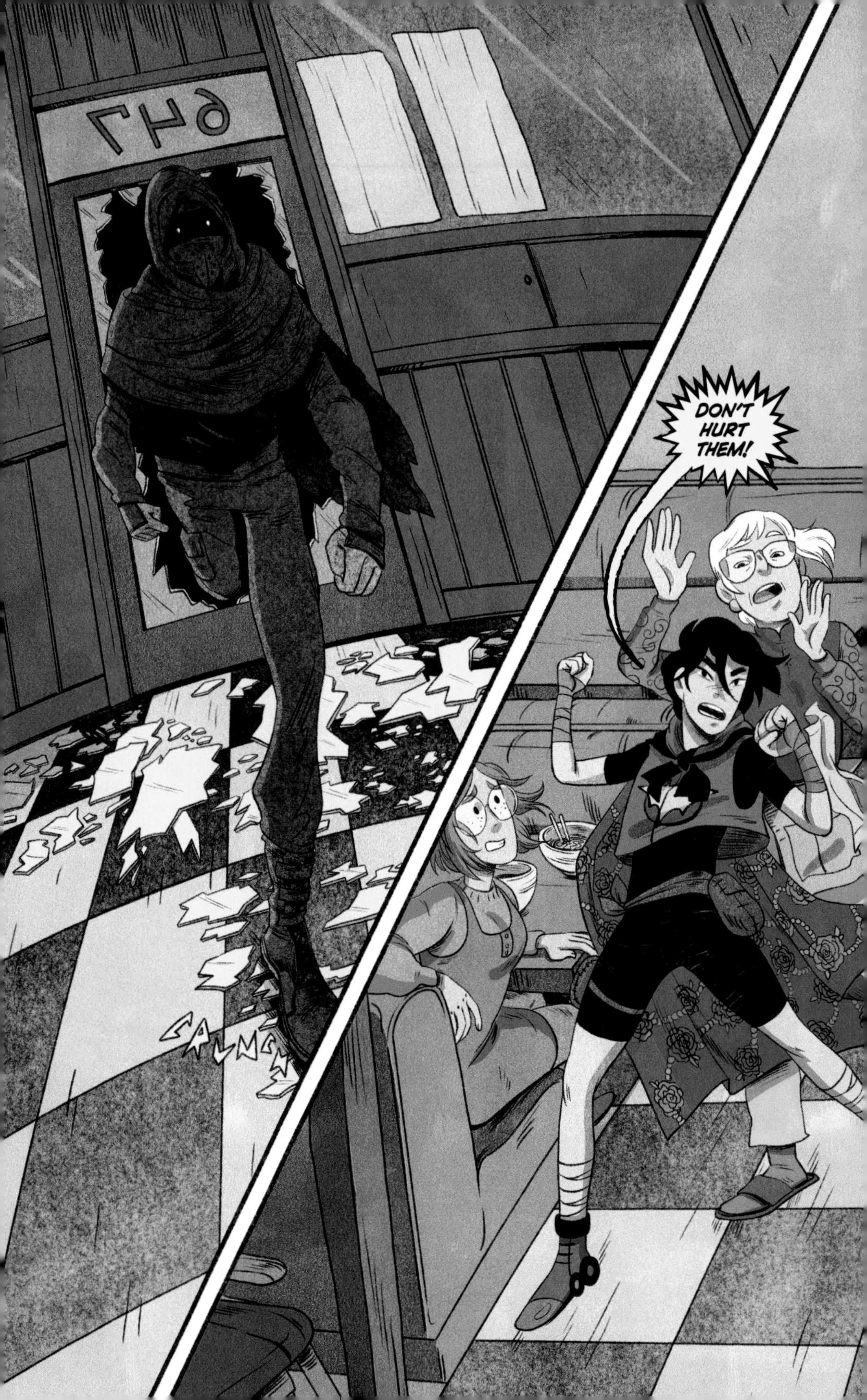
DON'T HURT THEM!

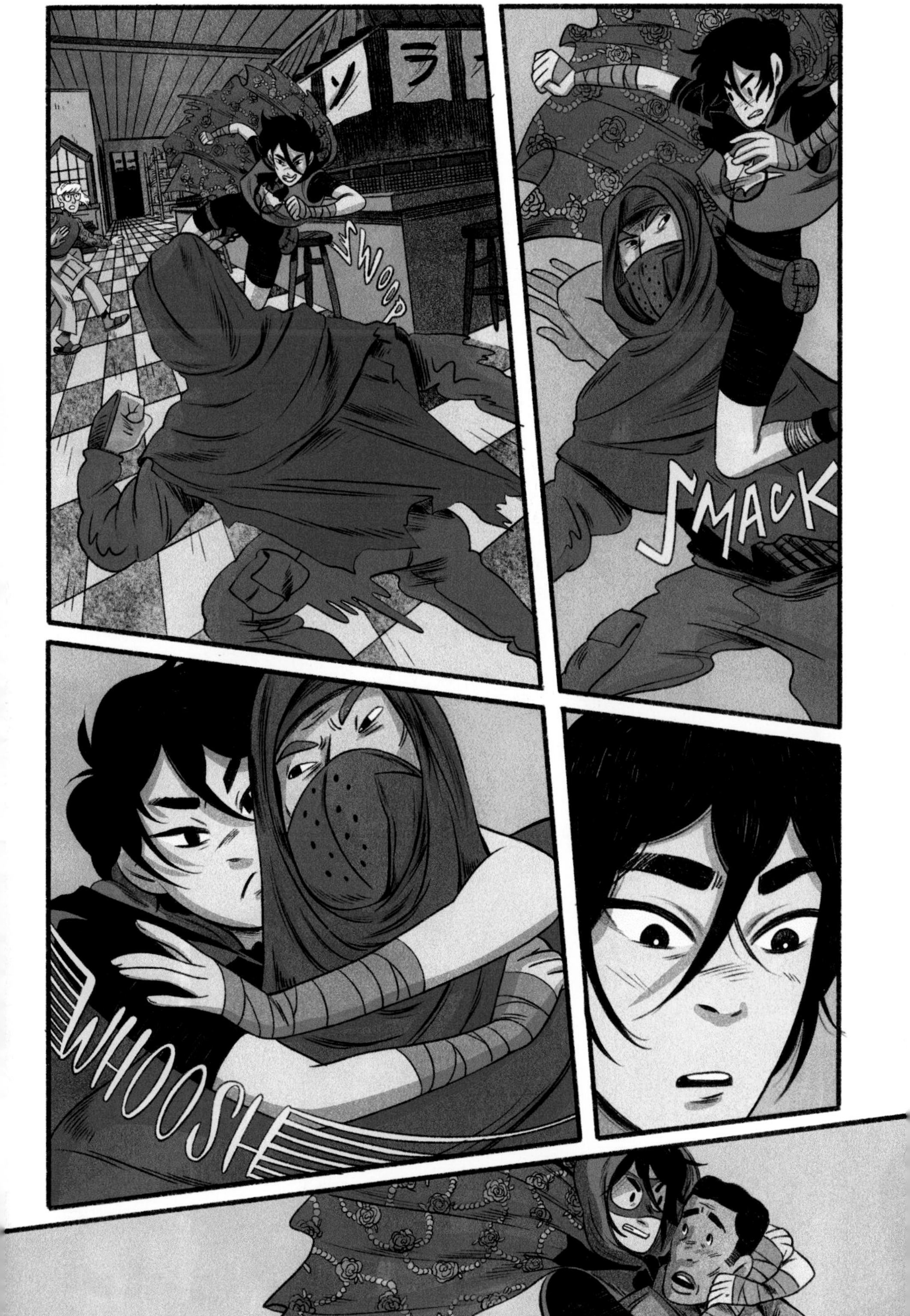
SWOOP
SMACK
WHOOSH

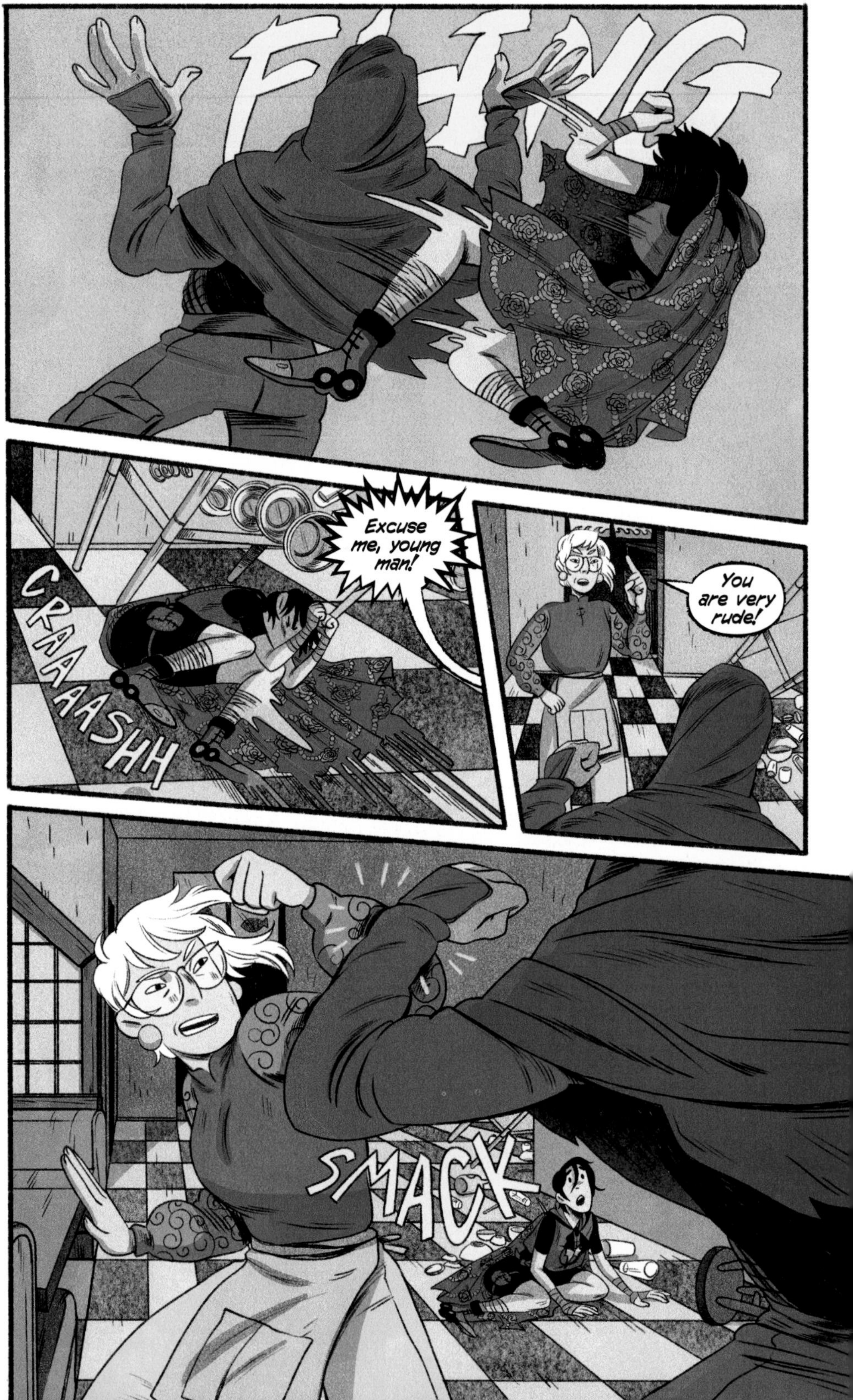
CRAAAASHH
Excuse me, young man!
You are very rude!
SMACK

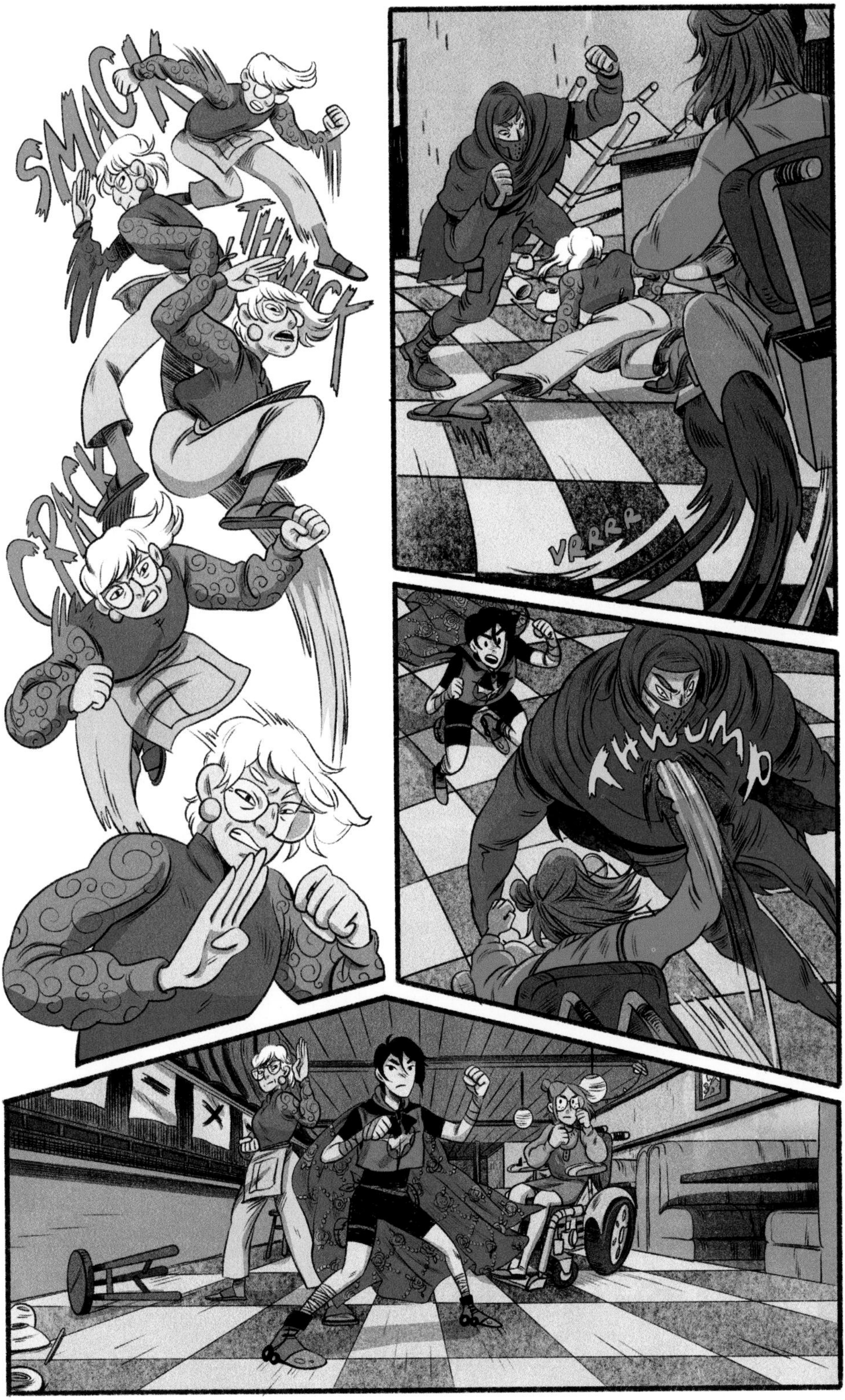
SMACK
THWACK
CRACK
VRRRR
THWUMP

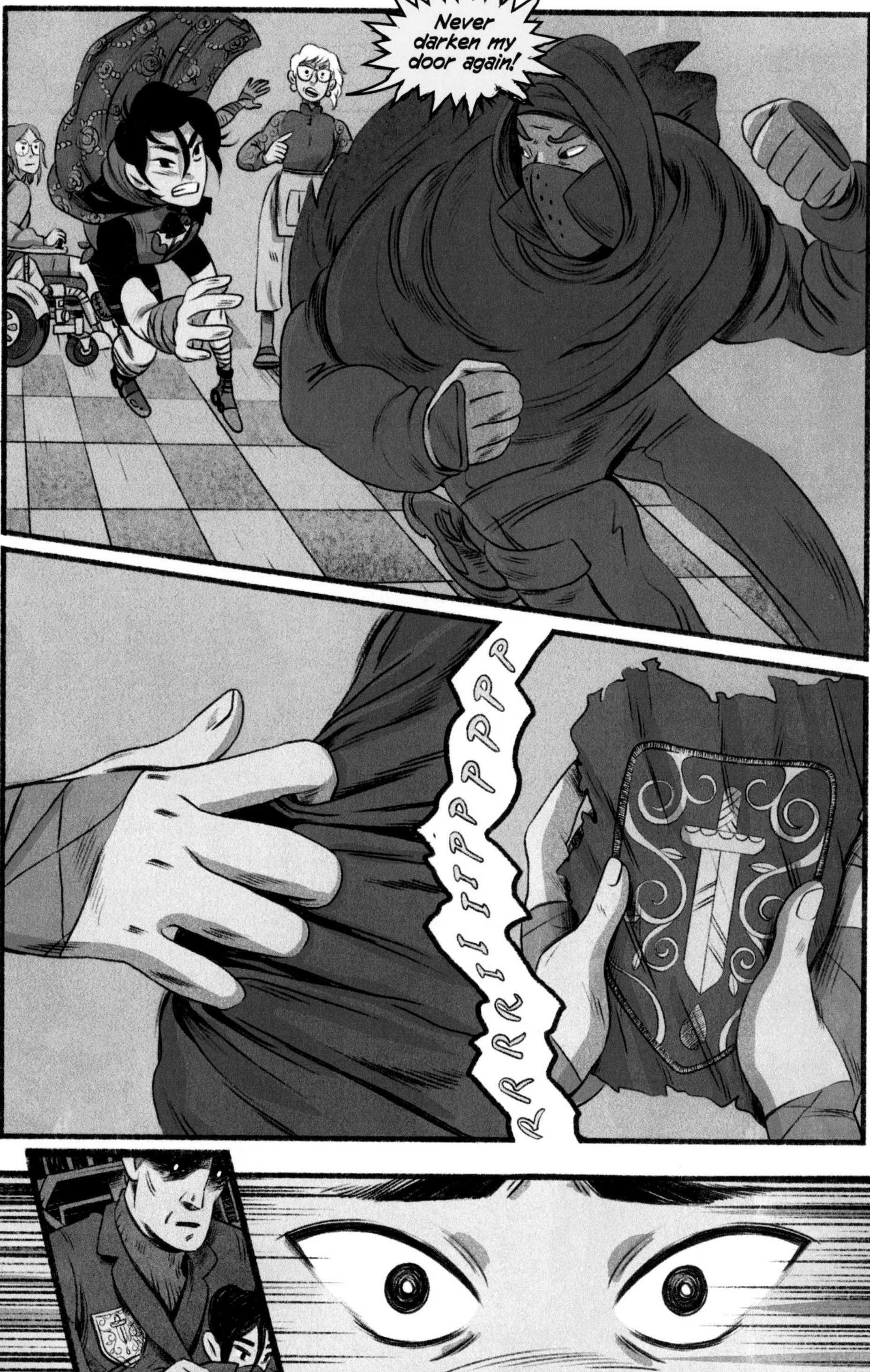
Never darken my door again!
RRRRIIIIPPPPPP

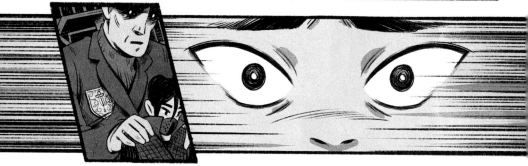

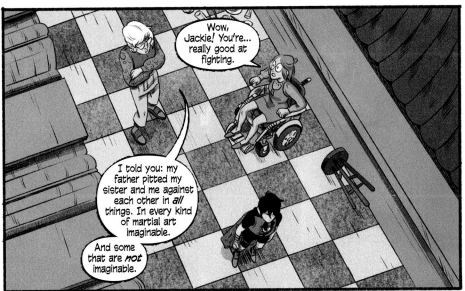

Wow, Jackie! You're... really good at fighting.

I told you: my father pitted my sister and me against each other in *all* things. In every kind of martial art imaginable.

And some that are *not* imaginable.

It was real this time...one of my father's soldiers. It wasn't in my head. I—

BEEP
BEEP
BEEP
BEEP
BEEP

Oh... wow...

What is it?

Oracle just picked up this video.

No, Cass, wait—

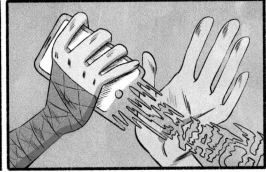

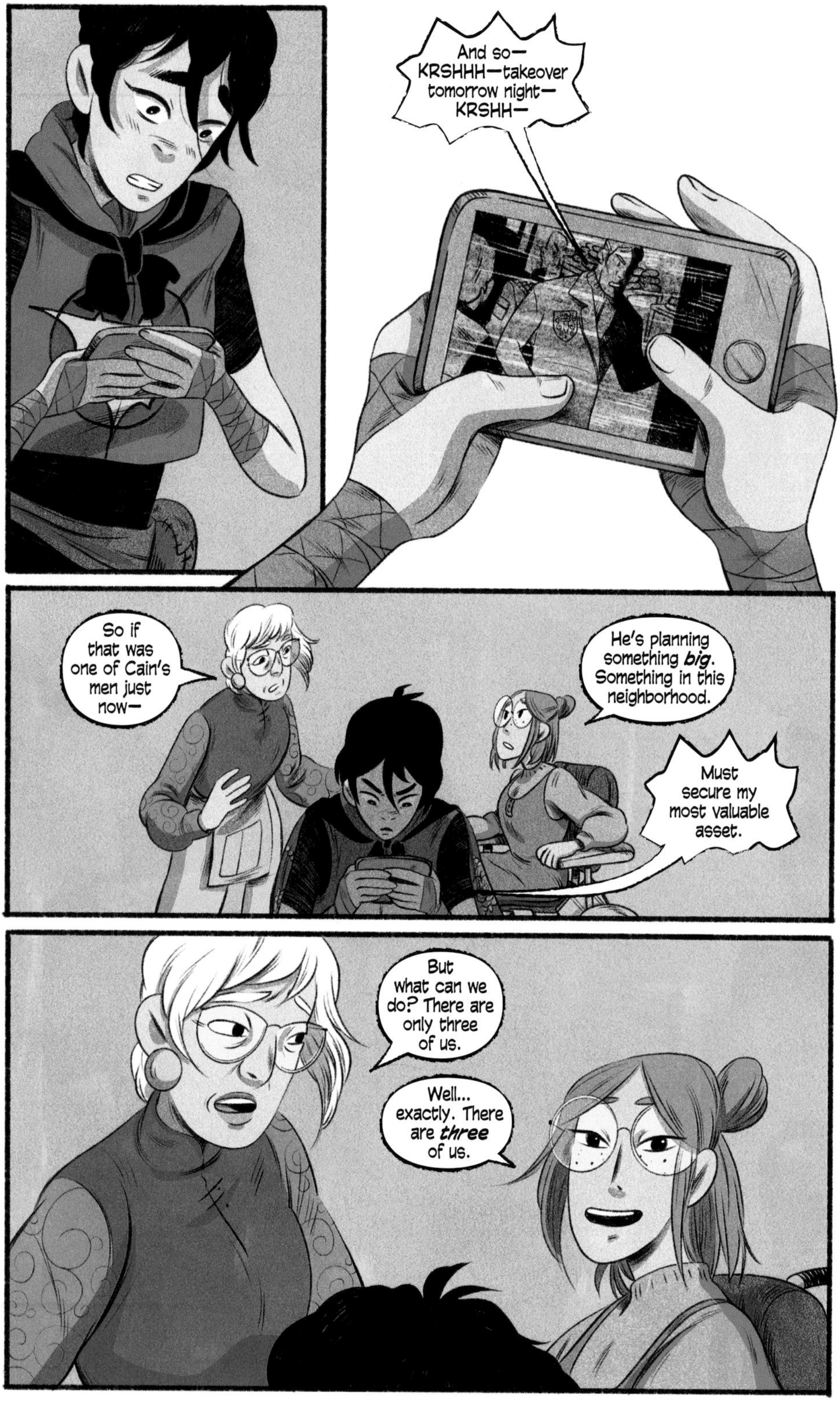
And so—KRSHHH—takeover tomorrow night—KRSHH—
So if that was one of Cain's men just now—
He's planning something *big*. Something in this neighborhood.
Must secure my most valuable asset.
But what can we do? There are only three of us.
Well... exactly. There are *three* of us.

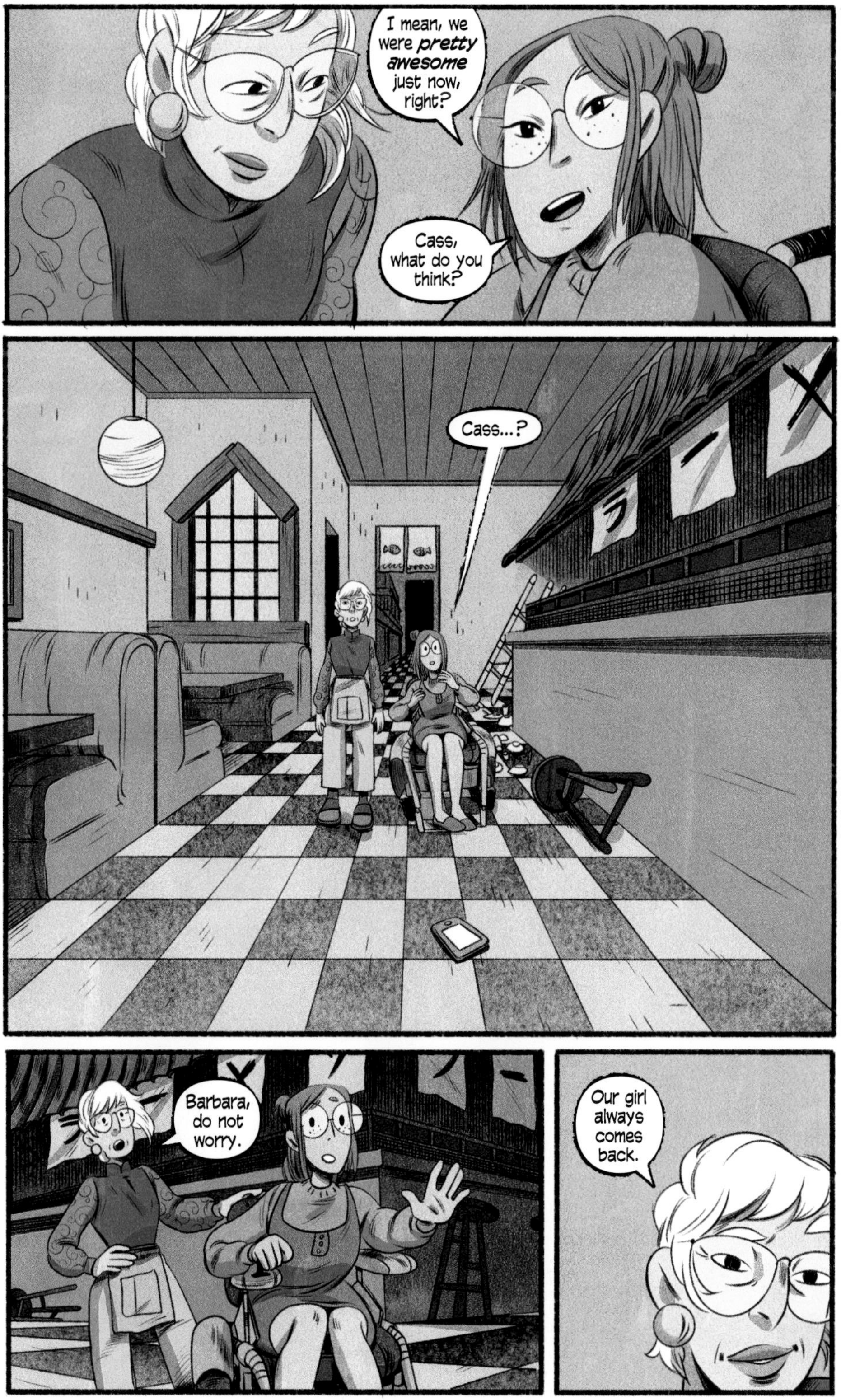
I mean, we were **pretty awesome** just now, right?
Cass, what do you think?
Cass...?
Barbara, do not worry.
Our girl always comes back.

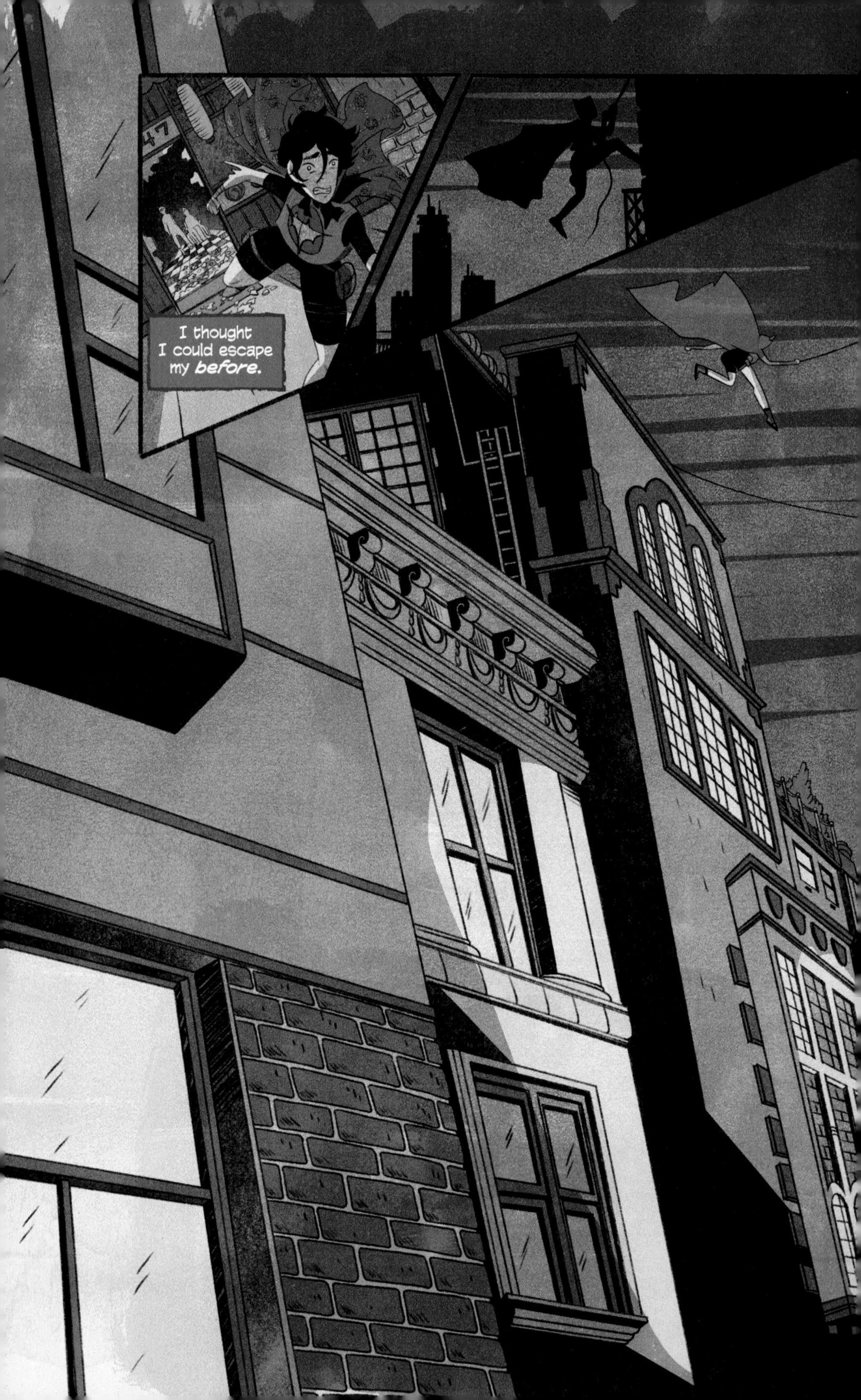
I thought I could escape my *before*.

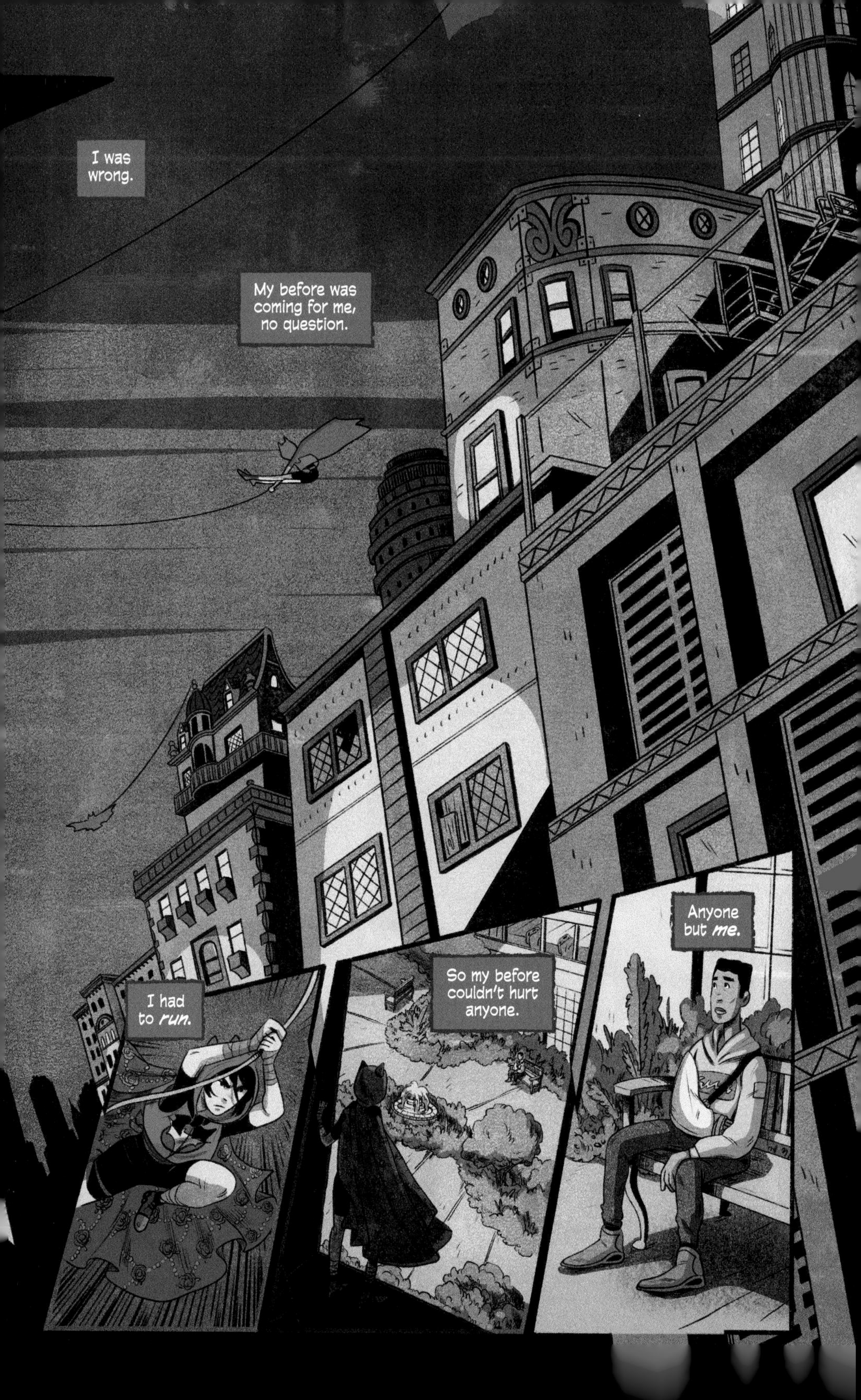

I was wrong.
My before was coming for me, no question.
I had to *run*.
So my before couldn't hurt anyone.
Anyone but *me*.

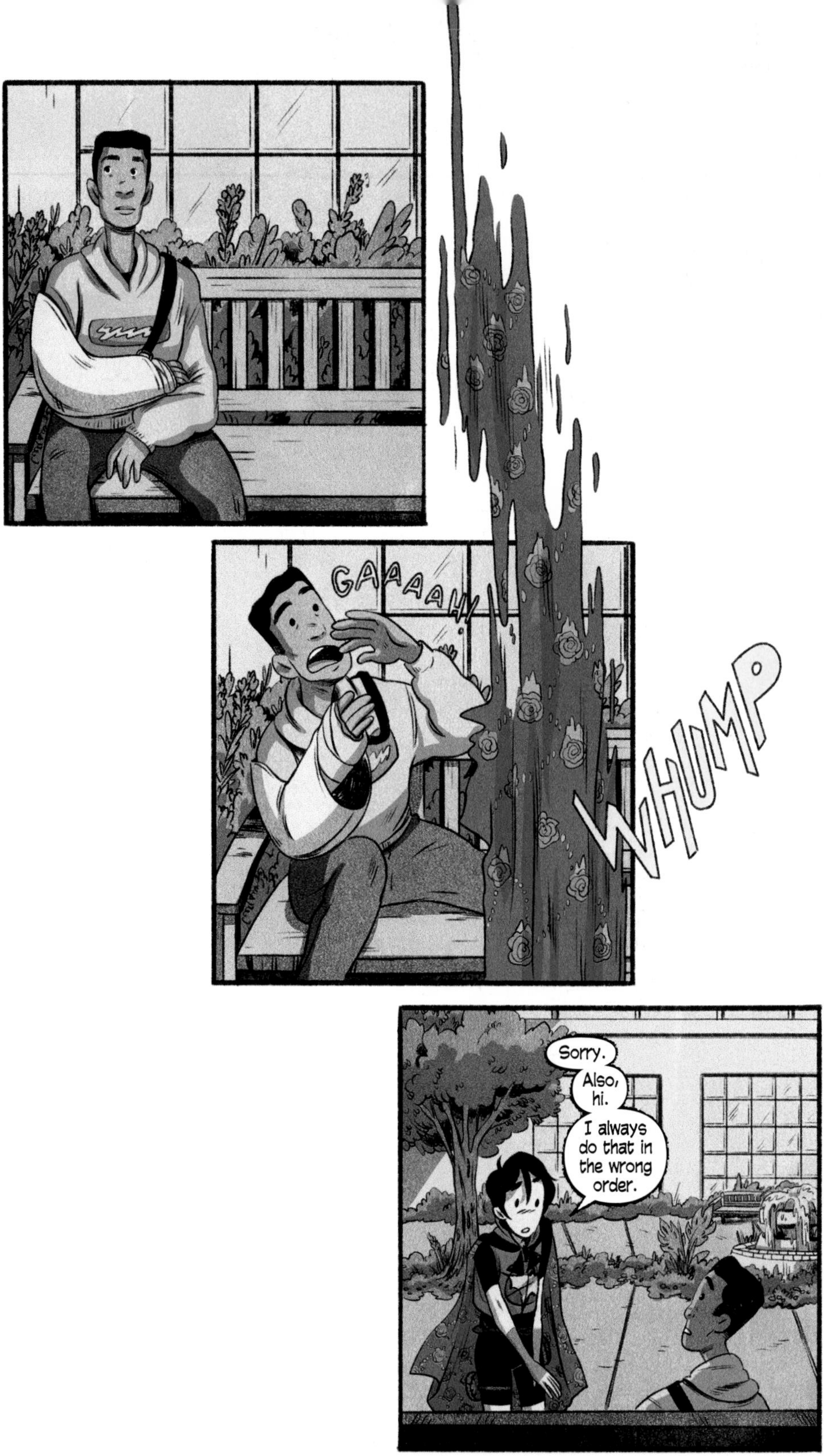
GAAAAAH!
WHUMP
Sorry.
Also, hi.
I always do that in the wrong order.

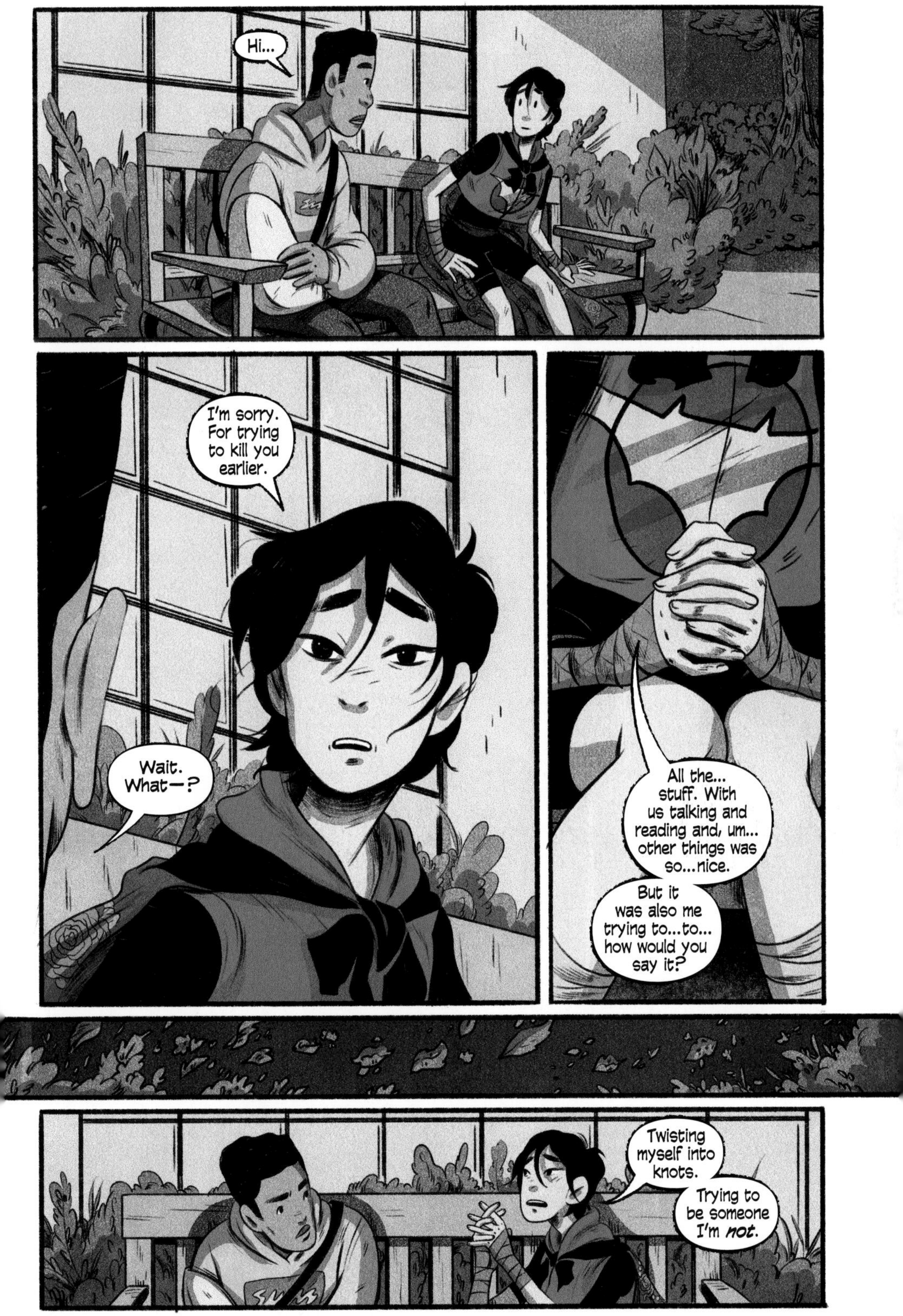
Hi...
I'm sorry. For trying to kill you earlier.
Wait. What—?
All the... stuff. With us talking and reading and, um... other things was so...nice.
But it was also me trying to...to... how would you say it?
Twisting myself into knots.
Trying to be someone I'm *not*.

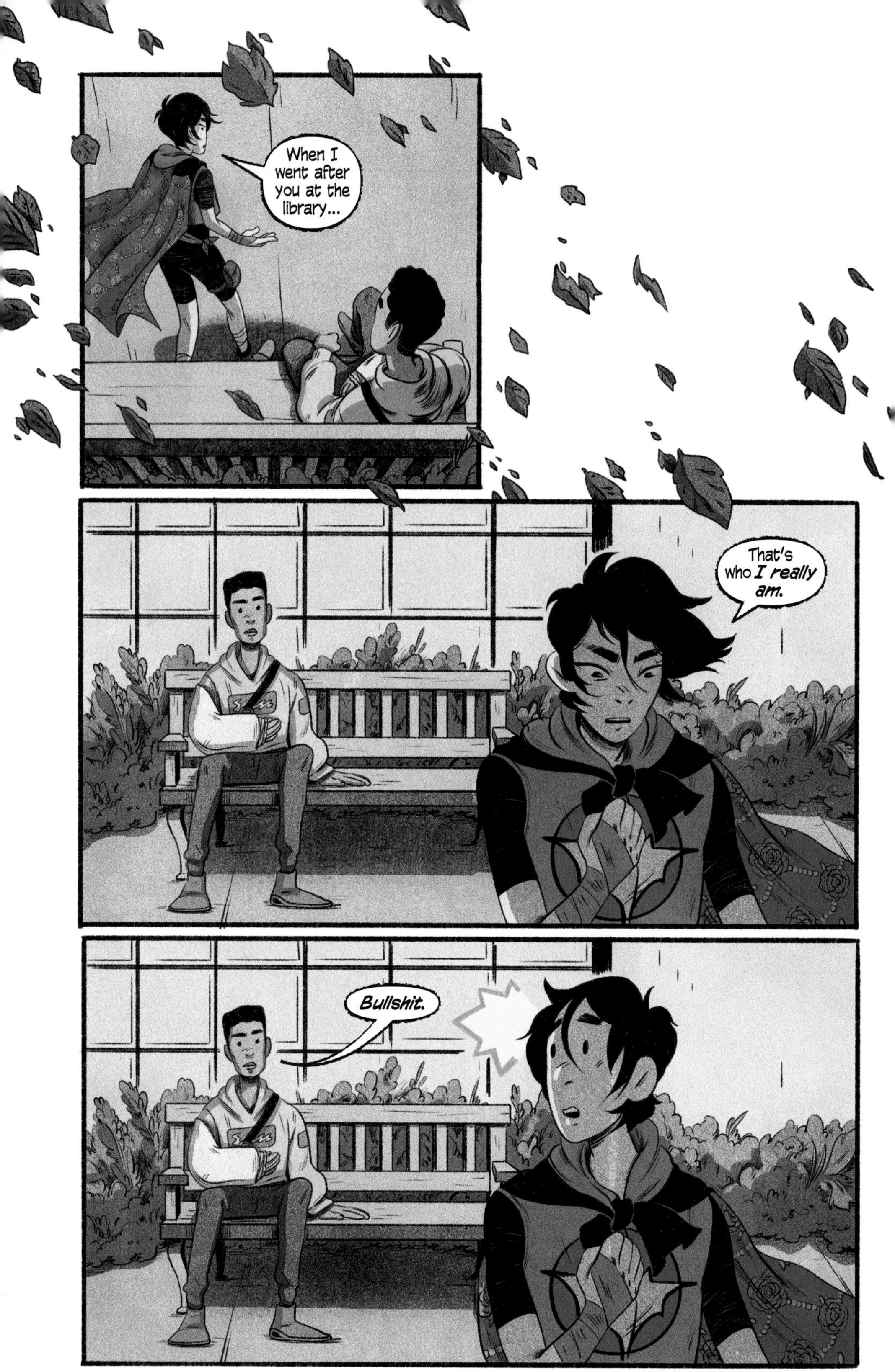

When I went after you at the library...
That's who I really am.
Bullshit.

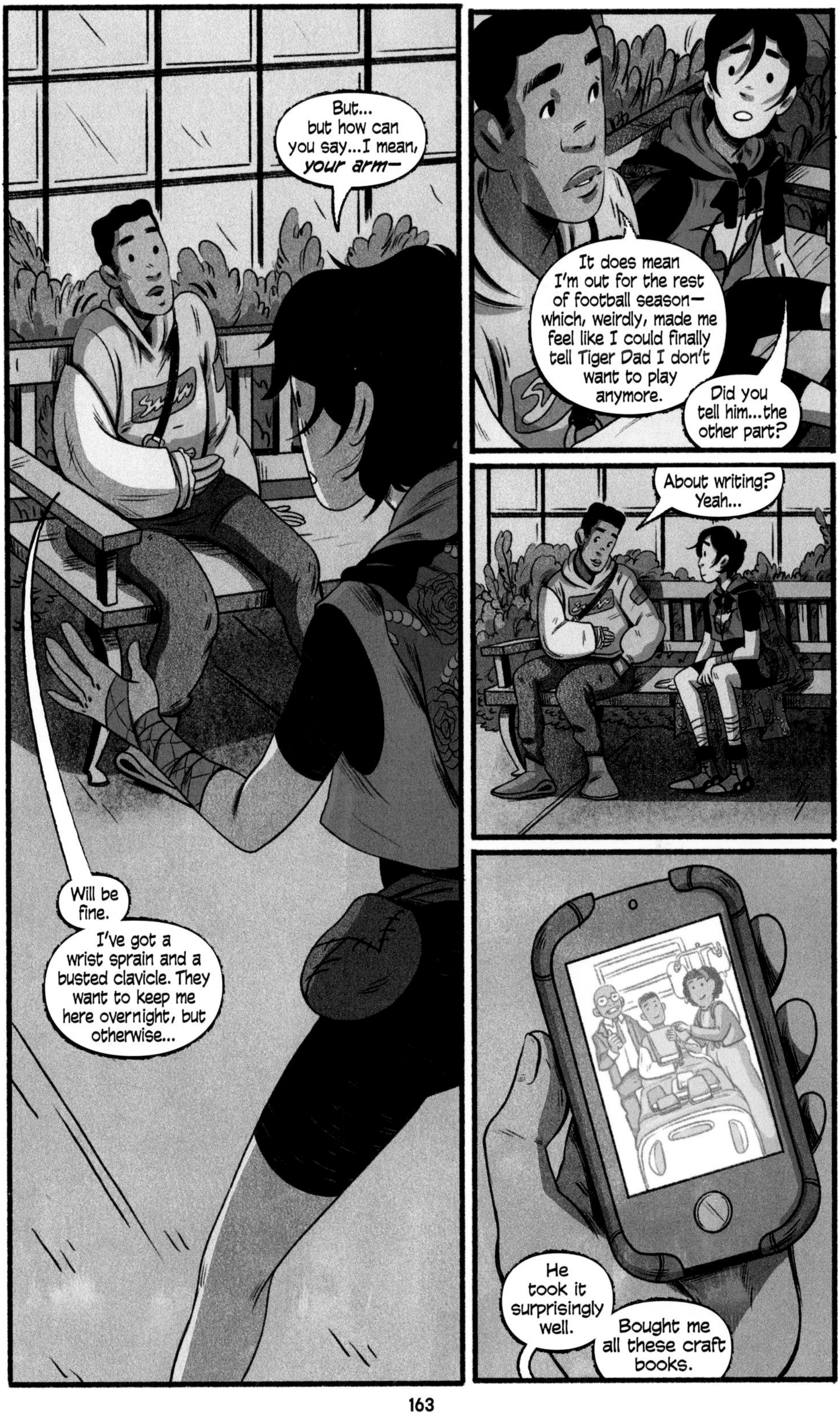
But... but how can you say...I mean, *your arm*—
Will be fine.
I've got a wrist sprain and a busted clavicle. They want to keep me here overnight, but otherwise...
It does mean I'm out for the rest of football season—which, weirdly, made me feel like I could finally tell Tiger Dad I don't want to play anymore.
Did you tell him...the other part?
About writing? Yeah...
He took it surprisingly well.
Bought me all these craft books.

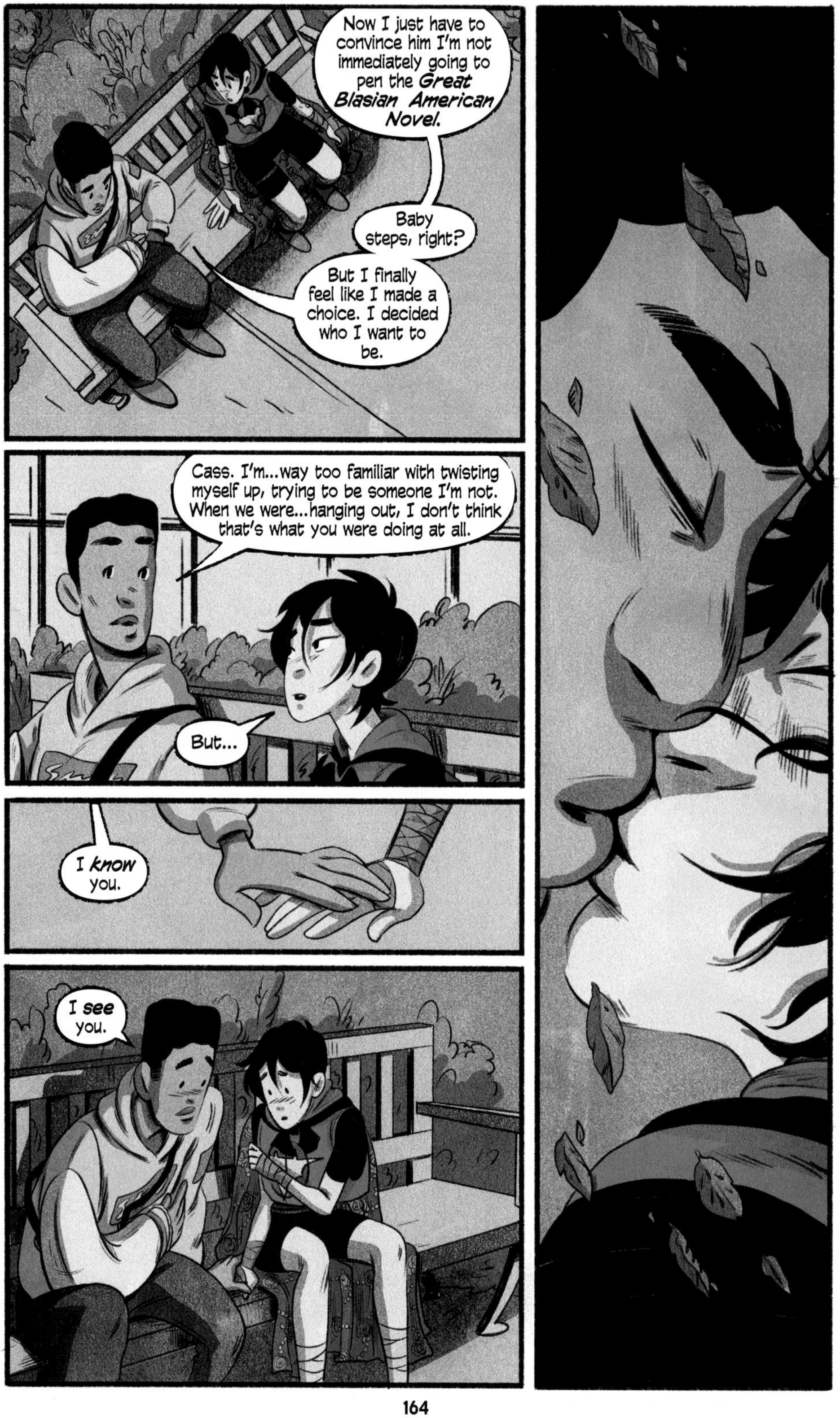
Now I just have to convince him I'm not immediately going to pen the *Great Blasian American Novel.*
Baby steps, right?
But I finally feel like I made a choice. I decided who I want to be.
Cass. I'm...way too familiar with twisting myself up, trying to be someone I'm not. When we were...hanging out, I don't think that's what you were doing at all.
But...
I *know* you.
I *see* you.

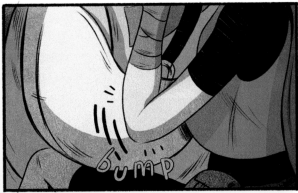

bump

OW!

I'm sorry... I shouldn't have...I have to go.

Cass...

I actually just wanted to say good-bye.

Just...please remember who you *really are!*

That's what I'm doing.

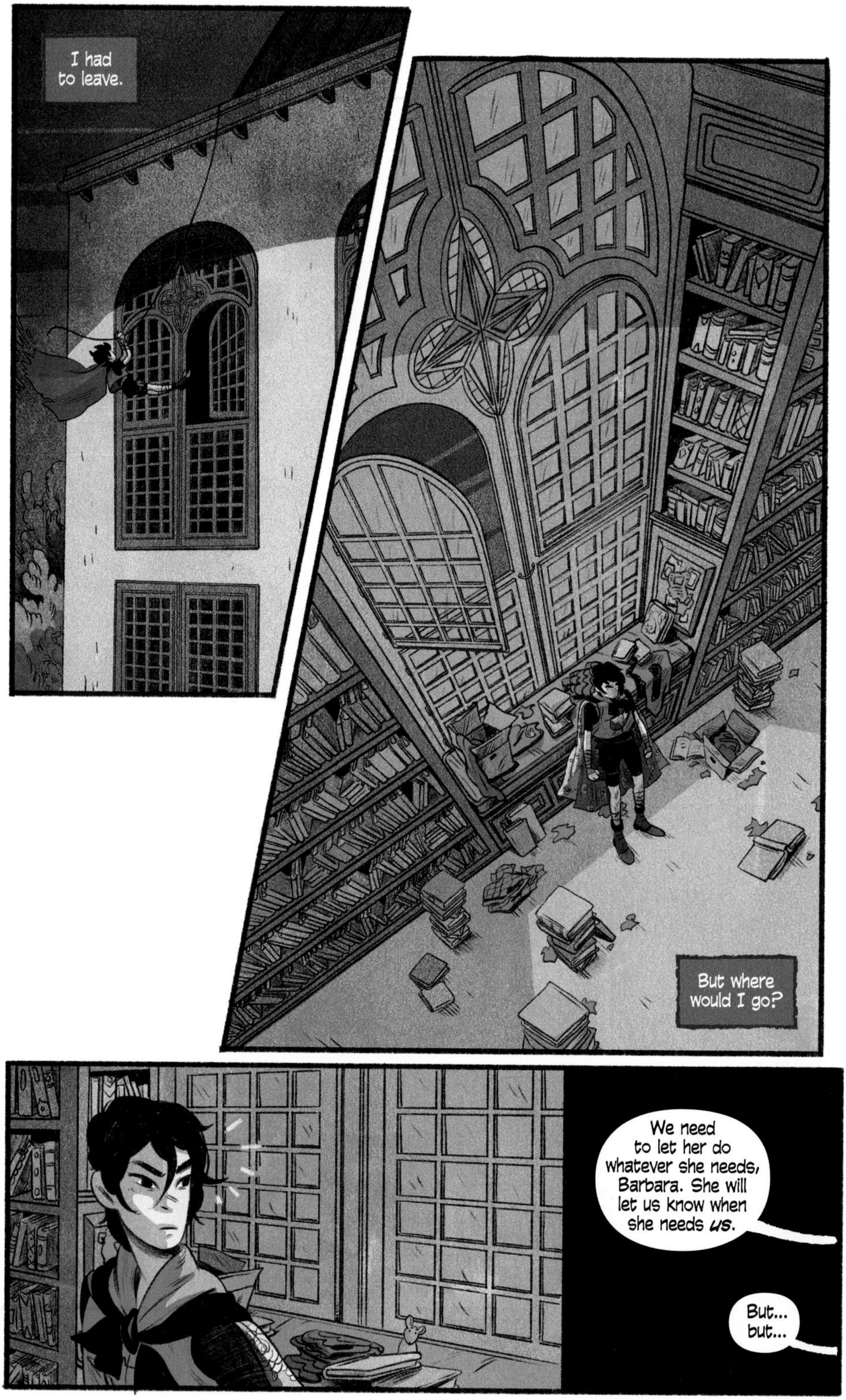
I had to leave.
But where would I go?
We need to let her do whatever she needs, Barbara. She will let us know when she needs *us*.
But... but...

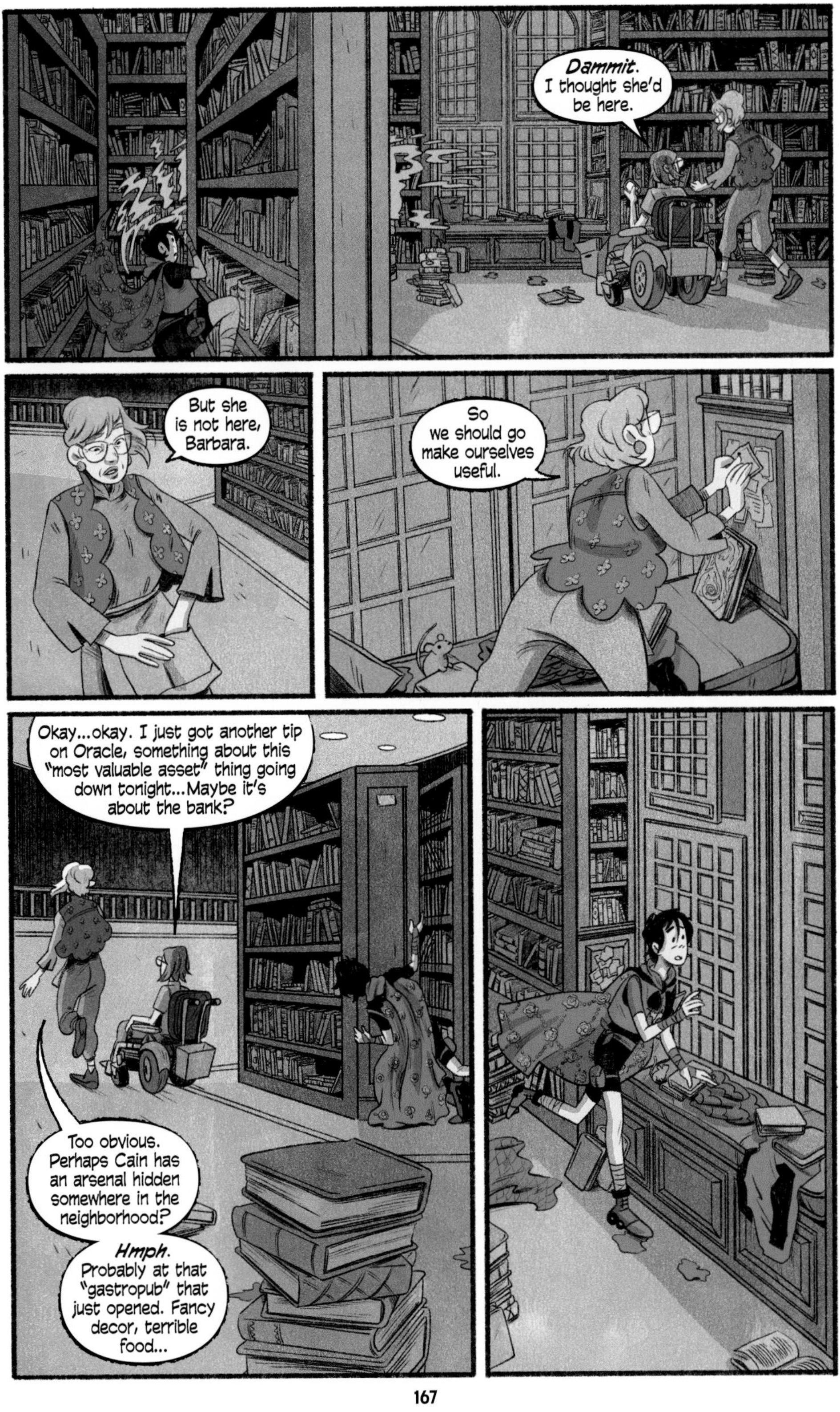
Dammit. I thought she'd be here.
But she is not here, Barbara.
So we should go make ourselves useful.
Okay...okay. I just got another tip on Oracle, something about this "most valuable asset" thing going down tonight...Maybe it's about the bank?
Too obvious. Perhaps Cain has an arsenal hidden somewhere in the neighborhood?
Hmph. Probably at that "gastropub" that just opened. Fancy decor, terrible food...

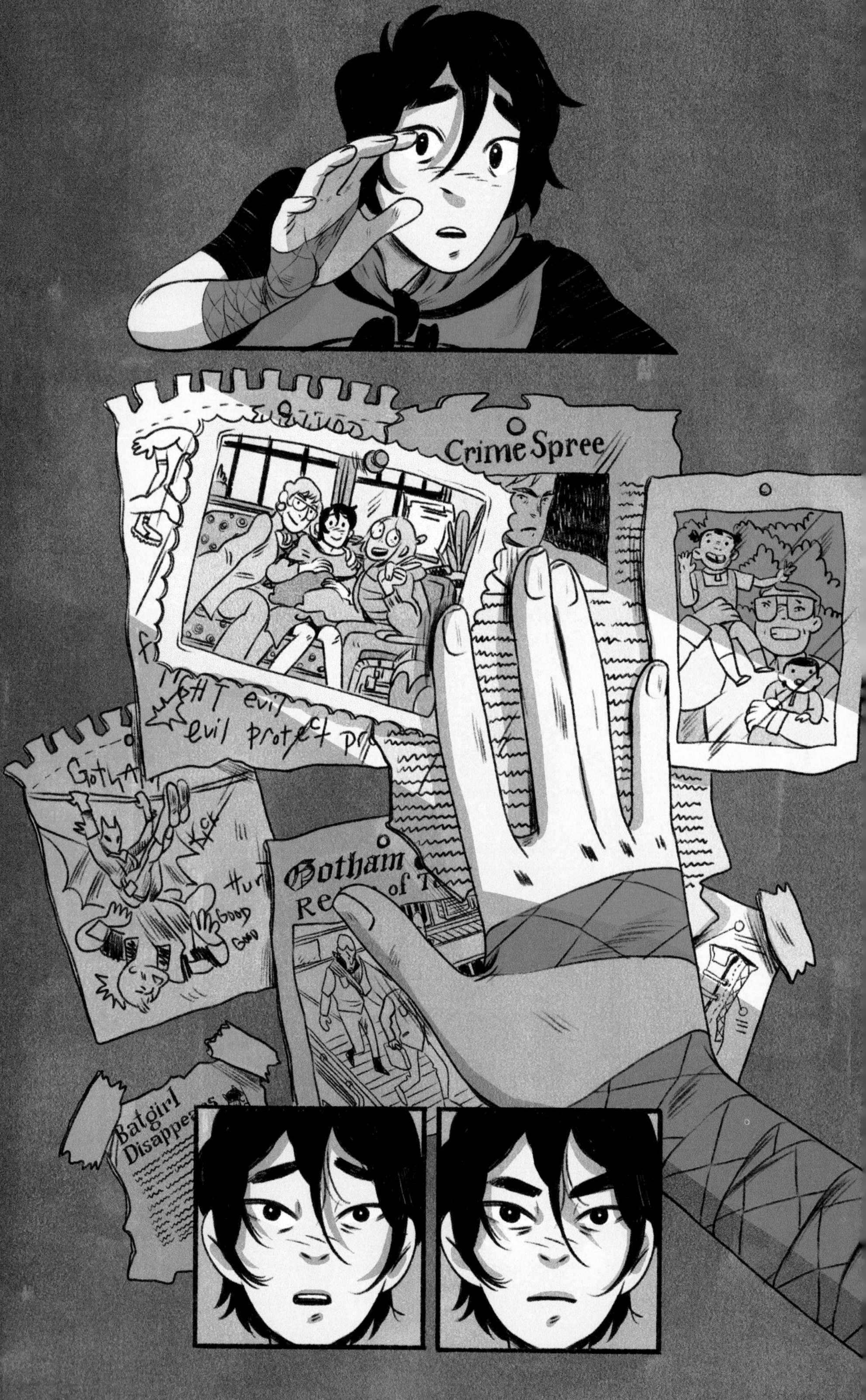
Crime Spree
evil
evil protect
Gotham
Kick
Hurt
GOOD
GOOD
Gotham
Batgirl

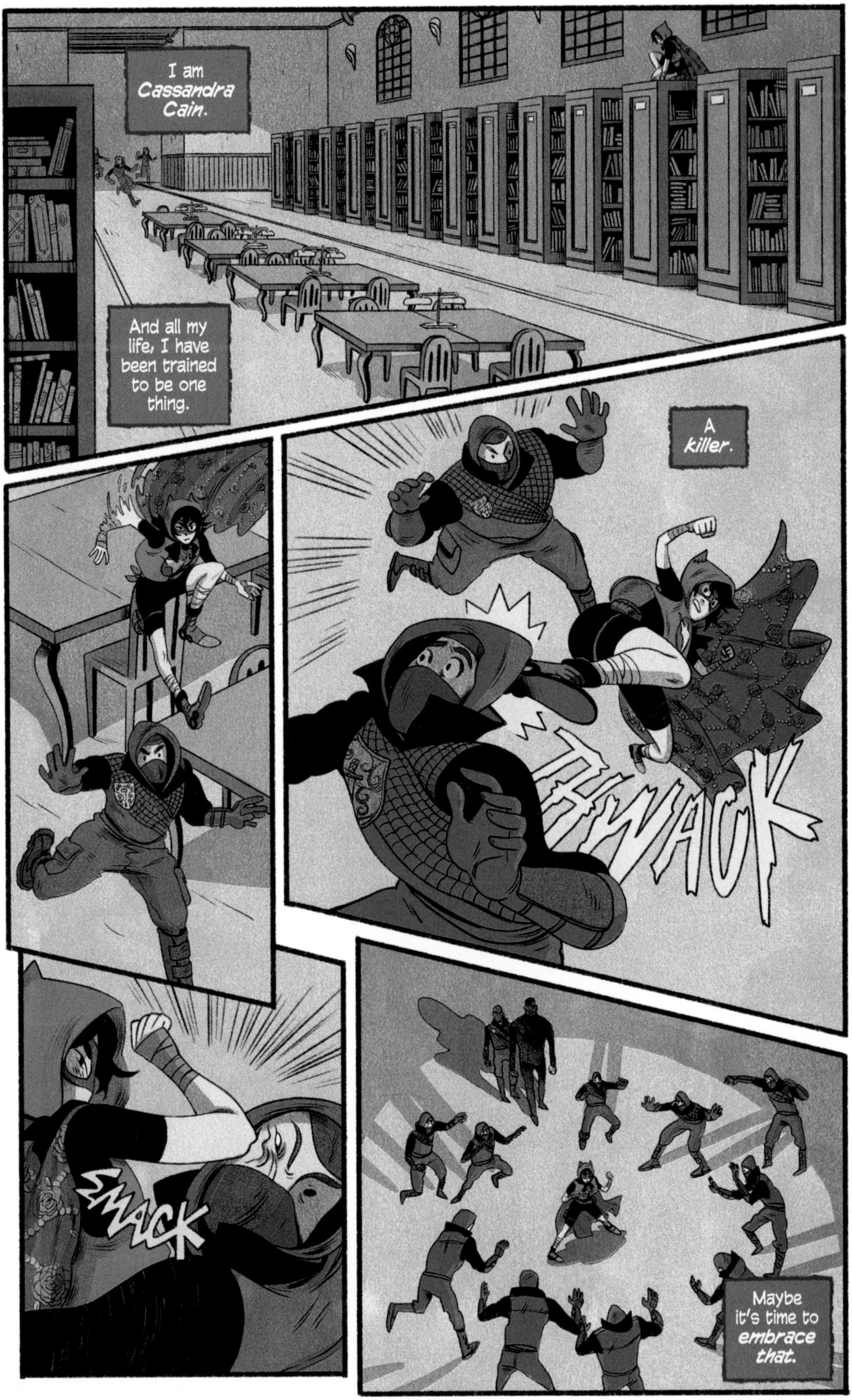
I am *Cassandra Cain.*
And all my life, I have been trained to be one thing.
A *killer.*
THWACK
SMACK
Maybe it's time to *embrace that.*

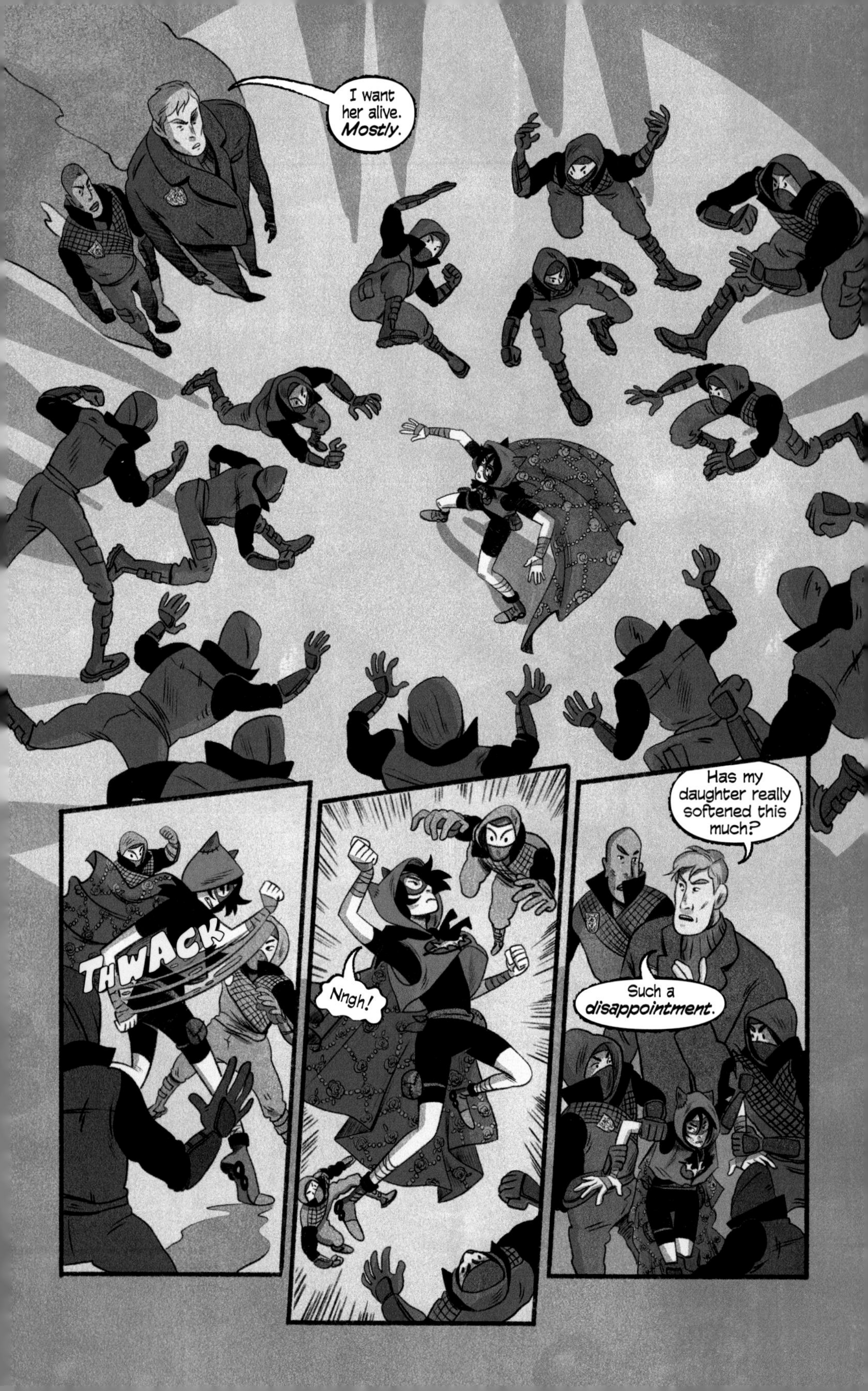
I want her alive. *Mostly*.
THWACK
Nngh!
Has my daughter really softened this much?
Such a *disappointment*.

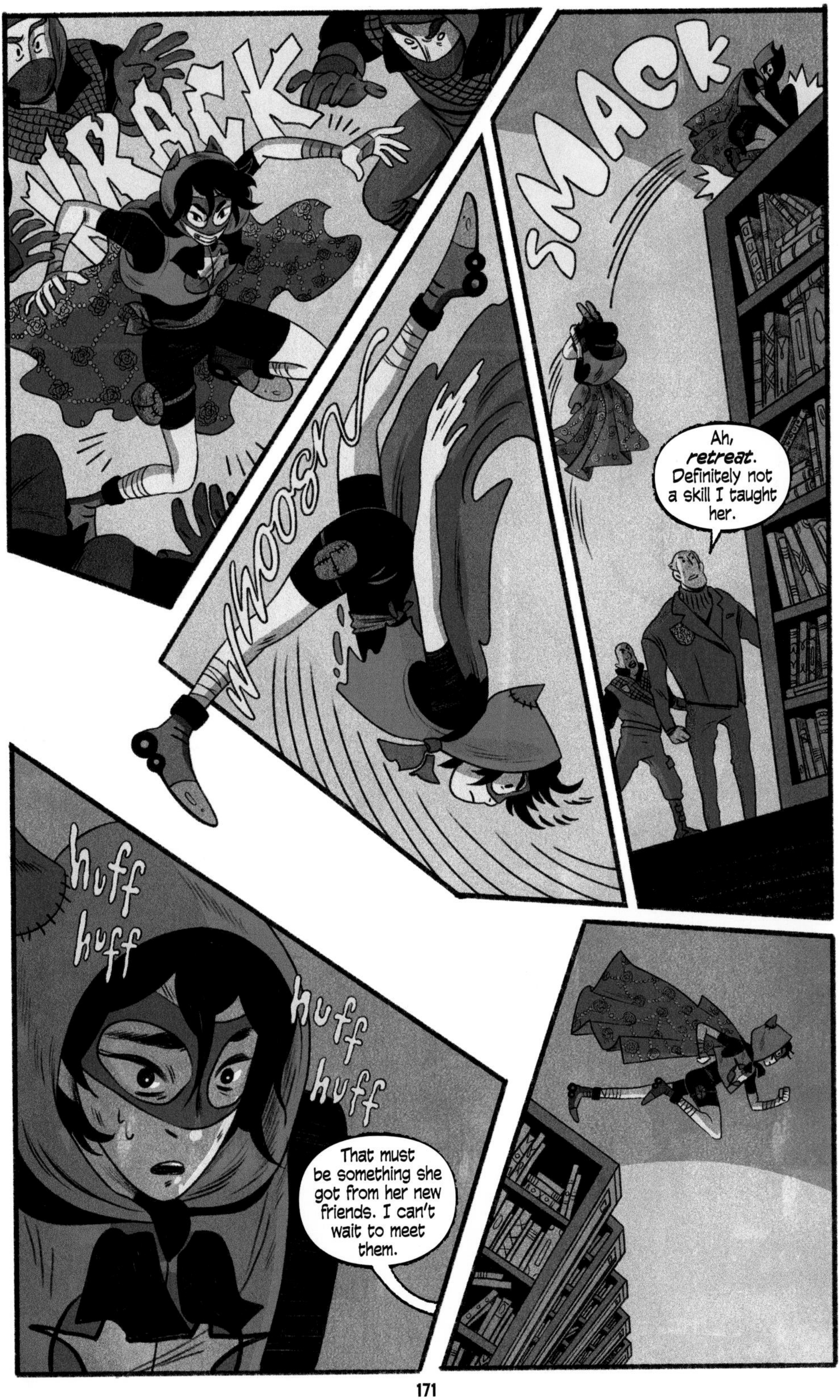
KRACK
whoosh
SMACK
Ah, *retreat*. Definitely not a skill I taught her.
huff huff
huff huff
That must be something she got from her new friends. I can't wait to meet them.

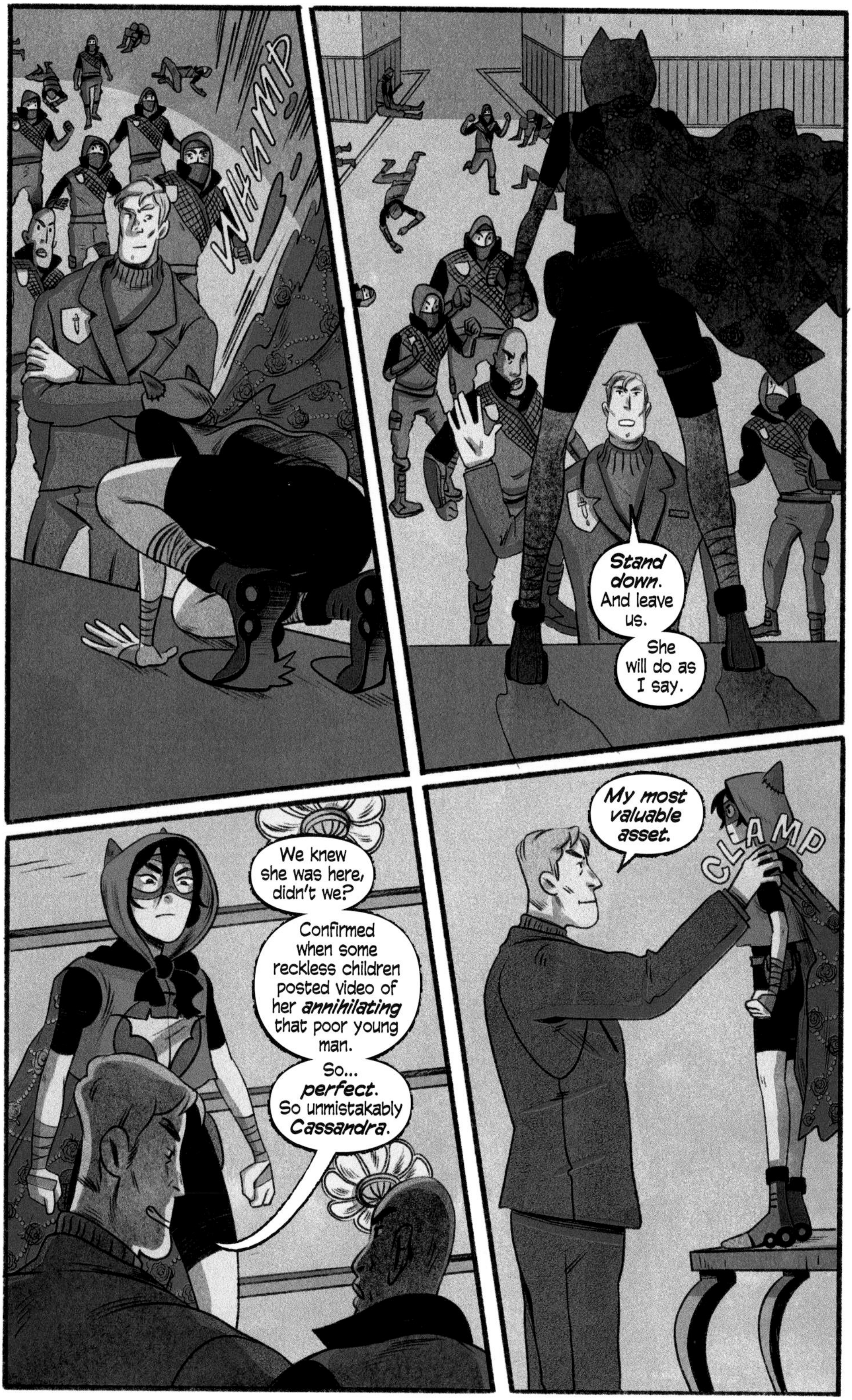
WHUMP
Stand down. And leave us.
She will do as I say.
We knew she was here, didn't we?
Confirmed when some reckless children posted video of her annihilating that poor young man.
So... perfect. So unmistakably Cassandra.
My most valuable asset.
CLAMP

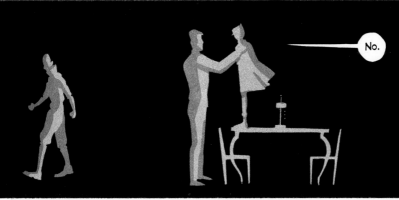

No.

You... you talk now?

Well, that's... *endearing.* As is this little outfit.

You must know, Cassandra: You can talk. You can put on a costume. But no matter what...

CLENCH

You're still *mine.*

NO!

173

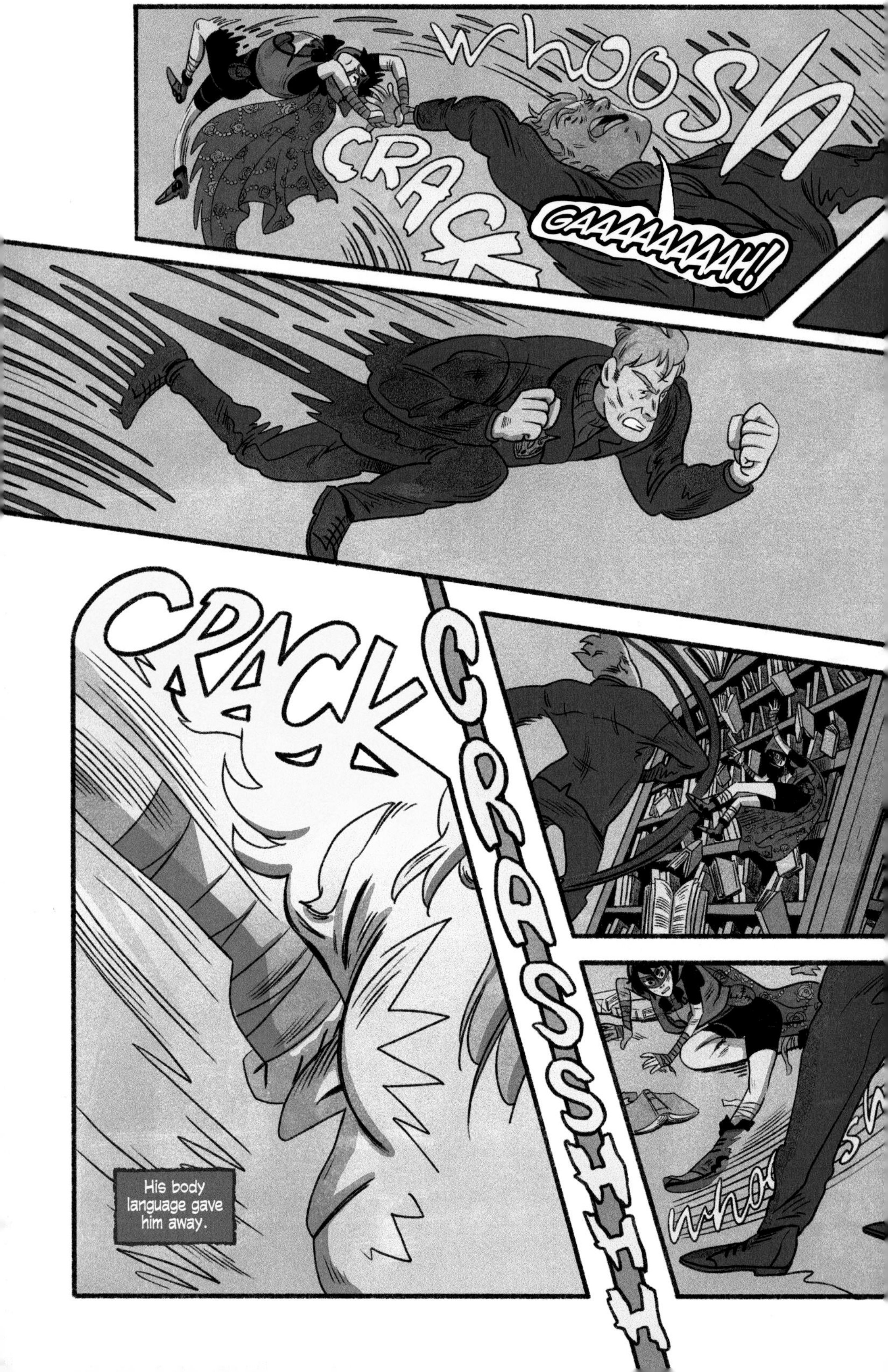
WHOOSH
CRACK
GAAAAAAAH!
CRACK
CRASSHHH
His body language gave him away.

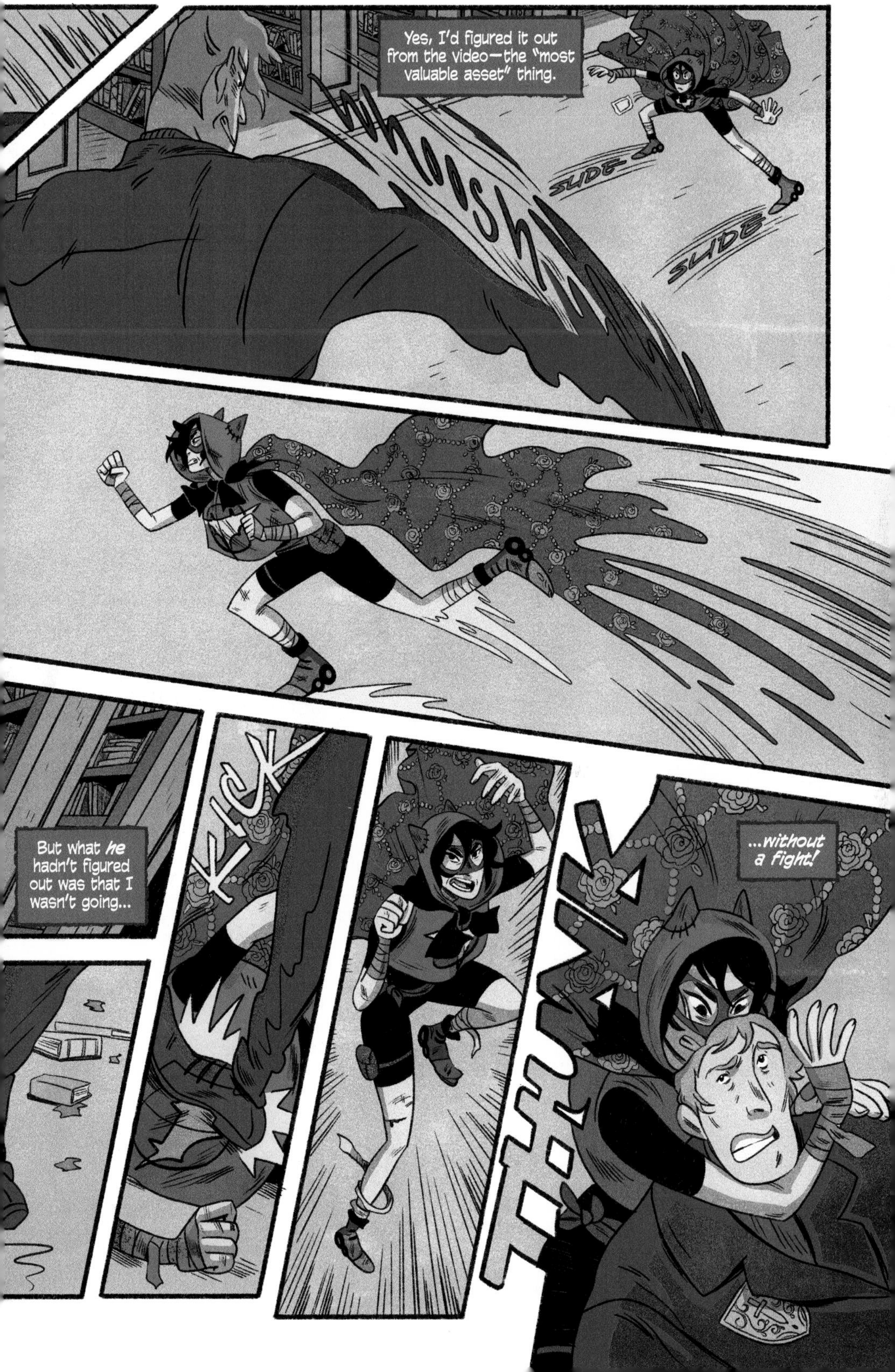
Yes, I'd figured it out from the video—the "most valuable asset" thing.
WHOOSH
SLIDE
SLIDE
KICK
But what *he* hadn't figured out was that I wasn't going...
...*without a fight!*
THWIP

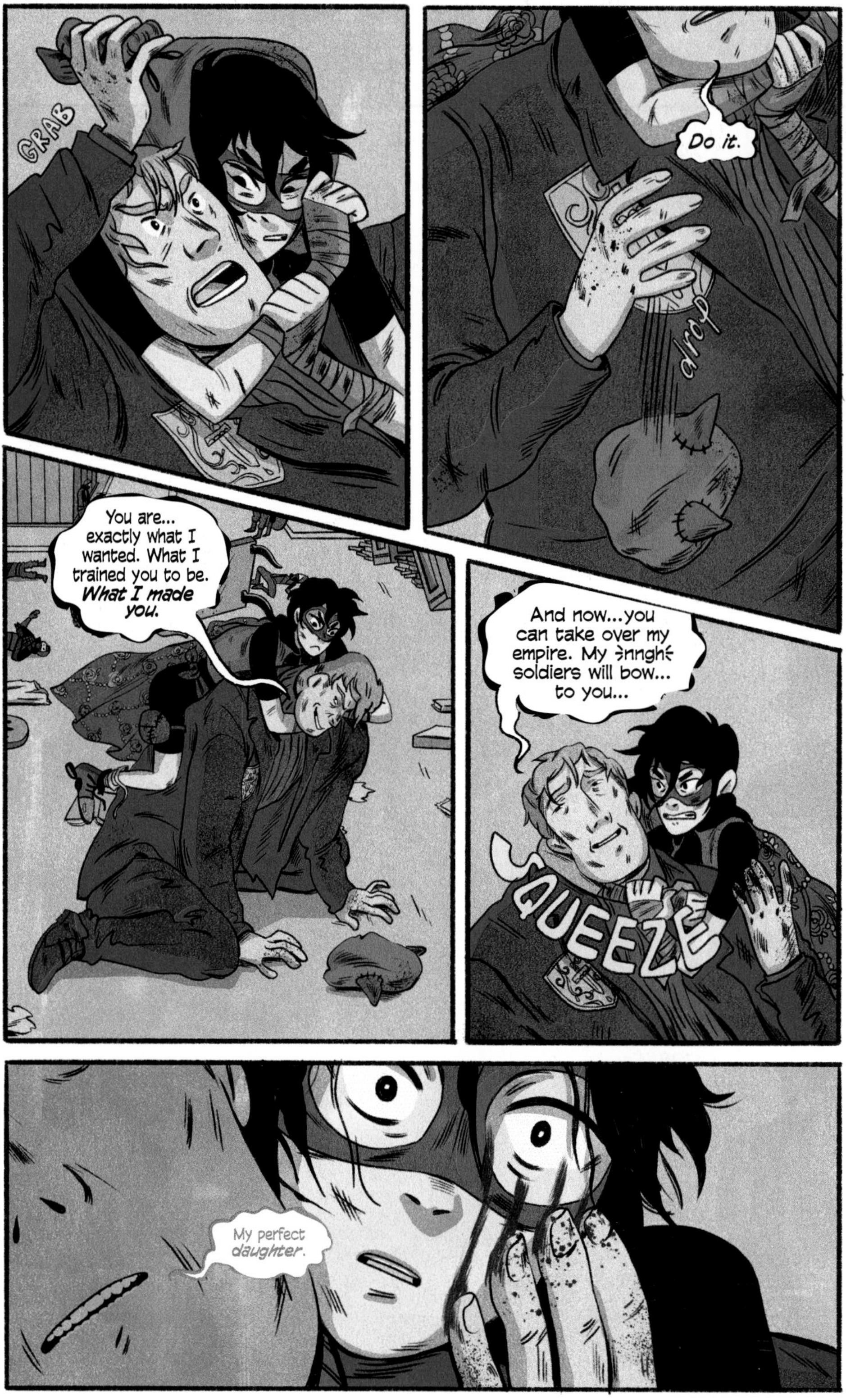
GRAB
Do it.
drop
You are... exactly what I wanted. What I trained you to be. *What I made you.*
And now...you can take over my empire. My ⫶nngh⫶ soldiers will bow... to you...
SQUEEZE
My perfect *daughter*.

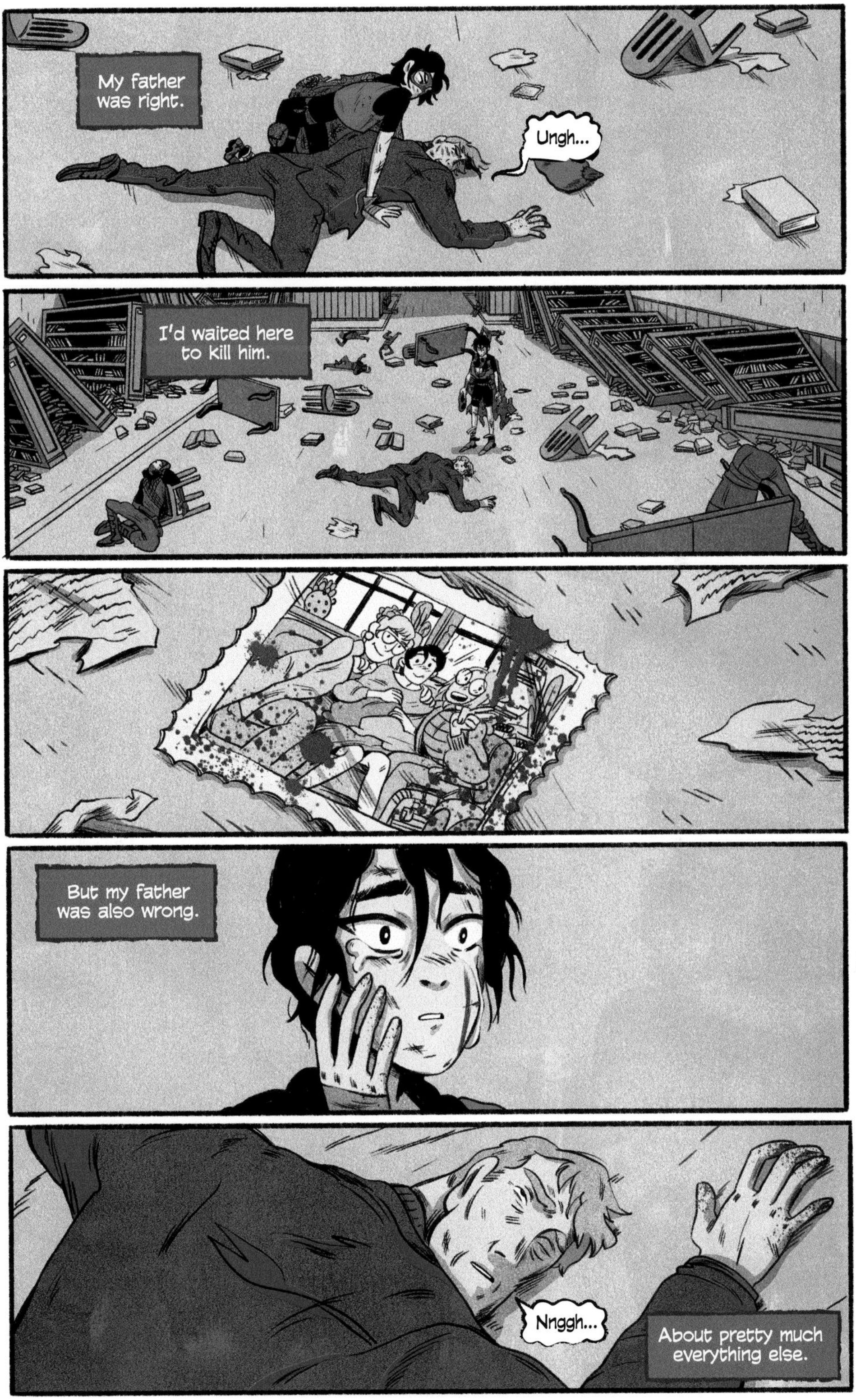
My father was right.
Ungh...
I'd waited here to kill him.
But my father was also wrong.
Nnggh...
About pretty much everything else.

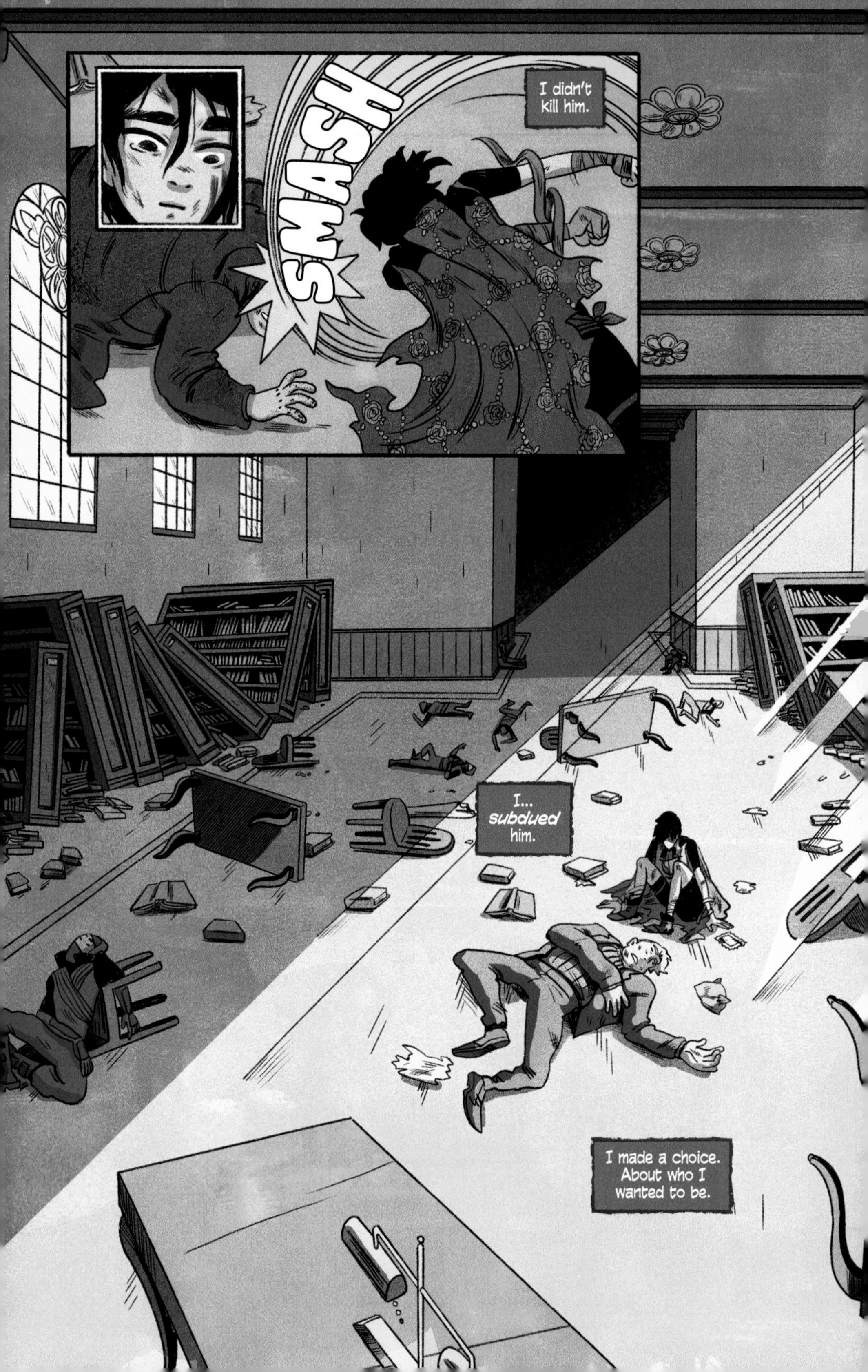
SMASH
I didn't kill him.
I... *subdued* him.
I made a choice. About who I wanted to be.

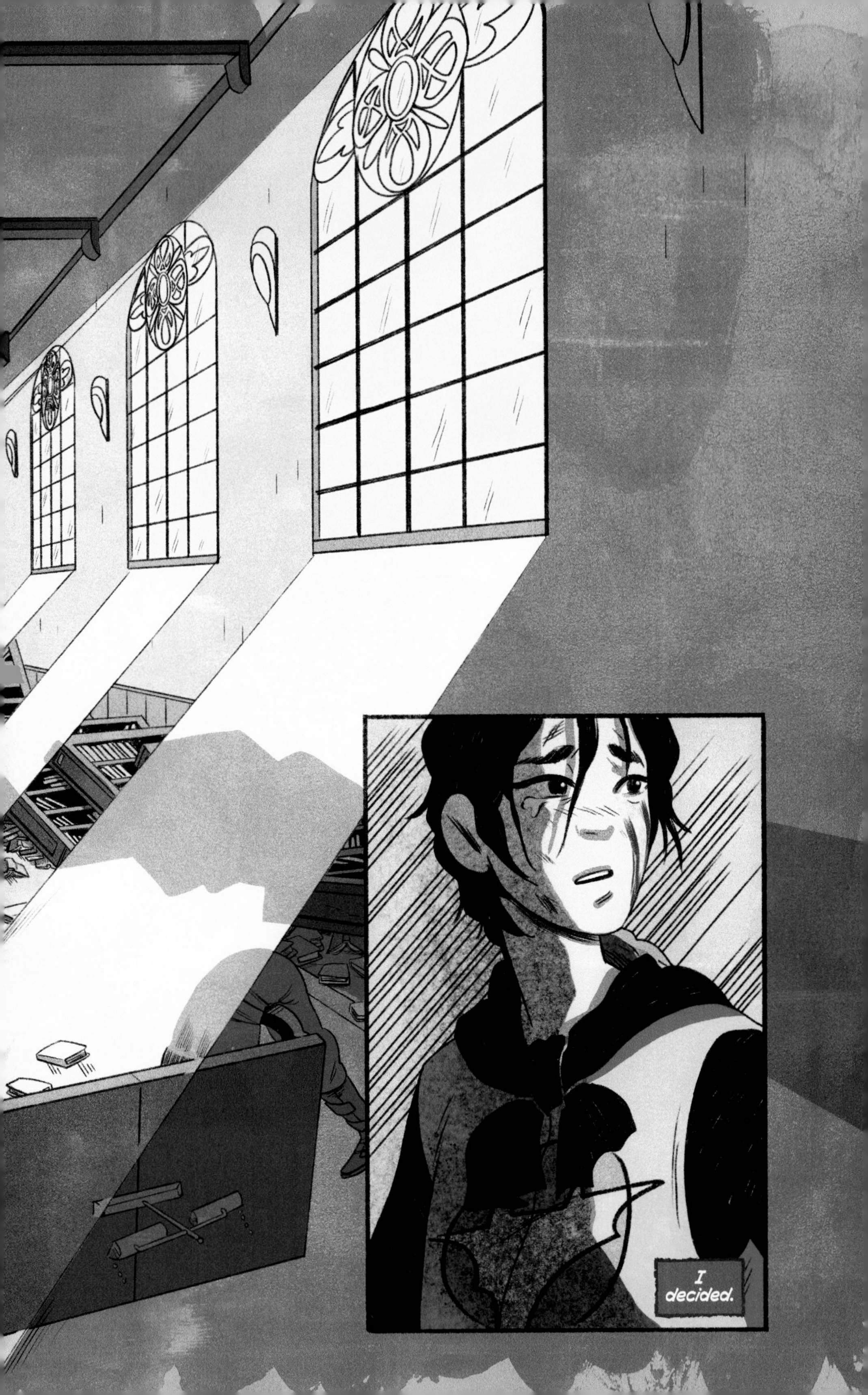
I decided.

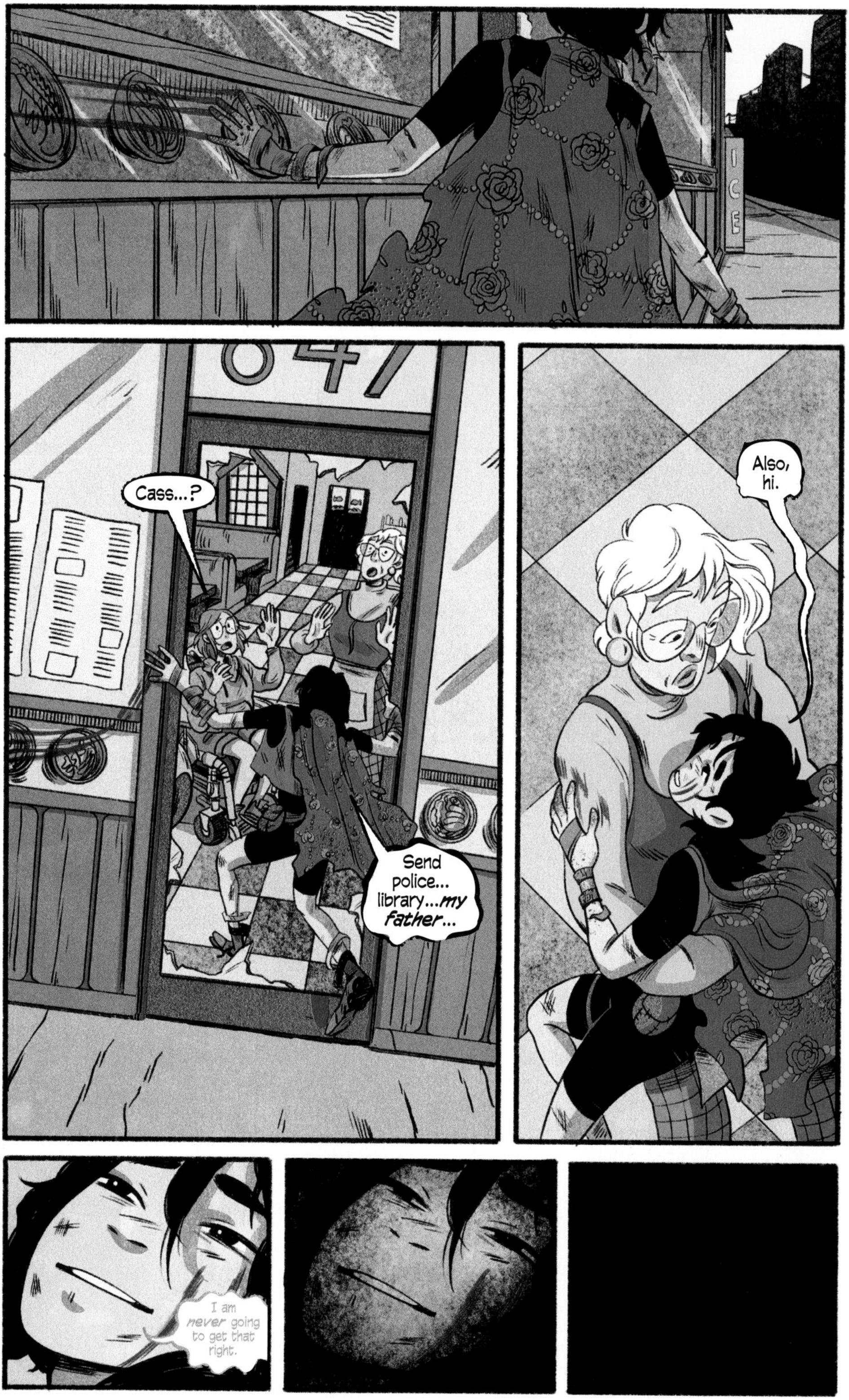
ICE
847
Cass...?
Send police... library...*my father*...
Also, hi.
I am *never* going to get that right.

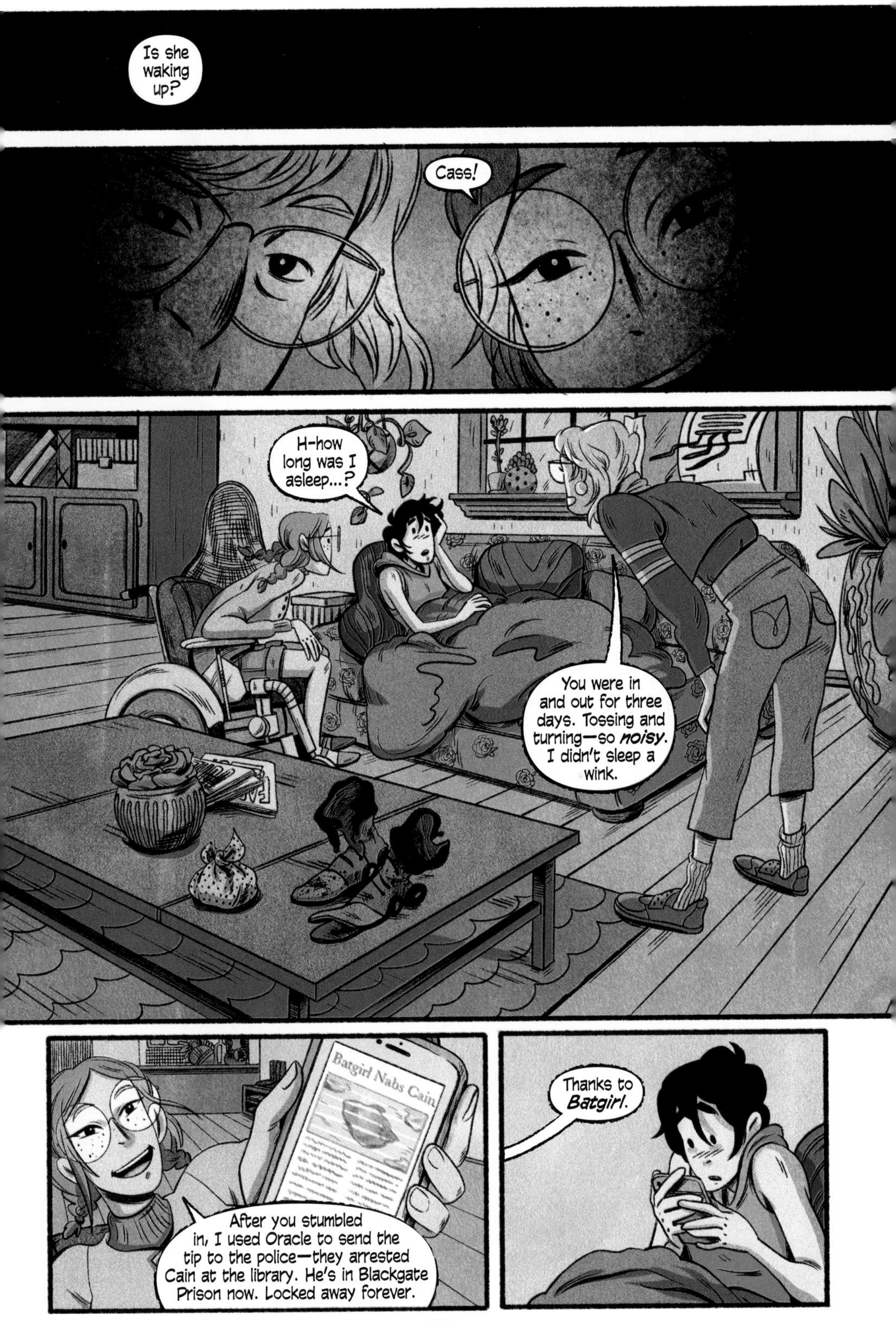
Is she waking up?
Cass!
H-how long was I asleep...?
You were in and out for three days. Tossing and turning—so *noisy*. I didn't sleep a wink.
Batgirl Nabs Cain
After you stumbled in, I used Oracle to send the tip to the police—they arrested Cain at the library. He's in Blackgate Prison now. Locked away forever.
Thanks to *Batgirl*.

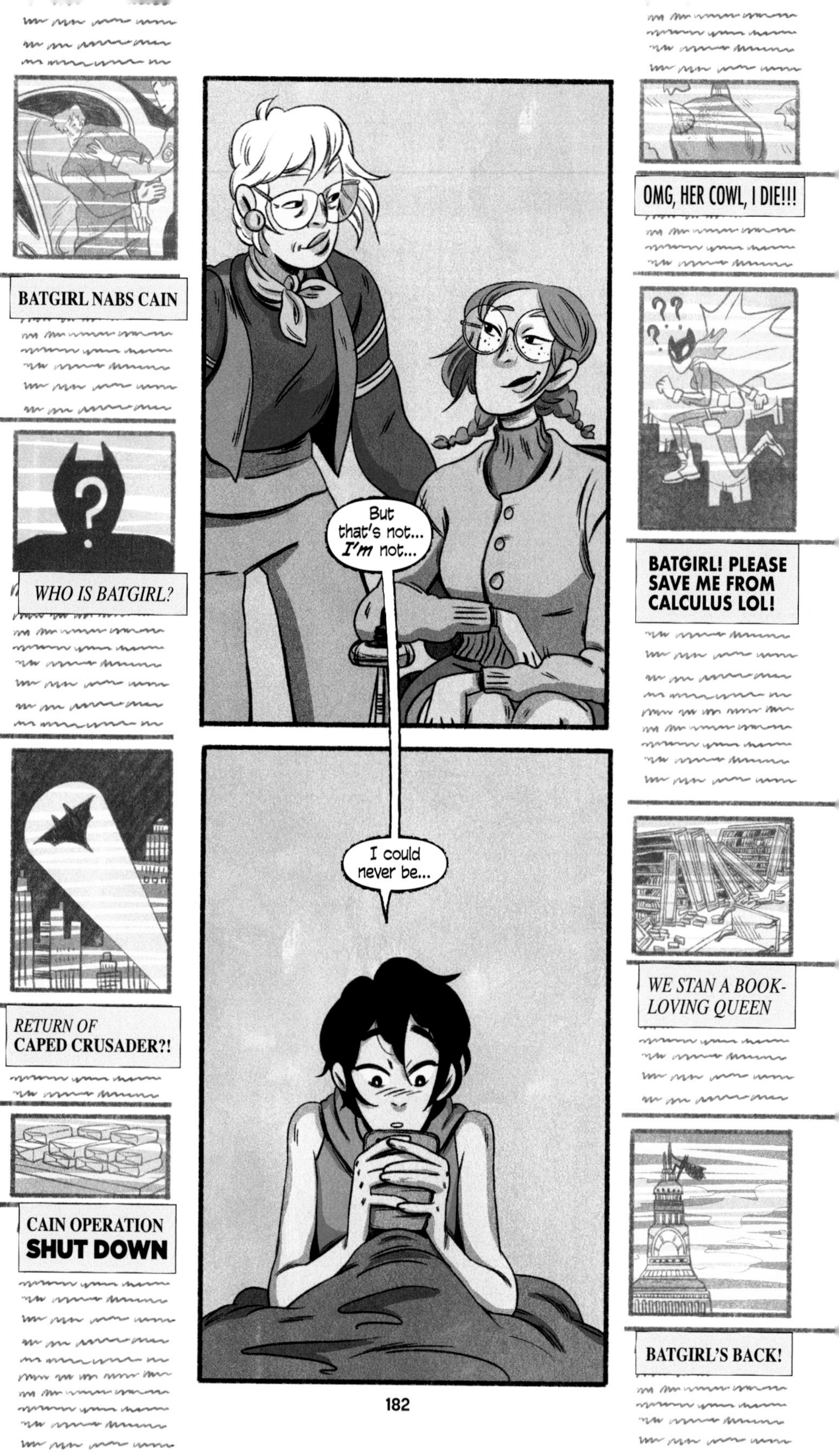

BATGIRL NABS CAIN
WHO IS BATGIRL?
RETURN OF CAPED CRUSADER?!
CAIN OPERATION SHUT DOWN
But that's not... *I'm* not...
I could never be...
OMG, HER COWL, I DIE!!!
BATGIRL! PLEASE SAVE ME FROM CALCULUS LOL!
WE STAN A BOOK-LOVING QUEEN
BATGIRL'S BACK!

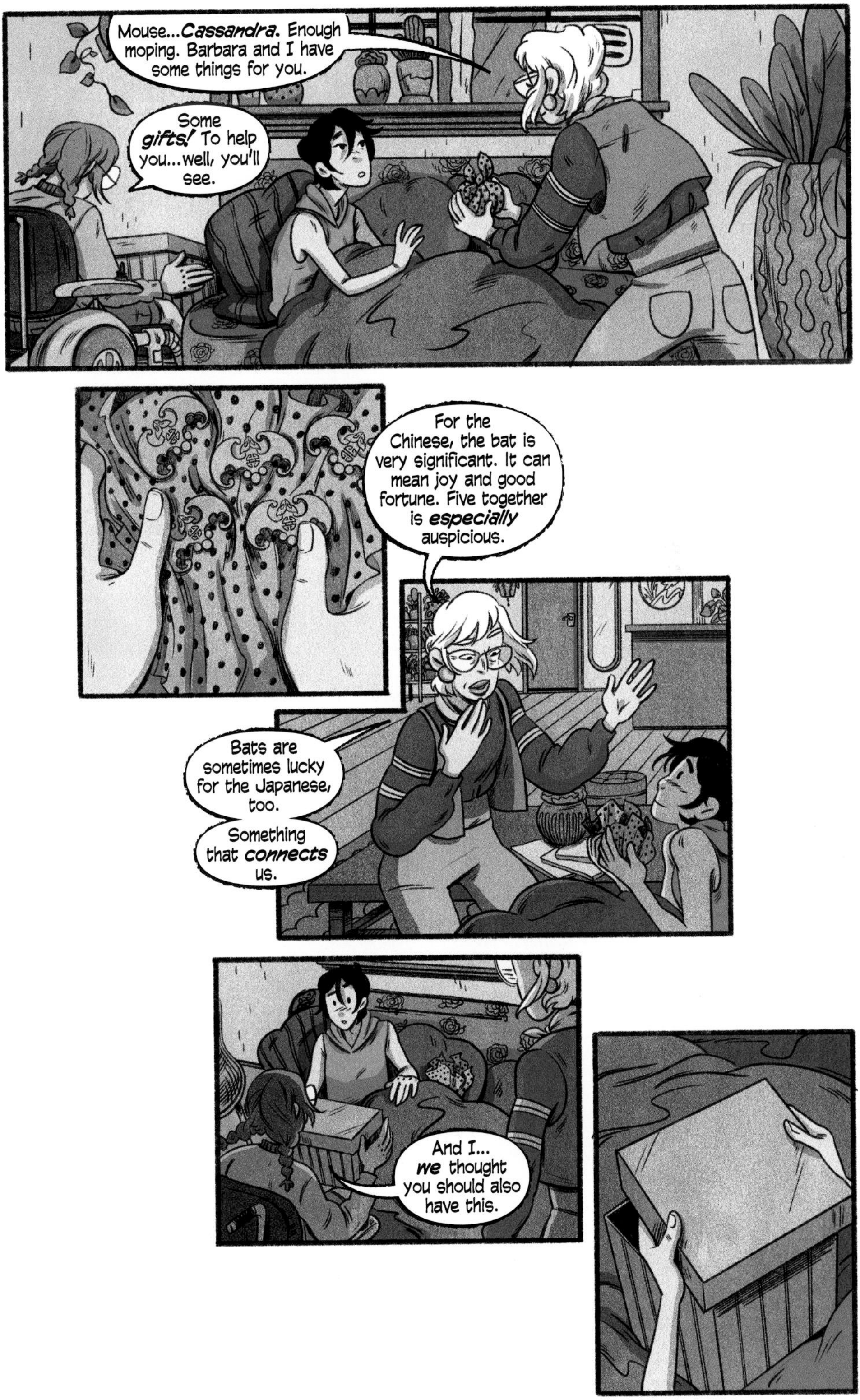
Mouse...Cassandra. Enough moping. Barbara and I have some things for you.
Some gifts! To help you...well, you'll see.
For the Chinese, the bat is very significant. It can mean joy and good fortune. Five together is especially auspicious.
Bats are sometimes lucky for the Japanese, too.
Something that connects us.
And I... we thought you should also have this.

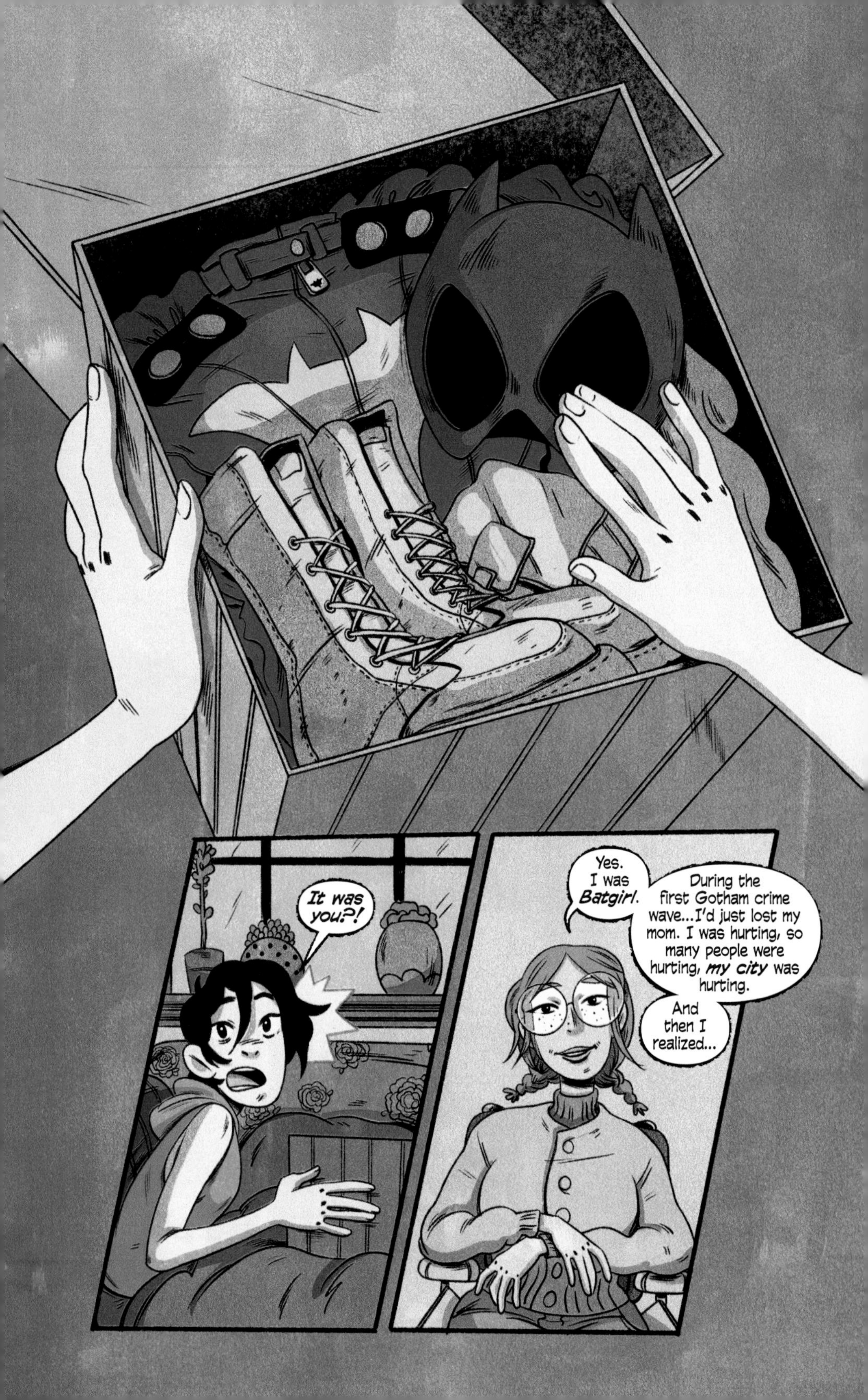
It was you?!
Yes. I was Batgirl.
During the first Gotham crime wave...I'd just lost my mom. I was hurting, so many people were hurting, my city was hurting.
And then I realized...

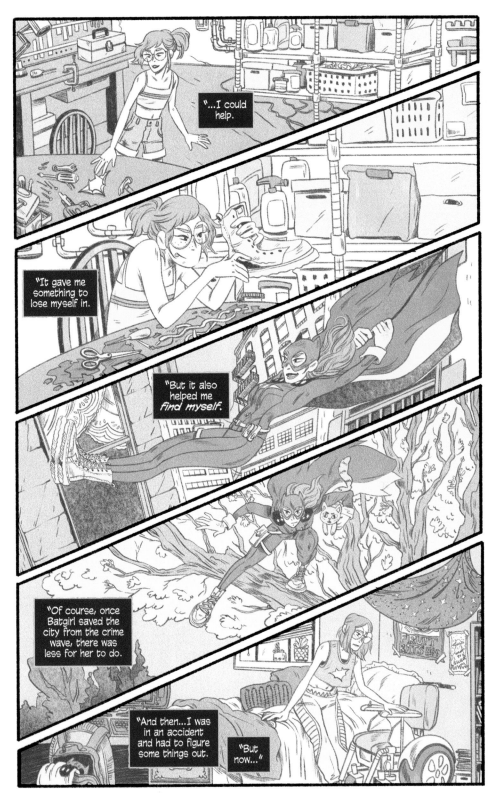

"...I could help.

"It gave me something to lose myself in.

"But it also helped me *find myself*.

"Of course, once Batgirl saved the city from the crime wave, there was less for her to do.

"And then...I was in an accident and had to figure some things out.

"But now..."

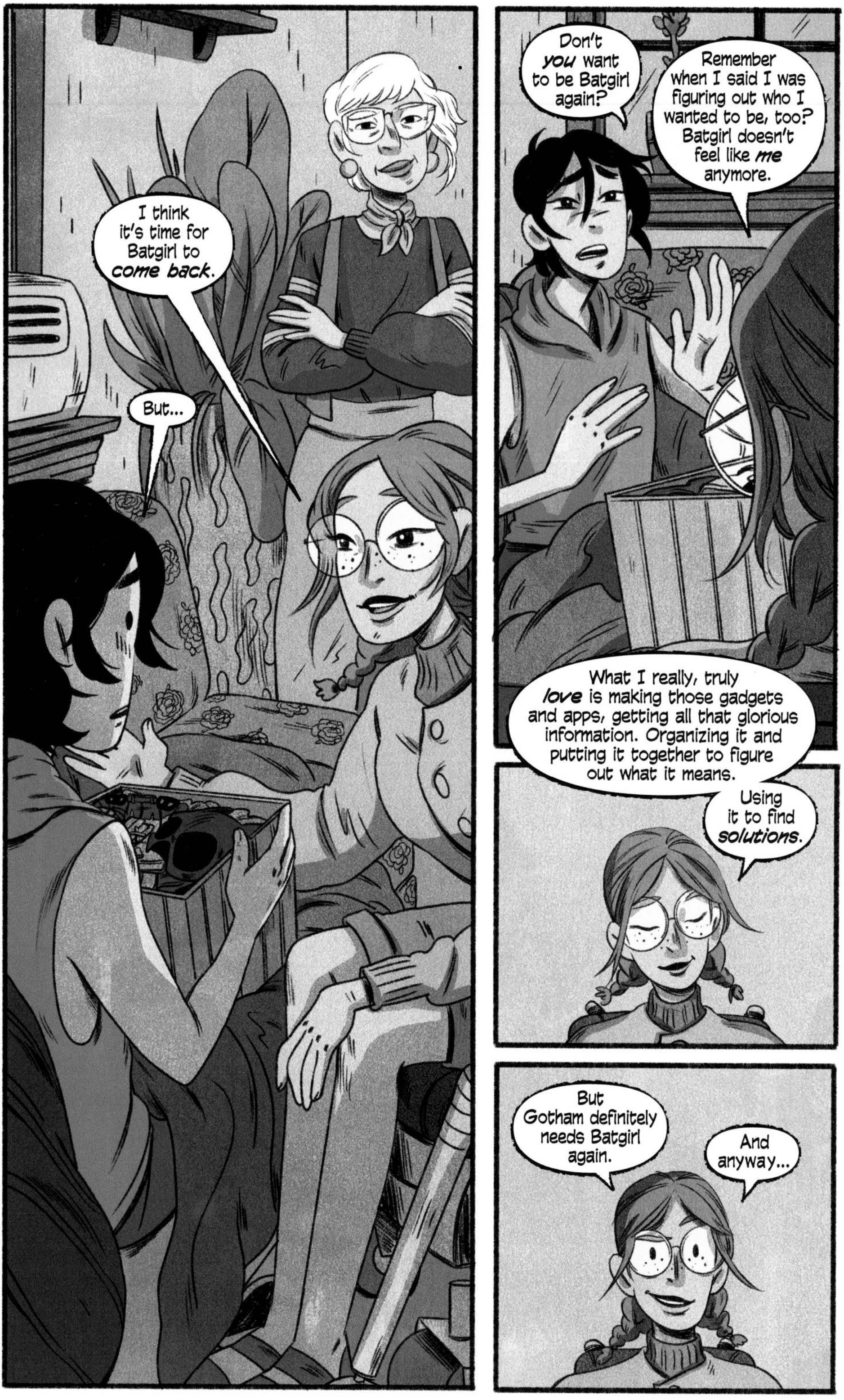
I think it's time for Batgirl to *come back*.
But...
Don't *you* want to be Batgirl again?
Remember when I said I was figuring out who I wanted to be, too? Batgirl doesn't feel like *me* anymore.
What I really, truly *love* is making those gadgets and apps, getting all that glorious information. Organizing it and putting it together to figure out what it means.
Using it to find *solutions*.
But Gotham definitely needs Batgirl again.
And anyway...

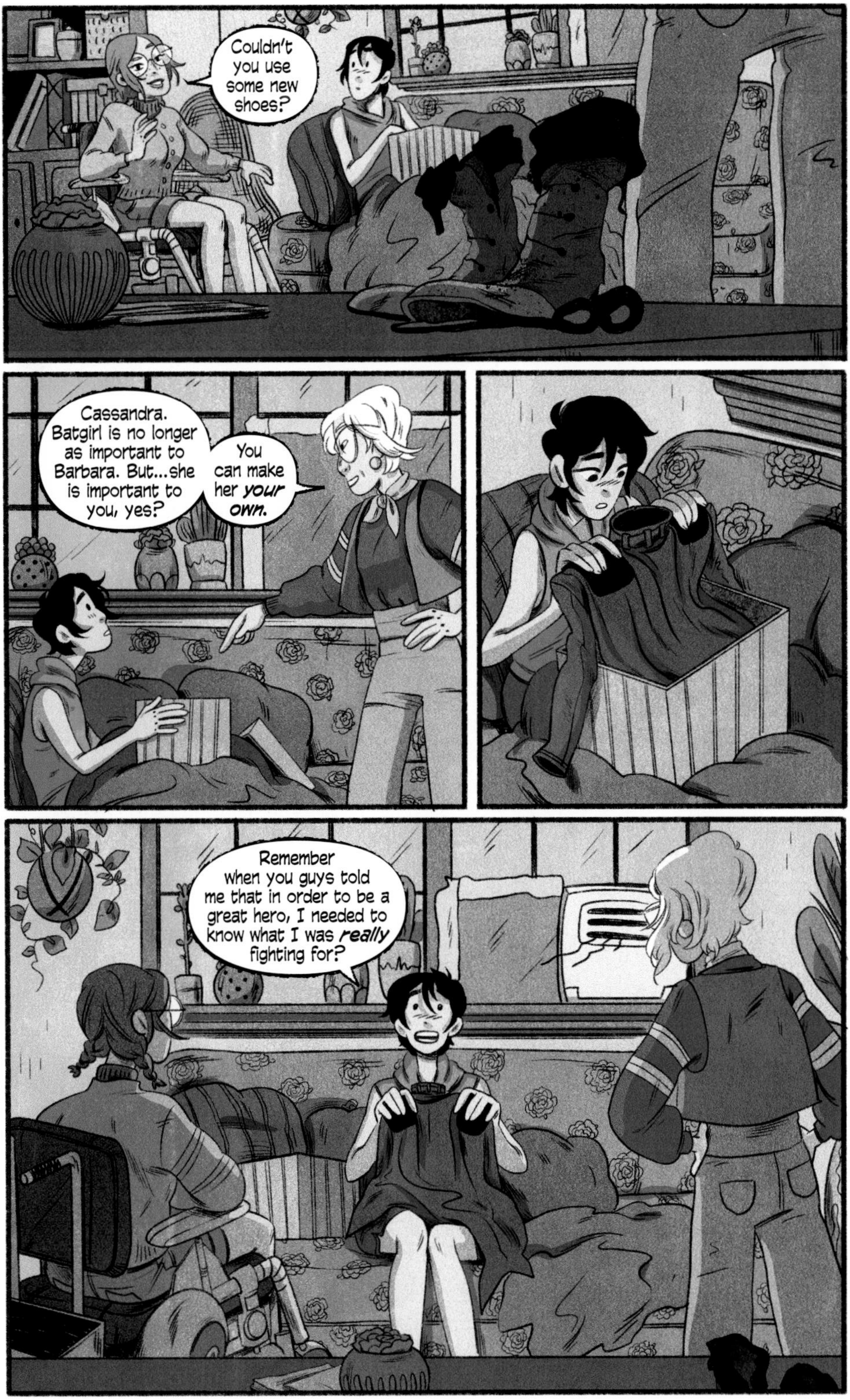
Couldn't you use some new shoes?
Cassandra. Batgirl is no longer as important to Barbara. But...she is important to you, yes?
You can make her *your own.*
Remember when you guys told me that in order to be a great hero, I needed to know what I was *really* fighting for?

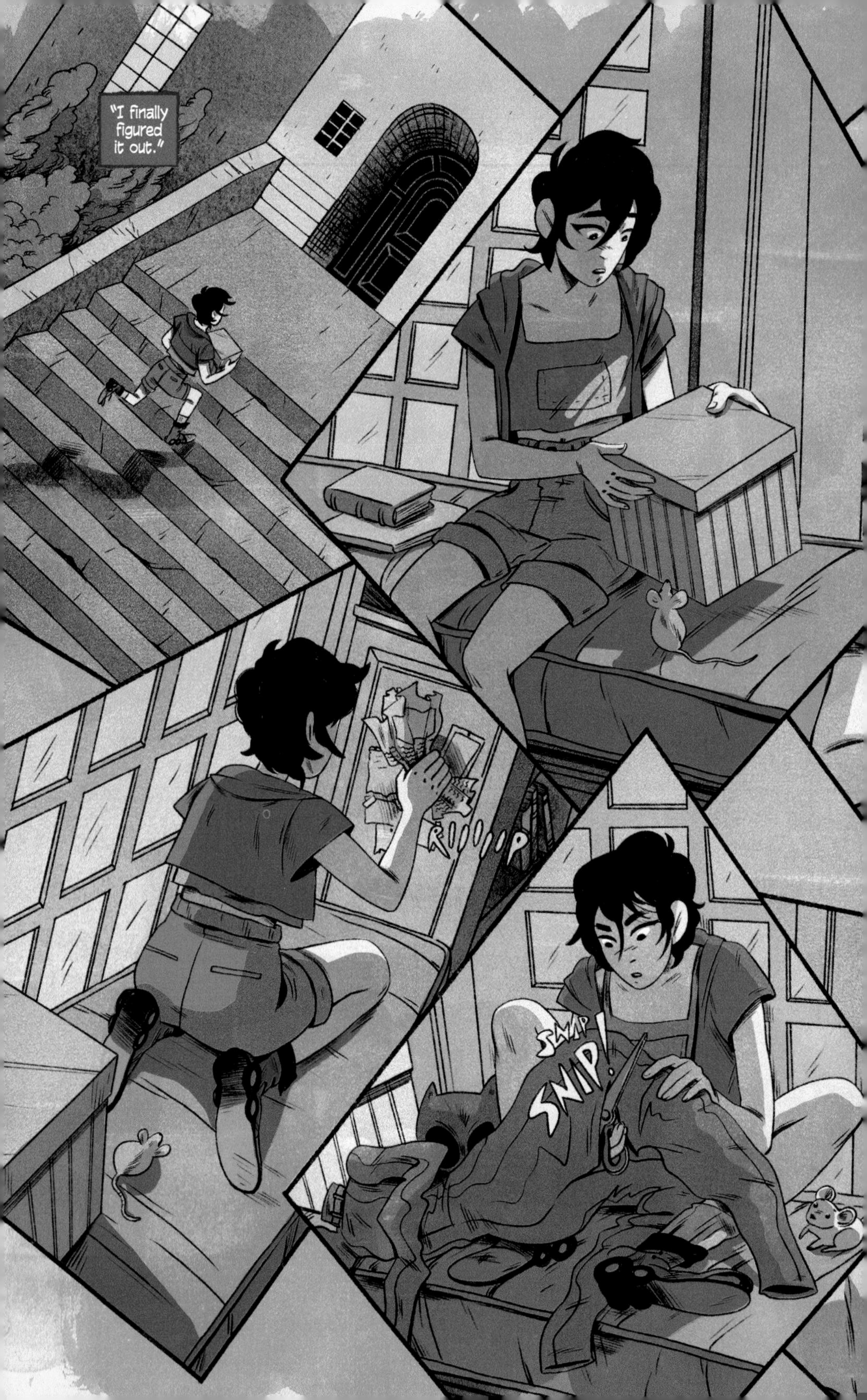
"I finally figured it out."
RIIIIIP
SNIP!
SNIP

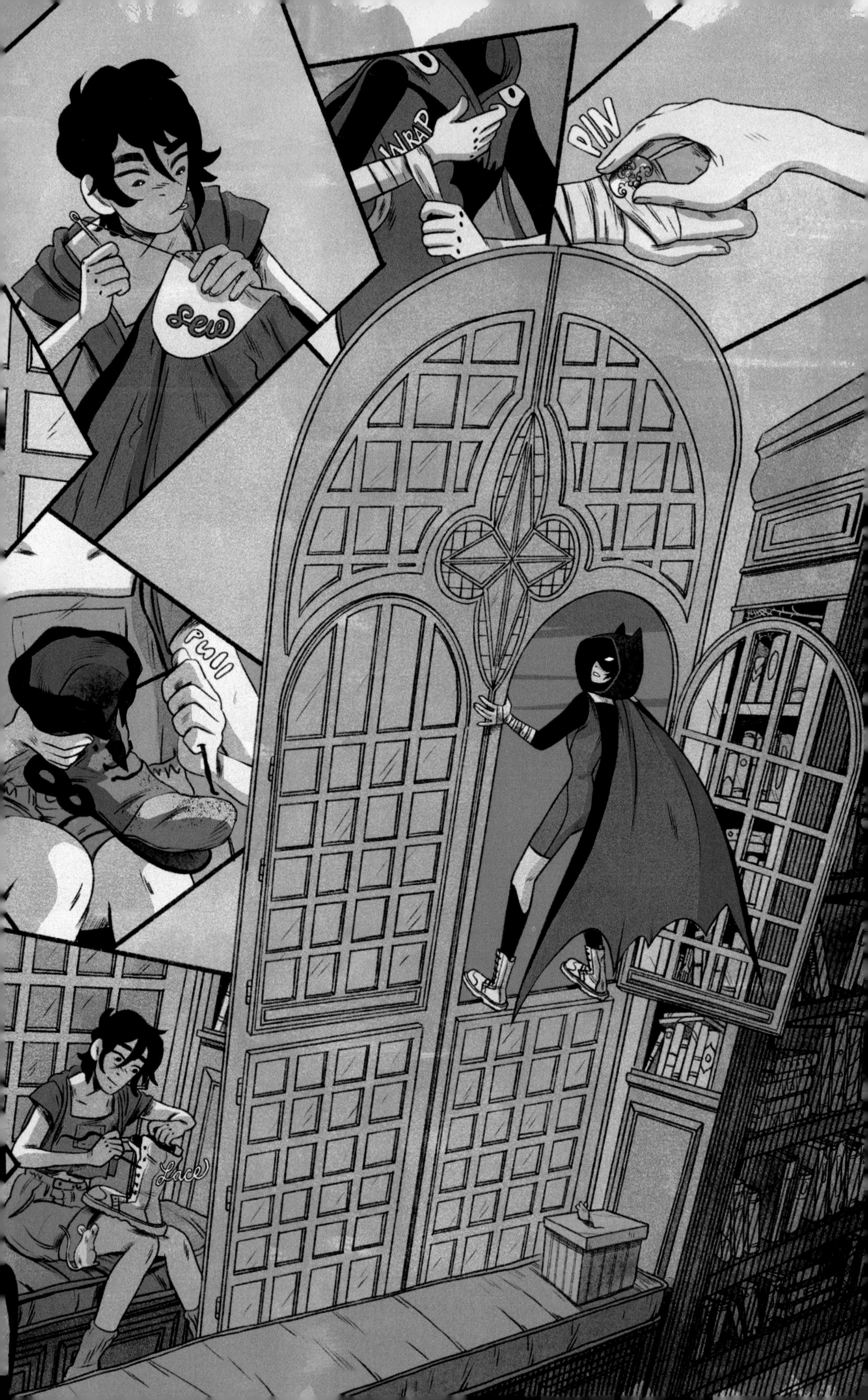

SEW
WRAP
PIN
PULL
LACE

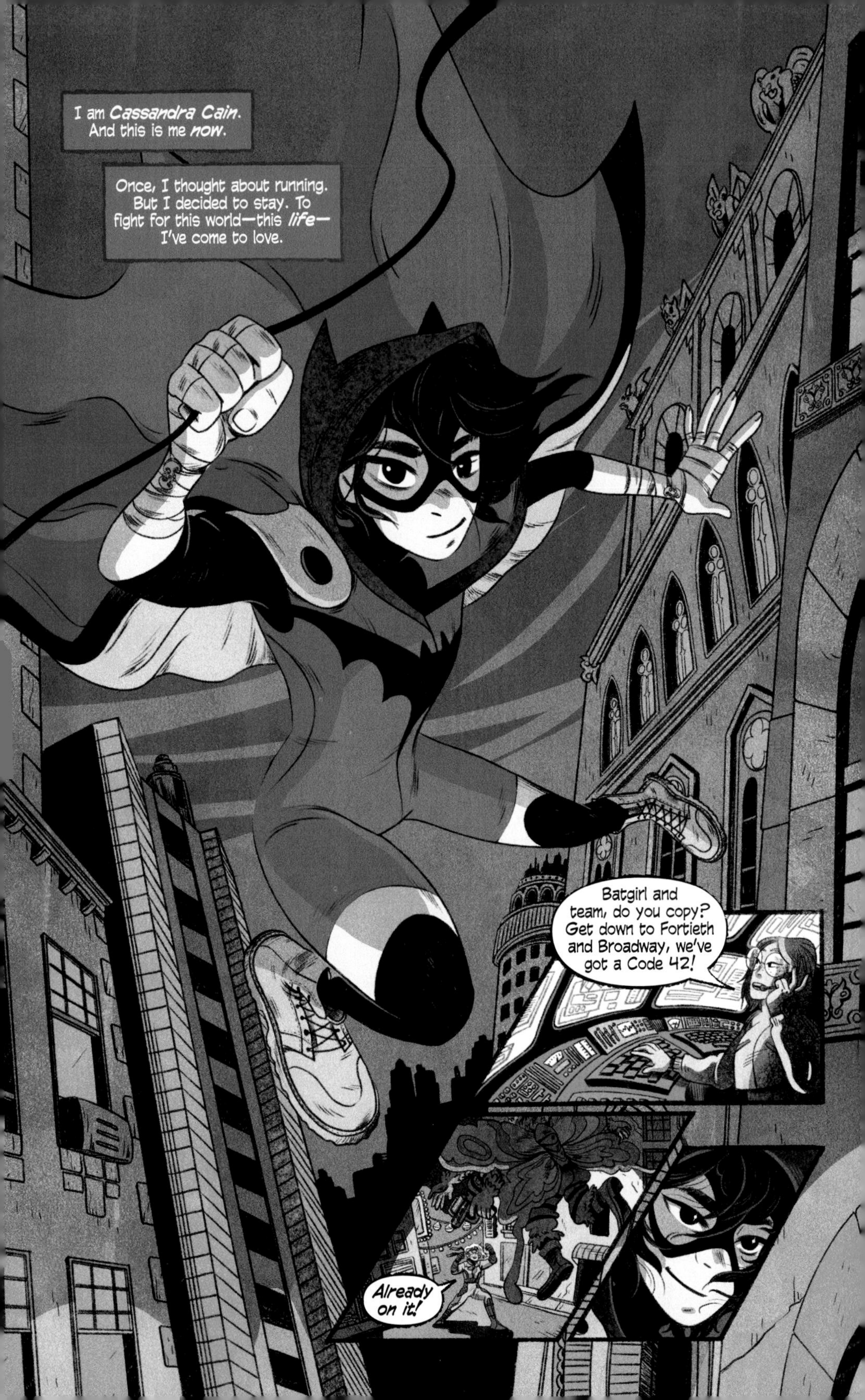
I am *Cassandra Cain*. And this is me *now*.
Once, I thought about running. But I decided to stay. To fight for this world—this *life*—I've come to love.
Batgirl and team, do you copy? Get down to Fortieth and Broadway, we've got a Code 42!
Already on it!

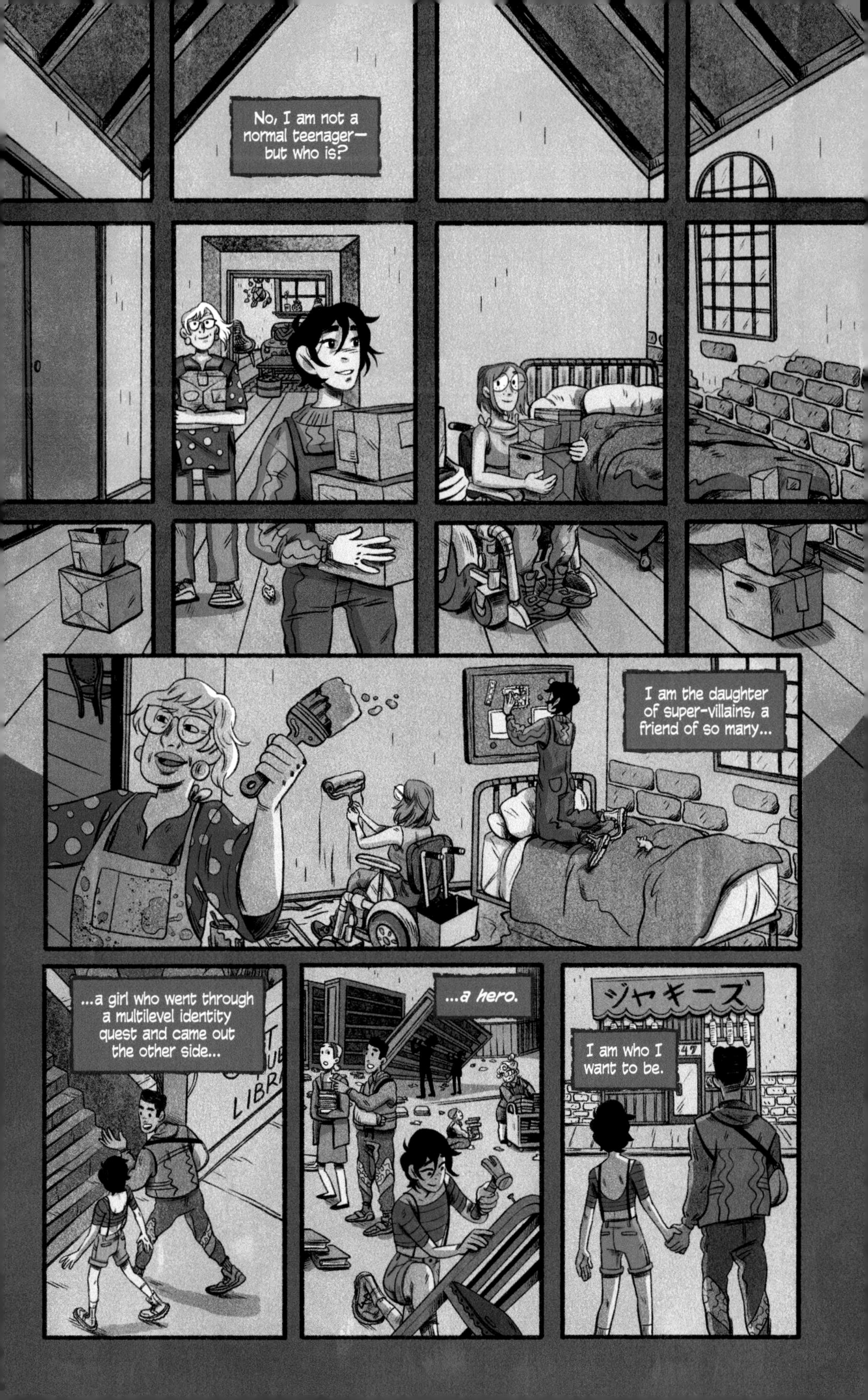
No, I am not a normal teenager—but who is?
I am the daughter of super-villains, a friend of so many...
...a girl who went through a multilevel identity quest and came out the other side...
...a hero.
ジャキーズ
I am who I want to be.

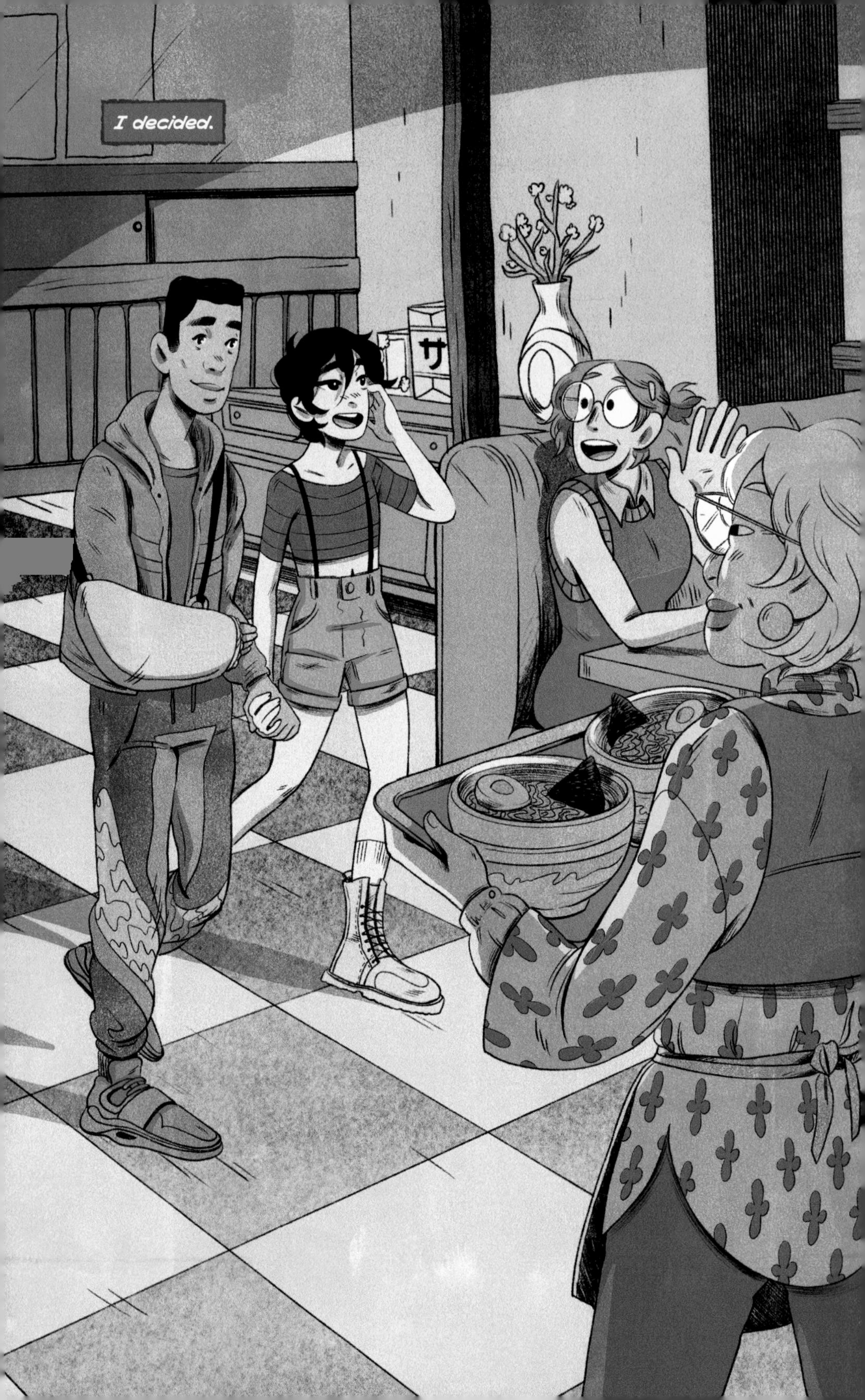
I decided.
サ

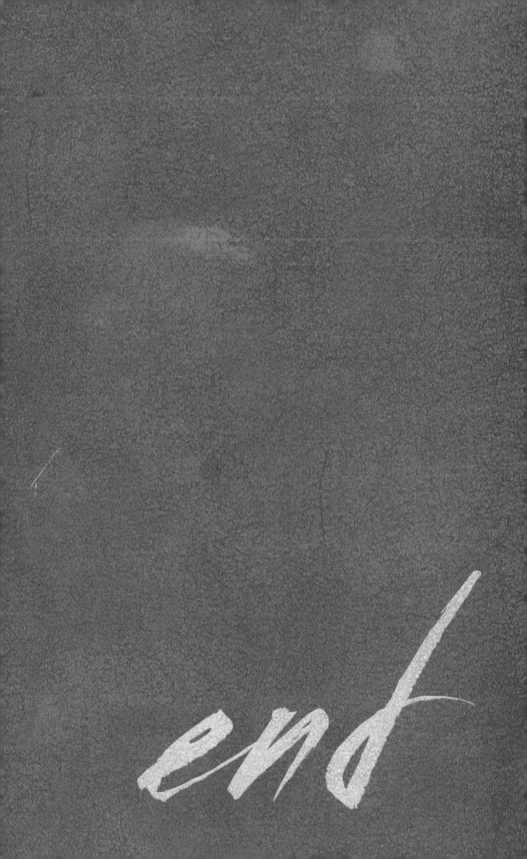

end

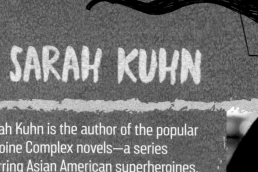

SARAH KUHN

Sarah Kuhn is the author of the popular Heroine Complex novels—a series starring Asian American superheroines. The first book is a Locus bestseller, an RT Reviewers' Choice Award nominee, and one of the Barnes & Noble Sci-Fi & Fantasy Blog's best books of 2016. Her YA debut, the Japan-set romantic comedy *I Love You So Mochi*, came out in June 2019 and is a Junior Library Guild Selection and a nominee for YALSA's Best Fiction for Young Adults. Additionally, Sarah was a finalist for the Astounding Award for Best New Writer and the CAPE (Coalition of Asian Pacifics in Entertainment) New Writers Award. A third-generation Japanese American, she lives in L.A. with her husband and an overflowing closet of vintage treasures.

Photo by CapozKnows Photography

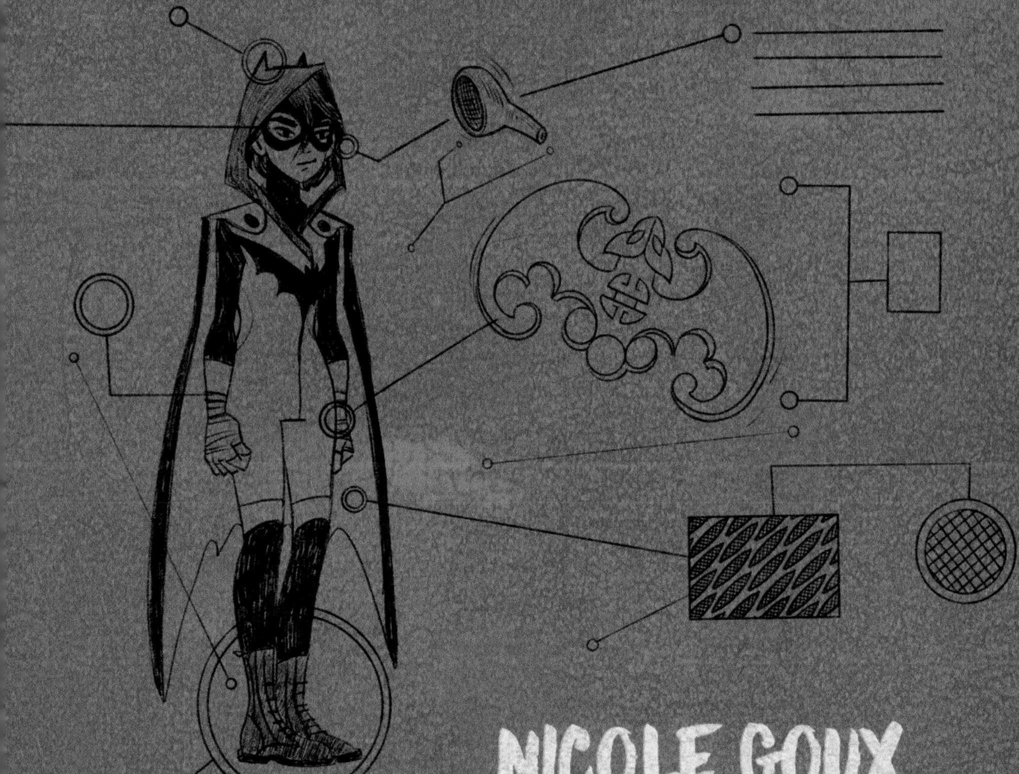

NICOLE GOUX

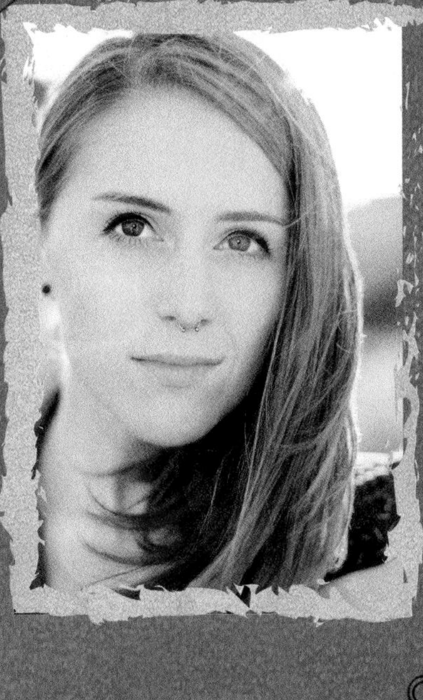

Photo by Justin Galligher

Nicole Goux is a comics creator from Southern California. She has been published by DC Comics, Hulu, Silver Sprocket Bicycle Club, IDW, Oni, Black Crown, Image, and Lion Forge.

When she's not making comics she's usually at a comics convention, or playing catch with her partner, Dave.

No, really. They just go to a park and play catch and talk about *Star Trek*.

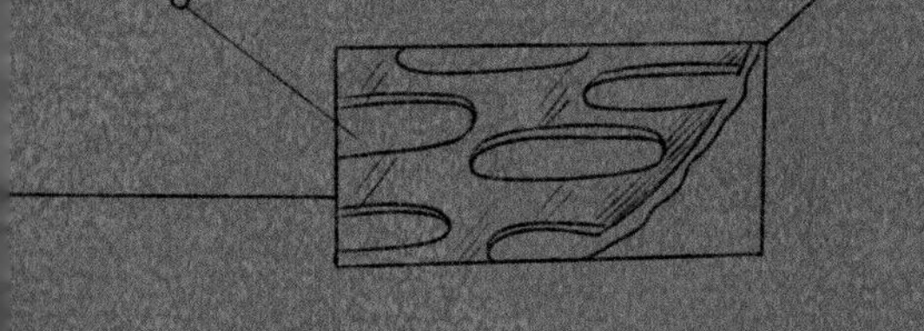

From the #1 *New York Times* bestselling author of *This Is Where It Ends*, Marieke Nijkamp, and artist Manuel Preitano comes *The Oracle Code*, a graphic novel that explores the dark corridors of Barbara Gordon's first mystery: herself.

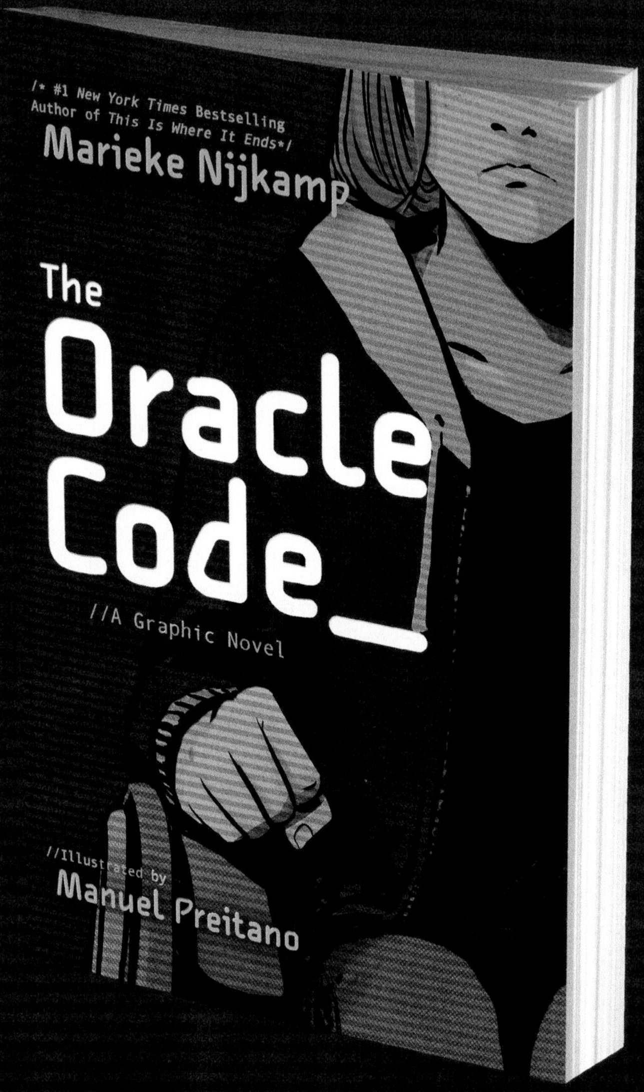
/* #1 New York Times Bestselling Author of This Is Where It Ends*/
Marieke Nijkamp
The Oracle Code_
//A Graphic Novel
//Illustrated by
Manuel Preitano

On sale March 10, 2020.

Read on for an exclusive sneak preview.

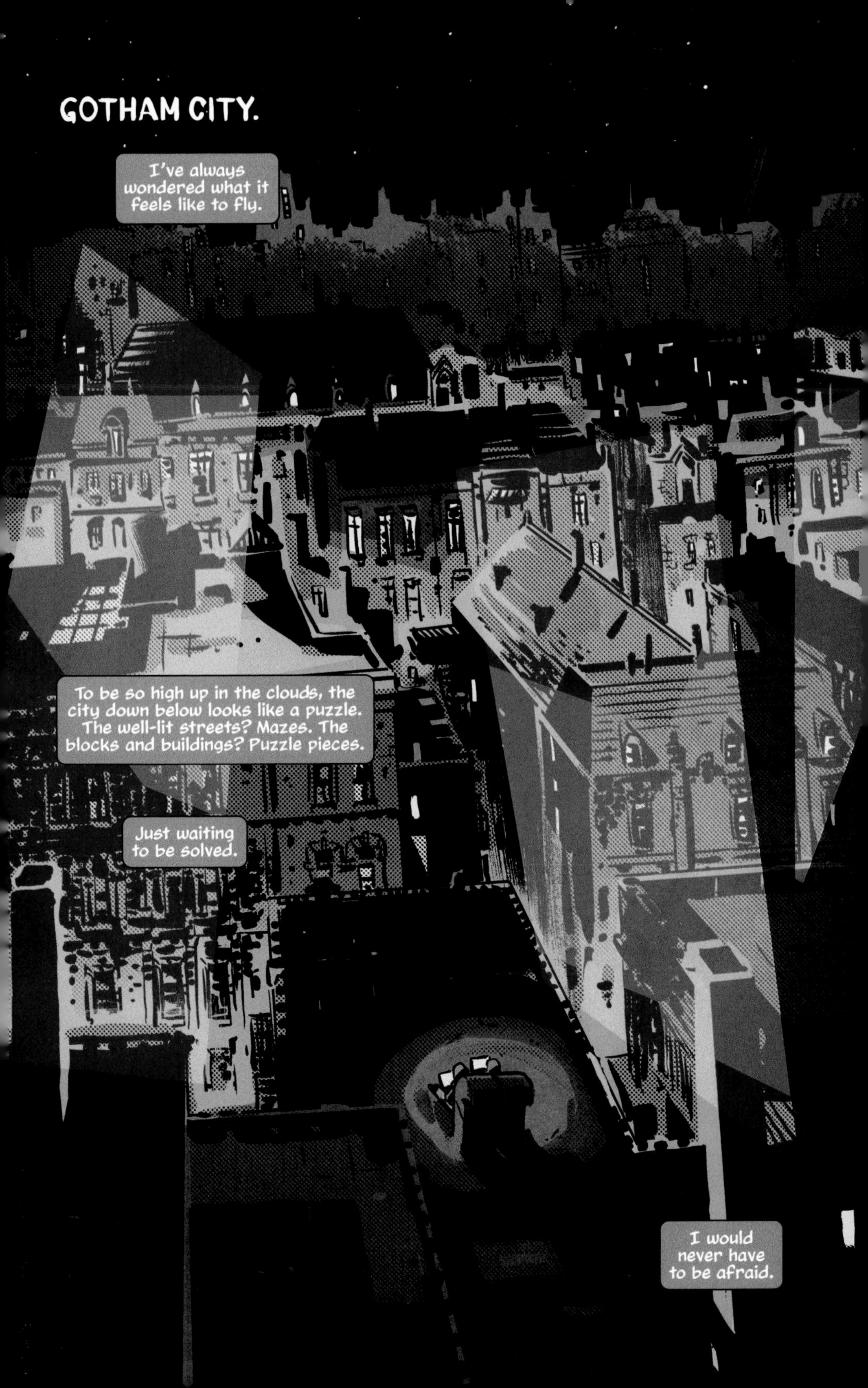
GOTHAM CITY.
I've always wondered what it feels like to fly.
To be so high up in the clouds, the city down below looks like a puzzle. The well-lit streets? Mazes. The blocks and buildings? Puzzle pieces.
Just waiting to be solved.
I would never have to be afraid.

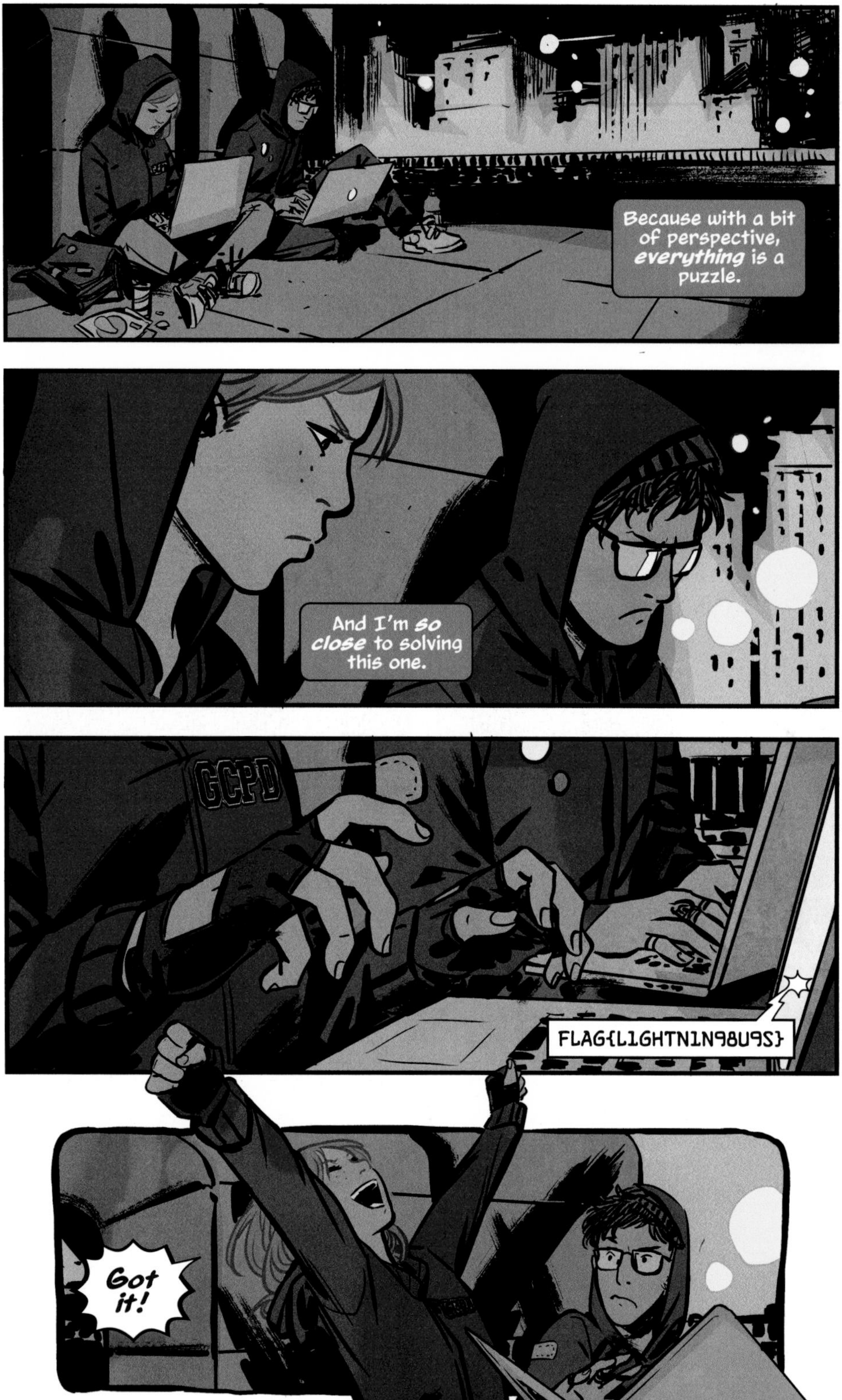
Because with a bit of perspective, *everything* is a puzzle.
And I'm *so close* to solving this one.
GCPD
FLAG{L1GHTN1N98U9S}
Got it!

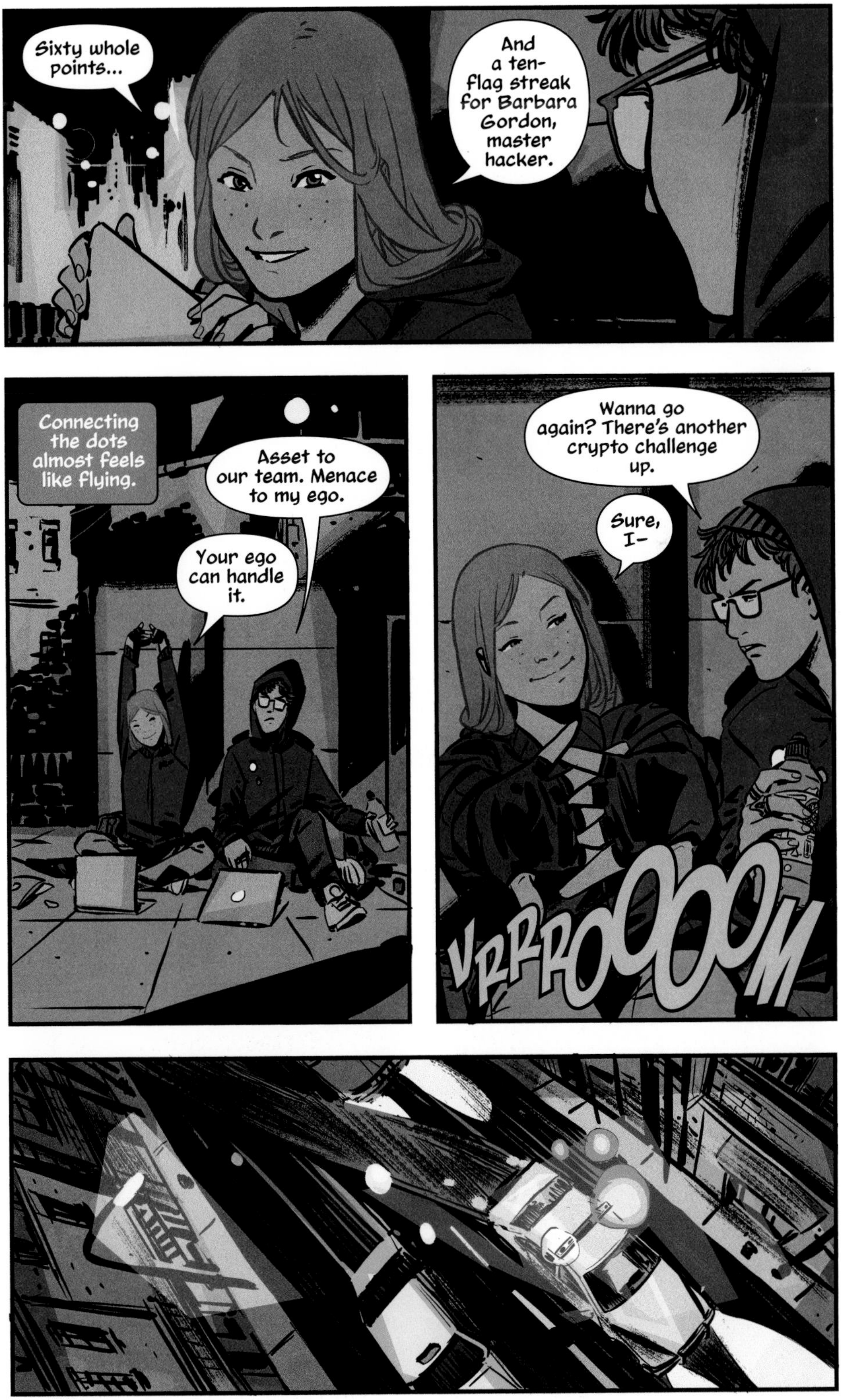
Sixty whole points...
And a ten-flag streak for Barbara Gordon, master hacker.
Connecting the dots almost feels like flying.
Asset to our team. Menace to my ego.
Your ego can handle it.
Wanna go again? There's another crypto challenge up.
Sure, I–
VRRROOOOOM

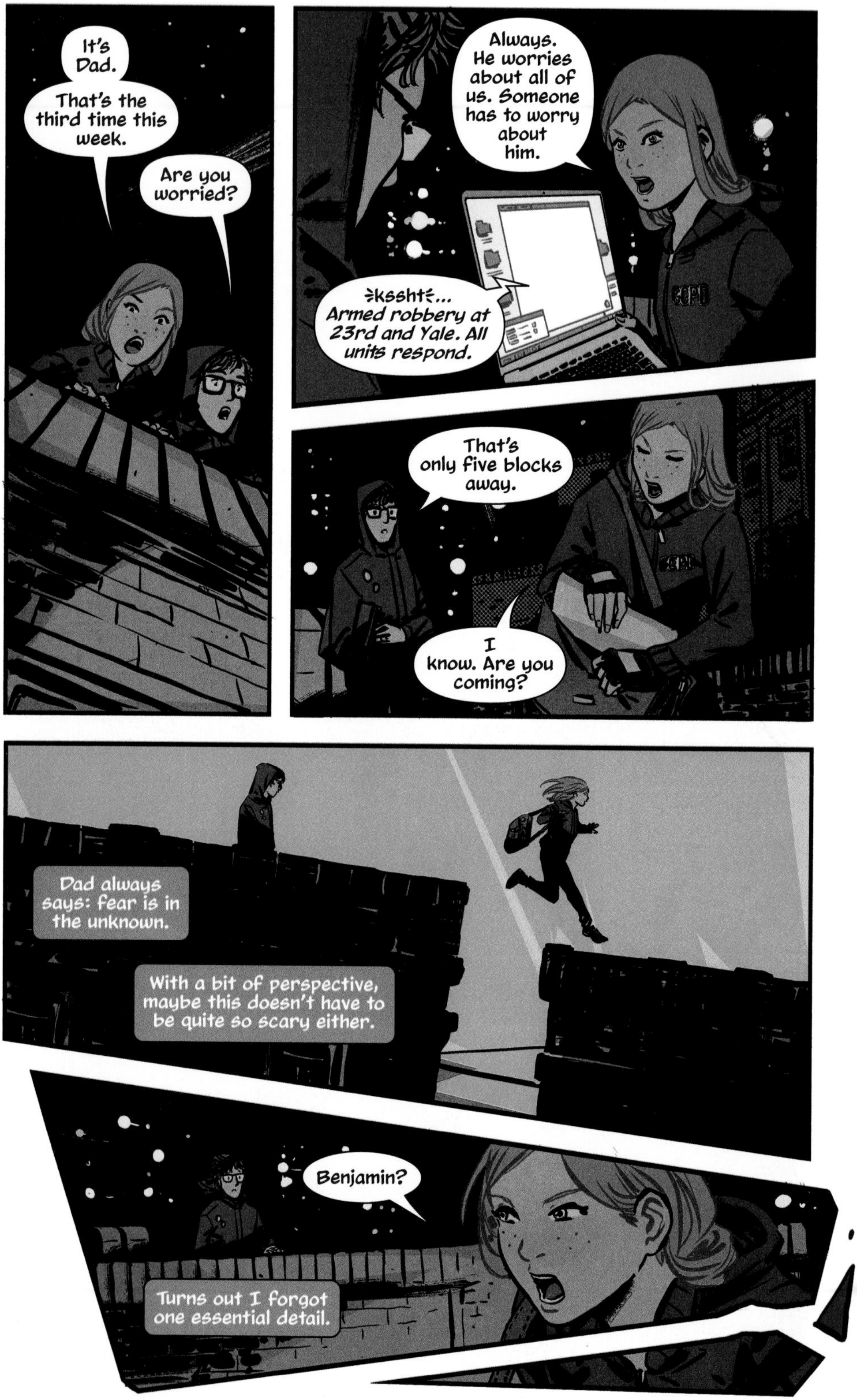

It's Dad.
That's the third time this week.
Are you worried?
Always. He worries about all of us. Someone has to worry about him.
⋞kssht⋟... Armed robbery at 23rd and Yale. All units respond.
That's only five blocks away.
I know. Are you coming?
Dad always says: fear is in the unknown.
With a bit of perspective, maybe this doesn't have to be quite so scary either.
Benjamin?
Turns out I forgot one essential detail.

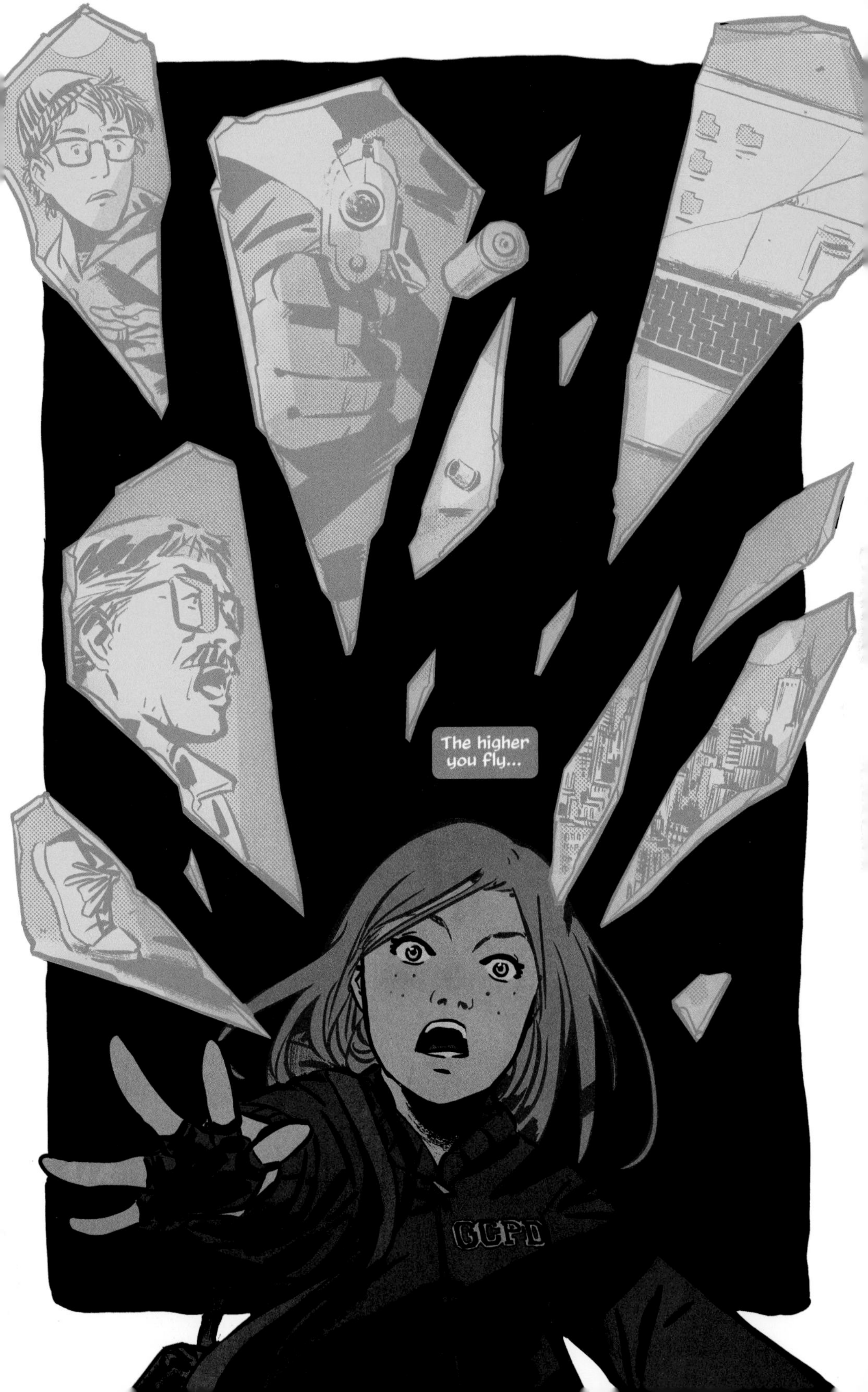
The higher you fly...
GCPD

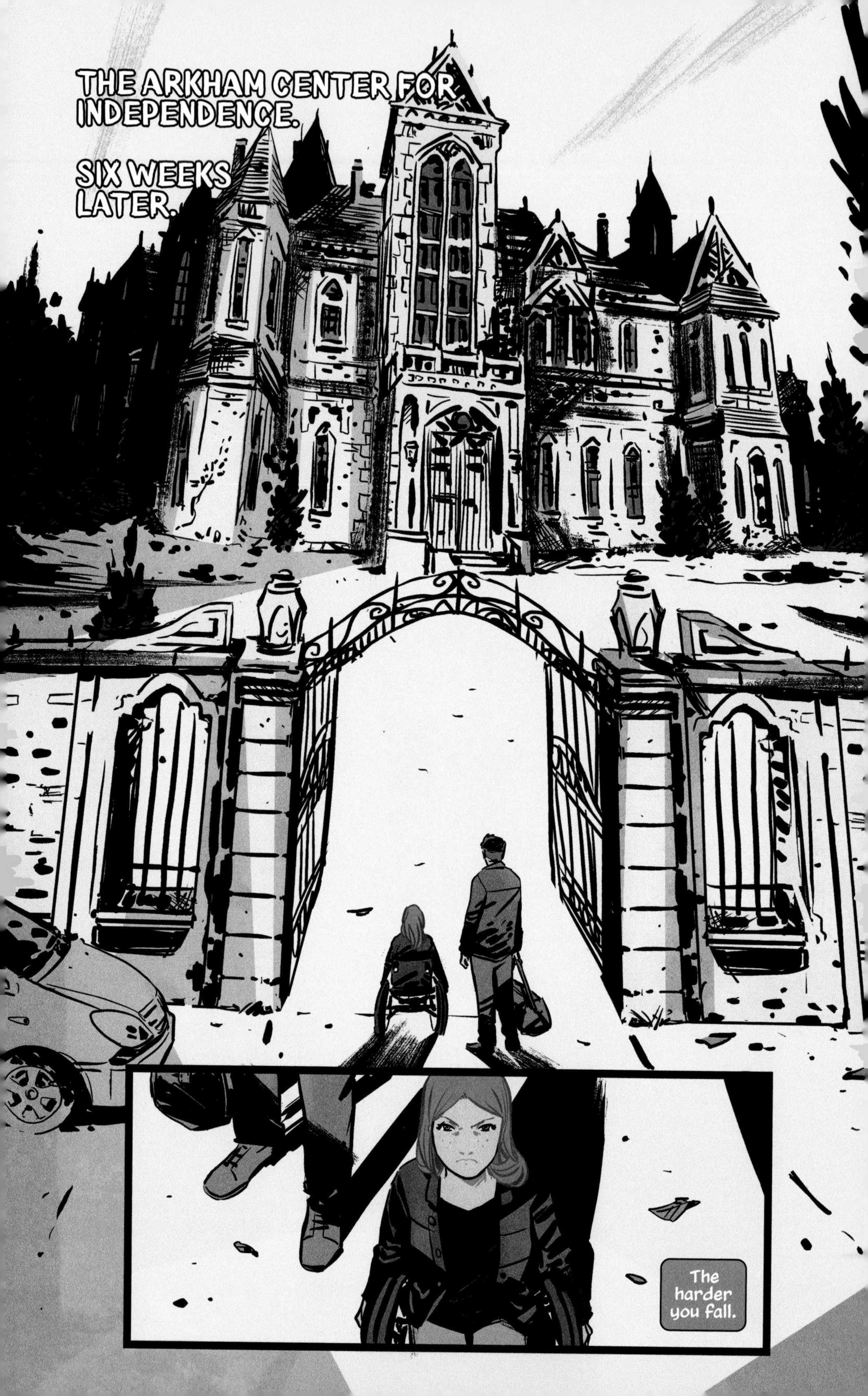
THE ARKHAM CENTER FOR INDEPENDENCE.
SIX WEEKS LATER.
The harder you fall.

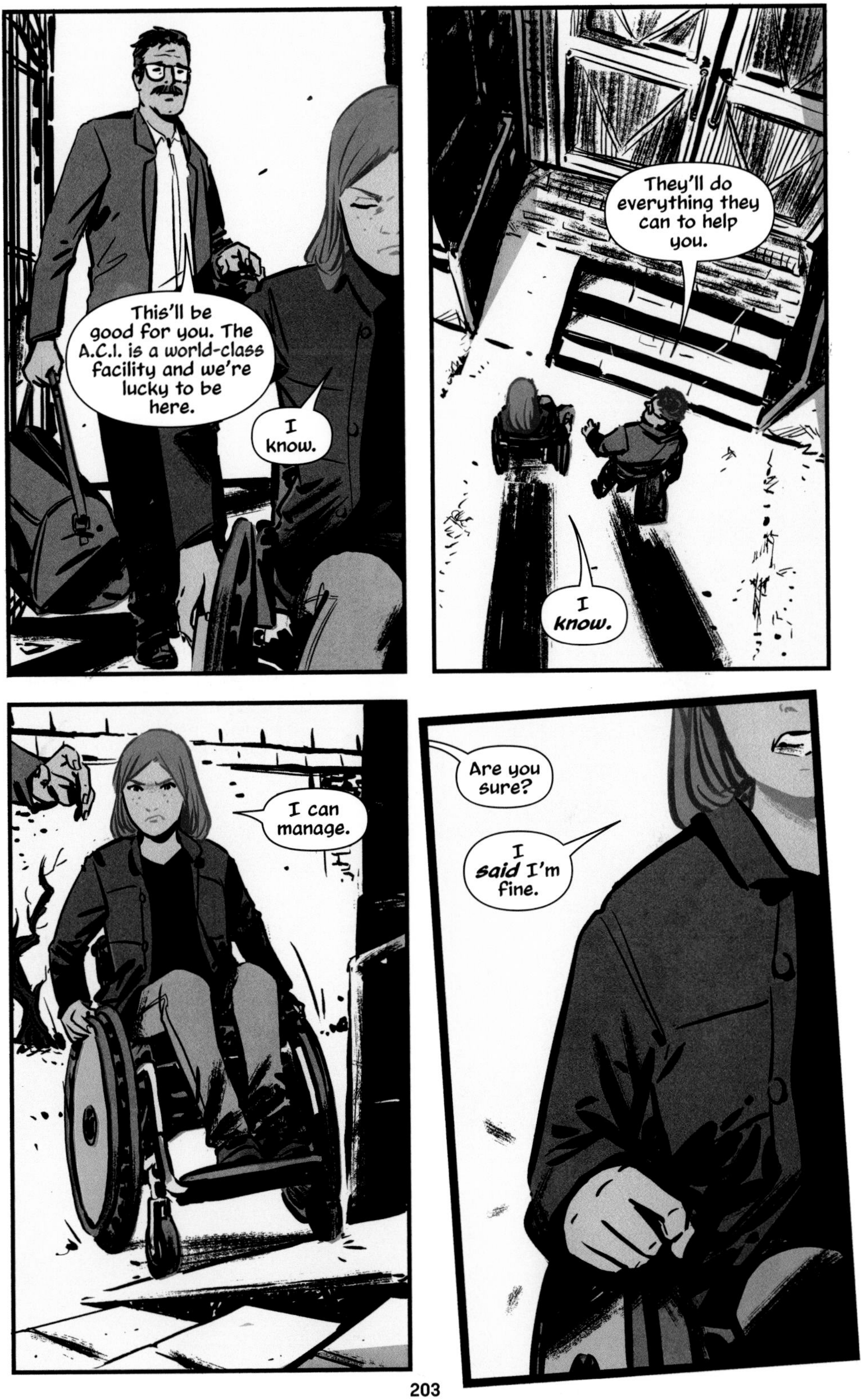
This'll be good for you. The A.C.I. is a world-class facility and we're lucky to be here.
I know.
They'll do everything they can to help you.
I know.
I can manage.
Are you sure?
I said I'm fine.

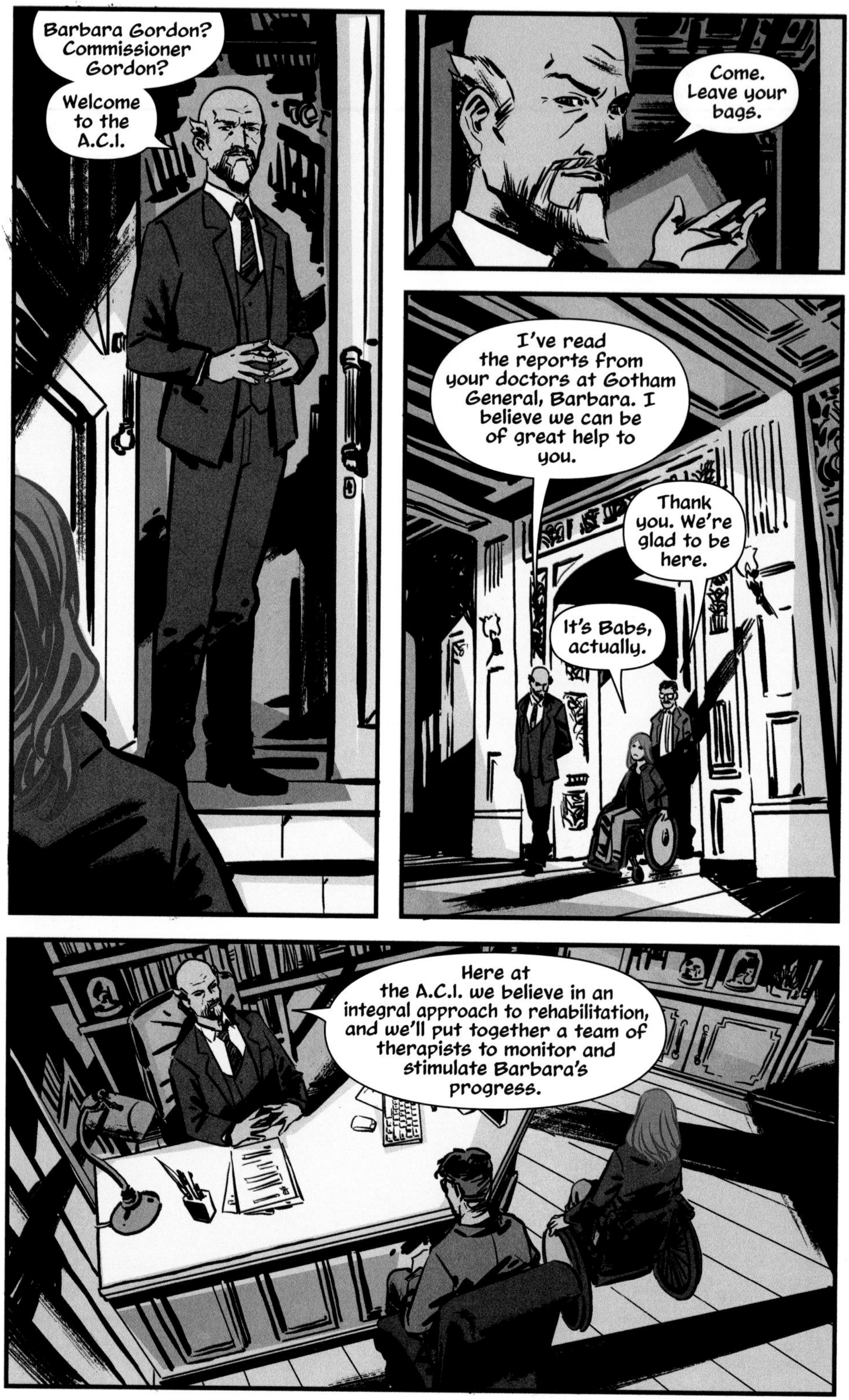
Barbara Gordon? Commissioner Gordon?
Welcome to the A.C.I.
Come. Leave your bags.
I've read the reports from your doctors at Gotham General, Barbara. I believe we can be of great help to you.
Thank you. We're glad to be here.
It's Babs, actually.
Here at the A.C.I. we believe in an integral approach to rehabilitation, and we'll put together a team of therapists to monitor and stimulate Barbara's progress.

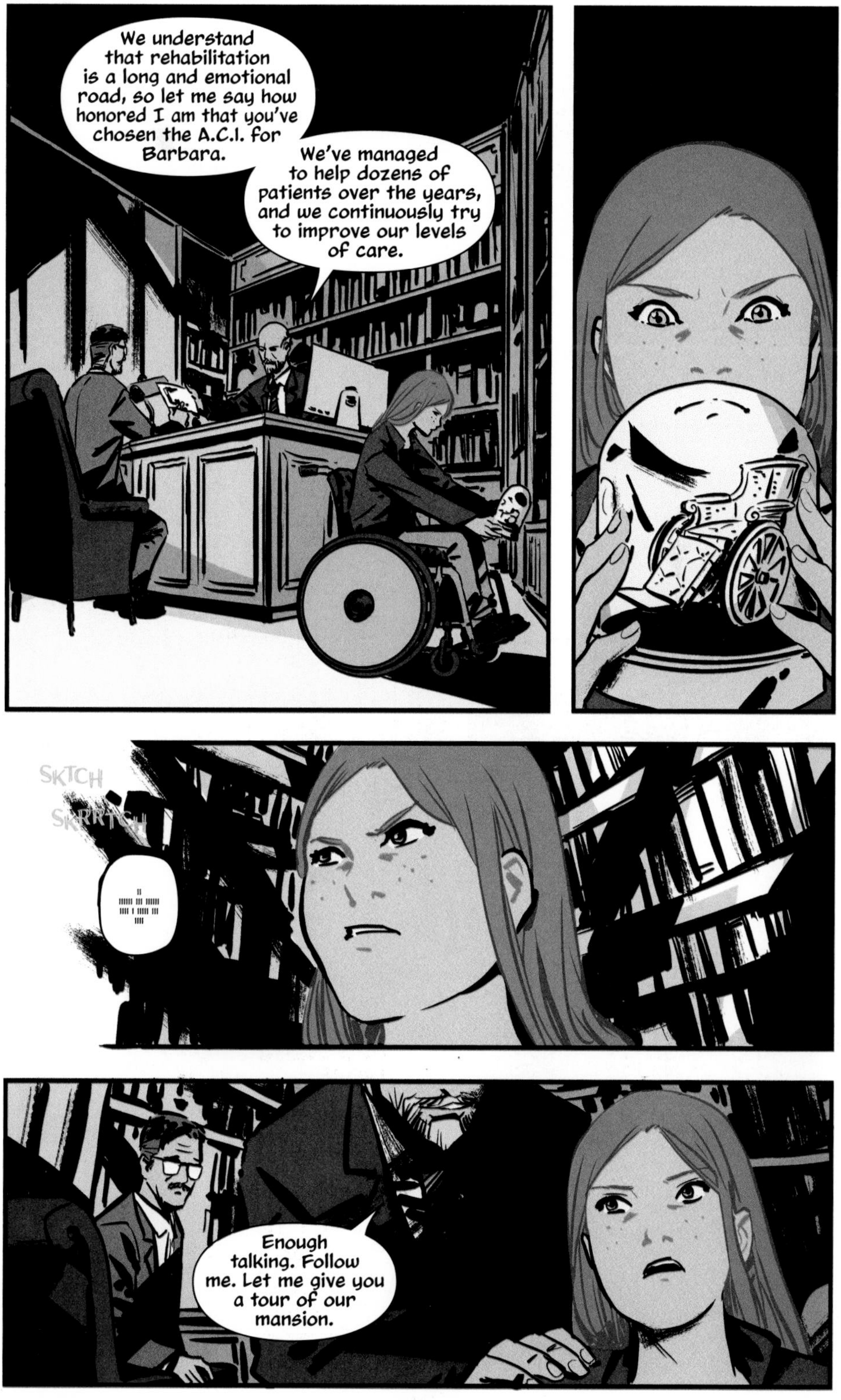
We understand that rehabilitation is a long and emotional road, so let me say how honored I am that you've chosen the A.C.I. for Barbara.
We've managed to help dozens of patients over the years, and we continuously try to improve our levels of care.
SKTCH
SKRRTCH
Enough talking. Follow me. Let me give you a tour of our mansion.

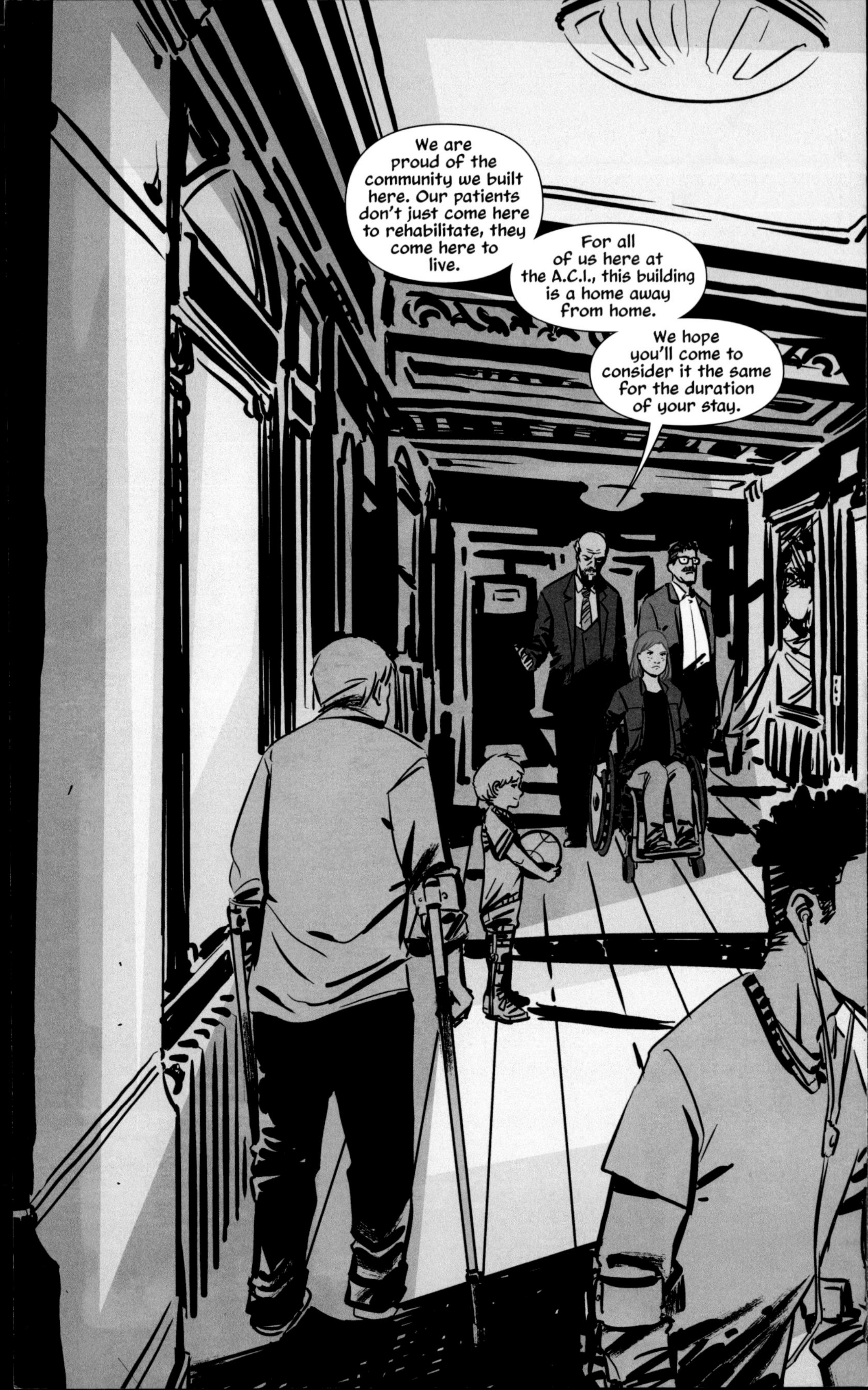
We are proud of the community we built here. Our patients don't just come here to rehabilitate, they come here to live.
For all of us here at the A.C.I., this building is a home away from home.
We hope you'll come to consider it the same for the duration of your stay.

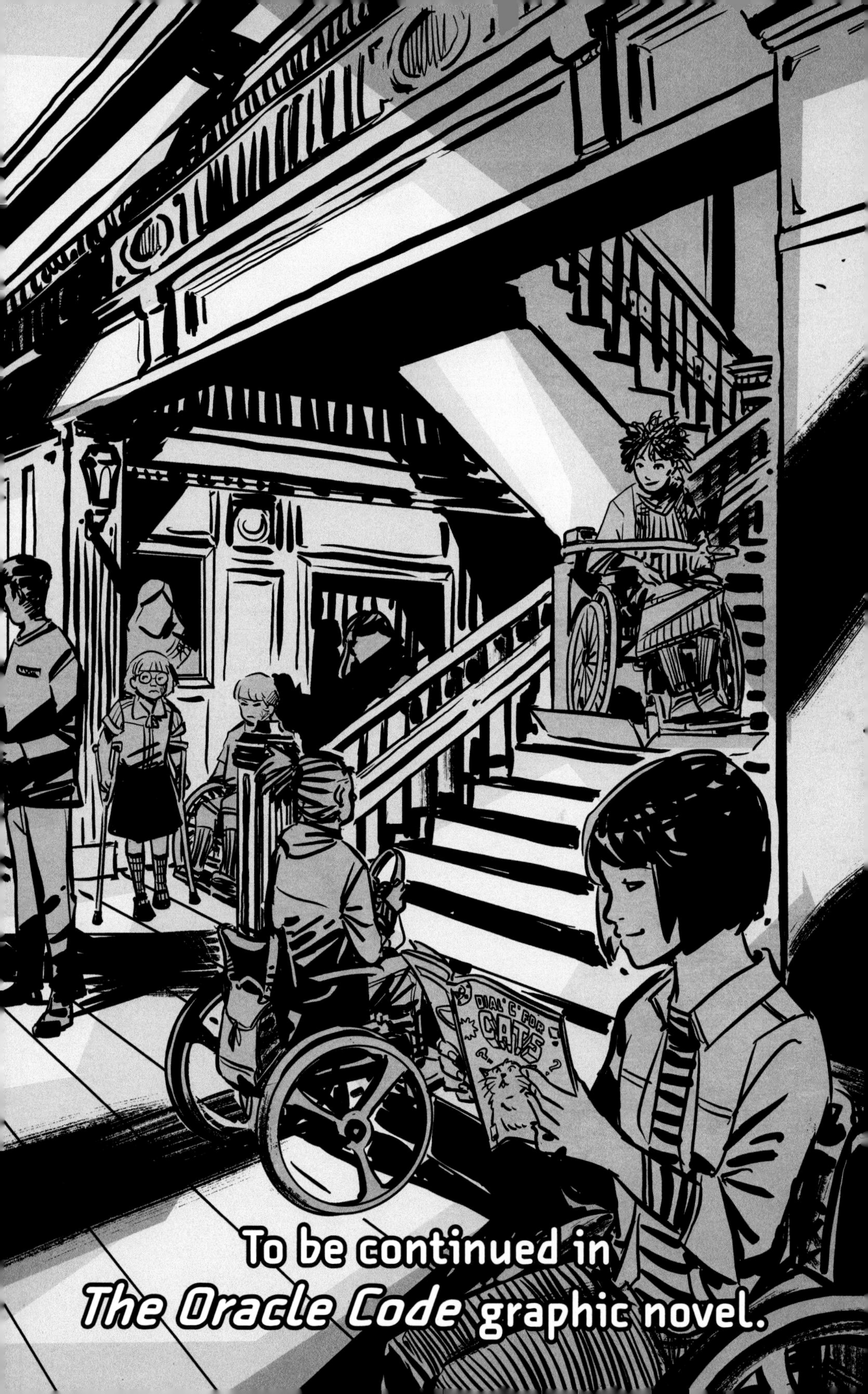
DIAL 'C' FOR CATS
To be continued in *The Oracle Code* graphic novel.